1989

A Jeremy Winters Adventure

Lisa Mortara

Foil Books

This book is a work of fiction. References to real people, events, establishments, organizations, or locales are intended only to provide a sense of authenticity and are used fictitiously. All other characters, and all incidents and dialogue, are drawn from the author's imagination and are not to be construed as real.

Foil Books

Cover design by Lynne Pierce
Photos by Lisa Mortara

Also by Lisa Mortara

Silver Blades

Snow Blind—Book Two in the Silver Blades Series

In the Shadow of the Eiffel Tower

Chapter 1

Vive la Révolution! Or not...

It was June and the Paris air shimmered with excitement over the impending bicentennial of the French Revolution. 14 July 1989: foreseen as the biggest celebration in Paris's history...or, the biggest hassle and inconvenience Parisians would ever suffer...or, to a select few, a flaming example of historical hypocrisy...

Jeremy Winters, if anything, tended to think it a hassle, though the whole business didn't concern him much. What mattered was the woman who had just rushed into the café where he was waiting and plopped down in the chair opposite him—out of breath, eyes like thunderclouds. Stefania Perin: his mark, his target, his professional responsibility, so to speak. An Italian exile living in Paris whom he was being paid to tap for information.

"What's wrong?" he asked in French, in a low voice that barely carried over the clinking cups, the hiss of the espresso machine, and the French chatter filling the little Latin Quarter establishment.

Stefania's eyes narrowed in tandem with the tightening of her full, sensuous lips. Jeremy guessed she was gauging him. Was it his trustworthiness she questioned? She knew him as a Belgian-American expat, but he needed her to trust him as a *friend*. For that was what this job required. He reached over and gave her hand a little pat.

Finally she seemed to relax a bit, hunching forward

1

over the table to engage him. "Do you see a tall blond *mec* standing somewhere behind me?"

From his seat on the banquette against the wall Jeremy glanced around the room. "The only men I see are standing at the bar."

"Then maybe he's there." Stefania drummed her fingertips on the table, evidently loath to turn around. "A big Viking type; I'm sure he followed me in here."

Jeremy scrutinized the individuals lined up at the counter, most of them there for a quick espresso, and identified a fair-haired man who had to be 1.9 meters tall or more, at least a head taller than Jeremy. "There's a tall blond guy at the bar but his back's to me."

"Probably him. He tried to take my picture on my way over here, *tête de con*. Luckily, now I'm facing the wall."

Inwardly Jeremy smiled at Stefania's pronunciation of the French word *dickhead*. Her Italian accent was ever present in their French conversations and he liked it, along with her more physical charms.

His studious eye returned to the so-called *Viking,* now stuffing what did indeed look like a small camera into his jacket pocket. The *mec* persisted in presenting them his back, bending his elbow to sip something or another. "The guy won't turn around but he just put a camera in his pocket," Jeremy confirmed to Stefania.

"You see?" she said, nodding hard to emphasize she was right. She stole a quick glance at the bar. "That's him for sure."

Jeremy shifted his perplexed gaze to the tall blond man, then back to Stefania. With her flowing red hair and lake-blue eyes, she hooked many a male eye in Paris. He had noticed it personally—the subtle, appraising stares, the occasional overt ogle. The problem was that Jeremy's own eyes were growing more and more covetous of this plucky, ginger Italian.

Yet he had an assignment to carry out. His work status as an American in France depended upon it. "So why is he following you?" he asked with a concerned frown.

"I have no idea, but he doesn't seem to care that I notice. What's he doing now?"

"He's leaving," Jeremy said, watching the man finally turn and send them a steely glance, before heading for the door. A Nordic type, Jeremy confirmed to himself as he observed the man slip out the door, cross the street, and melt out of sight.

"You can relax," he told Stefania. "He's gone."

Automatically she whipped round to check the room and the street beyond the plate-glass window. When she turned back to Jeremy her brow had softened and some of the turbulence had left her eyes. Still, she looked worried and remained hunched over the table.

He placed a hand on hers, this time letting it rest there. He wanted to reassure her, and she didn't pull away. "Have you seen this guy before?"

"No. I've no idea who he is." She exhaled a nervous sigh. "But he's been following me around all morning."

"Maybe he's just some nut who likes to photograph pretty girls," Jeremy said with a little grin. He didn't quite believe this, however, given the Viking *mec's* about-face behavior at the counter and his iron stare as he left. But he wanted to calm Stefania, keep her from getting up and bolting like a spooked rabbit. It was the first time she had agreed to meet him on his own, outside her group of friends with whom he was acquainted. He'd gone out of his way to arrange the encounter, following her to a supermarket in her neighborhood, feigning surprise at their meeting, making pleasantries and finally asking for a rendezvous for coffee, which he'd been surprised to hear her readily accept.

3

"With 14 July only a month away," he went on, "no doubt we'll see more and more quirky types out and about."

"Maybe," she said, sounding unconvinced. Gently she removed her hand from under Jeremy's. She sat back and pulled a face. "The bicentennial of the French Revolution: big bloody deal."

Jeremy smiled at her cynicism; at least she'd set aside her fear. "You're right," he agreed, "tourists already clogging up the streets, up to a million extra expected next month. He shook his head at the onerous thought.

It was good they could agree on the burdensome-ness of the Bicentennial, that he didn't have to pretend. The job unspooled easier when you didn't have to act. He lifted his beer for a sip.

"Affligem, hmm?" said Stefania, nodding at his glass.

"You know what I like to drink?" he asked, pleased at her guess.

"It's written on the glass." One corner of her mouth twisted in a mock smirk.

Jeremy flicked an amused glance at his glass, then raised it in salute. "It's excellent, you should try it."

"I might, if I liked beer...but maybe just for you..."

As Stefania leaned in and reached for his glass, her hair tumbled over her shoulder. Her T-shirt, stretched taught against her breasts, grazed the table. As she placed the glass to her lips she watched him, as he did her, until he straightened in his chair and glanced away. Abruptly he cleared his throat. "We haven't ordered anything for *you* yet." He raised his arm and motioned for the waiter.

The only way the French government would allow Jeremy to work at his night job was if he agreed to do the occasional "little job" for them during the day. For Jeremy had only American citizenship. His father had been American and his mother was Belgian, their marriage the fruit of a World War Two romance. And because of this particular hybridization, Jeremy could speak French and English with equal fluency. It helped that the family had lived off and on in both America and France during his formative years, though the reason behind that crisscrossing of the Pond had proved anything but a healthy experience for the boy.

He still spoke French with his mother, as well as with Stefania and her Italian friends, who referred to themselves as *Compagni—Companions*. If Jeremy could be called a willing émigré, Stefania and her Compagni counted among the "forced" variety: political exiles, Communists wanted for terrorist crimes in Italy. They had fled their country in the early 1980s and been granted refuge in allied France by the socialist government of François Mitterrand. The peculiar situation even had an official label: The Mitterrand Doctrine—designed to protect Italian Socialists and Communists from unjust prosecutions in Italy.

Still, *Monsieur le Président* was nothing if not shrewd, adjudging that these Italian Compagni bore watching by the Renseignements Généraux—the RG, the French intelligence service now tasking Jeremy to cozy up to Stefania. Specifically he was to discover what she knew about false passports circulating among the Italian Compagni. In return for this service, and his past little jobs, he was permitted to tend bar at Le Prince Blue Note jazz club.

"The Compagni trust you, Jeremy," his RG handler Benoît Rébert had explained. "They appreciate what you've gone through during your own life. And *you* know we all remember your father's struggle; they're aware high up in government, I've told you before."

What he'd gone through; his father's struggle—
Jeremy hated the references. He actually felt he had
betrayed Walt Winters in a certain way. But if Jeremy's
unfortunate history had somehow allowed him to live
and work in the only city where he felt remotely at home,
well, so be it—even though he wasn't crazy about the
idea of getting any of the Compagni in trouble. As a
group they had always honored his father's memory and
accepted Jeremy in émigré solidarity.

They were roughly his age, the Compagni (Jeremy
and Stefania were both thirty-four), and at least a
hundred of them lived in France, toughened veterans of
an urban guerilla war waged against the Italian state in
the 1970s. The Italian government had branded them
terrorists, every one of them wanted for armed revolt.
Stefania and her comrades insisted they had only taken
up arms to combat the Neo-fascists, who were rife,
according to the Compagni, in the Italian parliament,
and their foot soldiers every bit as angry and active on
Italian streets as the Reds. President Mitterrand
obviously agreed, claiming his Doctrine permitted
refuge only to those who had committed "political
crimes." So, what were these failed and embittered
revolutionaries supposed to do in France? *Keep their
profiles low and their noses clean*—period.

"You already know the Compagni through
Christophe Branger," Rébert had added while briefing
Jeremy on Stefania. "No doubt he long ago vouched for
your family history, that your father was a Communist
who knew his father."

Christophe Branger: Jeremy's childhood friend
from early elementary-school years in Paris, though he
and Jeremy had grown benignly apart during their adult
lives. Christophe, who along with his family remained
an inveterate French Communist and had been a
comrade of these particular Compagni since their arrival

in Paris in the early 1980s.

Christophe: *boyfriend* of Stefania, Jeremy reminded himself as he sat in the café giving her a measured look. Today's meeting he had planned as a purely social affair, a prelude to his eventual, casual mention of "passports." Now, however, this mysterious blond stranger had intruded on the scene.

"Be sure to let me know if he follows you again," Jeremy told her, wiping his right eye before a tear could leak out.

An irritating condition, his permanently watering eye. The ignominious result of a blow he had taken in a harrowing fight that haunted him to this day. The American doctor who'd treated him said his tear duct was damaged, with scar tissue blocking the eye from draining properly. And yet Jeremy considered his eye disorder—he could still see fine, after all—the absolute minimal consequence of that ruinous clash five years ago.

His conversation with Stefania drifted back to the Bicentennial. The 14th of July, 1989, would mark two hundred years since the original Bastille Day, when rioter-revolutionaries attacked the royal prison, chopped off the governor's head and placed it on the tip of a pike, and then launched themselves into the destruction of the prison, an achievement that took a subsequent string of years.

"Despite all that effort," Stefania complained, "the proletariat in their long trousers, clogs, and Phrygian caps failed to take down their bourgeois manipulators. If they had, this Bicentennial might mean something."

Jeremy cared little about failed politics of the past. And he lacked the university education Stefania possessed. He and his mother had moved back to Paris from San Francisco when he was fifteen, and he'd been tested and placed in a language lycée, where he'd

7

studied English, German, and Italian—only to pass all of his exit exams except German. He didn't retake the exam the following autumn, and so he had not received his diploma. Stefania, on the other hand, had studied sociology at the University of Bologna, though she'd chosen the revolutionary road rather than finishing her degree. Jeremy didn't mention he could speak school Italian, partly due to embarrassment at failing to obtain a diploma, but mainly in apprehension she might prefer speaking her own tongue, which would leave him grappling. He kept up with the language by following the Italian daily *La Repubblica*, but fluent speech remained a different animal.

In any case, both he and Stefania agreed on the garish face of Paris these days—the gaudy gilding of famous monuments, the esthetical failure of the newest construction projects belonging to President Mitterrand's "Great Works."

"The Opéra Bastille is the worst," Stefania maintained. "Still a month to go before it's finished, and so far it's nothing but a big ugly slab of concrete and steel. It disgraces the Place de la Bastille and the rest of Paris's architecture."

Jeremy concurred, his pulse ticking up with the subtle excitement of landing on the absolute same page as Stefania. "I'm not fond of the Louvre pyramids either," he offered. "Glass and metal, and totally out of place in the courtyard."

"And don't forget that the French government considered building a pyramid there for the *centenary* of the Revolution in 1889. Purely to honor Napoleon's achievements," Stefania added with a sour look.

Jeremy vaguely remembered this and so kept silent while Stefania continued.

"The pyramids are banal at best, their glass looks dirty, and you're right, the Louvre would be better off without them."

Jeremy grinned. "Yeah," he joked with carefree bravado. "Someone ought to blow up those blights on Paris!"

Chapter 2

Off and on through the afternoon and into the next morning Jeremy reflected on his *tête-à-tête* with Stefania. Once they had finished venting about the Bicentennial and Mitterrand's Great Works, their conversation had migrated toward food and the best economical restaurants in Paris. Stefania was living on a shoestring—a pittance of French government aid—and she missed the cheap, tasty pasta lunches you could get in Italian cafés. Jeremy had nodded in sympathy and fondness at her wistful musings, watching the blue in her eyes darken with melancholy. With his part-time work status he knew what it was like to scrape by though he didn't complain about it to Stefania. Nor, of course, could he mention how he depended on the subsidy of the Renseignements Généraux for carrying out their little jobs, the latest of which consisted of probing Stefania about false passports—she might know who possessed them and through whom they were procured. He felt he had achieved his modest goal of gaining camaraderie with her. But the surprise arrival of the Big Blond tailing Stefania had launched his feelings and instincts into protective mode as well.

"Protecting" versus "probing:" not mutually exclusive, Jeremy decided as he presently sat in a café with Rébert of the RG. Perhaps the *Viking* incident had proven a one-off occurrence; still it was worth mentioning along with the progress he'd made in cozying up to Stefania.

First, he assured Rébert of the latter, then he moved

on to the former. "By the way, someone seems to be following Stefania," he said in a casual tone, an eyebrow lifted to nudge Rébert's interest.

"*Following her?*" Rébert repeated, extending his pack of cigarettes to Jeremy. "In what way?"

Jeremy declined the offer, showing the palm of his right hand.

"That's right, you're trying to quit," said Rébert with an abrupt chuckle. The domestic intelligence agent was a few years older than Jeremy, genial for the most part and rather portly. Jeremy suspected he looked forward to their meetings (always in a café, this one already decorated with tricolors for the Bicentennial) as much to slip in a mid-afternoon lager as to hold their briefings.

"Trailing her around town with a camera," Jeremy explained. "The *mec's* a very tall blond with Nordic features. Late thirties, about your age," he added with a tilt of his chin at Rébert. "Heard of anyone with that description who might be up to mischief?"

Rébert angled his head in brief reflection then shook it. "No clue. Stefania *is* pretty though..."

"Mm," conceded Jeremy, aiming a shrewd look at Rébert.

"I mean, let's not overreact," the RG agent clarified with a subtle smile. "Men tail women all the time in this city. *You know,* it's mostly an innocent pastime."

"Right..."

"But if it happens again, let me know." Rébert took a draught of his Kanterbräu Gold followed by a drag of his cigarette. "Have you finished up that other job?"

"It'll be done tomorrow morning. I've got his routine down; always has a coffee at Les Fruits Des Bois in the Ninth before heading to work."

"*Très bien.* Make sure he gets the message."

Jeremy had to give Les Fruits Des Bois a crumb of credit

for at least trying to look woodsy, *wood* being the operative word. The dark paneling did need a fresh varnishing, though, and the framed wall prints of forest fruits a slight straightening; and he would have liked to turn up the lights in the place. Still, what mattered was he could keep his eye on the Weasel, who always ordered a café crème, smoked a cigarette, and invariably used the W.C. before leaving the café.

Weasel had been Jeremy's father's word, polite-company label for individuals whose treachery he had dealt with in the 1950s. In reality the man sitting in Les Fruits des Bois was called Raymond Blanc, and Rébert had deemed the matter highly sensitive, considering the bastard was blackmailing the wife of the assistant to the minister of culture. A little question of *sleeping with*, and then threatening to *tell*, or broadcast, or slip a letter to whoever might be interested, including the young lady's husband. Monsieur "Weasel Blanc's" grudge was classically simple and succinct: Madame had decided to close the portal to any further nookie.

He worked at an intimate little antiques shop in the Sixth Arrondissement. Jeremy had followed him there as well as to his residence in the Ninth, but deemed it convenient to confront him and set him straight in the café. Sort things out in at least a quiet manner, Rébert had instructed, if *friendly* proved out of the question. And above all, with discretion.

And so it went. At eight-thirty a.m., the salt-and-pepper-haired Raymond Blanc arrived at the low-lit Fruits Des Bois. When the clock ticked nine, obeying either habit or need, he rose to go downstairs to *les toilettes*.

Jeremy didn't waste time. On Blanc's heels, he entered the men's room, verified they were alone, and jerked the Weasel away from the urinal before he could get his zipper down. Blanc's brain, as reflected in his wide eyes, had no time to communicate with his vocal cords, for Jeremy spun him around by the shoulders and shoved him against the rolling towel dispenser.

His head clanged then rebounded forward. "What the hell!" he managed to yelp.

"No worries, we'll be finished soon," Jeremy answered, snatching the Weasel's fashionably narrow silk tie and yanking the man toward him. "You're going to cease threatening the wife of the minister's assistant. You'll never write or call her again, let alone attempt to follow her or contact her husband."

Instinct kicked in, and the man batted Jeremy's arm loose and landed a blow to his stomach. When his foe didn't flinch, and he again felt his head bounce off the towel dispenser, the Weasel's eyes registered the alarmed awareness that he was dealing with someone out of the ordinary. He cast Jeremy a doubtful frown. "Who the fuck are you, and why do you give a shit who I bang?"

Which was answered with a return blow to the man's unprepared abdominal muscles, then another to his side. Patiently Jeremy waited for the groaning, huffing-and-puffing Blanc to finally straighten. He allowed himself an instant to size him up, though he had done so before in the mornings he had watched him sip his crème and read *Le Figaro*. Now, however, he could perceive the man's arrogance, the barely-submerged smirk that was superseded by hostility and seething humiliation radiating through his grimace of pain.

"Who the fuck sent you?" he rasped.

Jeremy narrowed his defective right eye. "Who cares? All you need to know is I'll be watching you. And if you go to the newspapers with your sordid account of Madame you'll regret plenty more than this morning's encounter."

Raymond Blanc took a moment to study Jeremy.

Then he cleared his throat and reached down to straighten his tie, his wary gaze never leaving Jeremy's.

Was that a slight tremor in Blanc's fingers as he buttoned his jacket? Jeremy was amused. "I trust this will be our one and only rendezvous," he said, and elbowed the Weasel out of the way as he walked out wiping his eye.

Dealing with Raymond Blanc had been cut and dried, Jeremy later reflected. The Big Blond, if he continued to hound Stefania, might be trickier. He didn't look like one of those silly grinning gadabouts who trotted around Paris after pretty girls for distraction; those were mostly younger men, plying their immature, court-jester brand of charm in hopes of hooking a bit of promising eye contact.

Not the hulking Blond's modus operandi, as far as Jeremy had been able to discern. He was annoyed with himself for not pushing the point, sketchy as it was, with Rébert yesterday.

At length he forced his thoughts to the rest of the afternoon and evening to come. He had the night off, though his plans still involved spending time at his workplace, Le Prince Blue Note.

The jazz club, located on boulevard Saint-Michel, across the street from rue Monsieur le Prince, didn't open until six, but Jeremy wanted to pay an early visit to hear tonight's saxophone trio rehearse. Loads of sax players came through Le Prince Blue Note but the one booked this week held a special appeal for Jeremy. Like lots of jazz musicians in Paris the leader had known his father, Walt Winters, the American tenor saxophonist who had serenaded France and Europe, particularly once he'd been virtually barred from working in America.

At Le Prince Blue Note sentimental recollections of

Walt Winters trailed after Jeremy, though fortunately his colleagues didn't often remind him of his father's misfortunes. Unlike Rébert of the Renseignements Généraux, who chose select moments to commiserate over Jeremy's problematic youth, emphasizing how thoroughly the RG were in his corner—especially when they had work for him. Work that, so far, Jeremy had not found objectionable. Even this little passport job he didn't object to in principle; it just might prove a touch delicate.

After the blacklisting of Walt Winters in 1958, Jeremy's family moved to Paris, and from the start they'd felt welcome. In the same way the City of Light and Tolerance and Fraternity had made a home for Josephine Baker in the twenties, his father used to say with special affection for the American Black Pearl. No political hurdles to securing gigs in Paris, such as Walt had endured in Los Angeles, where he'd performed his music in clubs and assisted with film soundtracks.

Too bad Europe's depressed, post-war pay and economy didn't match the demand for jazz. And so the family returned to the U.S. in 1964, this time to San Francisco. The McCarthyite zeal had lost some momentum by then among conservative politicians. If only the same had applied to "the people." Even the proverbial "innocent babes" had caught wind of Walt Winters' infamy, their taunts of "Commie," "Pinko," and the more juvenilely earthy "Red-butt," contributing to the flowering slang of Jeremy's fourth-grade vocabulary. At seven years old, in France, he had started learning the saxophone. By age eleven, in San Francisco, his fists rivaled the instrument for extracurricular, hands-on activity.

Jeremy's walk to Le Prince Blue Note took him across the quiet, stately Île Saint-Louis and onto the rhythmic, tourist-laden Left Bank of the Seine. The June air quivered cool and sweet under a cloud-veiled sun as he wound through the maze of little Latin Quarter lanes off rue des Écoles, past the Pantheon and up to the club on boulevard Saint-Michel. By July Paris would undergo a siege, not only from a spike in tourists galloping in for the Bicentennial, but by an oppressive humid heat, mixed with heightened auto exhaust, hot air rising from the metro through sidewalk grills, and annoying blasts of noxious air spewing from the vents of restaurant buildings.

Suffice it to say Jeremy wasn't fond of Paris in summer, and not much in spring either when shoots of extending daylight blazed the way for summer's assault. When on the day of the solstice, night would not finish spreading its black cloak over the city until eleven p.m., all the while the bullying sun shining a relentless spotlight on his life. Unlike in autumn and winter when the soothing blue of twilight stole in earlier and earlier to gently shadow personal sins, and failures, and shortcomings.

When he arrived, Jeremy found the glass doors to Le Prince Blue Note unlocked. Quickly he passed the few small round tables and the short curvy wooden bar to head downstairs where the serious business of jazz unfolded. Framed wall posters of jazzmen flanked the way, one depicting his father, tenor saxophone clutched on his lap like his own child. Pierre, the manager of the club, said Jeremy looked like him.

And he might have been right at one time. Both father and son had dark, untamable hair (one reason Jeremy kept his mop close cropped whereas Walt had slicked his down with brilliantine), and Jeremy's eyes—the right one before taking its hit—probably resembled his father's brown eyes; Jeremy remembered the bruise-like patches under them when Walt was wrought with fatigue. He hadn't reached full height before Walt's passing, but his mother Béatrice claimed Jeremy's 1.8 meters (five-feet-eleven, as the Americans and Walt would say) equaled, if not topped, that of Walt in his day. "You're lean through the torso like *Papa,* but bulkier in the arms and shoulders." The latter, no doubt, from Jeremy's years of amateur boxing. His nose, however, mirrored *Maman's,* straight and high-bridged, a mark of the Belgian *famille* Martineau. With one slight variation that irritated *Maman* to no end; for due to a fight Jeremy's nose was no longer *completely* straight. "*C'est permanent, ce nez-là! T'es content de tes bagarres, Jérémy?*"

With a sigh he had conceded his shame. *Bien sûr,* another permanent branding from his brawls.

Jeremy pulled a chair off a table in the basement of Le Prince Blue Note and sat down to watch and listen. The trio was belting out "So Rare," in Jimmy Dorsey fashion though without the chorus. Once his drummer had hiccupped the song to a halt, Pascal Bertrand swung his sax aside and beckoned Jeremy, who rose immediately to shake the eager trio leader's hand and exchange a double grazing of the cheeks. He hadn't seen Pascal in at least three years and the fifty-some jazzman's hair had turned completely grey. Still, to Jeremy's sentimental relief, his blue eyes retained every bit of the keenness and luster of his music making.

"How's the son of Walt Winters doing?" he asked with a solemn hand on Jeremy's shoulder.

Used to this kind of nostalgic greeting from his father's contemporaries and former acolytes, Jeremy answered, "*Ça va, ça va, merci.*" *Things were fine. But never mind that.* "Your trio's brilliant," he quickly added.

But Pascal Bertrand wasn't to be rushed off the tender subject of Father and Son Winters. "*Quelle tragédie, quelle tragédie,"* he intoned (naturally, not for the first time), gravely shaking his head. "Just recently I was reminded of when your father played at Le Tabou in the late fifties and early sixties. *Mon Dieu*, how he executed "Temptation!"

Temptation: Saxophonists forty-five and older raved about Walt Winters' slow, sensuous rendition of the venerable standard, in a way that bound Walt and the song together as a legend in some Parisian jazz circles. Perhaps "Temptation" (which he played on the alto sax) would have been Walt's signature piece had he hit the big time. But he had not—neither in France nor in the U.S.

Jeremy sighed to himself. He had almost outgrown that fervent longing for Walt's life, and his own by hapless extension, to have turned out differently. Almost. At least he no longer shuddered inside when people lionized his father at length. He had been fourteen when Walt died, alone in his San Francisco apartment, and over the last ten years—from age twenty-four to thirty-four—Jeremy had gained the ability to compartmentalize, so to speak. *No*, nearly literally, for Walt Winters' tenor saxophone now reclined in its scuffed black case under Jeremy's bed, its musical enchantment suspended in Limbo.

"Will you be tending bar tonight?" asked Pascal, reeling Jeremy in from his musings.

"No, I'm off. I've got a date—"

"Bravo, mon vieux!" Pascal interrupted with a rakish twinkle in his eyes and a slap to Jeremy's back.

"And I'm bringing her to hear you," Jeremy finished.

While Pascal Bertrand rehearsed "I'm Beginning to See the Light," Jeremy tried to follow the master's fingering. At one time he knew notes well, could read music a little, played for friends and family, once even in public. He wished he could create that magic again—even transcend it...

He glanced at his hands, pictured his fingers scampering over the keys. Then looked away as he felt a flush of embarrassment, recalling the very real role his hands had played this morning in the men's room of Les Fruits des Bois. Mechanically he wiped a leaking tear from his eye.

Chapter 3

Jeremy Winters and Haley Morgan shared American citizenship, a passion for jazz, their parents' passing (his father and both her father and mother), and a lasting affinity for Paris. That is, she adored the city, come summer or winter, while he simply felt more at home there than anywhere else. They also shared her bed from time to time, which was where they found themselves after the Pascal Bertrand performance at Le Prince Blue Note.

"I've loved that club since 1979," she said as they lay on their backs, Jeremy having fulfilled his part in their lovemaking with the kind of intensity he desired to play Duke Ellington's "Half the Fun" on the sax.

"I saw your father's picture," Haley went on. "You must be proud he played there."

"He didn't. The photo's in homage to him. He actually played at Le Tabou, over on rue Dauphine. Le Prince wasn't built until 1971...he was already gone then."

"When did he die?"

"In '69, back in the States."

"You were fourteen..." Haley uttered quietly, after a pause allowing her to do the mental calculation.

Jeremy shrugged a bare shoulder, the one not touching hers. "You've had it worse. You were only two when both your parents died in that car crash."

"You've never told me how *your* father died..." she murmured. She turned onto her side to face him, stroking his chest with delicate fingertips tuned to a sensitive subject.

Jeremy's first instinct was to clam up and roll over to face the window. Yet he and Haley had been seeing each other for two months and he'd been dodging her inquisitiveness about such personal matters all the while. Skirting sentimental intimacy while still inching closer to her—one step backward and two forward, so to speak, with spontaneous spikes both upward and downward. He tended to view their relationship like a bar graph when in an objective state of mind. After ten years of living in Paris she was still so damned enthusiastic, so delightfully spirited, the way she spouted Paris's history, announced its latest exhibits and the newest hole-in-the-wall museum she'd discovered. Her hazel eyes—childlike though hardly ingenuous—and that lithe gait of hers as they gamboled about the city together filled him with a freshness he'd thought had long expired. Not that he considered the two of them particularly equals. He was two years older, but she proved his undisputed senior in material wealth. As for the latter, he had to remain on guard lest envy rear its ugly chartreuse mug.

So, in a symbolic gesture, he laced his fingers in hers and brought both of their hands to his side. And he confessed in a low, neutral voice. "My father shot himself. In his apartment."

Haley's hand slackened, and when it resumed an even tighter grip he focused his gaze on the slice of moonlight piercing the crack in the curtains, painting a white stripe on the bed between them. Matter-of-factly he continued, "He was separated from my mother at the time."

"How *horrible*. I mean...you weren't *there* when..."

He hadn't anticipated this question. Gently he removed his hand from hers. He wanted to roll away— off the bed, out of the room, into the sweet black anonymous night. But Haley had invited him to her home, he was subject to her hospitality, to her reasonable and understandable concern.

"No, I wasn't there when it happened," he assured her, continuing to fixate the strip of light between them. "I found him later."

"God, that's awful..." she whispered.

"The way of the world."

"Well," she stammered, "we know that's easy to say...I...I don't really remember my parents...but—"

He silenced her by turning and placing a kiss on her lips. "We do our best to move on," he said, then kissed her again as his hand slid down her abdomen.

They woke and had breakfast in Haley's tidy little kitchen. Everything about the flat boasted of the new and the modern: the shiny chrome features in the sparkling kitchen and bath, the parquet floors of the sitting room that practically reflected his dodgy looks. A desk stood in the corner of that room, splattered with books and papers pertaining to her project, a collaborative art book that would display photos of Paris's fanciful wrought-iron balustrades. Haley's partner, and the project's creator and photographer, happened to be the mother of Haley's former companion, Thierry Kérouac; now—conveniently for Jeremy—living in Buenos Aires. While Madame Kérouac snapped the balcony pictures and wrote the French text, Haley crafted an accompanying English translation. She was a ten-year veteran in the translation field and at one time even worked as a tour guide in the French capital.

Yes, Jeremy envied and admired her sense of purpose, along with her affluence. She rented a flat in the heart of the Marais, in rue des Archives near the medieval-styled turret of the Paris archives building. She was a purely voluntary expat, benefitting from a modest inheritance from her parents coupled with what her deceased grandmother had left her.

She didn't need to work. Although she did point out how Jeremy might achieve a more *stable,* as she put it, work status for himself.

"Have you thought about taking out French citizenship?" she asked in between lightly- crunched bites of her *tartine.* "It might help you advance, especially if you get tired of bartending. You've lived here off and on your whole life—more *on*—and what with your father's tragedy and all, you could very well get a sympathetic hearing..."

Tragedy and *sympathy*. The words loped after him eternally like two mangy hounds—well-meaning in their sentiment though irritating. Just yesterday he had received a dose of it from saxophonist Pascal; now he wished he hadn't told Haley about finding his father dead of a self-inflicted gunshot. As for bartending, he had never complained to her of wanting to do more. Yet somehow she'd sensed his restlessness...

His thoughts shifted to Stefania Perin. Now that he had finished with "Monsieur Weasel Blanc" he could devote his expertise to her. The thought produced an inward smile of anticipation.

"I'm not tired of what I do," he said. "And I've already considered applying for French citizenship. When I need to, I'll go forward with it."

Haley's brows drew together but thankfully she made no further comment. She didn't understand him, and he would not reveal more of his personal history to her. For instance, that up until July of 1984 he *had* possessed a full-fledged work permit issued by the prefecture of police. Unfortunately, upon return from his little trip to America that year, the Renseignements Généraux had intervened and made issuance of a permit for *part*-time employment contingent on his assisting them. As far as citizenship was concerned (of course it could further his career options), well, there he was stymied. *Not for the time being, the RG had advised; not with your U.S. conviction.*

Jeremy stopped fiddling with his napkin and looked up at Haley. She was gazing out the kitchen window at the golden city she had adopted out of sheer love.

"Nice how you still have a passion for Paris after ten years," he said, keeping his voice casual.

"Maybe I lived here in another life," she answered with a musing smile.

He chuckled then asked, "Have you seen other European capitals?"

"Oh, Rome, Venice, London, Nice—not all capitals of course—"

"With Thierry?"

"Mm-hm..."

"That's right, he works for Air France." Jeremy's voice was turning edgy; he could hear it. He knew she and Thierry Kérouac hadn't been lovers now for some years, that they had broken up after Thierry's transfer to Argentina. And yet, she was working on this balcony project with his mother...

He caught her sharpish look and quickly amended his tone. "Have you seen Brussels?" he asked with genuine interest.

"No...never really thought about it."

"Well it's great," he pronounced with a proud grin. "Architecture as interesting as Paris's, or more so. Plenty of museums; cafés like here—all the things you like."

Behind light-brown, large-framed glasses her hazel eyes brightened at the prospect. "Have you spent much time there?"

"Sure, often when I visit my mother, though she lives in the Walloon area."

"That's right," Haley recalled. For an instant her gaze turned pensive, then she beamed again. "You could probably get Belgian citizenship, no questions asked, and then doors could open for you all over Europe."

He allowed for a pause, then granted her it was something to consider. She was nothing if not enthusiastic. With her *joie de vivre* she could almost levitate him to her degree of gusto. Except the bar had now been set too high, and he was brought up short with this simple reality: when you've been convicted of assault, no doors open for you.

That night after work Jeremy lingered at Le Prince for drinks with Pascal Bertrand. After two Manhattans, the specialty cocktail Jeremy had modified for the other bartenders, Jeremy didn't even mind Pascal's repeating the same sentimental stories about Walt Winters. After his third drink, Jeremy called it an evening and walked with a lazy sway, like a boat in its moorings, to metro station Cluny-La Sorbonne. He caught the train, and with the one change at Gare d'Austerlitz, arrived at Place de la République, his *quartier*. Three minutes later he was mounting the stairs to his sixth-floor flat in rue de Turbigo.

His digs were humble compared to Haley's: wallpaper slightly peeling in areas, hardwood floors a touch scratched up (his doing), a brown and thoroughly seasoned punching bag hanging pugnaciously in his bedroom. Permission for the latter he had obtained from the owner of the building, Monsieur Henri, which was why Jeremy put off mentioning the wallpaper. Monsieur Henri, proud of his establishment, would have had it fixed in no time. But Jeremy had a tendency to procrastinate with that kind of thing, so he had never invited Haley to his place in the Third Arrondissement. Better her flat in the Marais, only about half an hour's walk from his, in the direction of the Seine.

He closed his door, dropped onto the sofa, and released a long sigh that mingled with the rising dust from the cushions. Despite his exhaustion his mind cranked out images of Pascal's virtuosity on the tenor sax. His deft finger play, like spiders' legs on the keys. His perfect synthesis with the members of his combo. The middle-aged *mec's* indefatigable passion for jazz old and new.

With another, more melancholy sigh Jeremy heaved himself off the sofa and plodded to his short, narrow strip of a kitchen to mix another Manhattan. He hadn't prepared ice in the mini-freezer of his midget fridge, so he made the drink room temperature in a small water glass and brought it back to the sofa.

Tomorrow would have been his father's sixty-fourth birthday, with 1989 marking the twentieth anniversary of his death. Pascal Bertrand hadn't mentioned either at the bar, and that was just as well with Jeremy.

So he raised his own silent glass to Dad. No doubt *Maman* in Namur would expect his call on tomorrow's anniversary.

Neither Dad nor *Maman* had explained to the three-year-old Jeremy what it meant to be blacklisted by the nebulous powers that were. In 1958 they had simply whisked him off to Paris, the city to whose liberation Walt had contributed as a GI in August of 1944, a place that had consistently welcomed his presence. Then back across the Pond to San Francisco when Jeremy turned nine. He could still speak English, the language he shared with his father, though a slight French accent betrayed him—a *smidgeon*, to use his father's kind words, but annoyingly perceptible to Jeremy now that he had been plunged into the depths of American life. Into school, in particular. As if the epithets Commie-kid and Red-butt hadn't sufficed, those precociously witty little schoolmates couldn't resist adding "Frog-balls" to the mix. Naturally, the boys dished it out the hardest, though Jeremy soon learned to silence them with ever-growing, dexterous fists that targeted blows to the nose and windpipe.

The tipsy reminiscence led him to put down his glass and examine his hands; rotate them from palms to backs. His mother liked to remind him that they were finely muscled like his father's while warning him not to ruin them with his amateur boxing. That he just might want to take up the sax again—as a hobby, strictly speaking, and not as a profession which she associated with boozing and philandering. Well, Jeremy was on hiatus from the boxing club for the summer (no air conditioning in the gym) and his hands and fingers looked the same as ever. No threat to the saxophone. Only to the person who had tried to deny it him five years ago.

The thought caused an involuntary shudder.

Walt Winters had hoped his son would follow in his footsteps in at least one form or another, something the boy aspired to under his father's tutelage in France. Then came the move back to America, with responsibility for saxophone lessons handed off to a teacher called Mister Carney, who sat gazing out the window like a birdwatcher, drawing idly on his cigarette while Jeremy sweated out what he had practiced all week. Squints and grunts came as feedback, leading to less practice and more brawling about the neighborhood, with harsh punishment at home. And Jeremy's growing need to distance himself from Walt Winters' image, both as Communist (which had got the family into their mess in the first place) and as stellar sax performer.

A distance made final the day fourteen-year-old Jeremy discovered his father in his bachelor apartment:

splayed out flat on his bed, his lifeless grimace staring at the ceiling, black blood coagulated on the pillow under his head.

He'd turned his back on his father and been abandoned in return. To this day he regretted his rebellion bitterly. By his mid twenties he longed to play the saxophone again in a way that might showcase him as his own man. If only he hadn't made that disastrous trip to America.

He tossed back the last of his rye whiskey and vermouth and shuffled to the bedroom to fetch Walt's tenor sax from under his bed. He hadn't taken it out in months. Tenderly he lifted the venerable artifact from its case and carried it back to the sofa. Images of a swinging, ecstatic Walt playing "Temptation" shimmered before his eyes, both of which were now red-rimmed and burning. He remembered the notes from long ago, though he shivered to think how horrid they would sound coming from a slob beginner—which would amount to his status after having laid down his own alto sax twenty-two years ago and allowed it to be sold. He pictured Pascal Bertrand, at one with the song "So Rare," and softly began humming the tune as he nestled the beloved brass body on his lap. Gingerly he made an attempt to finger the fine keys covered with mother of pearl.

Then, slowly and carefully as he had embraced the instrument he as swiftly jerked his hands from it. His breath came short, his pulse throbbing in his head. "Jesus Fucking Christ!" *How could he have committed such a crime in the presence of this object he so loved?* He snatched up the empty glass from the coffee table and hurled it across the room. When it shattered against the wall he gaped and shuddered. Gently he let the sax slide to the floor to rest against the sofa. Then he leaned back, shut his eyes, and waited for the Manhattans to resume their anesthetizing work.

Chapter 4

The following Saturday night Jeremy changed shifts with fellow barman Gilles to attend a party hosted by two Italian Compagni: Mirko Mazzini and Pietro Grimaldi, two exiles in Paris from the early 1980s and both good friends of Christophe, Jeremy's childhood friend. The invitation had not come from the hosts, however, or even from Christophe. Rather Stefania had called him. "I talked to them; they said they'd enjoy seeing you." The phone call continued to strike Jeremy as odd. Clearly Stefania desired to see him again and hadn't wanted to go through Christophe. Whatever the case, another occasion now presented itself to get closer to her, which served his RG purposes.

Like Stefania, Pietro and Mirko were both former insurgents of the communist and anarchic upheaval in Italy during the seventies. They had all battled neo-fascism and its official party in parliament MSI, whose symbol, an aspiring tricolored flame, conveyed the message that Mussolini's ideas were alive and well. Apart from armed street skirmishes with fascist gangs, the young Communists had made their reputation through armed robbery of "fascist" establishments (banks and jewelry stores *de rigueur*) and the firebombing of fascist newspaper offices and cafés. Pietro and Mirko had fought the guerrilla war side by side, taking refuge in Paris in 1983, with Stefania arriving a year or so later. And typical of refugees in a host country whose attitude toward them is ambivalent at best, they and other Compagni gravitated toward one

30

another.

As Jeremy looked round the living room of the flat he recognized people, both French and Italian, who knew the story of his father's blacklisting. Simply by virtue of its musical setting, the story had assumed almost mythic standing, with Jeremy lauded as the surviving noble son of an exotic comrade. Walt Winters: the saxophone hero who defied American capitalistic tyranny and told the McCarthyites to fuck themselves. European communists Paris-wide would have welcomed Jeremy into their circles had the apolitical young man (if anything, he swayed toward the center-left) sought them out. Never mind that neither father nor son had ever advocated violence on the part of the proletariat. They were American, they were charmingly different, Walt had been a great communist artist and was now a legend.

At the door Mirko greeted Jeremy and ushered him in, shook his hand, exchanged pleasantries, then handed him off to Pietro. The contrast between the two companions always fascinated Jeremy. Mirko, short and wiry, his intelligent eyes darting and glinting like refracted sunrays. He was an extrovert, unlike Pietro. Tall and solidly built, Pietro could snap Mirko in two if he wanted to, mused Jeremy. But his shy dark eyes, ever subtly admiring of Mirko, spoke otherwise. He reminded Jeremy of a great-trunked tree in a forest, inert and dormant in the shadow of Mirko's sun. He was Mirko's man, Mirko's intimate companion.

"Stefania said you were coming," Pietro said, hands retreating to his pockets as soon he gave Jeremy a quick, strong-gripped handshake. "I was surprised when she called, but I'm glad you could make it."

Jeremy didn't quite know how to respond. The request for his invitation coming from Stefania had obviously rung strange to Pietro as well. "It's been a long time," was all he could think to say. And adding a sweep of his arm to encompass all the guests present: "I'm happy for the chance to meet you all again."

Pietro nodded silently. It seemed he too had little to say. He shifted his weight from one foot to the other, and before Jeremy could ask how things were going he said, "Stefania's over there," his voice rising above the party noise as he pointed to the other side of the living room. "And drinks are in the kitchen."

Jeremy readily took the cue, thanking Pietro and nodding a "See you later." He wove his way through the clusters of guests cramped in the small, spartan flat, exchanging brief greetings along the way. When he located Stefania she was standing alone in a corner of the room, wearing the miniskirt he had last seen her in. As she sipped a drink she observed the room, its mostly bare walls and tiled floor echoing spikes of laughter and shouted conversation, the congenial hubbub boosted by the electronic rock of Étienne Daho's album *Pop Satori*.

She pushed a curtain of red hair away from her eyes in time to spot Jeremy's gaze, which she returned with a beckoning smile. In a few relaxed strides he joined her.

"Good to see you," she said, exchanging kisses on the cheeks.

"You too...I don't see Christophe," he commented casually.

"He's here," she replied, her tone flat and dismissive. "Off, who knows where..."

Jeremy registered his friend's temporary absence with a neutral "Mm." Inwardly he was glad to have Stefania to himself. Though the party was not the place to commence probing the subject of false passports, it at least offered a chance to advance his friendship.

And to admire her. As a warmness crept through him, over and above the June heat in the top-floor flat, he gave himself a tiny elbowing of self-reproval, then asked, "Like the music?"

Stefania's eyes hadn't quite stopped roaming round the room since he first spied her, and with distraction she answered, "It's one of my favorite songs."

"Mine too," said Jeremy, wondering whether she was looking for Christophe, who might be down the hall or in the kitchen.

"You like Étienne Daho?" she asked, focusing back on him with a hint of surprise in her voice.

"I do. In fact I own this album."

"So you're not just a jazz lover."

"No."

She smiled generously and he edged closer, inhaling a floral scent that mingled with the flowering smoke from the cigarette between her fingers. "You'd be surprised at my music collection," he added, his cheek brushing her hair as he leaned near her ear.

She offered him a pleasant nod, without flinching from his touch or his closeness. Then she returned a narrow-eyed gaze to the crowd, a few of whom were now gyrating to Étienne Daho's bass and drum-driven "Satori Pop Century." Something still preoccupied her, but before he could ask she met his eyes again and, with a teasing smile, raised her cigarette. "Still don't smoke?"

Jeremy flashed a helpless smile. "Trying not to, and I'm finding it especially hard here."

She glanced toward the thundercloud of smoke hovering above the partiers, then back at him with a coy sparkle in her eyes, her cigarette hanging suspended between them like mistletoe.

Impulsively he snatched it and took a drag. "Ahhh," he expelled, in tandem with a stream of smoke. "That's better." He wiped his eye before a tear could leak. In this room he practically needed a handkerchief.

Stefania's lips twitched playfully as she took back the cigarette. "Now I feel guilty."

"Only a bump in the road," he replied, savoring the feel of his lips on the moist, shared filter. He thought he had tasted a trace of her pale lipstick.

Their flirting had started back at that meeting in the Latin Quarter café, when *he* had offered *her* a sip of his beer and she had accepted with eyes locked on his. That it was now Stefania carrying the game forward pleased him in terms of his task but stirred his curiosity regarding her relationship with Christophe. His head tilted imperceptibly. Once more he wondered why she had invited him here. But Stefania was already regarding the room again.

"You look worried..." he finally said.

"What?" She gave a little start when a man whom Jeremy didn't recognize at all strolled past them. He brushed against Stefania, swiftly issuing her a smiling "Pardon" as he sidled back into the crowd.

"You know him?" Jeremy asked.

"No," she answered with a shrug and a crooked smile that seemed a silent scoff. Her eyes could turn hard, from welcoming to rejecting in one blink of her long dark lashes. He had noticed this before and chalked it up to her living practically hand to mouth in Paris for the last five years. According to Christophe, she, like the other Compagni, depended upon pitiful handouts from the French state; plus, in Stefania's case, help from her parents and sometimes from Christophe himself. Unlike her French boyfriend, however, she and the other Compagni were refused work permits. Unlike Haley, Stefania had no inheritance.

With an impatient sigh she drained her glass of the last of her white wine and asked Jeremy why he didn't have an Affligem beer in tow.

"I just got here," he said, wondering at her tone, "and I doubt I'll find Affligem; at best maybe Kronenbourg."

"Right," she said, looking around the room again.

Something wasn't right, and whatever it was, Jeremy suspected Stefania didn't care to communicate it to Christophe.

"Maybe I'd better try to find that Kronenbourg..." he said.

"Not yet." Stefania clutched his arm. A steely grip for a small hand. "Sorry," she said, her expression suddenly turning vulnerable, "but I half expect that Viking stalker to show up."

"You've seen him again?"

She nodded without making eye contact.

"Have you told anyone besides me?"

"No, and I don't intend to," she replied, her eyes now lasering Jeremy. "Christophe would want me to go to the police, and I *must not* have issues with them. The French can deport me at the drop of a hat. Jeremy, *you* know what it's like to be hosted at the whim of a government."

Instinctively he wanted to put his arm around her. Not, however, without doling out another dose of self-reproach. Christophe was here in the flat somewhere and his status as Jeremy's oldest friend could hardly be ignored. Granted, he and Christophe had drifted apart in their late adolescence, Christophe training as an electrician while Jeremy was sent to secondary school to study languages after he and his mother returned to Paris; Jeremy with his penchant for the jazz milieu, which Christophe didn't share, and Christophe looking forward to the weekend mainly to catch the next soccer game—different interests, new friends, separate worlds. And yet when Jeremy continued to delay retaking his German exam to receive his diploma, Christophe had offered solidarity in contrast to *Maman's* bitter disappointment. After two years of indecision Jeremy had acknowledged his mother's wisdom: that continued postponement would become perpetual; that his immature decision had led to nothing but stifled opportunities. Nonetheless, Jeremy couldn't deny Christophe's earnest, heartfelt support at the time.

Nor could he *not* agree with Stefania about the precarious state of her refugee status. He was about to answer her when a voice rang out in their direction. "*Salut, mon pote!*" An enthusiastic shout from Christophe himself, who steered toward them bearing greetings for his old pal Jeremy.

Stefania slid her hand from Jeremy's arm without, he noted, stepping away from him. "I'll tell you more later," she whispered. "I can meet you at Café La Gitane in your neighborhood, tomorrow at four."

Jeremy returned a quick affirmation, barely before the beaming blond Christophe arrived with an affectionate slap to Jeremy's back. "Haven't seen you in ages," he said, "and you're empty-handed. Come on, let's get you a beer; I need another one myself." As he took Jeremy by the elbow he glanced at Stefania. "Be back later," he flicked at her, without asking if he could bring her anything else.

As Christophe guided him through the crowd to the kitchen Jeremy looked briefly over his shoulder. With a level gaze, Stefania sent him the slightest of nods.

Which repeated itself in Jeremy's mind on the metro ride home. The Big Blond was tailing her again and she had chosen Jeremy as confidant. For whatever reason, it suited him, though the way she went about it continued to leave him with a vague sense of disquiet.

Comparisons with Haley dogged him. Not really fair, he knew, since both women had their positive points: one, a tall, leggy, confident brunette; the other a shorter, edgier, but very sexy redhead. Though her personality verged on aggressive at times, Stefania had revealed her vulnerability to him as a refugee. The very reason, perhaps, why she sought to confide in him. He found it personally touching. Even greater was a special magnetism she conveyed, for Stefania's dark red hair and deep blue eyes reminded him of Margie's. *Margie.* Twenty-seven at the time, she had become his father's girlfriend during Walt and Béatrice's separation. Her hair, her eyes, her high, teasing voice radiated a sensuality that raced through the fourteen-year-old Jeremy like an electrical current.

Unbeknownst to his mother, Jeremy and Margie had remained in touch after Walt's death. Until he and his mother moved back to Paris, and even then Jeremy kept Margie's San Francisco address. Once on his own, he struck up a correspondence with her. And when she announced a trip to Europe and Paris, inquiring if he could recommend a good tour guide for the City of Light, he sensed a fantasy was about to be realized. And it was. Everything about Margie, thirty-five-years-old at this point, seemed more intense—from looks to sensuality. She made him laugh and filled him with warmth as in the old days. And now, at twenty-two, he saw himself as a strong, fairly worldly man. They slept together in her hotel and he had never felt more confident—more primordially male.

The lightning affair taught him much about how to please a woman. And how to hurt one. When Béatrice discovered the liaison (from a woman friend who had approached Jeremy and Margie as they sipped cocktails at La Coupole), her anger spewed volcanic; her tears, it seemed, an unending flow of lava fueled by both rage and rekindled grief. Guilt and chagrin had rained down upon Jeremy in spades. He tried to make it up to his mother with redoubled attention, and maybe she was sincere when she finally said she forgave him. Still, for reasons she attributed to nostalgia and tranquility,

Béatrice eventually moved back to her hometown in Belgium.

Jeremy continued to court his mother's good graces. Yet Margie retained a magical place in his core, now to be joined there, if only through association, by Stefania.

Chapter 5

At four p.m. the next day Jeremy entered the café La Gitane d'Andalousie, diagonally across the street from his flat in the rue de Turbigo. He had a flash of surprise when he found Stefania already hunched over an empty espresso cup by the window.

"You got here early?" he said, rechecking his watch before sliding into a chair across from her.

"Had to calculate the metro." She shrugged and gave a casual smile. But things were not so casual these days, otherwise Stefania wouldn't have whispered the urgent need to meet him—and arrived early at the Gitane rather than late.

"Affligem Dark," Jeremy told the approaching waiter. Then, after offering minimal pleasantries, he got straight down to the business he assumed had brought her here. "So the big blond *mec's* following you again..."

She nodded gravely then cursed, "*Putain de* Viking."

"Camera in hand?"

"He's already snapped my picture. But I've struck back," she added, inhaling a triumphant breath and drawing herself up. "I took his too." She plucked a photo out of her purse and dropped it on the table.

For an instant Jeremy stared at her, impressed with her daring ingenuity. Then he picked up the photo and studied the long face with the high forehead and short white-blond hair. The pale eyes looked only mildly surprised at the flash that must have caught the man unawares.

"Yeah, he does look like a fucking Viking," Jeremy

echoed Stefania with a smirk. "Where did you take this?"

"In the Monoprix in my neighborhood. He didn't even seem to care."

"Did he approach you?"

"No—I was sure he would, if only to grab my camera. But he just turned and strolled away down the cosmetics aisle."

Jeremy shook his head in bemusement. He recalled his conversation with Rébert of the RG and the theory they had both entertained of a bored *mec* out admiring a pretty girl. "So he hasn't tried to flirt at all?"

"*Hardly*. He has the coldest stare you can imagine. You saw him when we met that other time," she reminded Jeremy. "Do you remember anything even remotely pleasant about him?" She shifted a distasteful look to the grainy espresso-film in her cup.

"No," Jeremy conceded, and welcomed the arrival of his ale, from which he took a long pull while his mind churned with both the mystery of the Big Blond and the question of why Stefania had chosen to confide her distress in him. He had planned to begin oiling the machinery for his inquiry into the passport business, but now realized that this Viking stalker might have to take precedence for the time being. "And you still haven't reported it to anyone, like the authorities who handle your refugee status...?"

"No way. For one thing, they'd probably think it's normal: 'a little admirer,' *wink, wink. Little, mon cul!*" For emphasis she lifted her demitasse and returned it to its saucer with a loud clink. "Or," she added, "they might doubt *me*. Remember what I said about deportation? I can't give them the slightest excuse to suspect me of anything shady."

Agreed. And yet she also failed to confide in Christophe, her boyfriend of almost a year. He needed to ask about that...

Instead, Stefania explained of her own accord. "Christophe tries, but he can't understand what it's like as an exile here—not being able to work, having to watch your every step, including walking against a red light, or who you hang out with..."

Unlike Christophe, Jeremy did understand these things. He wanted to point out just what he and Stefania had in common, though he hesitated when considering his situation was enviable compared to hers.

Once more she tuned in to his thoughts. "You get it more than Christophe does. Look at us: two foreigners, gypsies like the name of this café." She extended the illustration with a sweeping hand, indicating a wall mural decorated with three fiery flamenco dancers.

Though he nodded with a sympathetic smile, Jeremy remained silent, for at least he was permitted to work...for a price. And if he were crazy enough to wish to return to America, he could—unmolested, albeit the target of a fresh arsenal of prejudices.

"What if they're trying to get rid of me?" said Stefania. "The French government, I mean—spying on me." The question came out of the blue as she leaned in, her brow and eyes crinkling with worry. "I haven't made one false step but somehow I feel the French government breathing down my neck." She looked round the café with the gaze of a perplexed child, then insisted, "I'm not paranoid, Jeremy, but I've got a strong sense about this."

For a moment he paused to consider this speculation, then picked up the snapshot of the Big Blond. "Mind if I borrow this?" he asked.

"What for?"

"Just to keep an eye out for him."

"...I guess..."

"I won't keep it long," he assured her.

But she had obviously decided it didn't matter.

"Hang on to it," she said, and once more began scanning the café. This time Jeremy noted a shudder, a quiver in her hunched shoulders that invited him to take her hand.

"Maybe we should continue this away from prying eyes and ears," he said. "I could make you another coffee at my place across the street..."

With a smile Jeremy couldn't pinpoint, perhaps it floated somewhere between gratitude and collusion, Stefania inclined her head.

As they climbed the stairs in his building, a touch of curiosity floated through his head. Here he was, taking Stefania to his flat, when after two months of dating Haley he still hadn't asked her to his lean bachelor's abode filled with second-hand furnishings. Then again, Stefania's lodgings might easily prove even more humble. Plus she seemed to need him right now, which couldn't hurt his own agenda.

Once they settled in he offered to prepare coffee. Or perhaps she'd like a drink...

"Cocktail hour in America," she said, glancing at her watch and grinning. "A drink just might sort out my nerves."

"Well, you're in luck. At the risk of running you off by boasting, I make a pretty good Manhattan."

"And that would be...?" she asked, crossing her legs and wiggling into a more comfortable position on the sofa. She wore a pair of worn but form-fitting jeans today with a faded yellow T-shirt embroidered with the lonely image of a pink flower. Her sandals looked scruffy, and suddenly he felt an inexplicable pang of sadness that she didn't know what a Manhattan was.

"Whiskey and sweet vermouth," he explained with a dismissive shrug. "Something you'd get at Harry's Bar near the Opéra, or at my bar, Le Prince Blue Note."

"And you're an expert at making them?"

"Well," he said, almost by way of apology, "at the club I made a few suggestions, like using rye instead of Canadian whisky and a little cherry juice as opposed to bitters. No big deal," he concluded, deciding he had said enough about a skill that really meant nothing.

Stefania shot him an amused smile as she extracted a cigarette from the pack in her purse. "Well, now I know what a Manhattan truly is, though I've heard of your nickname—*Meester Manhattan*." She pronounced it in French fashion and Jeremy felt his cheeks flush, wondering where she could have learned of his silly sobriquet, before deciding it must have come from Christophe. He had a nervous urge to ask her for a cigarette but batted it down as he laughed off the comment and headed to the kitchen to make their drinks.

He returned with two stemmed glasses filled with the dark-amber cocktail. The ice situation he had remedied after that previous solitary drink at home. And for his special guest he had mixed and strained the cocktails into Martini glasses. A cherry, each, grazed the bottom of their glasses, something else he hadn't bothered with the night he'd drunk himself to sleep.

He passed her a glass and sat delicately next to her on the sofa, trying not to raise too much dust with his seventy-five kilos from the hand-me-down he'd received from his waiter friend Didier and his wife. "*Santé*," he said, clinking her glass.

"*Salute*," she responded in Italian.

He smiled indulgently, though once more he refrained from sharing his rusty schoolboy Italian.

She took a sip, then emitted a little cough. Something he hadn't expected, tough as Stefania presented herself in the face of her predicaments. "Sorry," she said, "I'm not used to strong drinks."

"My fault," he muttered. "I should have warned you...I can get you something else..."

"No—it's good, actually." She ventured another sip, this time swallowing smoothly. "Just what I need to unwrinkle my nerves."

They set their glasses on the coffee table, allowing a silence to settle while Jeremy searched her expression. "Are you frightened? Of the Viking, or the French government?"

"I don't like to admit it; fear's not usually in my nature...but I have a strong feeling that something's very wrong with this situation." Her frown turned from thoughtful to afflicted and when Jeremy took her hand he thought he could feel her anxiety through its heat. "Anyway," she went on, "I appreciate your support. As I said, Christophe's a French citizen, with a regular job as an electrician plus all the protections entitled to him. Yes, he's a fellow Communist, his father fought in the resistance like mine, but he's settled in terms of life."

She slipped her hand out of Jeremy's and reached down to stub out her cigarette in the ashtray on the coffee table. "*And,*" she continued, "he hasn't asked me to settle down with him—probably because he knows I could be deported at the snap of a finger." She aimed an intense, deep-blue-eyed stare at Jeremy.

"Then he must not love you enough." Jeremy marveled at his spontaneity. He half expected Stefania to edge away from him, when he himself longed to pull her into a robust, consoling embrace.

Instead she stayed put, her shoulders giving a tiny shrug while her gaze held his almost analytically.

When she prolonged the silence, Jeremy asked, "What about the other Compagni? Have you told them you're being followed?"

"Mirko and Pietro know. They're concerned, but what can they do?" In futility she turned up her palms to him. "They're in the same boat I am, but at least they have each other."

Indeed they did. Comrades in arms like the ancient Spartans, Jeremy reflected, surprising himself with this timely memory from his lycée history class. The frankness of the professor who had generously and solemnly treated his pupils as adults when he'd said: *In order to encourage the utmost loyalty and cohesion among the troops—deep, visceral union—particularly during times of war, homosexual love was approved between Spartan soldiers.*

Yes, that fit Pietro and Mirko to a tee. Each, in his own right, vigorous and masculine. Mirko, the senior officer, with the introverted Pietro granting this deference out of practicality, or admiration, if not adoration. Pietro, the dark and even brooding type, given to the blues, according to Christophe. Pietro, the follower of gleaming-eyed Mirko.

All of them, Pietro, Mirko, Christophe, and Stefania, had fathers who'd fought the Fascists. So had Jeremy's father, though on two successive continents and in two consecutive conflicts. They all understood one another, expressed solidarity and support; and yet, when all was said and done, only Pietro and Mirko seemed spared the terrible solitude endured by exiles in a big city.

"I'm here whenever you need me," he said, and lifted his glass.

Stefania followed suit with a glowing smile of thanks. "Definitely feeling better," she said after a swallow and a swish of the remaining spirits in her glass. "You're the man with the magic."

Flattery aside, Jeremy responded with a worried frown. "You might let me accompany you around town a bit...I'm free most every day until evening, and I'd like to get another look at this Viking..."

Stefania blinked a couple of times before laying a

hand on his arm. "I'd appreciate that," she said, her gaze turning sober. "Especially if anything were to go wrong. I know you can handle yourself..." She examined his face none too subtly.

"I hope the eye doesn't put you off," he said. That annoying, angry-red eye, which fortunately wasn't watering at the moment. It had made him shyer about women, with his mother insisting he had ruined his nice looks for good.

"Oh no," Stefania countered, giving his forearm a squeeze. "Gives you character, like a scarred cheek from sabers at Heidelberg...I did hear something about your little trouble in America, though."

"Ah," he muttered, blaming Christophe once again. Anything but dashing, this weeping eye, and hardly "little," the trouble that had landed him in jail.

Stefania continued to study him as if for clues on a patchy map. "But I imagine I'm missing the whole story..."

Quite so. In fact no one in Paris knew the entire truth behind Jeremy's damaged eye, the ignoble reality of his misadventure in America five years ago—apart from Rébert and the Renseignements Généraux, that is. Christophe believed he had taken on an American redneck. Haley accepted the line of "an accident."

Clearly Stefania expected an account as well. She went on observing him as she drained her drink, after which Jeremy gently commandeered her empty glass and set it on the table. He laid his hands on her shoulders. "Listen, whatever you heard about that incident, I'm not proud of it." Pausing to give her shoulders a delicate squeeze, he added: "I know you would take back what happened in Italy if you could, and I feel the same about my mistake."

For an extended moment they took stock of each other. Jeremy withdrew his hands, and although she didn't move, Stefania seemed to shrink into herself. A shadow passed through her eyes, an ominous cloud which darkened the blue like a lake deprived of its sun. Then her eyes softened, and glistened with unshed tears. At the same time a tear leaked from Jeremy's right eye and it appeared the two were perfectly synchronized in sympathetic grief. Or at least Stefania seemed to think so, for she suddenly embraced him. "Jeremy, I don't know what happened to you," she said, "but if it's half as bad as my being involved in that robbery...that led to that little girl's death, I..."

She collapsed in his arms, breathing in short gasps as if trying to keep head above water. He steadied her, kissed her hair, and with a free knuckle cleared his cheek of the tear whose escape he had failed to check while distracted. She was now burrowing her face in his neck. Too late to clarify things.

"I hate myself for what happened," she said, her voice thick and hoarse. "But I can't go back to Italy— they'd try me as an accomplice to murder at the very least. And I never fired a shot!"

"I understand," Jeremy said, sliding his hand from her hair to caress her back.

He really did comprehend her plight: both from Christophe and from Rébert of the RG. In 1980 Stefania had been involved in the robbery of a Milan furrier. A ten-year-old child had caught a stray bullet and died, which sent Stefania scurrying underground in Italy where she hid until fleeing to France. To François Mitterrand's doctrine of refuge for Communists at risk of Star Chambers. For this Jeremy now thanked *Monsieur le Président*.

Her lips, he realized, were brushing against his cheek and it took only a slight turn of his head to meet them with a kiss. Her eager response led him to guide her until they lay on the sofa, her head resting against the armrest. Her emotional state was fragile and he didn't want to push things, so he lifted his head to kiss her lightly-lined forehead. Instead, she pulled his head back to her and ran her fingers through his hair, slowly, probingly.

"I love your head," she murmured. "It's like a Roman bust, hair short, thick, bumpy. Did you know a woman can be turned on by a man's hair?"

The frisson he felt quickened his pulse and he slipped his hand under her blouse to let it wander over her warm, soft flesh. Her breathing seemed to dance with his and when his hand slipped beneath the waistband of her jeans she reached for his sweater, sliding it up above his shirt.

He kissed her neck then gradually pulled back, thoughts of Christophe returning like a slight case of indigestion.

"What is it?" asked Stefania, her head tilting lazily.

"I just...well, I know you're single but..."

"Christophe," she pronounced with a wise nod.

The name, stated aloud and matter-of-factly, filled him with an uneasy mixture of relief and disappointment. Time to clear the air.

Stefania edged into a sitting position, her expression unperturbed. "Have you ever been in a relationship where your mate stops being attentive—maybe stops caring?"

Attentive? Jeremy recalled Stefania standing alone at the Compagni party, how Christophe, when he returned, had whisked Jeremy off, leaving her isolated once more.

Stops caring? T'es barjot, Christophe—*crazy*, to risk losing her.

The tingling thought was joined by another. This one, a whispered reminder from quarters still braced by reason and duty. *The passports.* "Yeah," he said, with a sympathetic smile, "I think I might get it..."

"Good. I'd like you to understand me completely." And with a deep, indulgent breath she pulled him into another melting embrace.

"I could make us more comfortable elsewhere..." Jeremy murmured into her neck, and when she returned a complicit smile he stood and lifted her off the sofa.

Stefania was a vigorous lover. No joking when she said she wanted him to know her right then and there. Her kisses descended down to his abdomen and below. Gently he pushed her head aside before he could climax, and she climbed atop him. And then it was done. Before he could demonstrate any of his own specialties.

He wanted to do something for her as she lay contemplating the ceiling, her expression an odd blend of post-coital dreaminess and preoccupation. So after a few minutes he excused himself, got up, and went to fetch his boom box.

"I thought we could listen to some music while we relax, and *you* smoke a cigarette," he said, setting the boom box on the floor next to his side of the bed and plugging it in. On the bed between them he placed Stefania's cigarettes and lighter, then he popped *The Best of Miles Davis* into the boom box and clicked it to reeling.

The spry, saucy number "Well, You Needn't" began, and he thought it suited Stefania perfectly. "Do you like this sort of stuff?" he asked, giving her a quick kiss as he slid back into bed.

For a moment she didn't answer, her eyes fixed in a speculative gaze as she sat propped against the headboard. "I don't really know jazz," she finally said, turning to him with a helpless smile. "I'm used to rock and popular French and English-language music. But I'll listen to anything you like."

Encouraging words; all the same he felt disappointed. His jazz conversations with Haley wafted back on the wave of Miles' mercurial trumpet. Their shared love of "Temptation," in particular. After Pascal Bertrand's sultry rendition of the song on his sax, they had returned to Haley's place mutually eroticized. Haley...he tried not to think of her. Nor of Christophe, whose beaming grin added a dose of rocks to his belly. Instead, he stayed alert for a chance to segue into the illegal passport affair.

Miles' next number had veered off on random riffs. Stefania was staring blankly at Jeremy's punching bag, something they'd joked about upon entering the bedroom. The smoke of her cigarette curled and meandered indifferently along with the jazz, an ashtray from Jeremy's night table sitting dully on the sheet in her lap. He reached down and stopped the cassette. Too much for the uninitiated, especially for someone who dug the sturdy, straightforward melodies of rock.

"Why did you do that?" she asked with a tiny start.

"No worries," he said, giving her an affectionate peck. "But I think I've got something more to your taste." He rose and replaced Miles Davis with Patricia Kaas' *Mademoiselle chante.*

"You didn't have to," said Stefania as he snuggled back under the sheet beside her. "I'm always open to new experiences." Her voice verged on coy as she ran her hand through his hair again, then let her fingers trickle down his forehead to trace a delicate circle around his defective eye. "Would you mind telling me what kind of fight caused that?"

When he demurred she stared defiantly, then scooted away, pulling the sheet over her shoulders. "It's really not fair," she said with a wounded look. "You know all about my troubles in Italy, why I can't go back. I *broke down* in front of you...." She turned and stubbed

50

out her cigarette, placing the glass ashtray on the night table with a heavy *clunk*.

Jeremy sighed to himself. "True," he said. "But there's a difference. What happened in Italy was an accident while what I did in America...well..."

"*Well?*" The question rang both quizzical and demanding. When he continued to hesitate she pressed on: "I purposely took part in that robbery—no accident there—and if I hadn't, I wouldn't be feeling the guilt I do right now and that will probably torture me forever."

Her eyes became moist again. He reached out to cup her cheek and felt a warm tear wet his thumb. He dabbed it away and pulled her close. "I only meant to get it back," he mumbled into the dark-red cushion of her hair.

"Get what back?" she asked gently, wiping her eyes and lifting them to meet his.

He leaned over the side of the bed and cut Patricia Kaas off mid-song.

"What did you want back?" she repeated, nestling against him and stroking his chest.

He gazed into the distance, eyes half closed. As if in meditation. Or calculation. "My father's saxophone. After he died my mother lent it to my cousin, my father's nephew; he thought he was a budding Walt Winters." Jeremy barked a dry laugh. His cousin was even named Walter, thanks to his mother, Walt Winters' sister. "My father didn't care much for him or his father, who was my dad's brother-in-law. Both father and son spouted right wing garbage."

Stefania stiffened. "McCarthyites?" she asked in disgust.

"Extremely stale ones by 1984. I was already back here in Paris, so I left France for Norfolk, U.S.A., to reclaim what was mine."

"And then what?"

51

"Walter insisted my mother had given him the sax. I made the distinction between giving and lending."

That this sax was my father's and it was time it came back to me. The words thundered in Jeremy's head as if he had shouted them aloud, and for a moment he fell silent, letting the echo expend itself. Then he turned to Stefania. "Why don't you light us a cigarette."

She continued to watch him but did as he asked. When she handed Jeremy the cigarette he took a long drag and sighed out the smoke, recalling how Walter had hurled in his face: *You can't even play it. I'm in a band and making money off it.* But Walter was wrong. Jeremy had never intended to desert the sax forever; he'd planned to start lessons again. And if Walter was making money as a musician he could damn well buy his own instrument.

Stefania took the cigarette back and nodded for him to resume.

"Well, Walter said I'd have to pry the sax out of his hands, or something stupid like that." Jeremy couldn't remember every detail—maybe he had moved to call his cousin's bluff. At any rate, when Walter lunged across the living room where the saxophone sat propped in a corner on a stand...

"I went after him and we started to fight. He also called me a commie coward, and that did it."

No, that wasn't quite accurate. Walter's actual words had been: *Jeremy, you're a commie coward just like your father. Can't face up to your failures!* And *that* had been the clincher. He'd tried to restrain himself—*he really had*—knowing the potential of his trained fists. But the southpaw Walter landed a punch to his eye that nearly blinded him.

In the ensuing silence, Jeremy's head started to fill with static. Distorted, reproachful sounds accusing him of stupidity, of barbarity, of inhumanity. His eyes screwed up and Stefania sent him a fearful look. "Did what?" she asked warily. "*What* did it do?"

Jeremy plucked the cigarette from the ashtray and took another restorative drag. His face managed to relax but he kept his gaze trained away from her. In a hollow murmur, he said, "I let my fists fly. Broke his nose and his jaw, and..."

He had no intention of revealing the rest. How he had wrestled Walter to the coffee table and slammed his head on it over and over. That when he realized how much blood was sluicing from his cousin's nose and mouth he finally stopped and staggered back. And slammed by a tidal wave of fright and horror—*feeling* what he had done to his cousin—he called an ambulance, which sped Walter to the hospital in a coma.

The mind-static was back—*criminal*—and he flinched when Stefania squeezed his hand. "You didn't...?"

The softness of her touch and voice seemed to wind down the noise in his head. Did she believe he'd killed his cousin? No, she mustn't think that, he told himself. Calmly he looked at her and said, "He's not dead, if that's what you mean." Her worried eyes continued to sound him and so he granted her more. "He got through it. He's all right now, except for a scarred-up face like mine."

Another half-truth. Not only was Walter's face scarred, but his mind was as well. With permanent memory loss.

"...And what happened to you?"

"I spent three months in jail. The fight was ruled mutually instigated, and they took the damage Walter did to my eye into consideration. Anyway, I got to keep my passport and return here after I got out." He glanced longingly at the smoldering cigarette butt in the ashtray.

"Want me to light another one?" Stefania asked.

"No," he said, smothering the urge. Smoking had helped him get through this uncomfortable confession but he was prepared to go no further with the story. He hoped Stefania wouldn't ask how he now *felt* about the whole thing, about his terrifying loss of self-control. That she would now simply view him as even more trustworthy.

"Was jail rough in America?" she asked instead.

"Let's say it's degrading enough."

"And the saxophone?"

He gave a mirthless chuckle. "It's right under this bed. Walter's family sent it back to my mother at her request, and she gave it to me when I returned here."

"So do you—"

"That's enough about me." As far as Jeremy was concerned, he and Stefania had achieved parity in terms of sentimental confidences. She had nothing left to complain about and perhaps owed, in her own right, some explanation as to why she'd betrayed Christophe. Just like Jeremy, it appeared she had a private agenda, which reminded him that he'd missed the boat on broaching the passport business. Inwardly, he gave a sigh. Outwardly, he smiled and swept a strand of hair from her forehead. She *was* beautiful.

"I've got to work tonight," he said, "but I'll see you home first."

"You don't have to..."

"No, no, I'd like to see if the Big Blond shows up."

"Then you really want to accompany me about town, I take it..."

"I think I should, for a few days at least...if you don't mind..." *And if Christophe wouldn't mind*, he should have added. But on that score he remained silent. In fact, to avoid any awkward entanglements down the road, he should now limit his professional capacity with Stefania to friendship. Show her his strengths going forward, after having revealed the weakness in his past. A worthy resolution...he thought.

She tugged playfully at his hair, pulling his head to her face to kiss him. "Of course I wouldn't mind. How could I feel anything but totally safe with you next to me? Just one thing though"—and he tightened his lips, expecting the mention of Christophe—"Might you show me that fabled saxophone?"

Jeremy's lips relaxed into a half-hearted smile. "Some other time, maybe," he said; while one of his father's favorite expressions came to him: *let sleeping dogs lie.*

Chapter 6

So Walt Winters' saxophone lay perpetually snoozing under the bed, roused every so often when Jeremy wanted to have a look at it. Some people knew he possessed it, but he showed it to no one: not to Christophe, nor to Didier, his waiter friend at Le Prince, not even to Haley. They knew nothing of its regretful backstory. And as for Haley, she need know nothing of his indiscretion with Stefania either. He and Haley weren't engaged, after all, though they saw each other at least once a week. Which required declaring himself busy for five days, while he played escort to Stefania in the afternoons.

He took the endeavor seriously, to the point of exchanging his loose summer loafers for his dark-brown Richelieus—the former, airy but subject to slippage, the latter, tried and true Oxfords with closed laces that left the shoe perfectly stable in the event the strings came loose. They didn't look right with jeans though, so he donned corduroys and his tweed sports jacket in order to squire Stefania around town.

During that time he noticed the sparseness of her own wardrobe—the same jeans, a couple of T-shirts, a pair of two-inch leather sandals that doubled with skirts and trousers, a pullover sweater for the cool days of June. She tended to order the cheapest drink (espresso) in a café, and he had to practically force her to agree to see a movie, though he insisted on treating her.

Skies had turned overcast, dark clouds scuttling in, and one day they found themselves caught in a wind-whipped cloudburst on the boulevard Saint-Germain. They darted under the covered entrance to Café de Flore, but as Jeremy tried to steer her inside she stopped him.

"This is one of the most expensive cafés in the city," she protested.

"Come on," he insisted, "unless you want to get soaked to the bone."

With an irritated sigh she proceeded through the door he held open, hugging her arms as if defending herself against the very air of the tony café, polluted, as she must have perceived it, with the materialism of the haute bourgeoisie. They found no free tables on the enclosed, tourist-populated terrace so Jeremy led the way into the café's inner sanctum of elegance and formality: white columns, waiters in long white aprons with white towels draped squarely over their forearms, their crisp white shirts contrasting cleanly against black vests and bowties.

"I don't like you paying in expensive places like this," Stefania muttered.

"Not an everyday occurrence," Jeremy assured her. Which was true enough, although his wallet had begun to flatten significantly from the steady outflow of banknotes over the week.

"And you never let me pick up a check," Stefania added, a last futile complaint as she surveyed the inner café with disdain. Patrons sat cozy and confident on leather banquettes topped with brass railings, their glib chatter and easy smiles reflecting a comfortable insouciance regarding discomfitures beyond these walls, be it the rainy assault or the disgruntled state of the working classes. Denizens of the most bourgeois city in Europe, Stefania labeled the café's clientele in an aside as she and Jeremy wound their way through to a table. Jeremy didn't comment. He understood that

Stefania's attitude rose from her distressed conditions and her failed past as a revolutionary. She was no longer starry-eyed about communism, just resentful the experiment hadn't worked so far. And he certainly wouldn't rub salt in the wound by mentioning Tiananmen Square or the protests and anti-communist elections in Poland, which had exploded in the news earlier in the month. All the same, he'd become a little weary of the *bourgeois* refrain. Paris had taken in his family during the McCarthy oppression, and it wasn't lost on Jeremy that none of the Compagni he knew had seriously considered seeking refuge in the Eastern Bloc.

On the matter of Stefania paying, however, well, that was out of the question. "Remember, I've got a job," he reminded her as they sat down. "You're not allowed even that basic right."

For an instant her expression revealed regret, almost shame, thought Jeremy. Then it underwent a light-hearted shift, for she never wished to be seen as a poor-me type: "Yes, in that you're lucky, *Mister Manhattan*. And if you were fortunate to have inherited from your father—"

"*I didn't.*"

His brusqueness seemed to take her aback and her eyebrows rose in surprise.

"Sorry," he said, clearing his throat. "I mean, my father died in America and everything went to my mother."

Stefania's brows lowered into a quizzical frown. "Oh, then not like in Italy. There, you would've received your share of your father's legacy when he passed away."

"*Legacy,*" Jeremy echoed with a soft chuckle. "My father didn't exactly get rich going back and forth between France and America to make a living."

Stefania nodded in sympathy. "He obviously had it terribly rough in order to..."

She didn't need to finish for Jeremy knew what she was thinking. All of the Compagni were aware of Walt Winters' suicide, most assigning blame to the insidious persecution of McCarthyism. Jeremy had left them to their conclusions, never revealing Walt's money problems or the difficult dynamics in the Winters home. The fact remained that no one in the household could come up with a clear-cut reason for Walt's suicide; all the more fodder for internal feelings of guilt.

Deftly Stefania diverted the conversation. "My father didn't have a lot of luck either. Did I tell you he was tried for war crimes after World War Two?" Jeremy shook his head and she leaned in and went on. "Toward the end of the war he got caught up with a group of partisans that included some tough thugs—not all partisans' motives were noble, I know. Anyway, these particular thugs threatened to shoot a village midwife for treating a German soldier's wounds. They lined up her, along with her two daughters, ready to execute all three of them, when my father stepped in and convinced them to back off. Still, he was put on trial with the rest of them."

"Did he serve time?"

"No, but even so, *Papa* had trouble making a life under the Christian Democrats after the war."

"Is that why you eventually took up arms yourself?"

"That was part of it," said Stefania, her lips forming a bitter line. "My father, his partisan comrades, all the communist parties of Europe, were sold out after the war—and after having risked their lives battling the Fascists and the Nazis, some of the comrades ending up in concentration camps. By the seventies, like youths in Germany, we rebelled against the Christian Democratic Machine." She paused then puffed out a sigh. "A lot of good it did us in the end."

Thoughtfully Jeremy inclined his head. He was hard

pressed to imagine himself going to the extreme of trying to overthrow a government in his youth. Stefania had been brave indeed.

"Do your parents ever visit you?" he asked.

"About once a year. They come to Paris bringing things from home, a little money as well. My mother doesn't like to stay long. She doesn't approve of my past. *Papa* understands, though." She gave a slight shiver and Jeremy took her hand in both of his. At last the waiter came round to their table.

"Order something hot and strong," he suggested.

The next three days included a stroll through the Bois de Boulogne, a visit to the Natural History Museum, and a walk up the avenue de l'Opéra, where they derided the gilding added to Garnier's already flamboyant opera house. All, with no sighting of the Big Blond. Abiding by his renewed sense of professionalism, Jeremy did not invite Stefania back to his place again, though part of one afternoon they spent in her studio flat, which Jeremy had been curious enough to check out. There, they lapsed. A mutual weakening of the flesh, Jeremy was tempted to blame it on, though Stefania had again complained of Christophe's negligence. And Jeremy, who up until then had imposed his old friend's image on thoughts like an invisible chaperone, once more let sympathy morph into lust. The timing, however, of Stefania's grievances, was not lost on him, and he was determined to broach the passport business the next day—Friday, the last of their string of outings.

That day they planned a picnic in the Luxembourg Garden, at the Medici Fountain, with its rectangular pool surrounded by potted plants and slim, arching shade trees that permitted just the right measure of sun on this cloudless day.

July had arrived, with tourists swooping down on

the capital for the Bicentennial and strutting around like pushy geese. Patriotic posters had popped up all over, some depicting crimson Phrygian freedom caps atop fasces bound with red thongs, others stamped with tricolored streamers attached to crossed pikes pointing skyward. A more elaborate variation combined the two designs—the red-capped fasces in the center, flanked on either side by blue-white-and-red plumes, like wings bearing aloft an exultant phallus.

Anyway, that was how Stefania described the banner they had sighted on rue de Médicis, just before entering the Luxembourg Garden. *Liberté, Égalité*, and *Fraternité* for men, she emphasized, and those men mainly lawyers.

Of course she was right, Jeremy conceded, barking a laugh at Stefania's impish imagination. Before their picnic they had seen the film *Danton*, rereleased in the Latin Quarter, and one movie Stefania didn't want to pass up. A tour de force performance by Gérard Depardieu as Georges Danton, revolutionary leader and rival to fellow lawyer Robespierre. Within a year of Danton's beheading, Robespierre, his accuser, was toppled and marched to the guillotine in turn.

"At least that was *some* justice," Stefania commented, referring to Robespierre's comeuppance. "That prudish viper had absolutely no understanding of the fundamentals of the people or their plight." Jeremy agreed, though he wished Stefania might give the past a break and acknowledge the progress made since 1789 by women and all social and economic classes in France. She had to be somewhat grateful for her refuge here despite being banned from working. And yet without work, or some equal sense of purpose, what did life amount to? He wondered what Stefania ordinarily did with her days but didn't inquire, finding it annoying when people asked how he filled his own days.

Jeremy did, however, finally manage to work in a question about the false passports. Once they tossed their picnic leftovers into a rubbish bin, preparing to leave the Medici Fountain for an amble through the extensive gardens, he placed his hands on his hips and looked out toward the invisible horizon. "Do you ever feel the need to get out of the country? For a change of scene at least?"

Immediately he berated himself for the baldness of the question, which on second thought seemed launched out of the blue. But Stefania showed no indication of being thrown by it. She merely shook her head mournfully, and with a heavy-hearted voice said, "Of course I do. In all these five years I've only been as far away from Paris as Blois."

"Blois," Jeremy repeated. "A day trip."

"Yeah. If *only* I could take a holiday out of the country."

"Where would you go?"

She slowed to a meditative pace as they crossed the sandy paths heading toward the tennis and boules courts, and a frown of surprise caught on her face. "God, I really don't know. The only thing I've ever really wanted to do is visit my family and friends in my home town, and of course that's out of the question."

"But if you could meet them in a different country?"

"Like taking a *true* vacation," she said in a small, wistful voice.

"Mm-hm," Jeremy prodded. "So where would you go?"

"Well...maybe Spain—one of those nice big beaches on the Costa Dorada. Now that Franco's dead people say it's a paradise."

Jeremy rewarded her with a little laugh then moved back on point. "I'm sorry you can't have your wish," he said somberly. "I guess if you left, getting back into

France might be a problem."

"Christ, Jeremy—getting *out* of France is the problem. I'm not even supposed to leave the Région Parisienne. Plus I don't have a passport."

"*Oh*," he said in feigned edification.

Stefania let out an impatient sigh. "I'm not a French citizen so how could I be issued a passport here?"

"Right," he conceded, shaking his head in sympathy. "So no passport for any of you Compagni," he added with a helpless sigh.

Stefania shot him a raised eyebrow. "Not officially."

"*Ah...*" More feigned enlightenment on his part. "You mean..."

She returned an aloof squint. "Never mind," she said, and strode on.

Jeremy trailed a step behind her, silently analyzing his first bit of progress. Stefania had virtually confirmed the existence of false passports possessed by at least some of the Compagni. Though the information would be of no surprise to the RG, it was a start. Next, and this would take plenty of finessing, he needed to worm out names of fake passport holders and determine the black source of the documents. Lots more time and patience in store, and much relief to hear Stefania unwittingly acquit herself in the matter. The assertion that she lacked a passport sounded genuinely earnest. And Jeremy would have been at pains to report her to the RG if he had judged otherwise.

At the boules courts, an area of the Garden canopied with the tangled branches and leaves of enormous, age-old plane trees and chestnuts, they stopped to watch a quartet of players. One of them, a young lanky fellow, stood frowning in concentration at the constellation of balls on the lightly sanded court, arms crossed, feet shifting, while another player took measurements. The other two players, both well into their fifties, indulged in ringing banter and laughter, seemingly confident in their vaster experience.

"That guy, the half-bald one," Stefania pointed out. "He reminds me of my father. Same build and coloring. Similar gestures too. *Papa* loves boules. Back home he competes in amateur tournaments."

Jeremy noted the tenderness and nostalgia with which Stefania murmured *Papa*. He was no stranger to uncanny encounters with those who bore a remarkable likeness to a lost loved one. There was Stefania's resemblance to Margie, of course, though Jeremy didn't exactly consider Margie a long lost loved one. Rather, the time on the metro when a man in an old-fashioned overcoat sat down across from him—same close-set eyebrows above a ski-jump nose as his father's, dark eyes and wavy-brown hair, like Walt's, swept back high on his head. The materialization of a flesh-and-blood ghost was how it struck Jeremy, and all rational thought suspended itself like a wave frozen in its arc. Stupefied, he searched the man's face for further signs of recognition until reason at last resumed its flow. The man across from him had to be approximately the age of Walt Winters in *1969*, not in 1980. The frozen wave thawed and crashed down, drenching him in sadness, in deprival, and injustice.

Jeremy wondered whether Stefania might be experiencing something similar, for she stared at the players for a long while, listening to the companionable laughter of her father's lookalike. Then the play on the court resumed and she fished a cigarette out of her purse and lit it. Smoke streamed his way like a fragrant breeze. Oh, how he enjoyed a smoke in the outdoors. Inhaling his menthols was like breathing in cool mountain air. Since his last couple of lapses into smoking with Stefania he had been mighty tempted to buy a pack of les Royales. What kept him in check so far was the image of his grandfather Jérémy Martineau—wizened from lung cancer, a living carcass at the end, gasping in fits on his deathbed in Namur. A two-pack-a-day Gauloises smoker, he had passed away just last year.

That pinching reminder came right before Jeremy felt a poke in the ribs from Stefania. "*Putain*," she whispered, "he's here!"

Jeremy glanced at her then followed her gaze to the other side of the boules courts. There stood the Big Blond, drawn up in all his Viking bulk and bearing, one thick hand resting tranquilly on the trunk of a chestnut tree. He too was observing the boules players, or at least pretended to do so, which gave Jeremy a chance to take shrewd measure of the man—and amend his previous estimate concerning his height: the Big Blond had to be at least two meters tall, Jeremy concluded with a prick of unease. He wore a dark tracksuit today with a pair of Doc Martens, or similar shoes fortified with thick treads. But his features remained fairly consistent with the photo Stefania had snapped and with what Jeremy remembered from the café: high forehead, narrow blue eyes, and a long Nordic face that Jeremy now realized was tanned. A veritable Thor in short hair, having descended from Asgard to more mellow climes. What the hell did he want with Stefania, the Italian from Belluno, Italy?

Jeremy balled his hands into fists, then let them flex.

The Viking flicked a glance at him, bent over and retied his shoelaces. Straightening, he performed several stretches, ran a few steps in place, then set off jogging.

Jeremy sprang to follow him. "Stay here," he called back to Stefania.

Across paved pathways, sandy surfaces, and gravel, Jeremy raced through the Garden in pursuit, dodging strolling couples, frolicking children, and prams. Legs pumping like pistons, fists slugging the air, in all his fury he seemed to be gaining on the Big, long-legged Blond. What he would do once he caught him was less certain.

Then, in a ferocious sprint, the Viking headed toward the access gate at rue Guynemer, bounding out of the Garden and turning left onto the sidewalk hedged by the tall black iron fence. Jeremy strained to match his locomotive stride and now felt the first signs of flagging—thumping heart rising in his throat, thighs and lungs beginning to burn in rebellion. He wanted to shout, *Stop—I just want to talk!* but had to devote his waning energy to bolstering his throbbing legs.

Instead, irony of ironies, the Viking started to decelerate, his long tree-trunk legs prancing high as he gradually slowed to a halt. Casually he turned to face Jeremy with a stony expression that betrayed little evidence of the exertion just played out. When Jeremy reached him he wanted to thunder his protest, demand an explanation to what was going on, deliver his wrath in a spate of curses. But for the instant he was too winded. And in the two long seconds it took to catch his breath the Viking launched a kick to his left knee, a glancing blow made crushing all the same in the distance afforded. Jeremy gasped inwardly, feeling he had been struck with a hammer. His fists hardened and rose to respond. Only to face the Viking's back as he pivoted and shot off down the sidewalk again.

"*Putain!*" Instinctively Jeremy lurched to give chase but realized he couldn't run. He took a few steps. It seemed he could walk all right but in no way could he catch the big bastard, whom in frustration he now watched turn back into the Garden through another gate. His knee burned as though a slow fire had been kindled beneath its cap. Nevertheless, as readily as possible, he turned and began retracing his steps back toward the boules courts, hoping to get there before the Big Blond returned to pursue his agenda with Stefania. He wondered whether the bastard had lured him out onto the street simply to disable him and then return to finish his work. Christ, the *salaud* could run. And kick. *What the hell did he do for a living?*

By the time Jeremy approached the boules courts a lancing pain that screamed at him like an air-raid siren joined the fire in his knee. He found Stefania alone, *Dieu merci,* sitting on a bench and watching in his direction. The minute she spotted him limping toward her she rose and ran to meet him. "What happened?!"

"He got away," Jeremy said with a rueful grimace.

"But *you*?" she said, looking worriedly at his leg.

Jeremy sighed; self-consciously he shifted from his right to his left leg then wincingly back to his right. "I caught up to him. But before I could question him he kicked me in the knee and ran off again." *Kicked me in the knee*: it sounded like feisty girls at recess in grammar school. Only the Big Blond knew exactly what he was doing with those thick treads of his. Jeremy considered explaining that to Stefania but dismissed it as a lame attempt to defend his pride.

"I'm so sorry; Are you hurt badly?" she asked, alarm still lurking in her eyes.

"No. He just slowed me down. He hasn't come back here, has he?"

"No, thank God."

Jeremy nodded gratefully and Stefania clasped his arm, giving it an encouraging little shake. "Well at least you succeeded in warding him off. He's a coward and he fights dirty."

If only that were the end of it and they could dismiss the fleeing Viking once and for all. But they both knew this stalker didn't strike by whim; he had a motive, though it stubbornly remained to be established.

Fear had faded from Stefania's expression though she barely said a word all the way back to her place at the southern tip of the Thirteenth Arrondissement. Jeremy had insisted on paying for a taxi to accompany her home. Stefania objected, maintaining she was entirely capable of getting home safely on her own, that he should instead go straight to the pharmacy and see about something for his knee. In the end they had compromised, Jeremy limping alongside Stefania to a pharmacy on the boulevard Saint-Michel where he purchased painkillers and a supportive bandage. When the taxi arrived at her building he invited himself up. "I'll rest my leg for a bit then get another cab to take me home."

Serious regrets followed when it came to climbing the stairs to Stefania's flat, as the action involved initiating each step with his right foot, pulling the left up to meet it, then placing painful weight on his left knee before tackling the next step. Three flights of stairs, doable, though tiring, which made him grit his teeth at the prospect of his own six flights when he returned home.

Immediately Stefania ordered him to the sofa bed, bringing him water to take his painkillers and rolling up his trouser leg to bandage his swollen knee. But his knee hurt more when extended than flexed, so once she finished he sat on the edge of the bed, which in its unmade state allowed only a sliver of space for sidling around the room. Once more he was reminded of Stefania's hardships. The entire studio flat reflected her reduced conditions, including the closet-sized bathroom with cold running water. "Maybe we'll get consistent hot water by the time they finally bring the metro to the neighborhood," she had commented with a snort on the day he'd taken a chilly shower there.

The toilet had a pull-chain flusher, the carpet looked trodden on by the combat troops of both wars, and in the cooking corner a rubber nozzle hung attached to the sink's faucet for flexible rinsing purposes. Jeremy hadn't seen such an old-fashioned device in ten years. There was no armoire, just pegs on the wall, and a small dresser where Stefania kept most of her clothes, which seemed to migrate onto various surfaces around the flat. A tiny transistor radio sat on the dresser along with sparse pieces of costume jewelry, a small alarm clock, a slush of papers, and a stack of paperback books. None of the mess bothered Jeremy; perhaps the cold water a touch, and the fact he found *that* annoying caused him a wrinkle of shame. If he had at least been able to shake down the Viking for information he wouldn't have felt so useless and pathetic right now.

He stood up and hobbled toward Stefania who had just placed his water glass in the sink. Gently he laid a hand on her shoulder. "Don't go out at night," he advised, rubbing her back. "Unless you've got Mirko or Pietro with you...or Christophe, of course," he added after giving a little cough. She nodded absently, and her eyes were unreadable as she stared past his shoulder toward the Che Guevara poster on the wall. *Che*—replete with beret, fringe of black beard, and noble stare. Too bad he wasn't here to protect her, Jeremy quipped to himself. And Christophe—he was a union electrician with a nice flat, and yet he hadn't invited Stefania to move in with him when he must have realized she longed for stability. Jeremy wished he could do something to improve her living conditions. His own place swelled spacious in comparison; and in turn shrank when contrasted with Haley Morgan's model apartment. *Haley*: did she not have everything she wanted and needed? Maybe not, for that morning she had called him to invite him over on his next evening off.

"Will you be able to make it home all right?" asked Stefania. She had pulled away and was frowning at his knee, swollen and padded thick under his trousers.

"I'll be fine." His look was stern as he gazed past her, vowing to himself that if he caught the Big Blond again he would make him talk. And if the bastard attempted another underhanded coup like this afternoon's he would break his ribs.

Chapter 7

The Big Blond struck on the last day of Jeremy and Stefania's string of outings, afternoons that neither of them had proposed sharing indefinitely. The next day was Saturday, Christophe was off on the weekend, and Stefania had made no further complaint about her boyfriend since that little lapse into lust with Jeremy at her flat. Just as well. If she were toying with making Christophe jealous, Jeremy wanted no part of it.

The Big Blond was another matter. His menace loomed ever more concretely while his motives floated mysteriously out of reach. Jeremy's knee was proof of the former. "You need to stay off it for a while," Stefania had advised that Friday. "By the way, next week I'm meeting some Italian friends, so you don't have to worry about me." A hint that she could manage without him; nevertheless he'd felt a prickle of guilt. Plus a pinch of regret, for he longed to even his score with the Viking and, more importantly, to root out the man's scheme. Each hobbling step Jeremy took represented a piercing call to arms.

The pain had forced him to call in sick at work the evening of the mishap and he'd tossed and turned in discomfort all that night in bed. He should have probably stayed home the next day, but his knee felt better by afternoon and he had a scheduled rendezvous with Rébert of the RG, who rarely deigned to meet on a Saturday.

Luckily they had picked a café located across from

the Bourse, the Paris stock exchange, only four metro stops from the Temple station near Jeremy's building.

He couldn't avoid the metro stairs, however, and as he limped laboriously into the café, muscles pulling his face, perspiration leaking from his hairline, Rébert lifted his eyebrows in surprise.

With a grunt Jeremy sank into the leather booth across from him, muttering, "Sorry I'm late." Before Rébert could speak he slapped the Big Blond's photo on the table: "And here's why."

The waiter arrived. Jeremy lifted his hand to stall Rébert while he gave his order, let the waiter head off, then finally elaborated: "This is the *mec* who's been following Stefania and he's why I'm limping."

Rébert's mouth parted to form a question but Jeremy saved him the trouble: "*Twice* now I've seen him, and when he ran off yesterday I caught him (only a slight exaggeration), but he delivered an expert kick to my knee. And I do mean *expert*."

At last Rébert edged a question in. "What kind of damage did he do?"

"Not much," Jeremy replied, the two words exuding both self-pride and disgust.

Rébert examined the photo, shaking a baffled head. "Following Stefania again, I suppose..."

"We spotted him in the Luxembourg Garden, dressed in sweats like he was out for an innocent jog."

"I assume he got away after he kneecapped you?"

Jeremy's nod was grudging, and when his beer arrived he took a generous swallow. "What if he decides to move on Stefania when I'm not there; all he'd have to do is throw her over his shoulder like a sack of potatoes and dash off like yesterday."

"But he hasn't touched her..." said Rébert, a glint of skepticism in his eyes, a note of it in his voice.

Jeremy's lips tightened, containing an impatient

sigh.

"Has he even *attempted* to approach her or talk to her?" pressed Rébert. *If there were only something solid to go on,* his tone seemed to imply. "Did he say anything to you when you caught him?"

"...No." A resigned though reluctant response.

"And you're sure he couldn't have actually been out jogging? He takes off, then speeds up when he notices *you* tailing him; then he stops and gives you a kick to get rid of you...?" When Jeremy shot him an unappreciative smirk, he added, "Just playing devil's advocate."

"Listen," Jeremy said, "I know the police can't pull some guy in for just being in the same place as a woman, but could you at least pass his description around? I could get you a copy of the photo..."

Rébert cast a quick glance under the table toward Jeremy's knee. Then he slid the photo his way before pulling a camera from his side jacket pocket, attaching a flashbulb, and snapping a photo of the photo. "I'll keep an eye out," he said, handing the mug shot back to Jeremy. Camera stowed, he extracted a pen and notebook from his inside pocket. "You say he's tall?"

"About two meters," Jeremy said, still blinking from the flash. "Late thirties, pale hair and eyes, Nordic-looking as you can see—and *very fit.*"

"You say 'Nordic.' Anything else lead you to believe he's Scandinavian?"

"No, but he doesn't look particularly French."

"Hm," Rébert reflected. "What does a *Frenchman* look like?"

Touché, thought Jeremy with a shrug of his shoulders. Tentatively he asked, "Could someone else in the RG, or from another service, have added a monitor to Stefania?"

Rébert sent him a quizzical frown. "No—why should they?"

Because French security and intelligence services are a notorious labyrinth, Jeremy voiced to himself, then amicably said, "I'm just concerned with what this guy's up to."

"I understand. But *we're* still concerned about the circulation of false passports. Anything on that front so far?"

A sting of embarrassment drew Jeremy up in the booth, shoulders squared, tone formal. "I can say at this point your suspicions are justified. A number of Compagni do possess fake passports, though I haven't discovered any names yet."

Rébert returned a knowing nod. "Black-market documents are rife, always have been among the underclasses. If you ask me, it's a losing battle trying to combat the trade, but we've got to show we're trying—orders, you know. Anyway, Jeremy, you're obviously doing a fine job. And,"—almost as if in afterthought—"we'll be re-evaluating your work situation down the line."

"Pardon?"

"We're considering restoring you to full-time employment status."

Jeremy gazed at him with widening eyes. "Could I ask *when*?"

"Don't know yet. We're up to our ears trouble-shooting the Bicentennial. Once that's over I'll know more."

"Right," Jeremy acknowledged, his thoughts looping off as he gazed past Rébert's shoulder.

"Another thing about Stefania," said Rébert. "Has she mentioned reporting her Nordic admirer to the police?"

Regretfully, Jeremy shook his head.

"*No*," seconded Rébert, "I imagined not. Stick with her, Jeremy, she seems to at least trust you."

And not the French authorities. Obviously Rébert understood that; just as he made apparent his lack of empathy for Stefania's plight. It rankled Jeremy, particularly as Stefania's faith in him now seemed purely to benefit the RG. She suspected the French government had it in for her but Jeremy doubted that. Stalking games were not required to apprehend Stefania and ship her back to Italy. The sum of which, all things considered, again turned the Big Blond, now nemesis to both of them, into a Big, capital algebraic X.

He gazed out the window across the street, toward the classically-columned Stock Exchange. Inside the grand structure he pictured weekday swarms of worker ants in the guise of suits, ties, and briefcases, scurrying about making frenzied trades. Extended employment status was coming Jeremy's way, if Rébert could be believed, though he'd made no mention of the RG cutting Jeremy loose. For a moment he envisioned himself one of the workers in the temple of finance, humping off to his job from nine to six, caged and desperate to gain favors from the god Mammon. He'd take his flexible, eclectic RG job any day. As long as Mammon gave him a wink every now and then.

For the rest of the afternoon, thoughts of the Big Blond and an improved work status chased each other like clouds in the windy sky of Jeremy's mind. Once more he called in sick at Le Prince, hoping, since he had the following night off, he would be recovered for his next shift. The rest seemed to pay off, for he slept uninterruptedly through the night and the next day his knee felt much better. He was even limping less and considered walking the eight blocks, or so, down to rue des Archives, where Haley Morgan was waiting for him to spend the evening with her. But his better judgment convinced him to take a taxi, and all the way down into the Marais he fantasized how he could force the Big Blond to pay his cab expenses.

Haley's apartment shone spotless as usual. Not a fleck of dust on the glass coffee table, which she must have spray-cleaned before he arrived, the pillows on the over-stuffed sofa perfectly arranged, virtually awaiting a magazine photo-shoot. Who knew why such meticulous housekeeping bothered him, but before he and Haley managed to sit down he blurted, "Did you buy all this furniture?"

She blinked at him through the brown-framed spectacles that matched her short, chestnut hair. "Yeah..." she intoned inquiringly.

He gave a shrug, an ineffective gesture meant to mask his unease with Haley's relative affluence. Two days ago he had experienced Stefania's cramped, chaotic billet. And left her having failed to sort out the Viking. Furthermore, his knee was now pinching again after the climb of Haley's stairs. Regarding his limp, he'd told her he'd tripped on cobblestones near Beaubourg.

About the furniture, he went on to comment in a softer tone. "I was just wondering—everything's so modern compared to other French flats."

"Like yours, for instance? I still haven't had the pleasure." A touch of good-natured irony played in her subtle smile.

Jeremy wiped his right eye, a mechanical habit since the eye wasn't watering per se; a tic, perhaps, when he felt ill at ease, as opposed to the inopportune tear or two escaping when he found himself intensely absorbed in something.

"My place needs work," he said, "but of course I'll invite you over sometime." It was the first time Haley had addressed the subject directly and he didn't know what else to add.

"I've got a surprise," she cheerily announced,

relieving the awkwardness. "I haven't seen you all week and I've been dying for you to listen to something...sit down and I'll be right back."

He stripped off his jacket, draping it over the back of an armchair, then dropped heavily onto the sofa. Haley's flat really was comfortable, he admitted to himself with an umpteenth tinge of guilt regarding the meanness of an attitude he couldn't quite manage to shed. Embarrassment about his own flat notwithstanding, he still preferred to hang out here.

"I've discovered a new jazz album," she declared, entering the sitting room and shaking the music cassette before placing it in his hands and plumping down beside him.

"Gainsbourg," Jeremy grunted, faced with the French singer's close-up next to the cassette's title, *Du Jazz dans le ravin*. "This can't be new by the looks of him."

"True. The original album came out in 1964 but I found this in the Drugstore Matignon."

"Hm," said Jeremy, scanning the list of songs. "I'd heard Gainsbourg started out as a jazzman..."

"But you've never heard this album?"

He shook his head and handed her back the cassette.

Haley looked delighted. "Then I'm glad it's a surprise. Frankly," she said with a sheepish smile, "it bowled me over; I think it's become my favorite jazz album."

"You like it better than *Kind of Blue*? Jeremy asked in wonder.

"Just give it a listen." She rose to insert the cassette in the stereo, which sat on a metal-and-glass shelf, and pressed PLAY.

The first song made him blink inquisitively. By the third cut his doubts dried up entirely. The array of instruments, including a hot sax, the sizzling arrangements, plus plum musicianship, all held him in thrall. "You say this was released in '64?" he asked, his enthusiasm mounting to join Haley's.

"Right."

"That was when we moved back to America," he observed. "Didn't hear much French music there."

Practically every instrument known to jazz displayed its virtuosity, each spread sparingly throughout the album so as not to overload any one song. Each song soaring for about two tantalizing minutes.

Jeremy laid his head back on the sofa cushions and uttered, "This is delicious."

"Glad you like it," Haley said, snuggling closer to him in appreciation. "You can't really compare it to Miles Davis, especially with Gainsbourg singing in most of the numbers."

Haley loved Serge Gainsbourg, and Jeremy lifted his head to wink at her. "Yeah, *just for you.*"

In fact, the deep baritone was vintage Gainsbourg, smooth and sonorous, cool and confidential, and perfectly paired with the instrumentation. The lyrics glided from whimsical to edgy to provocative.

Jeremy rested his head back again. If *Kind of Blue* represented a *pièce de résistance*, Gainsbourg's short tangy numbers were the exquisite hors d'oeuvres you could make a meal of.

When the song "Black March" kicked in, he stirred and straightened. A fully instrumental cut, it featured a dialoguing trumpet and tenor sax: back and forth they went, the melody so clean and simple that Jeremy tried to follow the notes in his mind. *God, I could play this in no time if I took lessons again. If...*The word rang pregnant with the past, paralyzing in the present.

He sank back and let the next song seep into him like a soothing brandy. A slow, melancholy alto sax cozied to Gainsbourg's seductive croon, and Jeremy felt his blood rising with the heat.

"There's innuendo in this song, do you feel it?" he murmured in Haley's ear.

She drew a deep breath and released it warm on his neck. They kissed, and he wanted to taste her, to tickle her further.

"Shall we listen to the rest in the bedroom?" she whispered. "Unless your knee..."

Jeremy dismissed her concern with another kiss.

To a trumpet's wicked edge and the intoxication of the vibes, they plunged into each other, reveling in redoubled passion. When they at last surfaced and lay resting on their backs, the music was still with them.

Haley said, "The vibes are one of my favorite instruments—know why?"

Because they sound magical and intoxicating, he repeated to himself.

"Because they make me feel warm and less alone," she said. "The vibes give off a glow, especially when it's dark, when the days get shorter and it's easier to feel lonely. They're like bouncing balls of light that warm me." She turned to Jeremy and added in a misty voice, "Like you did when I met you."

Her description evoked magic itself, and for a moment he was so moved he remained speechless. He had an urge to tell her how much the sentiment meant to him, but instinctively shied from it. Instead, in a thick voice he said, "I felt special too back then. You usually surround yourself with French people..."

Together Haley's lips and eyes sketched a smile of reminiscence. "I had a British friend when I first arrived here ten years ago. He said it wouldn't be long till I'd crave to hear and speak English, embrace my native language like a lost treasure. Well, he was right. I'll always love French, but deep inside"—and her hand pressed her midriff—"English drives me. I don't know exactly how to put it ..."

With affectionate interest Jeremy watched her. Maybe he understood.

"For you it's different," she went on. "You've moved between English and French all your life."

True enough, and at this point he couldn't say which language spoke to him most at gut-level.

"Anyway, I'm glad you and I speak English together," she pronounced with a little laugh. "We've already established the superiority of your French."

He squeezed her hand and draped an arm around her.

As he prepared to leave the next morning, Haley pressed a cassette tape into his hand. "I made it for you yesterday before you came, hoping you'd like it."

It was a duplicate of *Du Jazz dans le ravin*—her marvelous Gainsbourg discovery—and she had printed the name of every song for him inside the cassette case.

He hadn't decided whether to take a taxi home. His knee felt better by the day and his spirits were high. So he left the building on foot, whistling up rue des Archives and giving the cassette in his jacket pocket a squeeze as if it were Haley's hand.

The eight-block hike to his flat left Jeremy feeling more taut discomfort in his knee than stabbing pain. Surely a sign of progress he decided, as he put on the new jazz recording and sat to listen and rest. Both sides of the cassette finished, he was back on his feet, finding the sax arrangements so stimulating that he needed to retrieve his father's instrument, attach its mouthpiece, and hold it in his lap on the sofa. His fingertips grazed the mother-of-pearl keys, shiny-opaque and so cool to the touch. He allowed his lips to brush the mouthpiece before inevitably pulling away like an apprehensive youth fearing his first kiss. His eyes closed and his brows rose high and tense as he imagined Walt Winters pealing out the climax of "How High the Moon"—holding the last note for those three or four long, enchanting seconds.

He opened his eyes and let his fingers slide fondly along the sax's body: little scrapes here, a tiny dent there, m-hm...

He stiffened, discovering a scratch he had overlooked or not paid sufficient attention to. He ran his thumb along it, then rose to collect a rag from the kitchen to try to buff it out. Nothing doing, and not for the first time Jeremy began the ritual of wondering and questioning how the saxophone had become marred in the various stages of its existence. Who was responsible for this bit of damage? His father, long ago? Cousin Walter with his greedy, grubby, clumsy hands?

Irritation bordering on anger, Jeremy stood, arms akimbo, and frowned at the inert instrument that lay cool, stiff and still as a porcelain doll on the sofa.

The phone rang. He started, then crossed to the entryway to answer it.

Stefania's voice—fresh with alarm. *Would he meet her at La Gitane?*

Of course he would, and quickly he packed up the sax and stowed it back under his bed, then headed down the stairs and across the street. Thoughts of the instrument dissolved like mist burnt away by a rising sun.

Chapter 8

*T*he French were persecuting her, the Viking, probably a big Norman employed by one of the security services to shadow her, then capture her, and next, God only knew what. "You know, the Normans *were* Vikings originally," Stefania added to her breathless litany, as they sat in Jeremy's neighborhood café La Gitane. *Oh, and by the way, how was his knee? Much better? Great.*

Stefania sat against the wall, her urgent gesticulations practically mirroring the flourish of the female flamenco dancers painted behind her. Jeremy found it all disconcerting, until she suddenly came to a calm halt and gave an understated shrug. "Anyway, I just wanted to alert you in case I disappear."

His mouth parted, his head shaking in puzzlement. "But you haven't seen him again...?"

"No, but after last Friday..."

Right, only three days ago; her nerves were understandably still raw. Christophe would have returned to work today, but what about the Italian friends she was supposed to be spending time with? Jeremy decided not to ask and flashing briefly on his tête-à-tête with Rébert, said, "But why would the security services be after you?"

"Why not—politicians and government represent-atives are always threatening to get rid of us."

"Get rid of you, Mirko, and Pietro?"

"Of all of the Italian exiles who fought in the seventies. You think Mitterrand really *enjoys* having us

82

here? Italy's always on his balls to return us, the French government has to keep an eye on us so we don't get into trouble—Mitterrand's Grand Politics are becoming a pain in the ass for him."

Jeremy shifted his weight, his thoughts whirring. No use further suggesting she report the harassment. She was paranoid about the government, and the RG— the intelligence arm of the state police—already had a copy of the Big Blond's photo. Shit, if she found out...

"I don't know what to tell you..." he said carefully.

Stefania shook her head in dismay. "There's nothing more you can do. At least you've taken me seriously, whereas Christophe hasn't, since he's never actually seen the big hulk. You stuck by me for five days and got hurt because of it. I've not gone out alone at night, but now I'm sick of it. Sick of acting afraid. It's not me."

Christophe: so he was finally aware of Stefania's stalker...yet what exactly did she mean that he didn't take her seriously? He wanted to ask but felt utterly embarrassed about Christophe. Still, he tried to frame a question...

"By the way, Christophe knows about us," she declared, paralyzing his thoughts.

"Oh...?" he muttered, glancing down.

"He's aware of our outings and therefore suspects we've slept together."

Therefore? Had Christophe made the leap of logic completely on his own? Somberly Jeremy regarded Stefania, wondering whether she had covered for them with a denial. Once more he voiced nothing, asking just one question of himself: *Why do I feel truly guilty only now that I may have been caught?*

"Anyway," Stefania went on, "it doesn't matter. I've given him plenty of hints about moving in together, even hinted at the marriage question. But he won't commit to anything more than what we've got going right now."

So she had been trying to make Christophe jealous. *Stefania, my dear,* Jeremy thought: *Christophe's a solid French citizen, one of the elect, a member of a cozy system that sacredly guarantees him his job. Your situation would be a millstone around his neck if he married you.* Of course the judgment was cruel, and Jeremy was glad he hadn't blurted out his half-assed attempt to ease his betrayal of Christophe. Even though he knew Stefania was of like mind regarding Christophe's privileged status.

About which she conveniently went on to complain. "Christophe was born here, he's got a good job, family, he can wear his communist badge without looking over his shoulder..."

Jeremy nodded, waiting for Stefania's venting to peter out, then finally speaking up on a different note. "Have you told him that you suspect one of the security services of tailing you?"

"Yes. And he thinks it's ridiculous. He says why would they follow me around like a lost dog when all they have to do is pick me up if they feel like it?"

Jeremy concurred, distinguishing his own RG role from the apparently random appearances of the Big Blond. A distinction he couldn't share, so at last he decided to pursue what Christophe knew about them and how he had found out.

"I told him that you only acted as my escort for a few days while he was working," confessed Stefania. "That you chased the Viking, or government agent, or whoever the hell he is, through the Luxembourg Garden. Your gallantry annoyed him, as much as he tried to hide it, and that's when he accused us of having an affair."

"Did you deny it?"

Stefania gave a couple of slow nods. "Problem is," and here she paused with an embarrassed, slightly forlorn look, "I love him." She leaned in, a warm hand on Jeremy's. "Which doesn't mean I don't still need someone to take my fears seriously, someone who understands...a friend."

Jeremy returned a faint though sympathetic smile. It was all right. Though she had used him to give Christophe a pinch of reality, as well as for protection from the Viking, Jeremy was nonetheless fond of her. And their fling had benefited them both, Jeremy having indulged his special nostalgia for the redhead Margie while making a dent in the passport business—*merely* a dent.

"Can I continue to count on you for solidarity?" she pressed, a hopeful note in her voice.

Jeremy nodded and squeezed her hand.

"*Friends*, then..." she said, holding his gaze as firmly as she returned his squeeze.

"Friends," Jeremy assured her. After all he still had work to do: both with the passport matter and with settling his personal score with the Viking, of which he hardly needed prompting as he flexed his left leg under the table and was reminded he still couldn't lock his knee without pain. He considered offering further escort services but instead suggested they meet for coffee again soon, after Stefania made the sensible observation: "I guess if the government truly wants me out of France they'll find a way to take care of it no matter who's in my corner."

She might have viewed her pronouncement as prophetic, if she had foreseen the content of Jeremy's meeting with Rébert two days later.

"I'm taking you off the passport job for the time being," said the RG man, "and putting you on something new."

Jeremy shifted irritably in his café chair. "You haven't assigned someone else to Stefania...?"

"No, something more immediate's come up."

"Oh?" said Jeremy, then listened to Rébert explain his new concern: two young graffiti artists whom he suspected (by way of a scruffy informant) of daubing anti-Bicentennial slogans on prestigious Parisian monuments. Allegedly they had already painted RÉVOLUTION BOURGEOISE at squares Nation, Bastille, and République. As soon as the banal catchphrase had been erased, the two had come back with another that was hardly more original: RÉVOLUTION RATÉE (*failed*), this latest sprayed prominently on François Mitterrand's new Opéra Bastille, scheduled to open on the very day of the Bicentennial—now only three weeks away.

Like most Parisians with leisure time, the graffiti aficionados frequented a favorite café, whose coordinates Rébert supplied to Jeremy with instructions to hang out there, try to eavesdrop, even make friends to discover the duo's further plans. Jeremy questioned how he would go about the job. He didn't know the two from Adam and it seemed doubtful he would overhear any damning confessions on their part. After all, who babbles their schemes in the open? Furthermore, they undoubtedly carried out their mischief at night when Jeremy was working.

Finally he sighed to himself: mere excuses on his part, and disappointment at being shunted away from Stefania and her Viking. No, *his* Viking, too. On the other hand, who said he couldn't pursue his project privately? And this new job, trifling as it appeared, would still earn him points toward the full-time work status Rébert had dangled in front of him like a longed-awaited Christmas present. On a lesser note it could also help clean up his neighborhood. RÉVOLUTION RATÉE had shown up on the plinth of the bronze statue of Marianne, female symbol of the French Republic, draped in classical robes and holding forth the olive branch of peace. At the center of Place de la République, she faced Jeremy's street in all her splendid majesty, and he hated seeing her defaced.

Jeremy and Rébert had met in a café a few blocks from Jeremy's house ("Glad your knee's better, *mon vieux*, but let's keep this walk a short one—you'll be doing plenty more when you get started on your new job"), and afterwards Jeremy paused at his neighborhood park, Square du Temple.

Faire le point—take stock—whatever you wanted to call it. Jeremy sat pondering. Yes, he would pursue the Big Blond bastard, his pride demanded it plus he wanted to put a stop to the stalking of Stefania, an even worthier goal, he felt, than simply settling his own score. So, perched on a dark-green bench amidst the more brilliant green of grass and fleshy plane tree leaves; against a backdrop of sculpted, balconied buildings and a foreground of frolicking children, he took out his notebook to prepare for the hunt.

He made a list of places Stefania most likely frequented, such as the Monoprix supermarket where she had snapped the Viking's picture, and other establishments common to all neighborhoods: nearest café, pharmacy, Laundromat, et cetera. If their nemesis had lurked in any of these places, someone—a proprietor, a clerk, a patron—may have noticed him, heard him speak, remembered something distinctive about him.

First things first, however: the graffitists.

As Rébert had advised, Jeremy found them at noon the next day in the Café du Moine Poilu. A sign above the door featured a scrawny medieval monk in shabby brown robes and ragged sandals. While in Western fashion he should have been clean-shaven and tonsured, he instead wore a thick beard that merged with wildly sprouting chest hair (hence the adjective *poilu*) and long hair spreading across his shoulders in a scraggly mantle.

Inside the Latin Quarter haunt, Jeremy matched photos Rébert had provided to two young men, no more than in their late twenties. And both with coiffures as abundant as the café mascot's, one with a long dark mane, the other sporting a blond Afro. There, the similarity to Hairy Monk ended, with the two clad in pedestrian jeans and long-sleeved T-shirts.

Jeremy took a seat at a table next to them and ordered an Affligem Blonde. After nursing the ale for forty-five minutes, watching the two do nothing but smoke, read the papers, and lazily mock celebrities in town for the Bicentennial, Jeremy decided to leave. The duo seemed to treat the café as their home, their gear spread out over two tables—keys, a comb, a wallet, in addition to their cups, ashtrays, and newspapers—and Jeremy wondered whether they had jobs. If they didn't it was just as well, since he would return tomorrow. As for today he considered his work complete. *Now, on to his own business.*

He caught the metro at Cluny-la Sorbonne, the station also nearest Le Prince Blue Note, and which had thankfully re-opened just last year after a closure of fifty-eight years. Jeremy considered the station's new ceiling one of the finer works of the Mitterrand period. In place of traditional white tiles you gazed up at a vault splashed with the signatures of famous Sorbonne students, among those the reproduced scripts of Georges Danton and Maximilien Robespierre. He recalled Stefania's disdain for the lawyers of the Revolution, then focused on matters of more consequence to both him and to her.

Stefania lived in the southwest sector of the Thirteenth Arrondissement, near the Gentilly cemetery and the southern border of Paris proper. A modest, hilly *quartier* that lacked a metro stop. Stefania had complained of this before and Jeremy, who didn't know the bus schedule here, now experienced the eight-block walk himself from station Tolbiac. Considering the similar distance he had walked home from Haley's a few days ago, his knee was holding up fine. As he arrived in Stefania's neighborhood he rearranged his collection of snapshots—the Hairy Monks, as he now nicknamed the graffiti pranksters of the Bicentennial, moving to the inside of his jacket, the Big Blond's photo taking precedence in his outside pocket.

Where to start? Not another café just yet—with the obligation to buy an additional beverage—but rather...Ah, the little Arab grocery store near Stefania's plain beige building.

To the bright-eyed, swarthy man behind the cash register Jeremy introduced himself as an insurance investigator, a convenient title when doing jobs for the Renseignements Généraux, as it never seemed to alarm people or arouse their suspicion. They never even asked to see identification. Nevertheless, when he plucked out the Big Blond's photo, he received a firm shake of the head and a polite *non* from the clerk. From there, Jeremy crossed the street to the pharmacy, where his display of the photo also netted a *non,* this time on the part of a white-coated female pharmacist, who added an apologetic *désolée.*

Upon leaving the pharmacy Jeremy longed to peel off his jacket and roll up his shirtsleeves, but he had to keep a professional profile while visiting establishments. Midafternoon, and the sun was a bonfire in the sky, gearing up for the 14 July blowout. He wiped his eye—the smog was back as well.

He crossed to the shady side of the street where he spotted a bank. Not likely the Big Blond would make himself visible there, with personnel alert to who came and went. Nor did Jeremy wish to show the photo to someone who might hold him to task. Banks were air-conditioned, however, so he nipped in for a fractional respite, then out again. Continuing down the sidewalk, he finally came to the Monoprix. But even there, clerks and patrons alike puffed out their cheeks and shook their heads at the Viking's mug.

Frowning over this latest disappointment he took another side street, where he found a Laundromat. Two women sat on a wooden bench along the wall, presumably waiting for the washers and dryers. To the droning and sputtering of the machines Jeremy studied the women, who were separated by a large space on the bench. One, middle-aged, glanced up at him from a booklet of crossword puzzles, a pencil poised at her lips. His gaze swiveled to the other, a younger woman immersed in a paperback. Her eyes refused to rise, so he thought he'd give her attention a little nudge.

Photo in hand he approached, planting himself in front of her. "*Excusez-moi...*"

Her distracted gaze left the final pages of her novel, and with an impatient look she flicked a strand of light-brown hair off her forehead. Jeremy's insurance spiel received, she granted the photo a quick frown, then—

"He's very tall," Jeremy urged before she could reply. "About two meters, and well built..."

But the young woman joined the ranks of the *non, désolée*, then curtly dismissed him by blocking her face with her book.

His shoulders had started to sag when he heard, "*Pardon, Monsieur.*" Down the bench, the older lady was motioning to him.

He joined her at once. "Madame?" he said in a solicitous tone.

Eyes on the photo in his hand, she laid her book of

crosswords in her lap with her glasses, then aimed an inquisitive smile at him. "You were asking questions...showing that picture..."

"Quite right," Jeremy replied, and quickly began his insurance investigator speech.

"May I see it?" she asked, fixing her glasses in place before he'd finished. "Sit down so I can get a good look."

He obeyed, settling next to her and handing over the Big Blond's snapshot.

She wasted little time scrutinizing it. "I've seen him. Big strapping fellow. Has the posture and air of a mountain climber and the looks of a young Max Von Sydow."

"You're sure..." Jeremy asked, practically suspending his breath.

"Saw him here last week, just sitting around—no laundry with him."

"*Sitting...*" Jeremy repeated. *No laundry.*

The woman slid her glasses off and handed the photo back. "He was staring out the window at the sidewalk. Got up, paced a bit, then sat down again. I asked him if he'd forgotten his laundry."

"You *spoke* to him," Jeremy said, stiffening in anticipation.

"Some small talk before I asked him if he had a pencil, since I'd forgotten mine."

"And he answered?"

"In a brusque German accent. *No pencil.*"

"*German,*" echoed Jeremy, disconcerted. "You could tell...?"

"I lived through the war, Monsieur," she stated with solemn eyes.

Slowly he nodded in deference. Madame had to be his mother's age to remember German accents during the war, yet she looked distinctly younger than Béatrice Winters.

"Did he say anything more?" Jeremy asked.

"Oh no. The conversation seemed to put him off, and he got up and left. May I ask what he's done?"

Jeremy returned the photo to his pocket. "It's confidential, I'm afraid, but I need to contact him."

He could sense her disappointment and continued curiosity, and when he asked if she remembered what the Big Blond was wearing, her eyes brightened with a keen glimmer. "A navy tracksuit, with a pair of heavy-treaded shoes," she said, holding his gaze in expectation.

"And you say he reminded you of a mountain climber?"

"Only an impression, I know, but a strong one. The build, the way he carried himself. My husband was a mountaineer. Plus this man was suntanned—ruddy-tanned, like he'd just come off the mountain, whereas not many people in Paris achieve that kind of tan until after they've gone on vacation in August."

True, Jeremy thought, although Madame's own complexion was golden-brown, her neck-length blond hair contrasting nicely with her tan.

Perhaps she caught his observation, for she airily explained, "On the other hand, I am retired and have the luxury to go to the mountains whenever it suits me."

Her smile was attractive. For an instant he pictured her in over-sized sunglasses, sunning herself on a restaurant terrace atop a grassy hill near Chamonix.

"Wish I could be of more help," she said, "but you obviously know what he looks like—and what he's done..."

Her tone remained expectant...perhaps she could be of further help down the line...

Jeremy gave her a kind but officious smile, then delivered a story he had prepared. "I suppose it wouldn't hurt to say we suspect him of hit and run. One of our client's cars was extensively damaged while parked."

"Well it's nice that you're on top of things, though I imagine the police are involved..."

"They've been notified, of course. Still we still have to proceed with our own investigation. In fact," he said, aiming an earnest frown at Madame, "if you happen to see this man in the neighborhood again, would you mind giving me a call?" He pulled out his mini address book and tore a sheet from it, scribbling his name and number. "I've left my cards at home, but please take this. It's my home number and I'd appreciate your news at any time."

She accepted the paper with pleasant smile, so he ventured, "If you wouldn't mind giving me your number..."

She didn't, and once the exchange was complete, Jeremy said, "You should probably give this fellow a wide birth, Madame"—he glanced at his booklet— "Cholot."

With that he rose, his weight shifting automatically to his right leg. Madame Cholot's gaze traveled from his knee to his face. When he proffered his hand she shook it firmly, and flashing his most affable smile he took his leave.

Chapter 9

Having received Madame Cholot's revelation about the Big Blond's German accent, Jeremy wanted to celebrate with another Affligem in the nearest café, where he had planned more inquiries anyway. But as he fingered the change in his pocket, which included a couple of ten-franc coins, he decided he was spending too much on beer. When he reached the café across from Stefania's building he ordered a simple espresso at the counter where he immediately engaged the barman with his spiel.

The man looked at the photograph on the counter and narrowed his eyes in recollection. "I believe I've seen him at least once..."

Luck begat luck, Jeremy affirmed to himself, then asked, "Did you speak to him?"

"He didn't come to the counter, but my colleague Mireille might've waited on him since we usually share this shift." Before Jeremy could ask to see her, the barman was already calling the young woman over.

She arrived with an empty tray in her hand, and after scanning the photo she pronounced: "*un très grand blond*."

All three met eyes and nodded, Mireille with certitude, the barman in concurrence, and Jeremy with enormous satisfaction. "Did you notice an accent when he ordered?" he asked Mireille.

She sat the tray on the bar and adjusted her brunette ponytail. "He didn't say much, but I remember thinking he might be Alsatian. Just a passing thought. I'm sure I was in a hurry, like I am now."

"Alsatian," Jeremy repeated, while Mireille gave the barman her order. "Because his accent was German?"

"Yeah, or something similar—just a thought," she reiterated as her tray was reloaded.

He watched her glide back through the tables, bearing an espresso, an Orangina, and a Perrier.

For Mireille, the *Grand Blond* spoke with a possible German inflection; for Madame Cholot the Teutonic accent was a certainty. In any case, he was no Viking Norman as Stefania had fantasized. At best a Frenchman from the historically German-speaking area of Alsace-Lorraine...*German*—the language that had scuttled him in school, now apparently spoken by the bastard who had almost done his knee in.

Jeremy gave an irritated sigh. Took off his jacket and rolled up his sleeves. No need to further canvass the neighborhood for now. He finished his near-cold espresso, paid, and left the café, mumbling "Now what?" Report his findings to Stefania? To Rébert—what would the RG agent think about this tidbit? Not much, probably, for his watchword had now become "War on Graffiti." And Stefania? he repeated to himself as he strolled down the sidewalk, directionless. No doubt she would dub the *Grand Blond* a German-speaking French agent, ever prowling the side streets in pursuit of her and her eventual deportation.

But the conspiracy made no sense. The French authorities needn't waste resources in pussyfooting around. There had to be something else going on, some other menace represented by this big blond mountaineer type. Jeremy looked at his watch: three-thirty. Since he was in the neighborhood he might as well pay Stefania a visit. She had no phone in her flat, so he couldn't warn her and hoped the surprise wouldn't annoy her. At the same time he could benefit from her hospitality to rest his knee for a spell.

He followed a young black woman through the entrance to the apartment building then hiked painstakingly up the three flights to Stefania's floor. He rang the doorbell—once, then once
more. She wasn't home. Maybe just as well; he didn't want to fuel her conspiracy fantasy.
Even so, he owed her this new information about the *Grand Blond* and he would try to find another opportunity to tell her.

Back on the sidewalk he continued to mull things over. Particularly the idea of an Alsatian identity for the *Grand Blond*. From what he remembered from his lycée German studies, he didn't think it was common for Alsatians in their thirties to speak German from the cradle. He thought of Madame Cholot, the original pinpointer of the German accent. She might have an idea, and he had her number.

He called her from the nearest phone booth.

"Ah, Monsieur Winters, something new about the case?" Like most French she pronounced his name *Weenters*, with stress on the second syllable. "I just got home; Come round for tea; you *do* like tea? If not I can make coffee..."

"Tea would be very nice," he said. She gave him her address and the security codes to open the building's entrance door and the following door to access the flats. If Madame Cholot hadn't already made her interest in the "hit and run case" so clear he would have wondered at such a degree of trust granted to him. It was clear she took a proactive interest in the goings on of her neighborhood.

She lived only a touch further north of Stefania, next to the Place de l'Abbé Georges Hénocque. The difference in architecture, however, was dramatic, with Stefania living in a drab six-story structure on the city's periphery, while Madame resided in a lovely redbrick building, enveloped by trees and enlivened by the verdant, flowery Place G. Hénocque. Once Jeremy got through the second door of the building he discovered Madame even had an elevator, for which he was infinitely grateful. It seemed recently installed, he noted, as he swung on his jacket and waited for the modern metal-and-glass cage to arrive at ground floor, next to the worn but polished wooden banister and steps of the stairwell.

An air of timeworn charm intensified when Madame Cholot opened the door to her fourth-floor flat, and Jeremy was ushered into a sitting room warmed by bookshelves, paintings, and oriental rugs. Madame swept her toned arm toward a velour-upholstered sofa whose curved, Louis-the-something legs, reminded Jeremy of his Belgian grandmother's furniture.

"Do take your jacket off if you'd like; with this heat I can't imagine wearing one," she said, then glided off to the kitchen to put the kettle on. Before settling on the sofa Jeremy paused in the quiet and cool of a cross breeze flitting in from two open windows. He let his gaze roam the room, taking in walls crowded with watercolors of mountain scenes and framed generational photos. A drum-table sat on one side of the room, its round wooden surface hosting two open dictionaries that flanked a booklet of crossword puzzles. On the other side of the table lay a maroon atlas, hard-backed and dog-eared like the dictionaries. He laid his jacket on the sofa's armrest and sat down.

"I see you enjoy crosswords," he said, as Madame returned and sat across from him in a matching chair.

"That plus knitting, and jogging early in the morning in the Parc Montsouris."

Jeremy's eyebrows rose with interest in a middle-aged French woman jogging in Paris. Though Louise

Cholot didn't look it she had to be at least in her mid fifties, he thought again. In the Laundromat she had worn a skirt and blouse, the skirt now traded for a pair of comfortable drawstring trousers. Perhaps she wore them when she ran.

"You're surprised that I jog?" she asked, a corner of her mouth turned up in amusement.

"Er...no..."

"In spite of my indoor hobbies I'm an outdoorswoman. As I told you, my husband was a mountaineer, and I've always been an avid hiker."

Jeremy was about to ask about her husband, when Madame quickly went on to explain: "Jean-Baptiste died while climbing near Ortisei, in the Italian Dolomites."

"I'm sorry..."

"Well, you know the saying about dying while doing something you love. I suppose it's most people's wish. It's how Jean-Baptiste would have seen it," she added with a gentle smile. "Anyway that was a long time ago, but I've remained fond of the sport and follow its news. Now," she said, turning her smile directly on Jeremy, "what's this new question of yours?"

The kettle sounded its shrill whistle and Madame Cholot sprang up and strode to the kitchen, returning with a tray topped with teapot and cups, lemon slices and sugar. She served Jeremy his tea plain, per his request, then plopped a sliver of lemon into her own cup before sitting back down. "So, more questions about the strapping blond in the Laundromat?" she said. "You know, I wouldn't even have been there if I weren't waiting on the delivery of a new washing machine."

Yes, her misfortune was his good luck. "As a matter of fact," he answered, "I've got some news. After talking to you I inquired about him in a café, and a waitress thought he sounded Alsatian."

"Alsatian...whoever concluded that must have spoken with him at length." Madame gazed skeptically over her cup.

"In fact he didn't speak much, and the waitress said it was only her impression. Still, I wonder..."

"Well," said Madame, putting her cup down, "then let me tell you my take on the situation. From the little he said to me, he definitely had a German accent. Could he be from Alsace? I suppose you can't completely rule it out, but considering how young he looks I would consider Moselle more likely, where there are still a number of native young German speakers."

Jeremy nodded in agreement.

"I, on the other hand," Madame continued, "still vote for Germany or Austria."

"Well, I've got to find out his name," Jeremy said.

"I hope you do. Wrecking someone's car and taking off shouldn't be taken lightly. Did you say earlier that I should also expect a visit from the police?"

"...Not necessarily. I mean the damage might not warrant it. At any rate, I've already shown them the suspect's photo." And technically he had, to Rébert at least. "And of course I'll also convey your information."

"Well, I'll be happy to share what I know," Madame said, a quizzical glow in her eyes. "Although I can't imagine the police being as agreeable as you, Monsieur Winters. Yours is an English surname, I believe..."

Jeremy confirmed the guess, something he had done many times during his life in Paris.

"And I do detect a slight accent though your French is impeccable."

"Correct again, Madame." And he gave her a cursory account of his peregrinations back and forth across the Atlantic.

"Well, I hope you're settled for good," she said with a warm smile.

Jeremy nodded, his right eye contracting with a sudden strong draft of wind through the open windows. He wiped a tear away.

Madame Cholot blinked at him and leaned in. "Excuse me if I've bordered on indiscreet..."

"Not at all. Just this defective eye, the result of a stupid accident."

"No need to explain."

Madame Cholot took what he said at face value and he appreciated that. She was inquisitive though not intrusive. Not even when she had the right to be, such as pinning Jeremy down about his identity as an insurance investigator; she hadn't even asked which company he worked for. It was as though she sensed he wasn't completely on the up and up but still trusted him and desired to help.

He left her building, his knee rested, his thoughts as muddled as ever. He couldn't help considering the hypothesis of the *Grand Blond* as a French national with German his native tongue. It could certainly jibe with what Stefania feared—the French government at her heels, and now using a hound with a German accent to throw her off. He needed to at least tell her about the accent, though perhaps he would skip the French part since he still saw no indication to feed her conspiracy worries.

He made a detour to Stefania's building. This time when he approached he found no one entering or exiting. She had no number-code entry system, like Madame's, so he simply rang the intercom buzzer next to her name on the stained plastic panel. No answer. Deciding to wait a while before undertaking the eight-block trek back to metro station Tolbiac, Jeremy took off his jacket and perched himself on a low granite wall next to the door. There he sat basking in this shady side of the street while observing the traffic and passersby on the sidewalk. It didn't take long to get his fill, and he was about to leave when a teenage boy exited the building and Jeremy slipped in behind him. Might as well give Stefania's door a couple of knocks in case she'd been visiting a neighbor in the building.

About half way up he heard someone clunking down the stairs. Heavy steps. Steps that could belong to an unwanted visitor. But probably just Jeremy's vigilant imagination. Then, as he rounded the second-floor landing and started up to the third, he stopped cold, his eyes widening. The man descending had halted with equal consternation, a look that quickly mutated into outrage. *Christophe.*

Jeremy could practically feel the tensing of his friend's neck muscles, the clenching of his jaw, then the high rasp of his voice as he demanded, "What the hell are you doing here!"

The unambiguous greeting left Jeremy tongue-tied. The normally sunny, back-slapping Christophe now stood rigid and pale as an ice-covered pond, his blue eyes reflecting a sinister moonlight. In a further tone of hostility he barked, "She's not home."

To Jeremy's ears the sound ricocheted off the walls like bullets, making him wince, then offer, "I was just..."

"What—stopping by to chat?" Slowly, and with a slight swagger, Christophe descended three steps in his heavy work boots. That left four between Jeremy and him, and Jeremy caught a sharp whiff of sweat rising between them. "I heard you ringing the bell, now why are you here?"

Jeremy could not even begin to answer. However he might explain his concern about the *Grand Blond* (Stefania's *own* worry which Christophe had apparently dismissed), Christophe would surely take things the wrong way. Including Stefania and Jeremy's current vow of simple friendship.

Christophe leaned toward Jeremy, his hand sliding down the banister. "Sniffing around for an afternoon fuck? That why you came?"

He descended another stair. They were too close to each other and Christophe's metaphorical kick to the teeth left Jeremy burning with shame and anger. He squeezed the jacket he held in his right hand as if strangling every drop of water out a rag. "No," he said, shaking his head vigorously, feeling a shortness of breath. "Not at all."

Christophe reared back with a sarcastic laugh. "So then why has the knight in shining armor arrived?" he said, one hand on his hip, the other sliding up and down the banister as if gearing up for a challenge.

To warn Stefania! Jeremy answered to himself, though that was an exaggeration. And yet, Christophe knew about Jeremy's *knight-in-shining-armor* chase after the Big Blond. Stefania had told him, and Jeremy now latched on to it for support.

"I just stopped by to see how she was doing, after that day in the Luxembourg Garden..." The response barely topped a murmur. Jeremy knew he sounded pathetic, knew he had handled things badly. If only Christophe had taken Stefania seriously about the stalking. If only he would offer her a solid commitment, a decent future in France. *If only, if only*—shit!

What else could he say without risking Christophe's wrath, except: "You've got nothing to worry about— Stefania loves you."

Two sentences, but perhaps two too many. Christophe's eyes flashed and his rasp turned jagged. "What goes on between Stefania and me is none of your fucking business. And if you want to remain my friend you'll stay the hell away from her."

Jeremy's grasp on his jacket tightened until he felt he was clenching pure fist. His heart was thumping like a bass drum out of control. He forced himself to release his paralyzed breath. "Then just act like you care," he muttered.

Something between a rictus and a smirk twisted Christophe's mouth. His eyes roved menacingly over Jeremy before he lowered himself to two steps between them and issued Jeremy an equal number of slaps to the cheek. *Whack, whack,* neither of them too hard...Was this the prelude to a duel? A brotherly admonishment? Shocked, Jeremy couldn't distinguish. He took no chances, dropping his jacket and reaching up to block another blow. "I've known you since we were six years old. I'm only speaking to you as a—"

Down another step came Christophe, and with a shove he knocked Jeremy against the banister. "Don't come back here!"

His weak knee buckling, Jeremy clung to the banister to keep from slipping down the stairs. Then swung himself back up and elbowed Christophe in the belly. "Look—"

Christophe's return punch hit an unyielding abdominal wall. "Don't!" Jeremy warned, braced by the banister.

Breathing heavily, Christophe glanced at Jeremy's balled right fist. "American middleweight," he spat, his hot breath brushing Jeremy's face. "Stefania told me the truth about how you got that eye. I heard it from *her*, while *you* lied to me." He grunted his disgust. "But now that I know what happened to your cousin I won't tempt fate," he added with a sneer. Then he pushed past Jeremy, treading on his jacket on his way down to the landing. This time without the swagger, but with a pace that appeared difficult for him to master—hurried, then halting, as though he longed to rush away yet still retain some dignity.

Jeremy waited until Christophe reached the ground

floor and he could hear the entrance door clang shut. Then he sat down on the stairs and exhaled a weighty sigh. Elbows propped on his thighs he rubbed his head back and forth in frustration, as though trying to scrub some sense into it. His shirt was soaked with sweat. He closed his eyes as a wave of fatigue and despondency settled over him. It took great force to scoop up his jacket and plod his way down the stairs and out of the building. His only consoling thought was he'd maintained control of his fists. But had he lost Christophe for good?

Chapter 10

Jeremy needed to walk, to breathe, to clear his head of the gunk that threatened to weigh him down with inertia. There was nothing he could do about Christophe for now, and he should go home and perhaps call Rébert. Tell him he had begun surveillance on the graffitist Monks, then add the tidbit about the *Grand Blond*. Perhaps this latest about a German accent might jog the memory banks of the RG.

Despite that testy moment on the stairs, his knee seemed to be fine so he decided to hoof it all the way to Place d'Italie. From there he could take metro line 5 to Place de la République, (no changes, thus fewer stairs); or, if his knee flared up, he could easily grab a cab from there. In any case he needed fresh air.

The rhythm of physically moving forward, the expanse of sky and steady breeze which invited deep breaths, the visual distractions, in concert exerted a relaxing effect on him.

And when he arrived at Place d'Italie he found an even more significant distraction. An enormous crowd had amassed at the roundabout surrounding the Place. Bicentennial flags rippled in the light wind, and as Jeremy tried to round the Place toward the metro entrance he was forced to a stop by a wall of people. He jockeyed through to see what they were watching, which turned out to be a man in a dark suit, his white collar open as he stood next to the fountain in the Place. A policeman with a radio flanked him, his official presence seeming to hold the undulating crowd at a distance across the street.

Jeremy squinted at the man, then asked a female spectator. "Is that—"

"*Oui*, Jean-Paul Belmondo."

"Why's he here?"

"Who knows, he just *is*." She spared not a glance for Jeremy, her do-not-disturb-me gaze locked stubbornly on the middle-aged but still boyishly-handsome actor, who in turn grinned, puffed on a cigarette, and jawed chummily with the policeman on this virtual stage. Then, as if Jeremy threatened to put a damper on her movie-star moment, the woman wormed away from him toward the front of the rubbernecking line.

And here I am gawking too, Jeremy chided himself in disgust. He wiggled his way out of the crowd, making his way to the metro station.

He found the train as packed as the assembly at the Place, and with no seats free he stood gripping the bar next to the doors. Hot, clammy arms jostled him, various voices spouting English, Italian, and German. And if the *Grand Blond* were merely a German tourist?

Then he wouldn't waste time hanging out in Laundromats on the fringes of Paris, Jeremy confirmed to himself.

When the train left the Gare d'Austerlitz station it suddenly felt like a sauna, and not simply from body heat. It was as though someone had turned on heating in the train, an impossibility since the Paris metro system was furnished with neither heat nor air conditioning.

After six long stops he emerged at Place de la République, his home turf, stretched as if freed from a cattle car, then headed toward La Gitane, where he rewarded himself with an Affligem and a rest of his knee before he had to tackle his stairs. All of the café's adjustable window-doors stood open, facilitating a heavenly cross breeze, something that he and other Parisians lived for in July. He undid a couple of buttons at the top of his shirt and let out a weary sigh. *Why did Stefania have to tell Christophe the true story behind the saxophone?* If she hadn't, Christophe might have been a little less hostile, less distrusting. When Jeremy's ale arrived he guzzled a good fourth of it, helping him to shove his concerns to the dungeons of his mind and instead contemplate the news he had for Rébert.

Would confirmation by two people of the *Grand Blond's* German accent reignite interest in Stefania? Somehow Jeremy doubted it, and as he took another long pull of his beer Christophe reared back up from the dungeon. *American middleweight,* he had hurled at Jeremy. The *American* part still burned like a hot poker, its implication that Jeremy didn't really belong here; that he was a dangerous Yank who couldn't be trusted—especially with someone's girlfriend. But Christophe was ignoring his own place in the equation, Jeremy now thought, and had better examine the state of his relationship with the co-conspirator—*no,* the *principal* conspirator—of his betrayal. Adopt a bit more sensitivity toward those who couldn't take a job and security for granted. The fact that Stefania still considered Jeremy a kindred spirit eased the pain of the poker. If anyone was dangerous it was that big blond Teutonic bastard, Jeremy reminded himself, flexing his knee and noting the lingering discomfort. And he would do his best to keep the brute from harming Stefania, especially since Christophe didn't seem to give a shit.

In one last satisfying guzzle he finished his Affligem, paid, and crossed the street to his building. Upstairs, he flung open his windows, yanked off his shirt, and tossed it in the hamper. Then he rang Rébert, who wasn't available according to the agent who answered. Jeremy left his number, then planted himself bare-chested in front of the window. From here he had a view of the bronze statue of Marianne in Place de la République. Leaving the metro station he had noticed more graffiti on her ornate plinth, this time: RÉVOLUTION BIDON. He wondered how many tourists understood that *bidon* meant *phony*. Whatever the case, the constant defacement of the statue irritated him. He liked his neighborhood, he liked Marianne's presence there, and he liked the Republic for which she stood.

He wiped a stray tear from his eye. Right now he wished he were in Belgium. Not visiting his mother necessarily but up north, near the sea. Bruges in July averaged about 20 Celsius—70 degrees Fahrenheit, his father would calculate if he were still alive. Antwerp, about the same. The forecast for Paris today was 33C— over 90 whopping degrees, Walt would exclaim, preferring San Francisco's more temperate climate. Today in the metro it felt like 100.

Jeremy went to the kitchen and opened the fridge, squatting to let the cool air caress his chest. Not a great maneuver for his knee, however, so he stood up and bent to check the fridge's contents. Having only consumed a crêpe from a street stand at noon, he needed to eat before going to work, yet he was loath to turn on the stove.

The telephone rang.

"What's up?" asked Rébert in a distracted voice.

"Listen," said Jeremy, lifting the phone's base off the table so he could pace with it while delivering his news of the *Grand Blond's* accent.

A pause from Rébert. "...How did you come to that conclusion?"

"People from Stefania's *quartier* heard him speak."

"So you're canvassing her neighborhood now..."

"She feels threatened." Jeremy had come to a halt, his feet planted wide apart, his grip tightening on the phone's receiver.

"And I'm sure you'd like to pay this guy back for your knee. Has he made another appearance?" Rébert asked.

"...Not lately."

"Mm." More hesitation from Rébert. "Do you know how many German tourists are in the city at this moment?"

Jeremy resumed his pacing, stretching the phone's cord as far as it would go. "Understood, but this *mec* doesn't look or act like a tourist."

"Let it go, Jeremy; the guy's made no move on Stefania, and nobody I've shown his photo to recognizes him."

Jeremy grimaced. "Be interesting if some Mosellan in the Services was tailing Stefania..."

Rébert gave such a loud sigh that Jeremy could almost feel the breath in his ear. "I'm aware of *everything* my branch does when it comes to the Italian Compagni." Then in commanding staccato delivery: "Stick to the *mecs* in the Hairy Monk café."

"Because they might admit to penning *Révolution bidon*?"

"Because they could be planning further mischief to screw up celebrations. And if you *do* uncover something more serious, it'll help your work status."

Jeremy squeezed the phone's receiver. "Can I hold you to that?"

"I'll do everything in my power, *if* you get something significant to report."

Jeremy muttered a *merci*, hung up, and headed to the bedroom, where he stripped to his shorts, donned a pair of practice boxing gloves, and began hammering his punching bag. Jabs of hope and excitement soon accelerated into a series of furious punches fantasized against the *Grand Blond*.

He attacked the bag until sweat trickled onto the

scuffed parquet floor. Then he plunged beneath an icy shower, its shock decelerating his inner engine to a low rumble. He ate a cold sandwich with a glass of Volvic water, his motor now humming with something like a fantasy, the possibility of achieving everything: saving Stefania, foiling a plot by the Hairy Monks, and finishing up with a job perhaps managing a jazz club, where he might eventually jam with the musicians.

That night a note of Glasnost swirled around Le Prince Blue Note in tandem with the jazz. A visiting trombonist from Czechoslovakia prided himself on his Jack Teagarden repertoire, along with his own compositions. Jeremy had made arrangements to go downstairs when Radek played "The Mole," one of Jeremy's favorite standards. Once more emotions collided within him as he stood discreetly at the back of the room—listening, lightly tapping a foot, silently clicking his fingers to Radek's swing. Within his heart, the high of passive enjoyment clashed with the hunger to reproduce the exhilarating sounds, plus the ecstasy he felt just imagining himself capable of the accomplishment. Before the show, the trombonist had confessed to something similar regarding his dream performance in Paris and his desire to live in the City of Light.

"*Meester Manhattan—trois!* called Jeremy's waiter friend Didier, once Jeremy was back behind the bar. Three Manhattans for who? Jeremy wondered idly. Americans, French? Unless he asked he rarely knew for whom the drinks were destined downstairs where the jazz sizzled. He imagined himself manager of Le Prince, floating up and downstairs all evening, getting involved in the booking of gigs as well. It was beginning to feel more than a recurring whim.

At the end of the performance patrons filed upstairs, and when he swiveled from his bottles to the counter,

Haley was standing before him with the mischievous smile of a child who'd pulled a fast one.

He beamed back at her. "How did you get past me? Didier didn't tell me you were here, and I didn't notice you downstairs."

"I told Didier I wanted to surprise you. And downstairs you probably would've expected to see me alone. Instead I've brought a couple of visitors," she said, gesturing to two young women approximately her own age, who now stepped up to the counter. "Remember my mentioning the Morrissey sisters, Bernadette and Kathleen coming over from Ireland for the Bicentennial?"

"Jeremy Winters," he introduced himself, offering his hand. His smile encompassed both girls and Haley, about whom he added, "She's an excellent tour guide, you know?"

"Haley's more than that, she's been our good friend for years," said the girl named Bernadette, the one with the outgoing smile and lively blue eyes; the elder of the two, Jeremy gauged.

The younger sister nodded. "*Ten* years."

"You didn't happen to order Manhattans...?" Jeremy asked.

"We did," replied Haley grinning.

"Yes, *Mister Manhattan*," confirmed Bernadette.

Jeremy chuckled, listened to their small talk about painting the town during the Bicentennial, then flashed on his evening with Haley and the Serge Gainsbourg jazz. He longed to see her alone, though amiably agreed to meet up with her and her friends later on during their stay.

On the metro ride home, thoughts of the visceral passion he'd shared with Haley kindled him. And again when he went to bed, stretching out atop his sheets in the damp-dark night.

The next day his priorities shifted dutifully back to the Hairy Monks. He entered their café in rue de la Harpe around the same time as his first visit. And saw neither one of them. He ordered an espresso and waited half an hour. Then he sighed and left—so much for Parisian habitualness. He would try again later.

In the meantime...yes, a trip down to the Thirteenth Arrondissement wouldn't hurt. He still owed Stefania the information on the *Grand Blond's* German accent—Christophe's territorialism be damned.

Jeremy boarded the metro at Cluny-La Sorbonne, got off at Tolbiac, and strolled the six blocks to Stefania's neighborhood. At least he could dress down today in a pair of mustard-colored chinos and a beige, short-sleeved linen shirt—nothing like linen to battle the heat.

But the stroll turned out to be in vain, once more Stefania's buzzer going unanswered. And preferring not to risk another counterproductive—to put it euphemistically—run-in with Christophe, Jeremy renounced waiting.

He should go back to the Hairy Monk and, if the Monks still hadn't shown up to wet their whistles, head home to do laundry; he only had two clean shirts left.

Laundry...the Laundromat...perhaps another chance encounter with Louise Cholot...

The frivolous thought pleased him as he clipped across the street and turned the corner. He pictured Madame, crossword in her lap, pencil thoughtfully at her lips; such a tanned, fit *dame* of a *certain âge*, so modern compared to his mother who no longer even wore trousers since she had moved back to Namur. Béatrice, who had briefly considered retirement to a *béguinage* lay convent when she moved back to Belgium.

He opened the Laundromat door and poked his head in—then did a double take.

Stefania was pulling clothes from a dryer.

He hastened in and stood with his hands on his hips. "Are you never home?" he half-joked, grinning.

Her head whipped in his direction. "Jeremy..." she intoned, straightening with a trace of hesitancy. She stuffed a final handful of freshly dried clothes into a large canvas bag, while he crossed over to kiss her on the cheeks.

"I've missed you," he said, giving her an affectionate hug.

"It's only been a couple of days," she said, easing away from him to collect an additional bag packed with clean clothes.

"And I've worried about you," he added, relieving her of one of the bags.

She responded with a placid smile. "I've been fine. Walk me home?"

He appreciated the invitation, of course, but mostly he was thankful for no mention of Christophe. Perhaps he hadn't yet tracked her down to vent about his confrontation with Jeremy.

Jeremy followed Stefania into her building and up the staircase, admiring the swing of her hips in tight jeans, the bounce of ginger hair on her shoulders, bare of all but two strips of tank top.

"I've got news about the Viking," he said, as they approached her landing.

She halted and cast a surprised glance behind her.

"I'll tell you when we're inside," he assured her. "You're not expecting anyone...?"

"No, why?" she asked, hurrying the rest of their climb.

"No reason..."

"What do you know?" Stefania demanded, her voice excited, once they were behind closed doors in her flat.

Jeremy lifted the clothes bag in mock helplessness.

"Sorry," she said, taking it and shoving both bags into a corner next to the sofa bed, which remained unmade, the bedding in a twisted, crumpled heap that suggested nothing had been tidied since Jeremy's last visit.

She flicked a distracted nod at the bed. "Excuse the mess, I've been busy."

Busy with what? Jeremy wondered.

She sat on the bed's corner and tapped the mattress next to her, fixating him with an expectant stare.

"Relax," Jeremy said, sitting down and patting her shoulder. "Nothing definitive. Just that I've learned our Viking speaks French with a German accent."

Stefania's eyes widened in shock. "How—"

"I found out in the café across the street. He's been in there."

"*Putain!* Did he ask about *me* in the café?" Her breathing seemed shallow. He felt her anxiety as if his hand were still on her shoulder, his fingers stroking her pulsing, dew-damp skin.

"No," he said. "I showed them the photo and they said he just ordered a beer and a sandwich. Might be from Moselle, someone mentioned."

"*Putain de merde!*" she doubly swore, jerking herself to her feet. "The French!"

He could have kicked himself for mentioning Moselle. "Even so, you haven't seen him again..." he stressed, in an attempt to stem the panic.

"No, but you know what this could mean!"

Gently he rose and countered, "It's still far from certain he's French, let alone—"

"Mirko's seen him too."

"Mirko? When?" Jeremy asked, staring back in surprise.

"He's seen him a couple of times."

114

"Has he—"

"Mirko hasn't been approached, but I'll be sure to pass your information on to him."

"So the Viking's following him too?"

"Not 'stalking' him, like me, but watching him all the same. Mirko says he's spotted him in a café and in a line at the post office."

Certainly no coincidence, thought Jeremy, but he couldn't decide whether this new development was a bad or good sign. He decided it at least meant Stefania might have another ally, though he didn't voice this aloud.

"Anyway," Stefania said, "I'll see what he says about your news. Maybe he'll come round to my way of thinking."

"So Mirko doesn't fear a French plan against you..."

"Not at the moment," she said, blinking in annoyance. "But we'll see." She had taken a step back, arms crossed, eyes gazing past Jeremy in an ominous frown. Detaching herself from him, it seemed, with her private thoughts.

Finally she looked at him. "Thanks again for the news. Now I'd better get on with my chores." She turned away and began busying herself with the bedclothes, her features tightening with each tug of the sheets. Jeremy gave her a hand.

"Thank you," she said when they'd finished, though she couldn't conceal the tenseness in her voice.

"Listen, I'm not done with that bastard Viking either," he stressed. "And you can still rely on me for help."

Stefania glanced at his knee. "I appreciate that, Jeremy, and I'm glad you're walking fine again. But I don't see how anyone can stop this man and whatever he's got in mind..." She finished the thought with a hopeless shrug. When she accompanied him to the door her smile was wan. "We'll keep in touch." She didn't sound certain.

Her lips brushed his cheeks, and he returned a searching look. Then he stepped out onto the landing and the door swung shut behind him.

Chapter 11

Perturbations flooding his mind, Jeremy left Stefania's building and sauntered across the street to the café. He plonked down onto a chair, letting his legs droop apart, unable to shake the feeling he had failed Stefania. And even with Mirko perhaps now in her corner, Jeremy still felt no better about himself.

Mirko: what did it mean that the *Grand Blond* was shadowing him as well? With an unsettled look he gazed up at the server, who had pulled up promptly with her tray. The same girl, who along with Madame Cholot, had identified the *Grand Blond's* German accent. Today, in place of the ponytail, her dark hair curled softly in a chignon. Her lipstick seemed redder. Perhaps she'd be meeting a beau this evening.

"An Affligem, if you have it...*Mireille*?" he ventured.

She returned a smile of recognition. "I remember you—the insurance investigator. Sorry, no Affligem, but we have Leffe...?"

"That'll do, *merci*."

She turned to leave, then stopped and pivoted back to him. "Oh, in case you're interested, that *Grand Blond* with the German accent was back yesterday."

Jeremy straightened from his slouch.

"And he dropped something on the floor on the way out—a card."

"What kind of card?" Jeremy asked, both hands now gripping the table.

"Some kind of club calling card. I gave it to Julien."

117

She angled her head toward the barman. "He might still have it."

Jeremy started to rise.

"You can wait here," Mireille assured him. "I'll ask him when I get your beer."

Jeremy dipped his chin to her and sat back down. He crossed his legs and craned his head back in the direction of the bar. Yes, there he was, the same barman who had served him an espresso before.

And in less than five foot-tapping minutes, Mireille was back, setting his beer on the table along with the item in question. At first glance it looked like a business card.

"Julien left it on the counter near the trash," she said with a tiny grin, congratulating herself on the card's rescue, thought Jeremy.

And indeed he was grateful. "*Merci bien*, Mireille," he said, one eye on the card. He nodded an appreciative smile and let her get back to her tables.

The card hot in his hand, he read: INTERNATIONAL MOUNTAINEERS OF THE GREATER ALPS. Topped with a clichéd image of azure skies and snow-capped peaks, the title appeared in four lines: German first, followed by French, Italian, and finally English, the lingua franca of Europe.

A club—Mireille was right—and *not*, unfortunately, a personal card with name and address. Nevertheless, Madame Cholot's perception had proved spot on; the *Grand Blond* seemed to be connected to mountaineering. From where this Germanophone hailed, on the other hand, remained to be determined. It was possible to find out, Jeremy reflected, for the organization's address and phone number in Innsbruck, Austria, were also stamped at the bottom. He turned it over: too bad, no notes written on the back.

Jeremy scratched his chin with the card's edge and

sipped his beer in contemplation. He was tempted to return to Stefania's and wave the card at her, but he decided against it. Better to wait and see what he could decipher.

He left the café, fingering the telephone card in his pocket. He doubted he had sufficient money on it to call Austria from a booth. He would have to make the call from home.

He studied his watch. Four-thirty: the return commute to his neighborhood would take close to an hour; the journey back to the Hairy Monk café a good half hour. Provided the Monks were there, he still couldn't idle about with them indefinitely, for he would have to go home, change, then metro back to Le Prince. On the other hand, a quick chat with Madame Cholot regarding mountaineering clubs...

"*Merde*," he swore softly at the payphone encased in its glass booth. The mini address book with Madame's number and entrance codes to her building lay tucked in the jacket he had worn yesterday.

After another mechanical glance at his watch, Jeremy set out with long, vigorous strides toward metro station Tolbiac. He had been prepared to call Austria tomorrow but now felt driven to get it done today; with luck the office of the international mountaineers would be open until six. He lamented his ignorance of bus routes and timetables of the Thirteenth Arrondissement. But the metro generally proved quicker, and with any luck he would arrive home before the club's office closed for the day.

Which he managed to do, jogging stiff-legged from the metro station to his building and reaching for the phone as soon as he entered his flat.

A young male voice answered in German. Although Jeremy occasionally read articles in *Die Welt* to keep from losing the language, he had even less confidence when it came to speaking German than he did Italian. So he tried French, and they soon settled on English. With pen and paper, Jeremy plunked down at his entryway table, sweat dribbling down his temples and torso now that he had come to a full halt. And when he wiped his eye with a clammy finger, the sting of sweat made it water all the more. Nevertheless, he felt satisfaction at having caught the young Austrian steward before he left the office for the evening. Using a corner of his shirt Jeremy staunched the annoying tears and got down to business.

The institution was indeed a mountaineering club, confirmed Herr Heider, although a small one. Most members lived in Austria and Switzerland, though a minority of climbers came from other countries.

"Such as France?" Jeremy asked.

"Of course."

"Might you have a member from Moselle or Alsace, an area in France where German is spoken?"

"It's possible. But I'm not at liberty to look up a member's personal data for you."

"Certainly," Jeremy conceded. He had no name to offer in the first place. "Perhaps you could simply convey the names of any members from Alsace or Moselle...?

"I'm sorry. I must protect the privacy of our members in this respect as well."

"I see." No chinks in that wall. Jeremy took a lesser tack. He asked about the relative experience of the club's climbers and learned that all members were in the advanced category. *Fit*, Jeremy commented acidly to himself, *with iron thighs and inexhaustible heart-lung capacity*.

He thanked Herr Heider, hung up, then immediately retrieved his address booklet and dialed Madame Cholot.

"Ah, Monsieur Winters. I still have your number,

but unfortunately I've thought of nothing else that could help your investigation. 'I have come up dry,' she said jokingly in English, the R in *dry* rasped in French fashion but with a feminine lilt.

With a genteel chuckle Jeremy said, "Actually, Madame, I've made an interesting discovery myself. Would you have time to talk?"

"Not for long; my son Hervé is due to arrive any time now. Could we make it tomorrow afternoon? Tea again..."

"*Bien sûr.*"

"Let's say three o'clock."

Jeremy hung up and sat on the sofa to rest his knee. So Madame had a son. How old? he wondered, with more than fleeting interest.

9 July, the humid heat ballooning in proportion to the burgeoning swell of tourists.

People looked away while they talked and walked, their eyes swinging up toward *this monument*, across the street toward *that church*, all the while tripping over your heels or sending you swinging as they clipped your shoulder.

This morning Jeremy had encountered a mass of rubberneckers blocking the sidewalk on boulevard de Sébastopol, his route toward the Seine. When he had asked what they were waiting for, one man gave a dull shrug. "Someone famous."

Jeremy had to zigzag through the spectators, but before making it through their lines, a chorus of stadium-style whoops shot up. "*C'est Jacques Cousteau!*"

Instinctive curiosity sent Jeremy's gaze swiveling toward the street, where a limousine coasted along, slowing to the languid pace of a strutting feline as it passed the crowd. Behind a weakly-tinted back window,

Jeremy made out a big beak of a nose. Then on glided the sleek beast.

"*Tête de con*," Jeremy had admonished himself, shaking his head at the idiocy of human nature, his own included. At the same time he silently bemoaned the vanishing coolness of the morning, its crisp air being steadily devoured by a steamy, haze-shrouded sun.

Now it was twelve-thirty and he had spent over half an hour in the Hairy Monk. The café in rue de la Harpe sat roughly mid point between his house and Madame Cholot's, and since neither Monk had yet to show up he felt he was merely killing time, rather than working, before his rendezvous with Madame. He finished the last bite of the croque monsieur he'd ordered, thinking of Haley, picturing her guiding her friends through the most congested parts of Paris—kicking up hot dust in the Tuileries, elbowing their way down rue de Rivoli through knots of tourists and revolving racks of sidewalk souvenirs. He missed Haley but didn't envy the endeavor. Once the Bicentennial was over maybe he would finally invite her to his place...

The thought scooted off when the café door opened. And in strolled the two Monks—the afro-haired *mec* and his pal, who reminded Jeremy of the Rasputin-like mascot who stood etched in stained glass in a nook in one of the café's walls. The two made for the bar and Jeremy joined them, following their lead in ordering a beer. To the barman's quizzical look he responded, "Add it to my table's tab."

The attention directed at Jeremy invited the Monks to give him the once-over, which in turn allowed Jeremy to smile and comment, "I've seen you here before."

And so the chain of pleasantries continued, with Jeremy at last reminding the Monks of their sardonic but astute observations on celebrities.

"Peacocking about the city," declared the *mec* with the blond bush on his head, drawing himself up and sashaying in imitation.

"Masses of ass-lickers in their wake," concurred the lank-haired Monk.

"You're telling me!" said Jeremy, drawing out an appreciative laugh. "Bunch of idiots—ballbusters, the way they clog up the streets; why just this morning..." And he went on to grumble about Jacques Cousteau in a way that exaggerated the drooling crowd and the inconvenience they incurred. Howls of laughter erupted at the golden-ager Cousteau, followed by a dose of outrage and sympathy for Jeremy, including from the barman who appeared to be buddies with the Monks.

Two other young men at the bar, gauged as regulars by Jeremy, joined in with their own stories. *Imbéciles*, *connards*, and the like, were roundly repeated, here with disdain, there with guffaws. By the time Jeremy finished his Jean-Paul Belmondo anecdote, replete with the blocking of the metro entrance (more useful exaggeration) by the multitude at Place d'Italie, he was on his way to being welcomed into the fold. *Bravo*, he congratulated himself: he hadn't even needed to invent his stories!

Jeremy continued on his roll. "And all this *putain* gilding of the monuments."

More whole-hearted agreement.

The machinery nicely greased, Jeremy asked the Monks, "You guys live around here?"

"In the Mouffetard," said Rasputin.

"Gobelins," reported the afro-king.

"No gilding in those neighborhoods," Jeremy affirmed, nodding with satisfaction.

"Would shock me dead in the Mouffetard," Rasputin stated. "And what the hell's left to shock you these days?"

Jeremy agreed, the Monks introduced themselves—Jean-Marc (Rasputin) and Renaud with the afro—and the two said they'd look forward to seeing Jeremy back in the Hairy Monk another time.

With an elated spring in his step, Jeremy arrived in Madame Cholot's neighborhood early. The Monks had scurried off after their beer, and now, with another hour to kill, Jeremy decided to take a stroll down to Stefania's street. Stopping in front of her building he stared for a moment, fingers twitching nervously in his pockets. He resisted the urge to ring, considering if she were home he would be hampered by his three-o'clock rendezvous with Madame.

He walked further south, passing under the bridge at boulevard Kellermann and down into the Gentilly cemetery. It was his first visit here, and though it was paved and housed with antique-looking tombs like its other Paris counterparts, he noticed the Gentilly cemetery lacked the lush foliage of Père Lachaise and the cemetery at Montparnasse.

Too hot to stroll any further, he decided. He would return to Madame's, punch in the door codes she had graciously confided to him, and spend the remaining twenty minutes or so sheltered in the coolness of the tiled foyer.

At three-o-three he rang Madame Cholot's bell, entered, and was ushered into the living room to settle on the sofa. The blue, white, and gold Russian teacups already sat waiting on a tray on the leather-inlayed coffee table. Madame wore a green, flower-patterned skirt with a sleeveless yellow blouse, and when she carried in the teapot, festooned with the strings and labels of at least three teabags, he noticed that her toned, bronze upper arms bore no tan line—a devoted outdoors woman indeed. The moment she finished pouring and sat down, Jeremy plucked the mountaineering-club card from his shirt pocket and handed it to her.

"The *Grand Blond* dropped this in a café near here," he announced, explaining how he had gained possession of the card.

Madame's eyes gleamed as they scanned it.

"I called the number in Innsbruck," Jeremy went on, informing her of what he'd learned from Herr Heider. "Of course he declined to provide names."

"Naturally," murmured Madame from her armchair, waving the card distractedly in front of her like a fan. "Still: Austrians, Swiss, French...the club will obviously count Germans and Italians as well..." She placed the card on the coffee table right side up, sat back and gazed into the middle distance between herself and Jeremy. She drew an audible breath, then looked up at him. "Yet I wonder about the interest of the French insurance system..."

At this point in his acquaintance with Madame, Jeremy had all but forgotten his charade and wished he could cast it off for good.

"And I still haven't received a visit from the police..." she pressed in a doubtful tone.

"And it's likely you won't," Jeremy hastened to remind her.

Her smile seemed amused. She uncrossed her sun-brown legs and leaned forward to pour more tea while Jeremy sat pondering her. She might very well suspect him a fraud, yet she remained eager to receive him, to talk, to help him puzzle out this *Grand Blond* business. He took a slightly nervous bite of biscuit, contemplating his next move if Madame were to insist about the police or ask for the name of his so-called insurance company.

Instead she picked up the card again, giving it another cursory glance then peering at him over her reading glasses. "I can't help focusing on the name of the club in Italian. The club represents the principal Alpine countries—"

"Yet the Blond's accent is German."

"Exactly. Have you not heard of the German-speaking Italians of the South Tyrol?"

Jeremy blinked and wiped his eye. *Of course!* Concentrating so hard on a French connection he'd all but forgotten his secondary-school studies. Before he could speak, Madame went on: "Since the end of the First World War, as specified by the Versailles treaty, South Tyrol has belonged to Italy—much to the dissatisfaction of many German-speaking people there. I mentioned that my husband Jean-Baptiste was killed in a fall in the Dolomites..."

"The mountains of the South Tyrol," Jeremy affirmed.

"Spectacular country." Madame expressed a wistful smile that floated past Jeremy in gentle nostalgia. "Jean-Baptiste and I spent much time there, an Italian region but with quite a bit of autonomy. The native tongue is still German and they consider Italian a second language."

She paused to take a sip of tea, allowing Jeremy to draw the obvious conclusion.

He had already done so. "So when they speak a foreign language, French for instance, it's with a German rather than an Italian accent. Thus our *Grand Blond* could very well be an Italian national."

"A South Tyrolese wanted for hit and run with *significant* damage to property; otherwise, why all the brouhaha?"

Stranger things have happened, Jeremy was tempted to reply, but only for about two seconds. This bullshit insurance game was starting to embarrass him. Madame did not deserve the blatant insult of his drawing it out. He leaned forward with deliberate soberness, arms resting on his thighs, fingers laced between his knees. "May I be frank, Madame?"

"Nothing I'd like more," she replied, her eyes creased with a knowing smile.

"This affair is actually personal for me." He coughed, glancing at the floor. "*The Grand Blond's* been stalking a friend of mine—an Italian friend."

At the sound of the feminine form of *Italian friend,* Madame's smile broadened. "So we'll dispense with the insurance business?" she said in a light-hearted tone.

Jeremy's nod included a silent *thank you.* "My friend is afraid this *grand mec* will harm her," he explained, opting not to go into Stefania's exile status and her fears of deportation by the French government.

"And she doesn't want to go to the police?"

"We've tried that route," Jeremy offered, with Rébert in mind. "But they say nothing can be done since he hasn't physically approached her. Twice I've caught him spying on her myself. Chased him through the Luxembourg Garden, only for him to disable me with a kick to the knee and get away."

Responding to Jeremy's sour look, Madame nodded at his knee. "I thought I noticed some distress. At any rate, if he's an advanced mountain climber he'll be strong and lithe as a puma, and able to run all day long." She pinched her lower lip in reflection. "And we know he hangs around cafés and Laundromats, waiting for...what is her name?"

"Stefania."

"I wonder if she suspects the *Grand Blond* could be Italian?"

"I don't know. I've only just told her about the accent." *But she should suspect,* mused Jeremy. *She should have when I informed her of the accent.* He recalled Stefania's various responses to the news: a moment of shock, then renewed panic about the French, then an almost resigned dismay...

Initially, perhaps she *had* suspected an Italian...*but why not tell him?*

"Has she seen *this*?" Madame asked, pointing at the mountaineering club card on the table.

"Not yet," Jeremy muttered. *But she soon will.*

As Jeremy left Madame Cholot's, he tried to interpret Stefania's yo-yoing attitude toward both her dilemma and himself: alarm, then fatalism; needing Jeremy, desiring him, then distancing herself while insisting he remain her "faithful friend." Then finally throwing up her hands as if no one on the planet could help her. Well, he was tired of the emotional acrobatics, especially now that the *Grand Blond* might be Italian. It was time she explained what *that* could mean, so he could decide whether she truly needed his help or had merely used him to further her relationship with Christophe.

Singed with growing chagrin he headed back to her flat.

Chapter 12

Prepared to interrogate Stefania about a possible *Grand Blond*-Italian connection, Jeremy arrived at her building and pressed her buzzer. He pressed it again, and again. *How's it possible she's never home, or does she just refuse to answer the door?*

Suspecting the latter, he tried another name on the plaque of listed residents.

"*Oui?*" croaked a man's voice through the intercom.

"I've got a delivery of roses for Mademoiselle Stefania Perin and she doesn't seem to be home. Could you buzz me in so I can leave them on her landing?"

A pause, before the distorted, echoing voice resumed. "...Maybe you'd better leave them next to the front door."

"Here on the sidewalk? In this heat they'll wilt if they're not stolen first."

A crackly, irritated sigh, then the buzz and click of the door opening. Jeremy slipped inside and climbed as quickly as his knee would allow up the three flights of stairs. He let his panting subside, then rang Stefania's bell. He gave the door a couple of hard knocks with his fist, instinctively tried the handle, then kicked the door for good measure before pressing his ear against it. Complete stillness from inside. On the way back down, he encountered a bald, middle-aged man braced in his open doorway on the first floor.

"Who are you?" he demanded with a suspicious scowl, hands planted on his hips. "I could hear you banging from down here—some *floral* delivery. You'd

129

better get out before I call the police!"

Jeremy flashed him a hostile glare. "Shut up and mind your own business."

The man's arms dropped to his sides. His surprised gaze seemed to catch on Jeremy's bloodshot eye. With an air of caution the gaze slid down to Jeremy's balled fists. The man took a step back into his flat. With mock patience Jeremy waited for him to retreat a second step, lower his eyes, and quietly close the door.

"*Merde!*" Jeremy spat, hurrying down the stairs and out of the building, before the forcibly humbled man could make good on his threat to call the cops.

It wasn't until the door clanged shut that Jeremy cursed himself for not checking Stefania's mailbox on the way out. At any rate, he made the rounds of the neighborhood: the café, the Laundromat, the stores. No sign of her. He considered calling Rébert, mainly out of frustration at not knowing what else to do, but decided better of it. The RG agent had dismissed any significance attached to the *Grand Blond's* German accent, likewise any nefarious motives on the stalker's part. What could Jeremy expect from the revelation that the man might be a mountain climber? Then again, Mirko had seen him too...but had not been approached, either. Even if the latter piqued Rébert's curiosity, what tack could he possibly take? Resurrect the passport business, assigning Jeremy to Mirko this time instead of Stefania, in hopes of discovering a forged document in the Italian's possession? That could prove a tangle regarding Stefania.

No—better to wait and see. And so once home Jeremy took to his punching bag, always good for dispelling broodiness, if not lifting his spirits.

Later at work, when not thinking of Stefania, he wished Haley and the Irish sisters would drop back in. Not likely, though, since they had so much else to do in

Paris. On his break he went down to the cellar to hear the pianist play Stan Kenton's "Interlude." Haley owned a Stan Kenton *Best of* and she loved this song, he recalled, a frisson running through him.

After work Jeremy knocked back a couple of drinks with his waiter friend Didier and the pianist, then headed to the metro station. Past midnight, the brightly-lit platform still teemed with milling night owls: a few silent, solitary types like himself, but mostly festive young people, hooting and crowing in pairs or groups. *Vive la Révolution!*

When a train arrived and its pneumatically farting doors opened, he faced a wall of humanity, only two or three souls leaving the carriage. He stayed put on the platform, letting this particular train whisk away with a mechanical *whooing* down the dark, narrow tunnel. Then he walked to the opposite end of the platform where the end-cars of the train stopped, usually with more room in the carriages.

But not this evening, he witnessed, as the next train clattered into the station. He strode rapidly back up the platform, checking each packed carriage, and finally squeezing into a center car just as the warning horn blared. Cursing the Bicentennial mania, knowing the Monks would agree, he gripped the slippery, hand-hot metal bar next to the door, holding firm as the train thrust forward. From there he shot idle glances at other passengers hanging onto vertical poles on his side of the car: a few tired-looking, sober-faced loners surrounded by chirping, laughing tourists, plus a couple of French youths attempting the Marseillaise in tipsy, off-tune chorus.

Might Haley and the Irish girls be merrily metroing somewhere at this moment, or had they decided to have an early night and indulge in girl chitchat in their nightgowns on Haley's comfy sofa?

His gaze drifted toward the opposite end of the carriage, skimming the center bench seats, which faced one another and were crammed with the usual mix of passive and animated commuters. At the far side of the carriage his eyes alighted on a man in an overcoat, sharing a metal pole with a cluster of fellow travelers.

An overcoat, Jeremy remarked to himself. *In July*. His suspicion aroused in a semi-conscious way, Jeremy twisted and edged his way through the crowd, down the narrow aisle between the bench seats. When the train jerked and swayed, he latched onto the horizontal bar atop a bench, his arm grazing a woman's hair. At the end of the bench seats he grabbed hold of another horizontal bar and held steady. He was now positioned within a meter of the guy in the overcoat, who on closer inspection seemed about forty and turned out to be half a head taller than Jeremy. Like many a solitary traveler he gazed blank-faced at the glass half of the double doors and the yellowish reflections they sent back, including that of a chattering American next to him. A Yank decked out in shorts, Hawaiian shirt, and a red Phrygian felt cap, the kind sold by sidewalk vendors next to the Eiffel Tower or across from the Louvre.

Another rollercoaster swing of the train, with Jeremy, the American, and the January-dressed man swaying with the turn. And the coated guy's hand opportunely on the move: sliding into the American's back pocket, plucking out a wallet, and slipping it into his coat, all as slickly as a snake snatching a small prey and spiriting it into its burrow.

Jeremy maneuvered up to him. *"Pardonnez-moi,"* he announced to those he would have to jostle, and to all within listening distance: "We've got a thief here." He then grabbed the pickpocket by the shoulders and pushed him against the back door of the carriage that connected to the next car.

"Open your coat!" he ordered, as the train slowed on its approach to the Jussieu station. The man twisted and stretched toward the doors, flinging an elbow into Jeremy's ribs and ploughing into the crowd. Jeremy caught him and, for his troubles, returned a blow to his diaphragm, just as the train came to a lurching halt, sending the doubled-up thief to the feet of the parted, gasping onlookers. Jeremy squatted and pulled the wallet from the heap of man and overcoat.

"Yours, I think," he said in English, looking up at the American.

The doors had opened but most passengers remained rooted in place, patting their pockets and checking their purses. The American, after uttering an outraged "Shit!" proceeded to thank Jeremy.

With the sound of the warning horn, the thief tried to scramble through the now-closing doors, but the doors sprang back open and Jeremy shoved him the rest of the way out onto the platform.

Those who had debarked with them stood gaping. The thief threw a head-butt, clipping Jeremy's left knee, and attempted to flee again—this time to be rewarded with two slugs to the stomach by a groaning Jeremy, who then wrenched open the overcoat and pulled out five wallets.

The train had filled again but the doors remained open. Two metro police jogged up, no doubt alerted by personnel monitoring the closed circuit camera system. The pickpocket lay sprawled on the waxed, tar-black concrete, Jeremy holding the wallets aloft and eager to explain. He received his chance as the guards marched the thief away, ordering Jeremy to follow.

Only as he limped behind them did his adrenaline start to dissipate, replaced by a feeling of tepid triumph. He almost wished the thief had fought back more.

The next morning Jeremy called Haley with a warning about the metro.

"Holy crap," she replied.

"Tell your friends to be extra careful, not just in the metro but everywhere. Only four days before the 14th, and they say the city's never been this packed in its history."

"Right," Haley agreed. "Anyway, Bernadette and Kathleen are in Brittany at the moment."

"Oh?"

"They wanted to visit the coast—Saint-Malo, then over to Mont Saint-Michel.

"Well, they'll be cooler there," Jeremy pointed out, concealing his contentment that Haley hadn't gone with them.

"I imagine so; anyway, they won't be back until the 14th."

He stirred inside. "Are you free tonight? I'm off work for a couple of days..."

She had all afternoon and evening open.

"Then let's meet at the Flora et Fauna—and bring your *Pariscope*."

Haley had every aid imaginable to help her navigate and enjoy Paris. She never left home without her *Plan de Paris par Arrondissement*, a thick booklet of maps of each *quartier*, plus metro and bus routes. Jeremy kept one in a drawer at home but couldn't be bothered to tote it around. And of course each Wednesday Haley bought a *Pariscope*, the guide that kept her informed of all movies, exhibits, plays, and whatnot in Paris.

After these last hectic days, Jeremy felt justified in imposing a day of leisure on himself, with just one quick noon visit to The Hairy Monk café, only for a peek inside, where he saw no trace of the Monks.

Now, at mid-afternoon, he sat with Haley at a sidewalk table of the Café Flora et Fauna. The greenery of a little nursery spilled out its doors next to them, its workers watering flowers, potted palms and shrubs; up the sidewalk, pet shop birds warbled in wicker cages outdoors; across the street, on its isle in the middle of the Seine, stood the Conciergerie, the fortress building Haley loved most in Paris, newly cleaned for the Bicentennial. A strip of shade, courtesy of plane trees along the river, slanted in Jeremy and Haley's favor, and only the cars shooting down the street in front of them could be accused of disturbing their oasis.

Haley had just finished her espresso with a satisfied sigh, when she said, "So, how exactly did you stop the pickpocket last night?"

Jeremy shifted in his chair. He sensed a different kind of disturbance in the works. "I told him to give up the wallet."

"And he just handed it over?"

Jeremy chewed a loose piece of dry skin on his lower lip, his eyes fastened on the steady river of rumbling vehicles heading east. "With a little persuasion on my part," he offered.

"How's that?"

He turned to see lively, inquiring eyes behind their spectacles, and expressed a little grin. "With a couple of slugs to the stomach—had to immobilize him for the police."

"Oh..." A thoughtful pause. "And the police were grateful?"

For an instant he frowned. Was the question meant to be serious or a touch mocking?

"Sure," he said with an uneasy shrug. The two cops in the Jussieu metro station had actually looked at Jeremy askance before they noticed his slight limp. And though they thanked him, they did so with thin smiles. Perhaps he *had* overdone it a bit.

His gaze returned to the traffic, an appraising eye

following a midnight-blue Maserati sedan as it glided dolphin-like down quai de la Mégisserie. "So you didn't drive your friends to Brittany?" he asked, a remote edginess to his voice.

"No, they took the train."

"Mm," he responded with a distracted nod. Haley had a car, lucky girl. A second-hand Citroën which she rarely drove in the city, but at least it was her own vehicle. By contrast, Jeremy had gained most of his driving experience behind the wheel of a taxi, back in his days of fulltime employment in Paris. Since his jail stint in the States he had dabbled as a bartender, a bouncer, and naturally as Rébert's assistant. Haley knew only of the first *métier*. But as he hammered down that involuntary spike of jealousy, he began to feel he should share more with her. And as she pulled out her *Pariscope,* paging through to the cinema section, he watched her with a sense of affection that verged on painful, given the shame of his jealousy seconds before.

Apart from music they both loved movies, so when Haley suggested seeing Orson Welles's *Touch of Evil*, an encore of the 1958 film-noir classic showing in the Latin Quarter, Jeremy praised her choice.

He wasn't disappointed. For one thing, the Latin-jazz soundtrack fired them both up, and after the film they set off in search of the album. On and off the metro they hopped, taking advantage of the unlimited monthly rides provided by their *Cartes Oranges*. First, to the big record stores, then back to the Latin Quarter to hunt through dusty boutiques specializing in vintage collections. When they ultimately bagged the Henry Mancini soundtrack, Jeremy insisted on paying for it. Haley countered, but he pointed out that she could make a copy for him. At dinner he would once more pay, since Haley had bought the movie tickets. That was their arrangement, that was their routine—Hayley covered the cinema, while Jeremy, who had a gallant streak, preferred to pick up the meal checks. It suited them like a pair of comfortable shoes that promised longevity, Jeremy felt, as long as he didn't ruin things with his streak of immature envy.

In the restaurant of the Drugstore Saint-Germain Haley informed him, "I've got to get back to my translation while Bernadette and Kathleen are away." The *translation*, of course, the English text she was preparing for Annie Kérouac's dual-language coffee-table book, showcasing photos of Paris's wrought-iron balustrades. Annie Kérouac: the mother of Haley's ex-companion Thierry, now stationed with Air France in Buenos Aires.

"I'm really excited," she went on. "Annie might have a publisher, a fellow called Garnier, who Thierry and I've done translations for."

Jeremy made a point of looking out the window of the eatery's upper floor, but couldn't resist asking, "Do you ever get a postcard, or anything, from Thierry?"

"Not in a long time."

He made his tone casual. "And if he moves back to Paris...?"

"With his job, I don't know when or even *if* that would be." Haley tilted her head. "Are you worried about something?"

He held her gaze for a couple of intense seconds, then responded with a firm "No."

"Good," said Haley, giving him a grateful smile.

That night they returned to her flat and put on the *Touch of Evil* soundtrack in her bedroom. The Latin rhythms made Jeremy's blood tingle, whetting urges of desire, but also images of struggle. He pictured his careening chase after the Viking, only this time backed by the hot popping of conga drums and the low register of a pounding piano. He flashed on Stefania—he needed

137

to contact her. He thought of the Monks—he must sort them out and be rewarded by Rébert. *He had to thrust forward.*

Then a slow number took him by surprise; the soft chiming of a vibraphone, the sound that filled Haley with warmth and light, the sensation she'd told him she felt when they first met.

He wanted to tell her he shared the same feeling for her.

If only, out of the blue, she hadn't brought up the saxophone. "Deep down you've got to miss playing it," she said, after they'd made love. "*I* would if I could play an instrument."

"Maybe someday."

"It might help you..." The pause was awkward.

"Help me what?" Jeremy rolled onto his side, propping himself on his elbow to face Haley.

"Well, after your clash with the pickpocket on the metro, and that ugly bruise you've got on your side..."

Yes, the bruise from the thief's blow was ugly, not big, but a bit painful, especially while he and Haley had made love. "*And...?*" he said testily, then reached to turn on the lamp on his side of the bed.

She squinted against the burst of light, blinked a couple of times and said, "Well, I only meant...you might need an outlet for your fists...I mean your hands..." Haley sat up, frowned, and scratched her head.

She wasn't even there, yet she's decided I can't control my fists. "I should have let him go, then?" he said.

"No, of course not." She stroked his shoulder as if he needed calming, then reached for her glasses on the night table and hooked them on. "I'd be glad to get my wallet back if it was stolen. I know what it's like to be robbed in Paris."

"Oh?" Jeremy said in surprise, and scooted up next

to her.

Haley shrugged and leaned back against the headboard. "Got my purse stolen in the movies when I first arrived here. That's how I met Thierry, and a friend of his; they helped me out." She paused for a moment. "Things were rocky for me that first year as a student."

"More than just losing your purse?"

"A lot more."

"Want to tell me?"

She glanced at him, then aimed her gaze across the room, her eyes misting over.
"Remember the U.S. hostage crisis in Iran?"

"1979-80. Who could forget?"

"Well," she began slowly, "I'd gotten to know this Greek guy here—turns out half-Greek, half-Afghan, with Iranian sympathies."

"Mm," murmured Jeremy, nodding for her to go on.

"His name was George...he was my friend—just a friend. We met only in cafés; talked politics, religion..." She gave a subdued little laugh. "Things virtual strangers shouldn't discuss, right?"

Jeremy smiled and shrugged his understanding.

"Anyway," Haley continued, "his mother was Christian and his father Muslim, but George couldn't seem to figure out where he belonged."

"So you talked..."

"Especially about the American hostages. He and I understood both sides of the issue, but his Iranian friends didn't. Some of them were connected with revolutionaries back in Tehran, and when they found out about our friendship they beat him up."

"They saw you as a representative of the *Great Satan*," Jeremy observed.

"Right. George should've stayed away from me after that," Haley confessed, shaking her head.

"But he didn't..."

"No."

Jeremy barely heard the utterance. Haley's gaze had withdrawn to her hands, which were folded on the sheet that shrouded her.

He cupped them with his own hand.

"One day George insisted on meeting in a café in the Marais. Thierry told me not to go, but I didn't listen. George talked of moving on, he'd broken with the Iranians, he was enthusiastic..."

Foreseeing a bad outcome to the story, Jeremy squeezed her hand in support.

When she continued, a film of tears formed in her eyes. She blinked them back. "He was happy when he left the café. Out of caution I let him get a head start before taking my own leave..." Haley squirmed, the sheets gave a nervous rustle, and she pulled them tighter around her. "I heard the car crash before I could get out the door. Hit and run. I found George, mangled...dying..." She lifted her glasses and quietly wiped her eyes with the sheet. "It's been ten years, and I've never gotten over feeling responsible for his death."

Jeremy took her in his arms, holding her until she gently extricated herself.

"Anyway," she said, "I've found over the years that the only way to deal with guilt is to channel your energies elsewhere. Keep busy, engage with other people, and above all try to forgive yourself."

"Sounds like good advice."

She grinned. "Imparted by a sage Jewish friend."

Once more he hugged her, then relaxed, leaving an arm around her. "I'm glad you loved Paris enough to still remain here—if not, we wouldn't have met."

"And I'm happy you've always returned after your various spells in the States. When was the last one, four years ago?"

Jeremy loosened his hand on her shoulder. He and

Haley had spoken casually of their comings and goings, her various visits to America, his previous visit whose purpose he had kept vague.

"How long did you stay in the States that time?" she asked.

Slowly he met her eyes; they were tear-cleansed and glowing. He saw in them acceptance and hope. Serenity coupled with perseverance. He almost caught the feeling himself.

"Long enough to retrieve my father's saxophone," he replied.

"Oh! You've got it here?"

He answered with a cautious nod.

"But that's fantastic! Do you ever..." Her voice trailed off to a respectful silence.

"I take it out from time to time." Then, after an indifferent shrug: "can't seem to bring myself to play it, though."

"Because of your father..."

"Not really...well, partly..."

"Tell me..."

And after heaving a great, determined sigh, he did: everything he had spilled to Stefania. It didn't come as easily, without an ulterior motive guiding him, but it came more honestly. Plus, he went one step further and confided to her about his cousin Walter's memory loss.

Haley said very little during the account, her eyes intense, her brow taut. Finally he broke the tension with a shake of his head and a fatalistic chuckle. "Lucky he didn't die, or you and I would be competing for the Academy Award for guilt."

She kissed him. And after a long pause in which she caressed his arm, she said, "Listen: I won't say that forcing yourself to take up your father's saxophone would be therapy. But you could try a different instrument. Like the clarinet—they say it's similar to the

141

sax—or even a different saxophone all together; a rental, maybe."

"Let's not rush things," said Jeremy, taking her face in his hands and kissing her hard.

She nodded. "You're right; things happen when you're ready."

They made love again, and afterward, as Jeremy fell asleep, he felt a fraction of the serenity he imagined Haley possessed. Life hadn't been a complete bed of roses for her either.

Chapter 13

The next morning, after setting a date with Haley for the 12^{th,} Jeremy walked the six blocks home while Haley headed off to Madame Kérouac's. He would shower, shave, and change, then, he hoped, catch the Monks in their café. His sense of urgency had become a constant thrumming under his skin. *Maybe another leg up today.*

His face was still warm as he prepared to soap his cheeks and shave. Then he dropped his hands and looked at himself askance in the mirror. Let the Monks see him scruffy with stubble—might help his credibility. He abandoned his trusty Oxfords for his loafers as well, and decided to time his visit to the Hairy Monk café half an hour later.

It paid off, for at 12:35 he arrived to find Jean-Marc and Renaud at their tables overlooking the café's sidewalk terrace. The window-doors were open, beckoning a breeze, while the Monks sat with their heads buried in the newspapers.

"*Salut*," Jeremy greeted them, a hand raised and an affable grin fixed on his face.

They looked up in distraction, then recognized him in tandem.

"What's your name again?" asked Jean-Marc, the stringy-haired one.

"It's *Jeremy*," the bushy-headed Renaud reminded him, with a broad smile for Jeremy. "Sit down," he said, indicating a chair across from their tables, which were littered, like before, with their personal effects.

143

Pleased with his reception, Jeremy squeezed through the cramped cluster of little round tables and straddled a chair. The waiter arrived and he ordered an Affligem.

"So you like Belgian beer," stated the lank-haired Jean-Marc. "Well you're in luck 'cause they've got a big menu here."

"I've noticed," said Jeremy, nodding his approval. Renaud offered him a cigarette and he was highly tempted to accept, if only to ride the Monks' wavelength as closely as possible. Then, at the last instant, he chose an appeal to sympathy, and told them of the loss of his grandfather to lung cancer. The confession required no acting, the Monks expressed frowning condolences, and Jeremy hung on to his ex-smoker status. He had pondered how to make further inroads with the two, considered inventing another celebrity story, but felt he needed a fresh angle.

Instead, Renaud conveniently reverted to common ground. "*Le Monde* has gone crazy reporting celebrity visits to Paris," he said, stabbing a copy of the center-left newspaper on the table in front of him with an accusing forefinger.

"Not *Libération*, *Dieu merci*," claimed Jean-Marc, who had the ultra-left-wing paper on his table.

Jeremy went with the flow. "I've had to modify my walking routes. Can't even get to work on the metro without planning an extra half hour. The other night my carriage was so packed with tourists it was a pickpocket's delight. I mean *literally*. Witnessed a guy pinch a wallet." He stopped there and waited to see what this last bit would yield. True stories always seemed the most effective.

"Idiot tourists deserve it," muttered Jean-Marc. "What've they got to celebrate? It wasn't *their* revolution."

. "People just want an excuse to party," said the more light-hearted Renaud. "Understandable, but I wish they'd join us when our unions protest; when factories and department stores close."

"You're right," said Jeremy. "Are you guys..."

"Unemployed," Renaud confirmed with a defiant look.

"Three cheers for the bourgeois state." Limply, Jean-Marc raised an empty demitasse. Then, with a conspiratorial twinkle in his eye: "That's why it's nifty when someone throws sand in the gears every so often."

Really? And what and who might that be? With an uptick of his pulse Jeremy nodded to the Monks in solidarity. "Need to do something when you live here and can't walk down the street."

Jean-Marc peered at him Rasputin-like past a lock of dark hair dangling over one eye. "Have you always lived here? You sound like you're from the North, maybe ..."

"Probably because my mother's Belgian, from Wallonia...I spent a lot of time there."

"And what's your surname?"

"Martineau," came Jeremy's tidy lie. He had used his mother's maiden name before when doing certain of Rébert's little jobs. "I've actually lived here longer than in Belgium—twenty years."

The Monks nodded blandly, and Jeremy charged on. "I'd like to bust up some of this Bicentennial bullshit," he said, shaking his head with a smirk of disgust. "Toss a firecracker, or something, into the mass of morons blocking the street."

The Monks snickered, Renaud's grin mischievous. "Or stick a banana in the tailpipe of a celebrity limousine, maybe?" He slipped Jean-Marc a quick glance, who returned what Jeremy perceived as a tiny smile of approval.

"Oh, that *would* be fun!" Jeremy replied with a broad schoolboy grin.

Renaud winked at him. "Trust me, it *is*. Hang out with us and you might get the chance."

"You've actually *done* it?" asked Jeremy in feigned awe.

"Yesterday," confirmed Jean-Marc, "in rue du Faubourg Saint-Honoré. Corazon Aquino's motorcade. We got stuck in a mess of fools trying to get a glimpse of her and her stupid yellow dress—"

"—I found a ripe half of a banana in a trash basket," continued Renaud, "shoved it in one of the limousines' tailpipes—and *oooh*!"

Renaud's miming of the act was rich in sexual innuendo, and Jeremy responded with an adolescent grin and guffaw—*"Bravo les mecs!"*—all the while groaning inside.

The three of them agreed to stay in touch, with Jeremy handing over his phone number. "It's *unlisted*," he specified, as though granting the Monks a special privilege, when he actually meant to discourage them from looking up "Martineau" in the phonebook, in case they lost the number.

He left the Hairy Monk café deciding to hold off reporting to Rébert. Considering their preposterous Corazon Aquino story, how could anyone take these two seriously? A pair of developmentally-arrested clowns attached at the hip. He would drop by the café again soon, but he sincerely hoped they would propose something more RG-worthy than bananas.

The disappointing encounter sent his thoughts scudding elsewhere. To Haley, who would now be working diligently at Madame Kérouac's, where she would also be staying for dinner as was her and Madame's custom. His thoughts touched on Le Prince, behind whose bar he didn't have to serve tonight, though he still wished he had somewhere to go.

...Like down to Stefania's in the Thirteenth, to try to find her at home for once.

When he arrived, he buzzed and buzzed to no avail, then once more set off searching for her in the neighborhood, dreading she might have fled in fear of the Viking. He tried the Laundromat—no sign. He weaved through the Monoprix, then out the door empty-handed. The Arab who ran the corner mini-grocery store recognized her physical description as well as her Italian accent, but reported not having seen her for some time. "*Ça fait longtemps.*"

The same answer from Mireille and barman Julien in the café.

Hot and exasperated, Jeremy found a phone booth, extracted the mini address book he'd been careful not to forget this morning, and called Louise Cholot. He desired a cool respite, and perhaps he might also benefit from Madame's unique insight into things.

She answered on the third ring and invited him over.

"I went out for an early run this morning," she pronounced, as she led the way into the sitting room. "The air's luscious at six-thirty. By one o'clock I'm done for the day."

"Must be nice in the Parc Montsouris," Jeremy said. "I've never been there."

"A bit of a walk from here but well worth it—so expansive and so much green. In winter I take the bus. Now," she said, as Jeremy took his habitual place on the sofa, and she her armchair across from him, "for a change of subject. It's about time you called me Louise."

Jeremy smiled in appreciation. "And of course you must call me Jeremy."

"*Jeremy*—yes, I remember from when you first

introduced yourself as an insurance agent," she said with a tiny wink.

"Right." He gave a little cough. "So now you know the *Grand Blond* has been stalking my friend Stefania..."

"The young Italian woman."

Jeremy nodded. "Well, I haven't been able to contact her for days now, and I'm afraid she might be trying to escape him." Granted, he hadn't called Christophe, or even Mirko about Stefania. As for Christophe, the thought made him recoil inside. But if Jeremy failed to find Stefania soon he would definitely ring Mirko.

Louise drummed her fingers on her chair's armrest in contemplation. "I recall your expressing hesitancy on the part of the police to get involved..."

"Well, now I'm starting to suspect she's gone missing. None of the merchants in the neighborhood have seen her for a while; I can't find her at home, and when I told her about the *Grand Blond's* German accent she went into a panic."

"Mm," Louise murmured. "What does she look like?"

Jeremy straightened his posture. "She comes up to my shoulder, long, dark-red hair, blue eyes, not heavy but not thin either..."

Louise shook her head. "I don't recall having seen her around the *quartier*."

They fell into a ruminative silence. Jeremy was aware of a clock ticking in the hall. Faint, measured clicks, unsettling in their suggestion of inertia and paralysis—going round in circles, spinning wheels, slowly, slowly...

His restless gaze went wandering; it noted Madame's shapely light-blue trousers and pink V-neck T-shirt, the Matterhorn in pastels on the wall behind her short, straight platinum hair, which was probably dyed, though she hardly looked more than in her late forties. He wished he had nipped back home and shaved before coming here. He really didn't know why he kept bothering her with all this. As a flush of discomfort began to creep up him, she finally spoke.

"I was thinking...we could perhaps go to the commissariat of police here in the neighborhood—it's not far—and it would be appropriate since Stefania's a resident of the *quartier*..."

Jeremy looked at her in surprise, then thought hard. Stefania would abhor the idea. *No cops—pas de flics—* was her everlasting refrain. But if she had gone on the run from the Viking with no one to help her—or worse, if the Viking had already apprehended her? *The fear she had shown in her flat...*

"All right," he conceded. "I'll look up the address and go over there."

"I'd better come with you. I can attest to living in the *quartier* and noticing Stefania's been missing." Louise gave him a knowing nod, leaving no doubt she had become Jeremy's ally.

They walked the few blocks to the commissariat of police. Louise owned a car, but like Haley she barely used it in the city. "Especially with this Bicentennial mess."

The layout of the station was reminiscent of others Jeremy had seen in Paris, an officer stationed at a high desk in the middle of the foyer to sort out foot traffic. He directed Jeremy and Louise to a cramped office, where a middle-aged officer with curly grey hair offered them each a chair near his desk, smiling graciously at Madame and nodding genteelly to Jeremy. Considering his stubbly chin, Jeremy was glad Louise was with him.

Jeremy repeated everything he had told Madame about Stefania Perin, minus the mention of a stalker.

Madame cast him an inquiring look but offered no comment other than her support of his declaration.

"Has Mademoiselle Perin no family in Paris?" asked the officer, after jotting down Stefania's address, which Jeremy had half-heartedly provided. If Stefania knew he was here she would slam the door on him forever.

"No," Jeremy replied, checking an urge to shift in his chair.

"Any friends or colleagues who've also noticed her absence?"

"I'm not sure about anyone else..." He glanced at Louise.

"The merchants of the *quartier* and I are seriously concerned," she offered.

The officer poked his pencil into his grey waves and twisted it; rather than scratching his head, he seemed to be giving his thoughts a stir. "What does Mademoiselle Perin do here as an Italian national?"

Avoiding Louise's gaze Jeremy rolled out a story. "She's conducting research for a book she's writing on Paris's fabled balconies and balustrades—taking photos, writing text, all for the Italian market." His eyes briefly strayed toward Louise, but if she was surprised she didn't show it.

"Well," the officer said, his own face retaining professional dispassion, "I'm afraid there's little we can do. Mademoiselle Perin may very well be absent from Paris, but she could be away on holiday for a few days. And unless someone suspects foul play..."

Madame turned a beseeching gaze on him. "I know this is asking a lot...but would it be possible for you to at least ask Mademoiselle Perin's concierge to open the flat and let us take a look around? We would of course request that you be present."

Jeremy stifled a cough in surprise.

"Officer," she added with an earnest smile not

lacking in mature, feminine charm, "if you would only grant us this *petite faveur*, it would assuage my conscience."

"Well," the officer replied, his aging features beginning to soften, "I might have a free moment…"

The three of them walked the short distance to Stefania's flat. By coincidence, one that made Jeremy curse to himself, the same man whom he had intimidated the last time he was in the building, happened to be exiting the front door. Jeremy gritted his teeth as the bald man held the door open in deference to the uniformed police officer. His eyes narrowed as Jeremy crossed the threshold behind Louise, yet he said nothing, and Jeremy exhaled his relief once they were inside the foyer and the glowering guy had left the building, the door thudding closed behind him.

Jeremy and Louise waited for the officer to emerge from the concierge's room, followed by the concierge herself, impatiently jingling the keys to Stefania's flat. Thank God the woman hadn't heard the ruckus three days ago.

First, they checked Stefania's mailbox, but instead of glass its locked door was made of wood, so they couldn't tell if anything had been abandoned inside. Then the four of them marched upstairs, the sixtyish concierge, with rollers in her hair, in the lead. She gave an embarrassed tap to her curlers, stressing to the policeman, "I'm only allowing you into the flat because you insist something might be amiss."

Jeremy and Louise expressed their many thanks. But when they reached Stefania's floor and the concierge got the door open, nothing seemed awry at all. Or *abnormally* awry, Jeremy thought, for they faced the same chaotic mess he had seen twice already in the studio flat. Bed unmade, a mound of clothes on the back of a chair, a couple of magazines on the floor next to the bed.

"*Quel bordel*," the concierge grumbled. Though the flat had only two rooms, she insisted on following Jeremy into every corner. The police officer lagged behind, more, it appeared, out of formality than interest. In the tiny kitchenette the dishes were put away, so at least Madame, the concierge, couldn't complain about a mess there.

Two people could not fit comfortably in the bathroom, so she stood at the entrance while Jeremy nosed around. She therefore missed his piqued expression as he noticed Stefania's toothbrush absent from the mug on the shelf above the sink.

She and the police officer stepped aside as Jeremy, his thoughts whirling, walked silently past them, back through the living area. He took a second, more concerted look around—impossible to pinpoint anything else missing since, according to her habit, Stefania's belongings lay strewn about all over the flat. Her watch was absent from the credenza but that meant nothing, as Stefania would be wearing it for whatever reason she left the flat. Earrings lay there, her books, her transistor radio...

Nonetheless, she could have grabbed some essentials, thrown them into a hold-all, and taken off. But where to? To Christophe's? Somewhere else? If the missing toothbrush served as indication, Stefania seemed to have left voluntarily.

"Anything look out of the ordinary?" the officer finally asked Jeremy. "Other than there's no toothbrush in the bathroom..."

So he actually *was* paying attention, Jeremy remarked to himself. "Right," he said, acknowledging the missing toothbrush. "No, nothing else." He exchanged an uneasy glance with Louise, who had stayed out of the way near the door the whole time.

"Then we'll lock up and I'll go back to the station and make a short report of your concern. We'll let a few more days pass, since she could be out of town, then, if she hasn't returned, we'll take it a step higher."

Back on the ground floor, the concierge stopped Jeremy and the officer. "I hope she hasn't abandoned the apartment. Before long, she'll owe me rent."

"Do you remember the last time you saw her?" asked the officer.

"It's been some days..." The woman blew out her cheeks. "What if I'm stuck with all her stuff?"

"I doubt that will happen," said Jeremy. "Has it been more than three days since you've seen her?"

The woman paused to think. "Yes, three or more."

So when he chanced on Stefania in the Laundromat three days ago, she was already keeping a low profile.

"And you're sure you've noticed nothing out of the ordinary?" asked the officer.

"Positive. Why are you so interested in Mademoiselle Perin?"

"Nothing for you to worry about," answered the officer with a reassuring smile.

They left the building, the officer heading back to the commissariat and Jeremy and Louise Cholot returning to her place. Though Jeremy congratulated himself on the coup of entering Stefania's flat, his worry over her whereabouts, coupled with concern about what conceivable trouble he might have caused her by getting the police involved, doused that brief flame of pride.

Chapter 14

It was four-thirty when Jeremy and Louise Cholot returned to her place, and as he hadn't eaten since breakfast, Jeremy was grateful for Madame's offer of tea and biscuits. He expected Madame had questions for him and he wished to be as forthcoming as possible after the significant help she'd provided.

"Thank you again for coming with me to the commissariat," he told her as they sipped their tea in the sitting room. "I doubt I would've been as lucky on my own."

Madame's smile was mild as she put down her cup and saucer. "Your friend Stefania seems to be a talented woman. Lovely idea, that photo album book. And she came to Paris expressly to work on it?"

Jeremy's lips tightened. Slowly he shook his head. "I needed the police to take me seriously, so I invented an important role for her."

"Mm, I suspected as much since you hadn't mentioned her accomplishments earlier. So what *does* she do here?"

"She just lives here," he answered, glancing down at his hands.

Madame gave a tentative nod of acceptance. "You *did* say you'd already reported the *Grand Blond* to the authorities, so I assume that's why you neglected to mention him this time..."

"Right—and I was told that nothing could be done since he hasn't approached her."

Madame watched Jeremy thoughtfully. "And yet

something is attracting him to Stefania; unless that's been invented as well..."

Jeremy straightened on the sofa and sent her an earnest frown. "There's nothing made-up about that. He's been following Stefania, and now that we've established he could be Italian..." Jeremy sighed and sat back. Both he and Madame gazed pensively past each other.

Finally Madame said, "If he *is* Italian, could she perhaps be on the run from him and not have told you? A bad break-up, maybe?"

Jeremy's lips parted in wonder. "It's possible," he said, annoyed that he hadn't considered this hypothesis himself. He knew nothing of Stefania's personal life before the start of her relationship with Christophe, nine or so months ago; had no idea who might have been her boyfriend before that. The fact that Stefania had proved manipulative with him now made him feel that anything was possible. She could very well have known her Viking in Italy, or even met him in Paris. A bad break-up? Perhaps. Though Jeremy now pondered a different theory. Given Stefania's stormy past, might the *Grand Blond* be some kind of right-wing enemy? Someone whose toes she'd stepped on—a lone wolf out for revenge for one of her political crimes? *Provided,* once more, he was Italian.

Madame seemed to have snatched the tail end of Jeremy's thoughts. "Well, our mountaineer's nationality is still up in the air, so you mustn't dwell on that too much. You look a touch haggard today. How about staying for dinner this evening?"

"No, Madame. *Louise,*" he corrected himself. "I'd like to invite *you* out for all the assistance you've given me today."

"I don't know how helpful I was, but thank you. Did you find any clues in Stefania's flat, other than the missing toothbrush?"

"No, but given that, she might've gone away without telling me..."

"Or she could be avoiding the *Grand Blond*," Louise finished.

Jeremy appreciated Madame's generous support, and nodded grimly.

They discussed the unlikeliness of a kidnapping, considering the missing toothbrush. They drank more tea, talked of family and current events, and finally Jeremy asked Louise to choose a restaurant for dinner.

"I always enjoy an evening out at the Brasserie Lipp," she said.

A venerable eatery, already a Paris fixture in Hemingway's day. Jeremy's experience there had been limited to a croissant and a café au lait, but all in all, the Lipp was smart and Louise deserved a fancy meal. "Sounds excellent," he said, then rubbed the stubble on his chin. "But I'll need to go home and shave first."

"Do you live far?"

"Near La République."

"Then don't bother. I still have my husband Jean-Baptiste's razor. You can shave here."

Jeremy felt a start of surprise, then gave an inward shrug. "That would be convenient, thanks."

"If you're hungry, we could get there early, say about seven...?"

That suited Jeremy perfectly, since his head was starting to ache.

Louise gave him a fresh towel and her late husband's razor. "Just to be on the safe side, since it's been in the drawer for years, I've doused it with rubbing alcohol and put a new blade in."

It was a safety razor, Jeremy was happy to see, after the image that had flitted through his mind of the mountaineer Jean-Baptiste—tall and tough as the

Viking, and scraping his coarse bristles with a straight razor. Jeremy took the towel and razor to the water closet, a typical room in old French homes, limited to a sink and toilet, the *bath* delegated to a room of its own. Madame had lathered up a mug of shaving soap and left it on the shelf above the sink. He wondered if he was the first to use this gear since Jean-Baptiste's passing. Perhaps their son Hervé had shaved here, since Madame had shaving soap on hand. She had told him earlier that Hervé lived in Dijon, far enough away to justify spending the night at *Maman's* occasionally. He was thirty, unmarried, and worked as a wine sales representative.

While he shaved Jeremy recalled the picture of Hervé that Madame had shown him, the man's long face and nose, the high forehead that gave glimpse to a receding hairline. Jeremy examined his own face in the mirror after he wiped it dry. Having four years on Hervé, and despite the latter's encroaching baldness, Jeremy deemed himself much older-looking, particularly given the imperfections life had saddled him with.

When he put his shirt back on and opened the bathroom door, he was mesmerized by a sartorially transformed Louise Cholot: full makeup, teased hair, and a flowing skirt that grazed her knees; the only signs of the athlete within were her firm arms and attractive, well-formed calves, which without stockings highlighted her healthy summer complexion.

"You look lovely," he said. "I wish I'd brought a jacket."

She granted him an assuring smile. "In this heat no one cares, not in this day and age and certainly not at the Lipp."

Nixing the idea of finding a parking place near Saint-Germain-des-Prés, they opted to leave Madame's car home and take the bus, which stopped near

Madame's building.

Although they arrived a touch past seven, the Lipp was brimming with early diners. Sounds of clinking glasses and spirited voices followed the maître d', Louise, and Jeremy through the restaurant, where the maître d' indicated a long, plush banquette occupied by fellow diners. Jeremy insisted Louise take the cushioned bench while he took the chair across from her. Mirrors, interspersed with painted panels, encircled the room. When Madame first suggested the historically famous Lipp, Jeremy had girded himself to spare no expense. Instead, he received a pleasant surprise when Madame suggested they order the Alsatian restaurant's *choucroute garnie*, a favorite dish of his with its blend of sauerkraut, sausages, ham hocks, and potatoes. She recommended an Alsatian white wine, and the repeated mention of the region and its German heritage led them easily back to the subject of Stefania.

"Rather than a relationship gone wrong, might she have done something in Italy to anger this stalker?" Madame wondered.

Ah, Louise was starting to reason along his lines. Jeremy felt he could trust her yet didn't want to go so far as to reveal Stefania's revolutionary past. He settled on neutrality. "That's a definite possibility."

"Sufficient reason to fear for her safety, then."

It was. Plenty reason for that and for suspicion all around.

He and Louise had almost finished eating, their bottle three-quarters empty, the discussion of Stefania having reached an impasse. He poured out the rest of the wine then asked, "How about a little stroll across the street for a digestive at the Flore?"

Madame agreed. When the check came, however, she wanted to pay for the wine. "I recommended it," she protested.

"No, Louise," he said warmly. "When one invites, one invites all the way." After scanning the tally he was glad he had stuck to his principals. He could afford this meal, though if he were to make a habit of chic restaurants he would need a better job. He thought of the Monks, Jean-Marc and Renaud. Would they ever admit to anything more grievous than graffiti and bananas? And if so—with the 14th only three days away—*when*?

Jeremy and Louise had barely left the Lipp, her arm hooked in his, when they heard shouts, and sirens in the distance.

"The Louvre!" a young man exclaimed, to all and to no one in particular. He then crossed the street and made his way toward a crowd heading in the direction of the Seine.

"Someone's bombed the Louvre," echoed a wide-eyed woman. "I can't believe it!"

Jeremy and Louise exchanged incredulous looks. Jeremy grabbed the arm of a man who was also getting ready to cross the street. "It is true? There's been an explosion at the Louvre?"

He shook his head in disbelief. "I'm heading over there to find out." As soon as he found a break in the traffic he was off, to follow the crowd now marching down rue Bonaparte. Once they crossed the Pont des Arts they would reach the Louvre.

"Must be some kind of mistake," Madame insisted. "Or a joke?"

Jeremy's thoughts flashed back on the Monks. "I hope you're right, Louise, but I've got to find out for myself." He aimed a concerned look at her. "Will you be all right taking the bus home?"

"I'm coming with you."

"But if it really is an explosion..."

"I'll believe it when I see it."

They took the same route as the crowd, past the École des Beaux Arts, thudding across the wooden decking of the Pont des Arts along with a score of other alarmed people. Reaching the Right Bank, they found the entrance to the Cour Carrée of the Louvre blocked by police with automatic weapons. They veered to the right and rounded the corner to the Louvre's southeast entrance, once more finding a barricading police presence on the sand-covered patch of hard ground. So far, no damage was visible.

"There's the Carrousel entrance," Jeremy suggested to Madame.

"I've heard all the entrances are blocked." The response came from a man milling among the crowd, one hand combing through his dark tousled hair.

"But is it true?" Louise asked him. "That there's been a bomb?"

The man nodded. "I hear one of the new glass pyramids has been shattered."

"*Mon Dieu!* And victims?" Louise asked anxiously.

"None that I've heard."

"I'm going to stay till I find out more," Jeremy decided.

"You might be here all night," said the man.

Madame looked at Jeremy and gave a helpless shake of her head. "He's right; I'm going to head back and find news on television."

"Will you be okay getting home on your own?" he asked her again.

"Jeremy, I was born and raised in this city and have seen worse."

Jeremy gave her shoulder a squeeze and they pressed cheeks.

Once Madame left, he retraced their steps, continuing along the sidewalk toward the Louvre's

Carrousel entrance, cars whizzing by him along the *quai*. He dodged more swarming bystanders, who shouted their alarm and curiosity. Finally at the Carrousel entrance, which eventually led to the pyramids, Jeremy was again blocked by armed, mute police, who had cordoned off all three arched, stone-sculpted entrances. He stood gazing skyward but perceived no smoke in the impinging twilight.

He strode onward, along the quai des Tuileries. When he reached the gardens at the end of the Louvre's west wing he crossed them and backtracked toward the Place du Carrousel, where he would be able to view the glass pyramids. But when he arrived at the Carrousel arch he found himself thwarted once more, the road stretching between the two wings of the Louvre also barricaded and patrolled by armed, granite-faced police. The pyramids lay mere meters beyond them, all but the tip of the large one screened by a fire truck and other emergency vehicles, everything steadily dissolving in the blanket of dusk. He wiped the sweat from his brow, wondering again whether anyone had been injured, or worse. Shouts and speculation from the crowds had still failed to indicate either way.

Ten o'clock: Jeremy decided to find a café with a working television, since his own was on the fritz.

The Hairy Monk café had a TV—that, along with two patrons who'd made Jeremy bristle with suspicion from the start. Could Jean-Marc and Renaud have made the leap from juvenile delinquents to ruthless bombers? They didn't seem the type, and yet Jeremy couldn't exclude the possibility that they could be somehow involved. In any case, he doubted he would find them dithering about the café at this hour, especially if they were even tangentially connected to the explosion. Just yesterday Jean-Marc had invited Jeremy to partake in their exploits. Tomorrow he would return to their haunt

161

and willingly play the sidekick.

He walked back through the gardens and out to rue de Rivoli, heading east. By the time he reached rue du Louvre he had made the complete circuit of the museum, finding its north-wing entrance barricaded as well. Up rue du Louvre he knew the owner of a café called Le Parapluie Anglais. He would stop there to check the TV news, then take the metro home at Les Halles.

Le Parapluie Anglais was dotted with low Formica tables and vinyl couches and chairs, which Jeremy bypassed to go straight to the bar. Behind it, proprietor Grégoire welcomed him with an extended hand then a shake of his head at the television mounted on the wall behind him. Jeremy froze in front of the screen as images shifted jerkily from firefighters to police to glass rubble strewn about the Cour Napoléon, and finally to one of the small pyramids with a jagged hole blasted through one of its glass sides.

"*Quelle folie,*" uttered the fortyish Grégoire, as if used to repeating his observation on the insanity of the attack. "And they have no idea who did it."

To Jeremy's relief he learned of only superficial injuries resulting from glass shards in the explosion. He took a seat at the bar, which was lined with beer taps.

"Affligem?" said Grégoire, his intonation more statement than question.

"Cognac tonight," Jeremy muttered.

After serving Jeremy and chatting as long as his packed establishment allowed, Grégoire turned up the TV's volume and got back to his customers, many of whom sat huddled at the bar in front of the TV along with Jeremy. Numbly, Jeremy watched the revolving images until he suddenly thought of Haley. Thank God she wasn't out with her friends, who weren't due back from Brittany until the 14th. All the same, he pictured her watching TV like him—and reeling. He would call her as soon as he got home. His thoughts then swung to Rébert. Jeremy wanted to hear his RG handler's take on the attack, but knew he probably couldn't get a call through to him tonight.

He took a stiff gulp of his cognac. *He needed something credible on the Monks.*

Twenty minutes later Jeremy left Le Parapluie Anglais and made his way to the metro station. Louise was surely home by now; he would call her as well.

It was after eleven when he flung open the windows of his flat to the cooling night air. He peeled off his shirt, went into the bathroom, and bathed his face in cold water. Then he pulled on a T-shirt and called Louise, hoping she hadn't already gone to bed.

"Not a chance," she said, affirming she was glued to the revolving reports. They exchanged their appreciation for the lack of serious injuries in the blast, Madame thanked him again for dinner, and Jeremy hung up and rang Haley, knowing she would still be awake.

"I tried calling you but you were out," she said, the instant he greeted her.

"I was at Le Parapluie," he told her, preferring to skirt his history with Madame Cholot, specifically how he'd gotten to know her.

"Who the hell could have done this?" Haley said.

Who the hell indeed. "I happened to be nearby after it happened. Couldn't see much but emergency vehicles."

"But what's it all about? Why today, the 12th?"

Who, what, why: over his cognac in Le Parapluie Jeremy had hammered himself with the same questions.

When he finished speaking with Haley, he returned to his sixth-story window. Outside, the sky glowed midnight blue, nocturnal passersby drifted down the sidewalk below, and Marianne at Place de la République stood illuminated for the coming Bicentennial. Only three more days to go, and considering the timing of this blast, Jeremy had a nasty feeling the job might not be finished.

Chapter 15

The next morning Jeremy listened to the radio news as he prepared his work clothes for the evening. Nothing about suspects in the bombing, though reporters bandied about the usual characters: Basque separatists, Corsica Liberation Front, Free Brittany. And of course, the habitual refrain from the authorities that "nothing can be ruled out." He waited until eleven to set out to buy a newspaper and then proceed on to the Hairy Monk, since his target Monks never deigned to put in an appearance before noon. He would arrive by eleven-thirty, giving him ample time to sound things out in the café.

The streets hadn't lost their volume of tourists, though some crowds seemed subdued, with frowns and puzzled looks. Up rue du Temple police were stationed in a string of vans all the way to Place de la République, typical behavior on their part when restiveness was afoot. When Jeremy got off the metro at Saint-Michel he noticed the same protocol, with police vans pooled all around Place Saint-Michel.

He swung into the Hairy Monk at eleven twenty-five, and found the place nearly deserted. No sign of Jean-Marc or Renaud, provided they even planned to show up today. Jeremy asked after them at the bar and perceived a cautious demeanor in the barman. "Haven't seen them." Not even a smile of recognition for Jeremy, who nonetheless ordered a coffee, took a seat, and opened his newspaper. *Le Monde* reported three foreign tourists among those injured by flying glass the previous evening. Once more he felt relief that Haley and her Irish friends hadn't been in the vicinity. Tonight was the 12th, Haley was coming to the club to hear pianist Claude Bolling, following which Jeremy and Haley would spend the after-hours together.

By twelve-thirty he had scoured *Le Monde* and eaten an omelet and fries, with still no sign of the Monks. He rubbed a frustrated hand through his hair, then rose and returned to the counter, where his question was answered with an uneasy shrug and a pinched look. "Who knows where they are. They don't *live* here."

"It's just that we'd planned to meet here soon," Jeremy offered, taking note of the barman's body language. Thin, pale, wispy-bearded, he looked about Jeremy's age.

"Well they don't report their every move to me," he shot back with even more irritation.

Jeremy pulled a toothpick from his pocket, removed the plastic film, and probed between a couple of teeth before letting the pick dangle between his lips. "You don't own this place, do you?" he asked the barman.

"No...why?"

"No reason...just that you're here every time I come in."

"It's my *job*."

Edgy today, aren't we? Jeremy commented to himself. He removed the toothpick and tossed it into an ashtray. "I'm a barman too," he said with a dose of bonhomie. "At Le Prince Blue Note, up by the Luxembourg Garden."

For a moment the weedy fellow eyed him askance. "A while back you were a bouncer...worked at...?"

"Le Cuba Libre," Jeremy quickly confirmed, though he couldn't remember crossing paths with this guy during his bouncer days three years back.

"Still work nights?" The barman sounded a tad less diffident. A connection was forming, tentative as it might be.

Jeremy nodded. "Tonight, as a matter of fact. Big doings these days, lots of tourists. And *bordel à gogo* after last night," he finished with a shrewd smile.

Either Jeremy's *shitload of chaos*, his sly look, or both, seemed to nudge the barman into a half smile, though it didn't quite reach his eyes. "Shocking," he said, his expression and shake of the head implying he was anything but shocked.

A bit more prodding was in order, and Jeremy was certain this *mec* would remember the previous bar discussion of noxious celebrities and gratuitous gilding of Paris monuments. Accordingly he listed the Monks' accomplishments. "Clever graffiti, fucking up politicians' motorcades...Renaud and Jean-Marc were supposed to keep me in the loop so I could participate..."

The barman finally granted Jeremy a friendly smirk. "If I see them, I'll tell them you came around."

"Wouldn't happen to know their addresses? I think Jean-Marc's in the Mouffetard and Renaud's in Gobelins..."

The man's eyes beaded before he gave a guarded nod. "Jean Marc's near the Contrescarpe and Renaud's next to Le Canons des Gobelins."

"Right," said Jeremy. Though he received no exact coordinates, the landmarks would narrow things down. "Remember, tell them Jeremy was in. And your name?"

The neutral smile returned. "Al," he stated.

Al, Jeremy repeated to himself. *Short for Albert? Alban? Alain?* Whichever, the Anglo-ness of the nickname amused him. He still lacked the Monks' surnames, yet declined to ask Al. No use arousing suspicion over something he might think Jeremy should already know.

So he left the café, setting out on foot for the Monks' neighborhoods. The Mouffetard quarter, where Jean-Marc lived, lay only a few blocks south of the Hairy Monk. The crowds were picking up and regaining their boisterousness. The blast at the small Louvre pyramid had been reported in one article of *Le Monde* as a possible gas leak. If so, it had fortunately occurred when the Louvre was closed, with only those outside affected. Jeremy hoped what he had read would hold true.

At the Place de la Contrescarpe, the heart of the quaint little *quartier* Mouffetard, Jeremy found a police van parked in front of a building with peeling paint and shutters in need of a fresh coat of lacquer. Inside the van he spotted two officers, a driver and his colleague whose stony gazes surveyed the sidewalk in front of the building. With a nonchalant gait, he approached the panel listing the residents, discovered the name Jean-Marc Robinet, then moved right along without pressing the buzzer. If the police were staking out Jean-Marc's place it might mean the Monk wasn't home, and in any case Jeremy wished to avoid undue attention. He hastened down rue Mouffetard and in twenty minutes reached avenue des Gobelins. The Monks lived about twelve short blocks from each other.

He hurried across the street to the Canon des Gobelins brasserie. Not only did the fabled locale feature a model of a cannon on its premises, which Jeremy had admired since he was a youngster, but more interestingly a police van sat in front of the Haussmannesque building next door. Jeremy swiftly checked the list of residents and identified the name Renaud Lenoir. *Police stationed at both Monks' residences*: he rushed back into the brasserie and paid to use the phone.

Rébert answered on the second ring. "I've been

trying to reach you at home," he half scolded Jeremy. "We've moved on the two graffitists; still trying to catch them."

"But you found their addresses—"

"Got them from an informant. More importantly, what've *you* got?"

"I've been on them through yesterday. Today they didn't show up at the café—"

"I'm about to send an agent there now," Rébert interrupted. "Already sent someone this morning to have a look around; now we'll ask questions."

"Don't!" Jeremy was playing speed-chess in his mind. "Their friend Al the barman will suspect I'm involved with you. He already said he doesn't know where they are but will remind them I'm supposed to meet them. Let me continue working on it."

A brief pause told Jeremy his offer was worth considering. "All right," Rébert conceded. "What else have you got?"

"Is this connected to the explosion last night, that I read might've been a gas leak?"

"We're not ruling anything out, but we've decided to round up the usual suspects. We checked out the graffitists' flats last night but it looks like they've bolted. Now, let's hear your end."

"Well," Jeremy started, "Jean-Marc and Renaud bitch nonstop about the Bicentennial, and yesterday they bragged about stuffing a banana into the tailpipe of one of the cars in Corazon Aquino's motorcade. They've agreed to include me in their next activity."

"Why didn't you report this yesterday?" demanded Rébert.

"Well, it was only a prank, and it seemed so childish..."

"*Putain*, Winters!" Rébert gave an irritated sigh, and Jeremy could picture him rubbing his face in exasperation with his free hand. "All right," he said, his tone calmer. "But they could be working up to something more serious if they haven't already. We've got units trying to find them, and I'll expect you to inform me of the least little progress you make with the barman."

Jeremy drew himself up. "I'm on my way back there."

The Hairy Monk was filled with patrons when Jeremy returned. Al the barman looked surprised and perhaps a touch interested to see him so soon again.

"An Affligem Blonde," Jeremy told him. "You've got the best selection of beer around."

Al pasted on his half smile as he fetched a goblet-style glass with Affligem stamped on it in stylized black script. He pulled the draught lever, eyes darting at Jeremy.

"Just back from Gobelins," Jeremy announced. "Police vans stationed there and at the Contrescarpe. Hope they're not looking for anyone we know."

At the mention of the police, Al gave Jeremy a hard stare. Slowly he set the brimming glass on the counter. "Doubt the boys are home," he said in a casual tone.

"I didn't bother to ring their bells, not with cops crawling everywhere..."

Al's lips parted, then a waiter arrived to place an order and he swiveled toward the espresso machine. "Don't think our friends'll be home for a while," he said as he banged out coffee grounds, repacked the cup, and twisted the machine's arm back into place.

"Since the 'gas leak' last night?"

"Mm-hm." Al set the espresso machine humming.

Jeremy waited for the returning waiter to take away the coffee Al had prepared, then exhaled, "*Merde*."

"Cops want to finger them for it." Al's mouth was set

in a firm line, his arms folded pugnaciously across his spindly chest. "So they've gone underground. Course, they had nothing to do with the Louvre business."

"No—not their style," Jeremy agreed.

"But maybe *yours*?" Al wondered with a tilt of his wispy-haired head.

Jeremy looked taken aback.

"Wanting to throw firecrackers at celebrities?" Al reminded him. "The boys told me about that..."

"Well..." Jeremy murmured.

Judging from his shrewd grin, Al seemed to be enjoying Jeremy's discomfort. "Just joking," he finally said. "You actually seem to be of a like mind to us: *Révolution ratée.*"

The waiter returned, requesting a Coca-Cola and a peach ice tea. Jeremy sipped his beer and took advantage of the pause to recall the other anti-bicentennial slogans daubed on Paris's venerable monuments. He considered Al's "Failed revolution" reference a confirmation of the Monks' guilt in the graffiti about town. But he needed more. He had to find the duo.

"*Ratée, bien sûr,*" he said with a nod and a knowing smile, once he had the barman to himself again. "If Jean-Marc and Renaud need a hand, tell them I could be of use."

Al placed his wiry hands on his hips and gave Jeremy a measuring look. "How d'you get that eye?" he asked with an upward tilt of his chin.

Out of habit, Jeremy dabbed his eyelid. "Fight. Nothing compared to how my opponent fared. Tried to steal what was mine and I put him in the hospital."

Al returned a cool nod, brows raised.

The waiter arrived to place another order.

"Well, as I said, I'm available." Jeremy pulled out his address book and tore out a page. He reached for a pen at the end of the bar to scratch out his phone number. "I've already given them my number but I'll write it down again. And tonight I'll be at work at Le Prince Blue Note, so I'll add that number as well."

Al scooped up the paper and stuffed it under the counter. "If they contact me I'll tell them."

As two women entered and sidled up to the bar, Jeremy drained the last of his ale and left the Hairy Monk, his thirst slaked, but his urge to make headway, not. Even so, he found the nearest phone booth and called Rébert, reporting Al's agreement to stay in touch about the Monks, for which Rébert offered approval and encouragement.

As Jeremy stood next to the phone booth in Place Saint-Michel, his unease regarding the Louvre explosion increased. His gaze skimmed the fountain of Saint Michael vanquishing the serpent Satan, and his speculation about what might happen tonight or tomorrow waxed equally dramatic. He felt he was at the eye of some unfolding hurricane; he needed to advance yet was forced into repose. And part of this interlude of calm included Haley, who would be at the club tonight. The thought made him nervous; he should go home after work in case the Monks called. He should head straight home right now, in fact, and wait. But the idea of sitting idle racked his nerves even more.

He looked at his watch. Three hours before he needed to be home to change, might as well check on Louise after their ultra-brief conversation late last night. He slipped back into the phone booth and rang her.

"Do come by," she stressed. "I tried calling you earlier with some very interesting news."

She told Jeremy just enough to make him straighten and square his shoulders. He would be right down— after a detour to Stefania's building.

"Yes," Madame agreed. "If she's not there, check

with her concierge again."

The metro ride, then the walk, terminated just as Jeremy expected, with no answer at Stefania's flat. When he buzzed the concierge, however, she let him into the building.

"Sorry, Monsieur Winters, I still haven't seen her," she said, speaking to him in the foyer. Today Jeremy had no police to vouch for him, yet the woman's attitude seemed amenable compared to last time. Dressed in a crisp linen blouse and skirt, lips glossed red and no curlers in her hair, she made his visit seem almost welcome.

"Mm," Jeremy replied, wishing he had brought along the *Grand Blond's* photo. Instead, he tried describing him.

Madame's eyes formed a far-off squint. "Yes, I believe I've seen a man who looks like that..."

"In the building?" Jeremy pressed.

"No, outside, standing near the entrance."

"You didn't happen to speak to him?"

"Oh no. It's lucky I even remember seeing him. Just that he seemed so tall and imposing. Does he have something to do with Mademoiselle Perin?"

"Maybe," Jeremy said, his gaze diverted past her.

"Should you inform the police?"

Jeremy nodded. "Yes, I'll be sure to take care of it. And thank you for your assistance."

He left the building, rubbing his neck in rumination. He would not be contacting the authorities. Rébert had his hands full right now, and there was still no indication any harm had come to Stefania. The missing toothbrush, however trivial the detail, attested to this. He turned on his heel and made a beeline to Louise Cholot's to hear the rest of Madame's intriguing account.

"Tell me everything," he said, perched on the edge of the sofa after having reported his conversation with Stefania's concierge.

"Well," Louise began, "as I said, I saw our mountaineer walking away from Stefania's building early this morning on my way to the park for a run." She paused, a twinkle in her eye. "Lately, I've been taking that route."

My delightful ally, Jeremy acknowledged to himself with a little grin. "And he was alone..."

"Yes. I waited across the street, screened by a parked truck. I don't know if he rang then turned to leave when she didn't answer, whether she was home or not...but he wasn't dressed in a tracksuit this time. Jeans and hiking boots this morning, and he had a rucksack slung over his shoulder."

Jeremy shook his head in wonder. *And if the Grand Blond had somehow gotten into Stefania's flat?*

"Anyway, I followed him..."

Jeremy gazed at Louise in disbelief; she hadn't dropped that detail over the phone.

"Most likely he has no idea who I am," she explained in an airy fashion, "so I wasn't particularly worried about his spotting me."

"*Still...*" Jeremy uttered in concern.

Louise waved a dismissive hand. "He happened to be walking in the direction of the park—"

"The Montsouris," Jeremy interrupted for clarification.

"Exactly. Then at Place Rungis he cut down to boulevard Kellermann, continued past the park, and kept on going. He took no buses, and of course there aren't any metro stations in the vicinity."

"And you didn't get tired keeping up with him?"

"*Jeremy*—compared to my runs, this was a morning of amateur boules."

"Right," Jeremy conceded sheepishly.

"We finally arrived at Porte d'Orléans, where there *is* a metro station, but he bypassed it. By now we'd entered the Fourteenth Arrondissement."

"Why walk that far?" Jeremy asked himself aloud.

"Precisely. He could have rented a car..."

After a split-second interval, they looked at each other and indulged in a laugh. "*And wreck another vehicle!*" Jeremy added, wiping a humorous tear from his right eye.

"*Necessitating another insurance investigator!*" After a mirthful sigh, Madame continued with her account. "Anyway, he finally stopped at rue Didot, at the corner of boulevard Brune. Do you know the neighborhood?"

"Vaguely," Jeremy said, recalling his taxi-driving days. "What did he do there?"

"Unlocked the door to a building near the corner and went inside."

"And you?" Jeremy asked, so caught up he expected Madame to say she'd followed the *Grand Blond* inside.

Instead, she gave a shrug. "I stopped, of course."

Jeremy shot her an approving nod. "What's the address?"

"112 rue Didot. Obviously I have no idea which apartment he was headed to."

"And you don't think he noticed you..."

"Not that I'm aware. There are lots of people beating those boulevards during the week, early in the morning. Plus he seemed absorbed in his own affairs, keeping his head down."

Jeremy barely heard this last bit. He was already projecting a visit to rue Didot. Not today though, he determined after taking a peek at his watch. He looked back at Louise with a broad smile. "I can't tell you how much I appreciate your detective work."

"Now, you'll take over, I imagine," she said with a conspiratorial wink.

He nodded. "But I hope I can still count on you in a pinch..."

"Now that I've come this far, Jeremy, I wouldn't have it otherwise!"

Chapter 16

Le Prince was sizzling that evening, people flocking to hear Claude Bolling work his piano magic just two nights before the Bicentennial. On the 14th the club would be closed for the big blowout—with everyone expected on the Champs-Elysées. Upon his return from Madame Cholot's, Jeremy had hoped the Monks or Al hadn't called in his absence, reassuring himself that Al had his work number. Now, as he stood behind the bar, his thoughts returned to the address 112 rue Didot, where Louise had followed the *Grand Blond*. In hopes the address might somehow lead to Stefania, he planned to investigate as soon as time permitted. Tomorrow, he added to himself, he would call Stefania's fellow Compagni Mirko, who had also seen the *Grand Blond*.

Haley was one of the first to arrive at the club, dressed in a gauzy summer skirt and matching blouse. In her high-heeled sandals she matched Jeremy's height, and when she approached the bar he wanted to plant a generous kiss on her lips. Instead, in his professional capacity, he limited himself to pressing cheeks with her. He'd thought about inviting her to his place for the night so he could be home for a much-desired call from the Monks. He decided to play it by ear. Not least of his concerns was the anything-but-romantic punching bag, suspended in his bedroom like a big slab of slaughterhouse beef.

Didier, Jeremy's waiter friend, emerged from the stairs leading to the cellar. "Caravan's" starting!"

"*Merci*," Jeremy called back, "but I think I'll stay up

here."

Didier cast him a *you're-kidding-me* look, to which Jeremy responded, "I'm expecting a phone call." Which netted another curious stare. "It's a long story," Jeremy said.

"Haley's down there," Didier reminded him over his shoulder, as he headed off to wait on a table on the upper gallery floor.

"I know," Jeremy said to his friend's back, then glanced mechanically at the phone behind the counter. His colleague Gilles gave him a quizzical glance as well, but Jeremy simply smiled, shrugged, and repeated, "Long story." If the Monks were to ring, they would ask for Jeremy *Martineau,* the surname Jeremy had given them so they wouldn't suspect him a foreigner. He'd been poised to lunge at the phone all evening to keep Gilles from answering it. When it came to Didier, however, Jeremy understood his friend's surprise. He knew Jeremy had looked forward to hearing Claude Bolling's version of "Caravan" all week.

So true, Jeremy thought with a sigh. *Caravan.*

With the lull in activity Gilles excused himself, and Jeremy listened to snatch muted bits of Bolling's piano downstairs. He gazed toward the cellar, listened, and dreamt back to his boyhood.

San Francisco, 1964: At age nine Jeremy had been playing the sax for two years. Then, a year later, Monty moved in across the street. Monty the drummer, who at ten could already play like Buddy Rich, or so it seemed to the starry-eyed Jeremy. Monty, who like Jeremy had a musical parent, his mother the locally-celebrated jazz singer Val MacLean. Before long the families Winters and MacLean were mixing as famously as gin and tonic, with Monty's father Tom, a glass contractor, taking the boys to games at Candlestick Park; an experience that intensified Jeremy's passion for baseball and the Giants, whom he still followed from time to time by checking their wins and losses in the *International Herald Tribune.*

The two boys jammed together after school at Monty's house, and Walt Winters often dropped in to watch and share a cocktail with Monty's mother. Within a year Monty's little sister Badge joined the boys on her mother's piano. The nine-year-old had badgered Monty relentlessly into admitting her—hence her nickname— though in Jeremy's appraisal, Alison MacLean more than deserved the honor of making them a trio. So much so, that by the time Jeremy turned twelve, Badge had caught up to him skill-wise in the execution of jazz, while Jeremy was on the downslide, more and more given to unruly escapades in North Beach.

And yet there came that one night, when the stars in the musical firmament aligned to make twelve-and-a-half-year-old Jeremy shine. An evening of youth jazz performers at the YWCA, organized by Monty's mother, would include the Monty-Badge-Jeremy trio, accompanied by a fourteen-year-old bass player. Under Monty's leadership the four had prepared Duke Ellington's "Caravan," and its success, recalled Jeremy, lay largely at the hands of the prodigious Monty and his dancing drumsticks. His performance bordered on furious: speed-juggling the various sticks, flinging his tom-tom mallets into the air and catching them. In contrast, Badge played in calm and utter concentration, while Jeremy sweated like a devil to hold his own. Thankfully, he and Badge shared the weight of the melody.

A few months later Jeremy dropped out of the group. Now that he looked back on it, he couldn't remember if he'd left before or after his mother Béatrice's stormy complaints. The whole six-month period seemed a blur, with Jeremy suspended twice from school (once for fighting, another time for smoking marijuana) and Béatrice accusing Walt of an affair with Monty's mother. Then came Walt's true mistress, Margie, when Jeremy was thirteen. And the following year, Walt's suicide.

With a concerted stretching of his neck and rolling of his shoulders, Jeremy shook off further reminiscence and focused back on Claude Bolling's quartet down in the jazz cavern. Bolling, the piano virtuoso who also crossed over to create several albums of classical-jazz fusion. His drummer Vincent Cordelette enjoying international fame as well. As for Cordelette, Jeremy expressed a secret smile as he listened to the percussion: a smile meant for Monty Maclean. For wherever his childhood friend might be at this moment, Jeremy was certain he could match, if not exceed, Cordelette on Caravan—stroke for stroke, beat for beat, flying drumsticks and all.

Jeremy let his thoughts move on to Haley at her table downstairs. Though she was too reserved to snap her fingers or undulate to the rhythms, he imagined her relishing every note of Caravan. A heady gleam in her eye, subtle nods of her head, a light tapping of her fingernails on the wooden tabletop...

He thought of her with desire and admiration...and tonight, if the Monks didn't make contact...?

The phone rang.

He jerked up the receiver and answered, "Le Prince Blue Note, *bonsoir*."

Silence.

"*Âllo?*" Jeremy said, one hand over his left ear to block the bar noise.

Another pause, then a man's voice: "So, this isn't the residence of Rosine Beaulac...?"

Jeremy blew out a sigh. "*Désolé*, you've got the wrong number."

"But I was sure this was her number..."

"This is a jazz club—no Rosine Beaulac here." Jeremy hung up and looked at his watch. *Merde— another hour to go.*

Jeremy and Haley left Le Prince at midnight, with an exasperated Jeremy deciding to spend the night at her house. The Monks hadn't called, and he figured they would probably now wait until tomorrow. *If* they planned to make contact. At any rate, he would return home early the next morning.

To get to her flat by metro they would have to transfer at Châtelet, a station practically as large as a city. At least five train lines converged there in a teeming subterranean hive that obliged you to take stairs, escalators, and people-movers. Then, they would have at least three more blocks to walk to Haley's building. Jeremy decided to splurge for a taxi.

"Thank God you don't live any farther east," said the cab driver once they were settled in the backseat.

"Why?" Haley asked.

"The explosion, of course!"

Haley and Jeremy exchanged startled looks.

"You haven't heard? *Bon Dieu*—someone blew out a window in the new opera house and they've blocked off the *quartier*."

Jeremy leaned forward, his stomach starting to roil. "The Opéra Bastille?"

"It's the only new one, right? Happened about half an hour ago."

"But it's due to be inaugurated tomorrow night," Haley said in dismay. "Was anyone hurt?"

"Don't know yet. Let's see if we can get more news." The driver turned on the radio and began twisting its knob.

But Jeremy's mind had already shifted gears. *Where are those fucking Monks?*

"I'm going to leave you at your place," he said to Haley. "I've got to check on something."

Haley shook her head in confusion. "At this time of night? Can't we just find some news on TV?"

"You do that. Sorry, but I've got to look into this myself."

Lips parted, Haley stared at Jeremy's dark silhouette. They had started speaking English and the cab driver eyed them in his rearview mirror. When Jeremy noticed, he said in French, "Pull over and let me out—you can continue on with mademoiselle."

"So soon?" the driver asked, his bemused gaze darting back and forth from the mirror to the road.

"Yes, *here*," Jeremy ordered, digging out his wallet as Haley continued to gape at him.

The driver stopped next to the curb on boulevard Saint-Michel, just down from the Cluny Museum, and Jeremy paid him. "This should cover mademoiselle's fare home."

"Jeremy, you're talking about me like I'm not even here!" Haley protested.

"Sorry again, but I've got to go. I'll explain later," he said, giving her arm a confident clasp with one hand then opening the door with the other. "Trust me, I can't stay," he added, sliding out of the cab. He nodded at her, said good night, then shut the door and tapped the car's roof to send the driver on.

Then he made straight for rue de la Harpe, the little lane parallel to the Boul'Mich, and in less than five minutes arrived at The Hairy Monk. He yanked open the door, his pulse beating in time with his quick strides as he crossed the room. No trace of the Monks, of course. But neither of the barman Al, who Jeremy had hoped might be working the late shift. The café looked set to close, a few chairs already stacked on tables.

He approached the counter anyway, where the night barman, a clean-shaven, stocky antithesis of Al, looked at him with a tired expression.

"Closing?" Jeremy asked, grasping at any contact with the man he could.

"All but locked the doors."

"Just a quick question: I was talking to the day barman Al, earlier today—"

"You the barman from Le Prince Blue Note?"

"Yes," Jeremy replied. *Yes, I am!* He gave his fists a hopeful squeeze.

"Al dropped by about fifteen minutes ago; gave me a message to relay to you—said if you came back in to call him." The barman plucked a piece of paper from his shirt pocket. "Here's his number." Then he picked up the telephone from behind the bar and placed it on the counter next to the scrap of paper.

Jeremy continued to watch him in surprise, something the barman must have taken as a request for privacy, for he stepped away to wipe down the counter.

No one answered at the number Jeremy dialed. Hanging up, he asked the night barman if he knew where Al lived.

"He commutes from Montrouge, that's all I know."

Merde, Jeremy muttered to himself. It would take Al half an hour to get home. "He didn't say anything more? Maybe something about a couple of our mutual friends...?"

"No, nothing."

"Do you know a pair who hang out here during the day, Jean-Marc Robinet and Renaud Lenoir?"

The barman shook his head, shooting an obvious glance at his watch.

Jeremy thanked him and left. His own watch read twelve-thirty. He could lay heavy odds that Benoît

Rébert was not sleeping at this moment. But would he be home or out on the streets? Jeremy crossed over to Place Saint-Michel and used the pay phone to try Rébert's residence.

"*Âllo*?" responded an anxious female voice.

Rébert's wife, Jeremy concluded. He excused himself for phoning late, then identified himself and asked for her husband.

"He's working..."

"Right," Jeremy said, in his gravest voice. "That's why I'm calling. Might I be able to reach him at his office, then?"

Madame Rébert assumed so. Jeremy thanked her then dialed Rébert's RG office.

"He's out in the field," responded a colleague.

Jeremy left an urgent message for Rébert to call him at home as soon as the RG agent came back to the office. Then he hung up and crossed the Place to the metro station, noting the tourists who chatted and licked ice cream cones under the streetlamps, the lot of them seemingly unaware of the chaos on the other side of town.

As a trickle of travelers disembarked from a metro train, Jeremy hopped on and nabbed a drop seat by the door. There, as he sat in the bright glow of the carriage, the train jerkily picking up speed through the dark tunnel, he was forced into a quiet contemplation of the situation. Other than the barman Al's attempt to contact him, Jeremy had nothing concrete to report to Rébert. More importantly, Jeremy wished for insight into what the RG agent himself knew at this point. According to Al, the cops had put the Monks in the frame for the Louvre explosion. Might Rébert have something new on the duo? Jeremy began tapping his foot on the gritty carriage floor. He couldn't wait to speak to both Rébert and Al.

He thought of Haley. Would she be home in bed by now? Tomorrow he would call and somehow explain his behavior, though it wouldn't be easy.

And Louise Cholot? Had she heard about this latest attack on a French monument, just two days before the Bicentennial extravaganza? He would call her too when he had time.

Inside his flat, he dropped his keys on the entrance table next to the rotary phone, picked up the receiver, and started dialing. One-thirty, and still no answer from Al. He dialed the RG office.

"Rébert," came the response in a growl.

"Jeremy here. Did you just get in?"

"*Just*," he confirmed. "Another explosion and we still haven't found Lenoir and Robinet," he said, referring to the Monks by their surnames.

"Any injuries at the Opera?"

"No. One window blown out. Where the hell are you with these two?"

"Their friend and barman at The Hairy Monk, a guy called Al, is trying to contact me, so I won't stay on long. I've offered my help and they might want to take me up on it." Given Rébert's harried tone and Jeremy's need to free up the line, he didn't ask for possible details supporting the Monks as suspects. There'd be time for that later.

"Well, call me the minute you've got something," Rébert said, and rang off.

No sooner had Jeremy placed the receiver in its cradle, than did a *tring, tring* shock him into snatching it back up.

"Jeremy Martineau?" asked a cautious male voice.

Jeremy smiled to himself. "*Oui*, is this Al?"

It was. "I tried to get hold of you earlier; you need one of those modern answering machines."

Jeremy conceded the point, then listened as Al

offered him a miracle—the Monks wrapped up as a gift. "I'm calling on their behalf," he said in a tentative voice. "They'd like to know if they could stay at your place tonight, and till dark tomorrow."

"Where are they now?" Jeremy's pulse was ticking up, his right hand sweaty on the receiver.

"Up in Barbès, but the place is crawling with cops after this latest explosion and they need to get out of there. Of course they're innocent," Al made a point to remind Jeremy. "The police just want to make a show of arresting someone."

That remains to be seen. "Yeah, sure they can stay with me while they sort things out," Jeremy assured him.

"That's exactly what they're trying to do, but they'll explain once they get to your place."

"*Bien sûr.* I'm at 72 rue de Turbigo, near La République. Sixth floor." Then, just in time, he added, "Tell them to ring Jeremy *Winters*. The management fouled up the residents' names and haven't fixed them yet."

Hesitation on Al's part. Jeremy closed his eyes, hoping he hadn't raised suspicion.

"...How do you spell that name?" the barman finally said. And Jeremy exhaled his relief.

"Okay," said Al, "got it. I'll call them now. They'll get there on their own."

For a minute or so Jeremy stood staring at the receiver cradled in the phone's base. The Monks had to be apprehended. Even Al had admitted his pals were responsible for graffiti about town. They'd boasted to Jeremy, invited him along to indulge in their mischief, which now might very well involve planting explosive devices—regardless of Al's insistence on their innocence. The unemployed Renaud and Jean-Marc resented Mitterrand. In Jeremy's presence they had vilified the president and his government for the unemployment rate, plus they despised the Bicentennial. A role for them in the targeting of two monuments credited to Mitterrand's administration, near the culmination of the celebration, could therefore ring reasonable. Particularly given the limited damage to the Louvre pyramid (already repaired) and the Opéra Bastille, with only light injuries inflicted at the former and none at the latter. Albeit perversely, this spoke to the Monks' ethical parameters. At the very least, the two needed to be rounded up and vetted properly as suspects. Jeremy reached for the receiver and dialed Rébert again. Time to hand this off to the RG.

After hanging up he dropped down onto the sofa and went over in his mind how he had set this critical moment into motion. The Monks and Al barely knew him and yet they trusted him. Had that been due to a feat of manipulative engineering, or were the Monks and Al just *pauvres cons*—poor schmucks? Jeremy didn't waste time trying to decide. He got up and opened the window, leaning forward and resting his hands on the black wrought-iron railing. He looked to the right and gave a silent nod to the moonlit statue of Marianne at La République. At least those fools Jean-Marc and Renaud would stop mucking up his neighborhood.

Jeremy massaged his face, unbuttoned his shirt, and sat back down. Now all he could do was wait. *Wait...*

He drummed his fingers on the sofa's armrest, then got up and shut off the living room lamp. His flat plunged into darkness, he returned to the window where he breathed in the still black air. In the building across the street, late-night lights from televisions winked at him through open windows as scenes shifted on their screens. His gaze floated over to his neighborhood café, at ground level across the street. La Gitane was still alight with neon, and nocturnal customers continued to enter and exit. His gaze swept the street as he wondered whether he would recognize signs of the police arriving to set their trap. They would surely come in unmarked cars. As for the Monks, if they left the Barbès *quartier* even five minutes ago it would take them at least fifteen to arrive here, regardless of their mode of transportation. He had time to get himself a beer from the fridge. *And he could really go for a cigarette.*

But Jeremy's feet didn't want to move. His eyes caught a vehicle pull up and commence parking on his side of the street, three car lengths from his building's entrance, in the direction of the Place. Once the car was in place, a lone man stepped out and set off in the opposite direction, past Jeremy's building, toward La Gitane. Two more cars whizzed by, then a third. A group of young revelers, loud and gesticulating, kicked an aluminum can along the sidewalk as they passed under Jeremy's window. He looked back at the lighted entrance to the Temple metro station, squinting to make out the two people emerging. One headed toward the Place, the other toward La Gitane. And if the Monks arrived *before* the police? He would have to let them in and act as their protector until Rébert's brigade busted in. Jeremy didn't want to face the two. Let them be picked up on the sidewalk and think the cops had followed them.

Another car stopped across the street, squeezing into a parking spot by lightly bumping both the car in front and behind. Jeremy watched the headlights go off, but no one got out. It was too dark to see inside the sedan, but could it contain two, three, maybe four officers of the Renseignements Généraux? Or maybe just Rébert plus a couple of cops to back him up? Then again, it might simply be a young couple returned from a date, parked to continue chatting or making out until the girl's curfew.

He lifted his watch close to his eyes: he'd been standing at the window for ten minutes. He had to take a leak; even so, his feet remained nailed to the floor. His hairline was damp and he drew an audible breath through his nostrils. His gaze continued to sweep the sidewalks and the entrance to the metro station in the glow of the streetlights. And still, no one had emerged from the tightly parked sedan across the street. His eyes followed two silhouetted individuals exiting La Gitane. In the café's terrace lighting Jeremy could make out that they were male. Now they were crossing the narrow street to Jeremy's side and he could pinpoint their freshly cropped coiffures—and as they neared Jeremy's door, the newly shaven cheeks and chin of Jean-Marc.

The Monks stopped, looking up in unison, and Jeremy instinctively withdrew into the darkness. He never heard his buzzer sound. Car doors opened and slammed shut, and when Jeremy peered back out he saw Rébert's crew, four strong, charging across the street. Two seconds later a police van pulled into the street in front of Jeremy's building, its brakes and brief bitonal siren shrieking in announcement.

Jean-Marc and Renaud stood frozen like startled wax sculptures, as two uniformed and two plain-clothes agents surrounded them, armed and barking orders. The clacking of handcuffs echoed up to Jeremy's window. He saw Rébert overseeing the operation, though the RG agent never sent a glance up to the sixth floor. But as he and his men began marching the Monks to the police van waiting in the street, Jeremy had to fall back again, for Renaud and Jean-Marc were once more craning their necks in his direction.

Chapter 17

The night passed fitfully for Jeremy. Toward morning, dreams of his father, which rarely visited him these days, returned with Walt back in their San Francisco home. All three family members were together, though Jeremy noted strange changes in the house's décor, and Walt remained mute. With comingled joy and pain Jeremy asked him where he'd been all these twenty years, with Walt's sole reply a distant smile, after which Béatrice turned her back on both husband and son.

The dream lingered when Jeremy woke, and he felt a heaviness of both head and body as he pulled himself out of bed; an unsettling feeling that made him take out Walt's saxophone from under the bed and give it a doleful inspection.

Then he called Rébert's RG office.

"Don't worry," Rébert assured him. "They won't find out that you tipped us off."

Jeremy wanted to believe Rébert, but Al had called back about half an hour after the Monks were taken away the previous evening. They were supposed to call Al when they got to Jeremy's place. "I told him that the cops picked them up on the street; that they must've followed them, but that was all I knew. I'm not sure he bought it."

"*Al*—right," said Rébert. "We're keeping an eye on him."

Obviously Jeremy could be of no further use in the matter, so he didn't ask how the RG was undertaking this job. Nor did Jeremy bring up his work status. He couldn't imagine how he might have acquitted himself better regarding the Monks. Even so, he would wait until things calmed down with the arrests, giving Rébert a week or so to bring up the subject of his own accord. If he didn't, Jeremy would address it himself. In the meantime he hoped to hear nothing more from the barman and bosom buddy of Jean-Marc and Renaud.

Two explosions in as many days. And today was the 13th of July, one day before the culmination of the Bicentennial festivities. By all rights he should be rejoicing in his role at apprehending the Monks, but Jeremy couldn't let go of certain nagging thoughts. Mainly, whether Rébert had called off the search for other suspects in the attacks. He hadn't said, and Jeremy hadn't thought to ask.

Then there was Haley. He called her and they agreed to meet at the café Flora et Fauna at noon, where he would deliver his excuse for abandoning her in the taxi. He considered giving Louise Cholot a call before leaving the house. Then there was his plan to visit the building where she'd tracked the *Grand Blond*...

Both could wait. He needed to explain to Haley. And frankly, his frustration over Stefania was edging further and further into a recessed corner of his mind, into a sort of room destined for half-finished projects and all their clutter, but whose door remained slightly ajar. For an instant, the metaphor roused something vague in Jeremy's mind...as though something he couldn't quite identify peeked with a glimmering eye from the clutter behind that cracked-open door...

He shrugged and went to the window to close it before leaving the flat; you never knew when it might rain in Paris. His street was a different world this morning. Calm seemed to reign, with residents in the building across from him watering their window boxes of geraniums and petunias, while others, who had proper balconies, were out sweeping. How many of his neighbors had witnessed the ruckus last night?

On his way to the Flora et Fauna Jeremy crossed the Marais, sticking to little lanes perpetually shadowed due to their sheer narrowness. Every so often a trickle of water struck his head from an overly filled potted plant above him. Upon first experience, the sensation could be unsettling, but when you realized it was just friendly plant water, you welcomed the droplets as a tiny gift of cool relief from the heat.

And now, after deliberating this morning, he welcomed the idea of coming clean to Haley about the Monks. His surveillance of the two required little sensitivity compared to dealing with the blackmailer of the assistant to the minister's wife, for which Jeremy had been sworn to secrecy. Which meant he would also have to tell her he did jobs on the side for police intelligence—either that or invent a lie about his dealings with the Monks. He'd chosen the truth. Another fresh step forward in his vow for more transparency. At least he hoped so.

When he got to the Pompidou Center, commonly referred to as Beaubourg and branded the "Big Blue Blight" by Haley, he dodged the crowds by clipping over to ultra-narrow rue Quincampoix. And yet, Haley's moniker for the modern art museum snagged on his thoughts. The Big Blue *Blight*: that third word rang distantly familiar, from a different context he couldn't quite pinpoint, though he felt he should.

On the rue de Rivoli tourists reappeared like locusts, confirming once more that the blast at the Opéra Bastille had done nothing to discourage celebration—probably because no one had been hurt and because this morning's radio broadcast had announced the arrest of two suspects. *Two males, known to the police, caught on the run in rue de Turbigo near Place de la République. No further details for the moment.*

And just as well, thought Jeremy, hoping his address would not appear in the papers.

When he reached the café across from the Conciergerie, with its potted palms and caged songbirds along the sidewalk, Haley was already seated. He joined her at her outdoor table, ordered an espresso, gave a sigh and a weak smile, then started in on the revelation of his unorthodox part-time employment, and the latest little job it had entailed.

Haley's eyebrows rose above the brown plastic rims of her glasses. "You work for the intelligence services?"

"On and off," Jeremy answered, his tone modest. "Though I'd like to keep it between you and me; my mother doesn't even know."

Haley's deep nod suggested she was impressed. "And you figured out that these 'Monks'—the two that were arrested last night—set the explosions at the Louvre and the Bastille?"

"They're still only suspects at this point."

"But you were *spying* on them..."

"I guess you could say that." Jeremy told her how the Monks had gone missing after the first explosion, how he'd gained their trust through Al after the Bastille bombing, had lured them with the promise of shelter at his flat, then waited for the trap to snap shut on them.

"And all this after you left me..." Haley marveled.

"Yeah, you should have seen it: one minute I'm watching a normal nighttime scene from my window and the next, sirens blaring and cops swooping down on the two right when they're about to ring my bell."

"Amazing." Haley said, shaking her head. "So that's that, then...?"

Jeremy's expression turned pensive as he gazed

across the street at the white towers of the Conciergerie. "I'm not sure. The Monks are still only suspects, and the crap they pulled before was really trivial compared to the bombings."

"Well, at least they won't have the chance to get up to anything else."

"Mm," Jeremy replied," his gaze shifting to the *bouquinistes* along the *quai*, one bearded displayer of art prints and old books lifting his little terrier onto a stool next to the sidewalk wares.

"You don't feel guilty about turning them in, do you?" Haley asked.

Jeremy turned back to her with a slight frown. "No...but I can't be sure they're responsible so I keep feeling something else could happen."

Haley gave a stoic nod. "I guess I was comparing how I felt when George died. I didn't tell you before, but I'd agreed to sort of spy on him...collect information."

Jeremy's eyes widened in astonishment. "On your friend, the one who was murdered by extremists?"

As Haley's gaze wandered toward the Seine, her voice came distant and halting, as though wafting off the rippling river then winding through the grinding traffic. "I've always suspected that his friends found out...and that's why he was killed."

"Found out you were *spying* on him," reiterated Jeremy, sitting erect. "I thought you two were just friends..."

"We *were* friends, and we did have friendly conversations. Only a CIA agent caught on and paid me to pass him information on what George said about his Iranian associates."

"I see." Jeremy tried not to sound as shocked as he felt. Haley embroiled with the CIA: *how the bravery of this girl continued to astound him.*

She sighed, a resigned, weary murmur that

suggested the past is the past and nothing can change it. "I'll never be certain these Iranians knew what I was doing...anyway, I only mentioned it because I relate to what you could be feeling."

Jeremy nodded, sensing a new affinity growing between them. "In this case of mine, I'm counting on the intelligence services to get it right. If the Monks are innocent they'll be set free."

"And I guess we'll only be sure of that if no more explosions take place."

"...Right..."

Haley's head took on a studious slant. "But you've got reservations..."

Jeremy shrugged. "Well, I never heard the Monks even mention the Louvre pyramid or the Opéra Bastille. *But,*" he drew out, "they blame Mitterrand for their joblessness."

"Disgruntled *chômeurs,* Haley echoed. "And those two targets are among Mitterrand's Great Works."

Great Works, Blights on Paris. Jeremy's eyes narrowed as he now remembered having once used the latter term himself. "Remind me of the other Great Works," he said to Haley, knowing she would be able to recite them as if she were still working as a tour guide.

"Well, besides the Opéra Bastille and the entire Louvre renovation, there's the Orsay Museum, the Arab Cultural Institute...Let's see," she said, pausing with her thumb and index finger extended as she counted. "There's the Parc de la Villette, the finance ministry building at Bercy, the Grande Arche de la Défense." All five fingers of her right hand were now satisfactorily displayed. "Oh," she added, "and now he's working on his gigantic new National Library, but they're only at the digging stage as of now. Anyway, he's almost as obsessed with building as Napoleon III and Haussmann were—"

Haley halted and peered at Jeremy, who was staring

at the sidewalk with ever-deepening furrows in his brow. "Do you think that's what the bombers are after?" she said with a start. "Mitterrand's Great Works?"

Jeremy shot her a worried glance "Maybe. Though a plot like that would be beyond the Monks, in my opinion. But they *could* be part of a bigger group."

"So far only two of the Works have been hit," Haley pointed out.

"And if we're talking about all seven," Jeremy speculated, "it would have to be an ongoing operation planned months ago. In that case, more buildings should've been targeted before now, considering the Bicentennial will be over with tomorrow."

"And they could have waited till tonight to attack the Opéra Bastille," Haley added thoughtfully. "During its inauguration. As it is, the concert's supposed to go ahead as planned."

"They wouldn't want casualties, or at least none that are serious," Jeremy stressed. "To me that fits with what I know about the Monks."

A pause settled in, both Haley and Jeremy retreating into reflection.

Getting nowhere with his thoughts, Jeremy finally resumed, "So we're left with the Arab Cultural Institute, the Orsay Museum, Bercy, La Défense. La Villette isn't even finished yet..."

"Right," said Haley, visually shivering at the mention of the Orsay with its Nineteenth- Century masterpieces.

Blights on Paris. Jeremy squirmed in his seat, remembering the rest of the sentence he had cavalierly uttered just a month ago. He would never repeat it to Haley. Instead, he offered, "Buildings the bombers don't like the looks of..."

Haley returned an incredulous smile. "Really? So the bombers are aesthetes?"

"I'm just mulling things over. So far they've damaged the new Opéra, which a lot of people think is ugly. Many think the Louvre pyramids are out of place…"

This time, a troubled frown from Haley. "People have criticized the design of the Orsay museum…but thank God not many condemn it outright. Because with all that Impressionist art…" She grimaced and shook her head. "The destruction of just one painting by Monet would represent not only tens of millions of dollars, but would be an assault on the conscience and morale of art lovers worldwide.

Christ, Jeremy agreed to himself. Yet he couldn't remember any mention of the Orsay during that bravado-filled conversation that took place last month. "There's also the Arche de la Défense," he said. "Loads of people hate that concrete and glass cube."

"But it's not in Paris proper…it's tolerated because it's located across the river. Even so, it's to be inaugurated tomorrow. Then there's the centennial of the Eiffel Tower this year—big celebrations for that too."

Not to diminish the importance of the Eiffel Tower, Jeremy had his reasons for adhering to Mitterrand's Works. "So far the bombers have shown they don't care about inauguration dates," he said, in reference to the blown-out window of the Opéra Bastille. "And the Louvre pyramids were finished last year."

"If it's a plot, it's hard to make sense of it."

"Mm," Jeremy assented, though things *were* beginning to suggest a kind of sense to him.

"If they're right-wing fanatics they might want to attack the Arab Institute."

"No proof they're right-wingers." *On the contrary,* thought Jeremy.

Haley gave a skeptical smile. "Okay, then we're back to band of aesthetes. If Pompidou were still president we could include that blue mangle, Beaubourg."

"True. But let's just say the bombers are somehow *both* aesthetes, as you say, *and* Mitterrand haters...there's the Ministry of the Economy at Bercy..."

"I haven't heard it was considered ugly for a modern building, and its location isn't inappropriate either. So that would leave the unfinished Villette, and who could get satisfaction in attacking a park designed for the common people of the Nineteenth Arrondissement?"

An area that used to be the slaughterhouse district, Jeremy agreed to himself. Haley was right, and he hoped that meant there would be no more bombings.

"So you say the Monks are leftists?" asked Haley.

Jeremy's lips twitched, a faint, rueful smile. *Oh, how he wished he could confidently blame this whole rotten business on Jean-Marc and Renaud.* "Yes," he said, hoping he didn't sound cagey; he could not reveal his new suspicions.

"Well," Haley went on, "if we rule out the Arab Institute, which would amount to an attack on Islam rather than on Mitterrand, and the Villette and Bercy..." She paused, then aimed a pointed look at Jeremy. "You *are* going to inform your Intelligence contact about all this...?" It was more a dutiful reminder than a question. "I've learned it's not a bad thing to cooperate with the authorities..." she added, with something like a smile of regret.

Mechanically he nodded his head, then told himself: *all in good time.*

Chapter 18

They parted ways, with Haley informing Jeremy that her Irish friends had changed their plans and were returning to Paris that afternoon, reminding him that they all needed to get together before the girls returned home to County Tipperary. Jeremy agreed, then gave Haley a quick kiss goodbye.

After she left, down to the Pont Neuf metro station, he cursed himself for not asking to borrow her booklet *Paris Par Arrondissement*. For he knew exactly what to do next: seek out the address Louise Cholot had provided him for the *Grand Blond*. He knew it was in the Fourteenth Arrondissement, but he would have liked a map to pin it down exactly.

He found a phone booth, took out the mini address book he now carried daily, and called Madame. After listening to ten rings he hung up. He would take the metro to Tolbiac, and by the time he walked to her neighborhood Madame might be home.

It took half an hour, and when he reached the phone booth he'd used previously, he let seven rings go by before hanging up, then heading for the café across from Stefania's building. On the way, with a fool's eternal sense of hope, he stopped and tried Stefania's buzzer. He gave it two long presses, waited about five seconds, then turned on his heel and left.

At the café he didn't spot the waitress Mireille, but Julien was at his post behind the bar and said he had not sighted the *Grand Blond* since the last time he'd spoken to Jeremy. As far as Julien knew, neither had Mireille.

His stomach rumbling and gnawing at him, Jeremy sat and ordered a lunch crêpe with a small carafe of tap water. Then he refocused on that piece of clutter which had been hiding in the mental room of half-finished projects, and now flapped like a signal flag at his memory: Stefania vis-à-vis the explosions.

On the metro ride down, he had dwelled on the possibility of the *Grand Blond* leading him to Stefania. And now, as his food arrived, he once more reconstituted that month-old conversation with her during their first one-on-one meeting in the Latin Quarter. Namely, how they'd shared their dislike of two of Mitterrand's Great Works: the Louvre pyramids and the Opéra Bastille. *Those two exactly, bon Dieu!* The new Opéra amounted to nothing but "an ugly mass of concrete and steel." Had it been Stefania or he himself who'd said that? He couldn't remember. The building was a "disgrace to the Place de la Bastille." Those had been Stefania's words, for certain. And what had they said about the pyramids? "The Louvre would be better off without them." Again, Stefania's quote. And yet, Jeremy's own joking pronouncement screamed loudest in his head: *Someone ought to bomb those blights on Paris.*

Christ, Stefania, what could you be up to—and why?

Jeremy finished his crêpe while deliberating what to do once he got to the *Grand Blond's* building. He hoped Stefania would be there, even if it meant she'd been kidnapped, for it might exonerate her from the explosions. But again, *why* would she be kidnapped?

He had to get to her, hoped he could rule her out as a suspect and not have to report her to Rébert. One thing gave him a sliver of solace: he and Stefania had discussed only two offending Mitterrand monuments, the Louvre pyramids and the Opéra Bastille. If Stefania had been involved in the blasts, things might very well have run their course.

Jeremy paid his bill and left the café for another phone booth. This time he took out Mirko's number. But his call went unanswered, and that filled him with unease as well. Did Mirko know about Stefania's disappearance?

He exited the booth and stood on the sidewalk glancing up at the heat-hazy sky. He pulled at his shirt, which was sticking to him, then finally turned, took a deep breath, and re-entered the phone booth, where it was even hotter than outside. He didn't need his address book to dial this next number, for he knew it by heart.

"Christophe," Jeremy ventured cautiously, when his friend picked up. "*C'est moi...*"

An ominous silence. Then Christophe's voice, cool as a block of dry ice. "What do you need, I'm trying to finish lunch and get back to work."

"Well..." Jeremy began, clenching his fist against what might follow, "has Stefania been in touch lately?"

He had delivered the question in the gravest tone possible and was now poised to jerk the phone away to save his ear a shrill chiding. To his surprise, nothing of the kind took place. Rather, Christophe almost whispered, "You mean you haven't seen her?"

"...No...I mean not for a long time...I assumed she was with you..." Only then did Jeremy realize that Christophe had presumed the opposite, perhaps hoping Jeremy could assure him that Stefania was all right.

"Then why are you calling?" Back to his former crankiness, with a touch of that menace familiar to Jeremy from their face-off on Stefania's stairs.

"...I'd heard there might be trouble involving the Compagni," Jeremy quickly invented. "I've tried calling Mirko and Pietro but they don't answer."

"What kind of trouble?"

"Some of them, not sure who all yet, may be involved in some illegal activity, and I wanted to warn Stefania before the police got wind."

"Who told you this?"

Jeremy was running short of inventiveness. "Please, just tell me whether you've seen Stefania."

In the painful pause that ensued, Christophe's voice began to soften. "I'm worried," he said. "I haven't seen or heard from her since before you and I met at her place. I've wanted to tell her ...um...things."

"...I understand," Jeremy said. He really did have an idea of what this heartfelt admission could be costing Christophe. "If I track down Mirko, Pietro, or her, I'll pass the message on."

"I tried going to the police in the Thirteenth. They already know she's missing."

Another silence, this one excruciating as Jeremy waited to hear from Christophe of his and Madame Cholot's visit to the commissariat. He wiped his brow with the back of his hand.

But Christophe merely continued in a worried tone. "They say a neighbor reported not having seen her for some days now."

Silently, Jeremy breathed his relief.

"So you're trying to contact Mirko and Pietro too?" Christophe asked with a tinge of hope in his voice. "I haven't been able to reach them either..."

"Well, I'll keep on it," Jeremy said.

"What kind of trouble could they be in?"

"Don't know if it's them per se, but I've heard the police are looking for foreigners holding false passports." Jeremy was glad for the convenient response, but even more thankful he wasn't talking to Christophe in person. "Anyway, let me know if Stefania gets in touch." And to forestall further awkward questions, he added, "I'll do you the same courtesy."

He hung up with feelings of both increased alarm regarding Stefania and gratitude for Christophe's mellowed attitude. Perhaps they would remain friends after all.

With relief he left the phone booth, then he set off for the *papeterie* he had spotted during his previous reconnoitering of the neighborhood. He entered the sellers of school and office supplies and flushed out a cheap tourist map of the city. Once he identified rue Didot in the Fourteenth, he folded it back up and took it to the clerk to purchase, where he also asked about bus routes. Having made a sale, the man was eager to convey his knowledge. Jeremy declined a bag, folded the map into a tight little square, jammed it into his back pocket, and left.

The bus stopped on rue Didot, conveniently across the street from number 112. The neighborhood seemed normal enough, with a café on the corner at boulevard Brune, its doors open, garrulous conversation spewing out, while next door to number 112 a florist exhibited bouquets on the sidewalk. That was the limit of Jeremy's survey of the block, and in four strides he crossed to the opposite sidewalk and stood scrutinizing the plaque listing residents and their corresponding buzzers. Two occupants had German surnames, one Romain Schoenberg and a certain Horst Gruber. The former having a French Christian name led Jeremy to try the bell of the latter, his phony cover as insurance investigator, as well as a fake name, at the ready. He wasn't sure whether either would serve him.

No one responded when he rang. Impulsively he tried again, knowing full well that his nervous habit of late proved ridiculously futile. Then he tried Romain Schoenberg's buzzer. No answer there either. For a couple of minutes, very long ones it seemed, he waited and watched for who might enter or exit the building.

But the florist next door, attending to her sidewalk displays, kept eyeing him. So he left, walking past her up the sidewalk where he waited at the bus stop. Five minutes later he was on his way back to the Thirteenth Arrondissement. This time, when he arrived and called Madame, she answered and invited him up.

She had just returned home and still wore a smart skirt and blouse. "I've been to lunch with friends," she said. "Fortunately the restaurant was air-conditioned." In fact she looked quite fresh, though her face gave off a luster, no doubt from the sultry heat of her commute.

It didn't take long for her to address the latest explosion at the Opéra Bastille, shaking her head as she handed Jeremy a cold bubbly glass of Perrier, a wheel-slice of lemon floating on the surface. "First the Louvre, then the Bastille; what the devil is going on?" she intoned, as she lowered herself gracefully into her armchair. "Someone trying to ruin the Bicentennial. So many dissidents living in the city—always have in Paris—and with as many different agendas..." She shook her head again. "But at least no one's been hurt this time and the police have two suspects in custody."

Jeremy agreed, skipping comment on the arrests to instead report his trip to number 112 rue Didot.

"And did you see the name 'Horst Gruber' on the list of residents?" Madame asked before he could finish. "I've been back to have a look myself."

Of course she had, Jeremy said to himself with a private smile of admiration. "I did, and I rang the bell but no one answered. I rang the name Romain Schoenberg too—no one home there either—though I'm leaning toward Horst Gruber to be the *Grand Blond*."

"As am I," Louise said, gazing in reflection past Jeremy. Suddenly she arched her back and cocked her head. "You don't think *Gruber*—if that's his name—could be involved in these explosions?" Immediately she shook her head. "No, that's ridiculous. Why would some foreigner want to disrupt the Bicentennial?"

Madame sank back into her meditations while Jeremy stiffened imperceptibly. Unwitting as Louise's idea might seem, it struck Jeremy as an intriguing possibility. Given the Viking and Stefania's connection, why had it not occurred to him that they could be working together, or at least have been formerly in collusion, only to fall out at a later date? But Louise was right; he could think of no reason why the *Grand Blond*, or Stefania for that matter, should choose to take after Parisian monuments. Particularly Stefania, who was so desperate not to get deported.

Madame interrupted his musings. "So, still no leads about Stefania, I assume."

Jeremy shook his head.

"And you still think this Gruber—or whatever his name is—may have taken her..."

"I wish I knew."

"I'd be happy to accompany you back to the police, but all we have to go on is that the *Grand Blond* appeared in front of Stefania's building two days ago."

"Right," Jeremy acknowledged absently. He had no intention of returning to the neighborhood commissariat.

Madame sipped her Perrier then said, "I still think you should concentrate on what your friend could have done in Italy to warrant a possible reprisal against her. Where is Stefania from, by the way?"

"The Veneto area—Belluno."

"That's in the northeast. Jean-Baptiste and I visited there; a beautiful mountain town not terribly far from the German-speaking South Tyrol..."

So, back to a private settling of scores among Italians—not an unreasonable hypothesis if you excluded the explosions. Jeremy's thoughts swung back to the Monks. If no mayhem occurred tonight, he could perhaps lay his worries to rest.

"Does Stefania have a regional accent?" Madame asked.

"Well," Jeremy said, grappling with the precision of the question, "an Italian accent for sure—not German..."

Madame nodded. "A regional Italian accent would be hard to identify in someone speaking French. Jeremy noticed her watching him and returned an inquiring gaze.

"Sorry," she said. "Every now and then—not often, mind you—I notice *your* slight American accent. But don't worry, it has its charm."

Jeremy smiled. "I'm told I've also got a hint of a French accent when I speak English." Haley had been the latest to mention it. "Result of living back and forth between the two countries, I imagine."

"And if I remember correctly you have a French-speaking *and* an English-speaking parent."

"My father was American, but he's deceased. My mother lives in Namur." As a matter of fact, Béatrice had called him this morning. She'd tried getting hold of him after the Louvre explosion and had been worried for two days that her son, finding himself in the wrong place at the wrong time, could have been hit by shards of glass from the hole blown in the pyramid.

Jeremy appreciated his mother's concern but couldn't stop comparing her to Louise Cholot. Béatrice, so Catholic, so long-suffering about her husband's affair—*affairs,* she had pointedly informed Jeremy when she'd discovered his own fling with Walt's former lover, Margie. Béatrice would be astounded, then irrationally worried, if she knew of her son's little jobs for the RG, which of late might have outgrown the qualifier "little." His mother had asked him when his next visit would be. He hadn't been to Namur since

Christmas. Soon, he'd told her, as he always had.

His gaze settled back on Louise, poised though relaxed in her armchair.

"How did your parents meet?" she asked him.

That had always been an interesting story to Jeremy, though he feared it might sound banal to someone as sophisticated as Louise Cholot. All the same, he recounted the story of Walt Winters playing tenor saxophone in an Army band at the end of World War II. The young corporal was only twenty but had stayed on to tour the continent after the Liberation, and met Béatrice Martineau at a dance club where he was playing in Namur. She was only seventeen and they had had to part when Walt and his band moved on to Luxembourg, then back to Paris. Still they wrote to each other, even while Walt and the band went back on tour. Walt stayed in Europe for five years, all the while making visits to Béatrice in Namur. Finally, before his planned return to the U.S., they married, though according to Béatrice, Walt had worried about how he could support her.

All this Jeremy told Louise, minus the fact that as a youngster he had wondered how his mother had failed to conceive all those years, as he wasn't born until 1955. Such a devout Catholic, she no doubt eschewed birth control and he couldn't understand how he didn't have a slew of siblings. When he grew up, well after his father died, Béatrice confided that she and Walt had tried for more children but had just not been blessed. After discovering Jeremy's dalliance with Margie, she told him she was glad to have had no more children with an adulterer. At first, Jeremy was taken aback. Yet as the years rolled on, he developed a sympathetic though slightly fatalistic understanding of Béatrice, and her confessed failure in love.

No, to Louise Cholot he didn't reveal the sticky side of his parents' marriage. Yet just thinking about it now made him feel he should call his mother back soon, and arrange for a visit—after this mess in Paris got sorted out.

"So your family moved here after you were born?" Madame pursued with warm interest.

Jeremy gave her a mild smile; he wasn't in the mood to tell the story of Walt Winters' ignoble blacklisting and the shame of a forced departure from the U.S. Rather, he said, "My father had experienced success with his music here; he knew happiness in Paris."

Madame clapped her hands together. "Sounds absolutely charming: your father playing Big Band throughout Europe and your mother falling for him as a devoted fan. I was a teenager myself when the Yanks came here, and I can picture it well."

Thus, in turn, Jeremy pictured Louise Cholot circa 1944: shin-length skirt and double-breasted jacket, the top of her hair rolled-up like two croissants. Though he esteemed her romantic memories he preferred her present look. Her recent pluck at tailing the Viking. Her clever initiative in getting the police to open Stefania's flat to them...her short skirt and firm, tanned legs.

"Do you miss anything particular about America?" Madame asked.

The question took Jeremy by surprise, given where his musings had landed. And yet, his answer came almost automatically. "Baseball," he said. His San Francisco Giants were expanding their winning streak, and sports pundits in the *International Herald Tribune* predicted they might go on to win the pennant. He remembered the Giants' lineup back to 1965: Mays, McCovey, Haller, Lanier, et al. The gymnastically high kick of Juan Marichal on the mound. The balletic beauty of the double play. The sublime orchestration of the defensive game.

Madame gave a vague nod in recognition of the

sport. "Would you like more Perrier?" she asked.

"No thank you, Louise. I should get going," he said, standing up.

"Will you be manning the bar at Le Prince Blue Note this evening?"

"I will, in fact."

"Fingers crossed, we'll have no more disruptions," she said, taking his arm as she walked him to the door.

Fingers, toes, and eyes, he told himself.

Chapter 19

After returning home, Jeremy sat staring out his open window at the red flowers bent with rain on the balcony across the street, seeing right through them into the anxious thoughts gyrating in his mind. On the way back from Madame Cholot's he had half hoped—with a good dose of guilt, of course—that Stefania had either been captured by the *Grand Blond* or was holed up somewhere in hiding from him—and therefore *not* a bomber on the run. If there were no explosions tonight he would be thankful, though Stefania's fate continued to nag at him. He had tried Mirko once more, letting the phone ring into the double digits, to no avail.

His thoughts circled round to the litany of President Mitterrand's still undamaged Great Works: the Arab Cultural Institute; the finance ministry at Bercy; the unfinished Parc de la Villette; the Grande Arche de la Défense; the Orsay Museum. None jibed with the former two targets in terms of poor aesthetics and sense of place. Only the Orsay, perhaps. Located across the Seine from the Tuileries and just downstream from the Louvre, it had provoked some aesthetic criticism in the past. Various people had disapproved of the way the old Orsay railway station had been redesigned to house Nineteenth-Century art. The museum retained too much of the hardware style of the station, he recalled the complaint, therefore detracting from the art. Jeremy liked the building, apart from some of the gallery spaces that felt a bit boxy to him. Nonetheless, he could not remember either Stefania or himself so much as *speaking* the word "Orsay" in that frivolous conversation; that ridiculous moment in which he wished to achieve a sense of camaraderie with her in line with his RG role. So, no reason to bomb it. But once again, *why bomb anything?*

Nothing but frivolous talk, he repeated to himself— *nothing to worry about.* And still he sighed heavily as he rose to make a cup of tea before getting ready for work. As long as nothing sinister happened tonight he could perhaps relax a bit and try Mirko again tomorrow. He wondered what Rébert had gotten out of the Monks. Considering what Al had said, the two would surely protest their innocence. On the bright side, when Jeremy had emerged from the metro at Place de la République this afternoon, he had seen no silly, anti-Revolution slogans defiling Marianne's monument.

He put the kettle on and walked over to the window. He thought back on his mention of baseball to Louise. He hadn't gone into his brief stint in Little League as a catcher. How the coaches initially preferred him in that position because of his overall unflinching-ness. Other boys found it a challenge to keep their masked faces pointed at the plate when a hardball bounced up at them. Instinctively they would jerk their heads away and often end up with a badly bruised and painful jaw. Jeremy had no problem facing down the ball to trap it. Nor did he flinch from aggressive runners barreling round third base, their cleats flying at him as they slid in to home plate. He defended his domain like a soldier, though at times he was reprimanded for using excessive force. At one point the coaches moved him to right field. But he coveted his role of catcher—ultimate defender, positioner of the field, caller of pitches—so at age eleven he left the team.

The mugginess of earlier had swelled into bloated

grey clouds that, wind-whipped, finally rent and produced rain on his way home. A cool breeze now floated into the flat, stirring the sheer curtains into a gossamer dance, while, outside, a gentler rain pattered down. It fluttered the leaves of the plane trees along the sidewalk, beckoning him to lean out the window and catch a tickling droplet with his cheek. Though he couldn't stretch beyond the eaves, the aroma of washed stone and asphalt filled him with a sense of peace and respite, a renewal of spirit.

The kettle alerted him like a drawn-out train whistle and he left his reverie to make his tea. Later, when he set out for the metro station, there was music at Place de la République. It wafted from loud speakers in the fresh, rain-rinsed air to mingle with the celebrating crowds. This was *his* Paris weather. *His* home. And he would not give up his hunt for those who would do it harm.

The night passed, uneventful, with Jeremy switching on the radio as soon as he rose the next morning. He learned of a successful inauguration of the Opéra Bastille, with the President of the Republic hosting 2000 guests at the concert, including thirty-three foreign heads of state. With great relief Jeremy called Haley and agreed to meet her and her Irish friends for lunch at the Pub Winston Churchill. The Monks seemed more and more the authors of the previous attacks, and even if not, it seemed no one wished to sow further chaos.

When he emerged from the metro at the Arc de Triomphe he had to wade through a sea of rubbish discarded from spectators of the morning's military parade. He had attended previous 14 July parades—troops on foot and on horseback, tanks, flyovers of the French Air Force trailing tricolored smoke above the Champs-Elysées—and knew that Haley and her friends would have had to get to the Champs at dawn to see this *Bicentennial* parade.

In fact, as he and the girls sat in the Churchill, munching burgers and chips, the older of the Irish sisters cheerfully confirmed just that. "We saw mostly other tourists and jutting tank cannons, but if you jumped up and down you could catch a glimpse of the troops."

"Then I guess you missed President Mitterrand riding in his vehicle," Jeremy said with a chuckle.

"Yes, but there were helicopters," the younger Kathleen chipped in. "For the first time, we were told. All quite impressive."

Jeremy smiled fondly at them, and admired Haley for accompanying them to the parade no matter at what ungodly hour they'd had to rise. And after his previous three days at grips with the Monks and the explosions, he relished the carefree, enthusiastic spirit of the sisters and the elated atmosphere it produced.

"The Opéra Bastille was inaugurated with great success last night," said Haley with a significant look at Jeremy. "And we were out and about in the midst of the partying and street dances."

Jeremy wondered if Bernadette and Kathleen had learned of the explosions. But since they hadn't mentioned them, neither would he. "Too bad I had to work," he said, wishing he could have been with them.

"Everything's been lovely," said Bernadette, her blues eyes gleaming.

He listened to the girls tell of their initial encounter with Haley in 1980, when Bernadette and Kathleen had first come to Paris and Haley had offered to be their informal guide. How Haley had visited them in Ireland and attended Bernadette's wedding. That this visit to Paris was a *sisters* outing and reunion with Haley, who added how lucky she felt living in a city where you could meet people from other countries on a daily basis. She pointed out that Jeremy came from an international background himself.

"His mother's Belgian," she said. "And he's got Italian friends as well as French."

This sent Jeremy's thoughts wheeling back to Mirko. Though Haley was vaguely aware Jeremy had Italian acquaintances, he had never mentioned any of the Compagni.

Absently he heard Kathleen say, "We haven't an international community in Dundrum."

Followed by Bernadette: "The whole population of the village is less than two hundred, so we love it when we get the chance to travel."

The girls talked on, Haley too, but Jeremy simply nodded and smiled, his thoughts fastened on Mirko and what he might know about Stefania's disappearance. He had tried Mirko's number again this morning, once more hanging up after losing count of the rings. The night had passed with no attacks, things seemed less urgent, and yet Jeremy couldn't shake the idea that Stefania might still be in jeopardy, his anxiety rekindled each time he recalled that not even Christophe could reach her.

Jeremy parted from Haley and her friends, having made a date to meet them later in the evening in a café near the Champs-Élysées. With Le Prince closed tonight, he would join them for the second parade on the Avenue, this one of a cultural-international flavor.

Then he took the metro to the Twentieth Arrondissement where Mirko and Pietro lived, only two blocks from Père Lachaise cemetery.

The two Compagni had their own revolutionary history in Italy: Pietro was wanted for a string of politically-motivated burglaries and Mirko for his part in the kidnapping of a local neo-fascist leader. Along with Stefania (on the run for her role in the inadvertent death of a child in the furrier robbery) both Compagni kept a very low profile in France. All the more so, considering the Italian government had conducted certain trials in absentia, a tactic which further offended President Mitterrand's sense of justice.

When Jeremy rang the Compagni's buzzer, an answer came almost immediately. After all those unanswered phone calls he hadn't expected it, and for a disconcerted moment he stared at the intercom, wondering whose metallic-sounding voice he had heard. Then, an irritated "*oui?*" was repeated, and he identified himself and asked whether he was speaking to Mirko.

"He's not home," came Pietro's succinct response.

Jeremy asked if he could come up all the same, and the door to the building clicked open.

The tall, muscular Pietro offered Jeremy his usual firm but brusque handshake, and as Jeremy followed him into the kitchen, he couldn't help observing that the Italian looked like he'd just rolled out of bed: dark wavy hair spiking out at drôle angles, stubble peppering his chin and cheeks, his white undershirt sporting a couple of cigarette-burn size holes.

"Haven't been out enjoying the festivities, eh?" Jeremy said with an ingratiating smile.

Pietro gave a grunt of a laugh, indicated a chair at the kitchen table to his impromptu guest, and slowly—diffidently, it seemed to Jeremy—slid into the seat opposite. The flat was larger than Jeremy's place but almost as run-down as Stefania's. He recalled the party there last month; how Christophe had left Stefania in a corner of the room as he ushered Jeremy off to the kitchen for a beer, taking his time, showering Jeremy with chatter, while Jeremy thought of Stefania alone and brooding in the other room. Privately, he shook his head. Despite Christophe's seeming change of heart, as revealed by their phone conversation, Jeremy still blamed his friend for taking Stefania for granted.

Pietro glanced at his watch, running a hand through his coarse hair. "I've got business to take care of so I can't give you much time...what is it you want to talk about?"

Jeremy sat forward, his arms on the table. "I've been looking for Stefania..." he drew out in an inquiring tone.

Pietro blinked in hesitation, then gave Jeremy a long look. "Stefania, huh? Haven't seen her in ages."

"Since the party last month...?"

"Not since then."

Pietro's eyes had narrowed, and Jeremy thought he perceived a subtle defiance in them. He had never found Pietro loquacious but had always considered him at least genial, in a shy way. "I think she might be in trouble," he said. "She mentioned being followed..." He made a quick decision to convey his urgency, and added, "Before she disappeared."

"*Disappeared?* What makes you think that?" A neutral tone, not *concerned*, as might be expected, but rather aloof.

Parsing his thoughts, Jeremy settled on a type of neutrality as well. "Christophe can't find her and he's worried too..."

"*Christophe*. He knows you're looking for her?"

Jeremy gave a cautious nod, and repeated, "He's worried."

"Well, I don't wonder." Pietro looked Jeremy up and down with an amused smirk.

He knows about Stefania and me, Jeremy said to himself, tensing automatically. "What about Mirko?" he asked with a steady gaze. "Has he seen her?"

"I can't speak for him."

"Will he be back soon?"

Pietro folded his arms and sat back. "He's out of town; wanted to get away from this Bicentennial chaos."

Without you? As close as the two of you are? "Know when he'll be back?" Jeremy asked.

Pietro shrugged. "He said he'd call."

Deliberate apathy. *Phony* apathy, Jeremy amended to himself. He leaned in further and raised his brows in innocent curiosity. "*You* haven't been followed lately, have you, Pietro? I know Mirko's seen the same tall blond *mec* who's been tailing Stefania..."

"Me? No, not at all...and Mirko hasn't mentioned anything like that either."

"*What*: he hasn't *seen* this guy or he hasn't been followed?"

"I haven't heard either way."

Really? Jeremy resisted a cynical smile. *Was it possible that Mirko had shrugged off his two Grand-Blond sightings, or maybe just kept them from Pietro so as not to worry him? Whichever the case, why no interest in the tailing of Stefania?*

Well, time to provoke some interest, thought Jeremy, and he proceeded to relate the prolonged stalking of Stefania. "She's told both Christophe and me," he specified, hoping to avoid further snide looks regarding himself and Stefania. For the same reason he ruled out revealing his own encounters and pursuit of the Viking. In this reporting fashion, he went on: "Stefania's afraid this guy might work for the French authorities, that they want to arrest her and send her back to Italy, though no one's sure what to make of the *mec's* German accent."

Jeremy had noticed a subtle stiffening in Pietro, a twitch of posture, at the first mention of the *Grand Blond's* accent. Now the Italian was scratching his chin. "Why would she think he works for the French authorities?"

Lisa Mortara

"Because he tracks her but never speaks; like he's waiting, watching—just for the right moment to snatch her up. And she can't do a thing about it."

Pietro's expression remained overtly puzzled. "Well, maybe he *is* from the security services—just keeping tabs on her."

That was my job, Jeremy quipped to himself, though he couldn't totally rule out Stefania's fears. For the moment, however, he was curious about Pietro's attitude. His seeming indifference to the fate of his fellow comrade and countrywoman. Could he be *that* offended by her unfaithfulness to Christophe? And why was he so evasive about Mirko?

Jeremy settled back against his chair and offered, "Christophe tells me he's been trying to contact you and Mirko about Stefania. Have you talked to him?"

Pietro turned his palms up and gave an accommodating smile. "We've been out a lot lately. But if Christophe *does* catch me at home I'll be sure to tell him you were here and that you're very worried about Stefania." He checked his watch again. "Now I've got to get ready to go out."

Jeremy descended the stairs to the lobby, the muscles in his torso girded against an imaginary punch. Whether Pietro would immediately try to contact Christophe really didn't matter, he told himself, trying to relax as he walked to the Père Lachaise metro station. He had discussed nothing with Pietro beyond what Christophe already knew. But if the two did speak, Jeremy hoped Christophe wouldn't bring up the bit he'd told him about the false passports.

Back in his flat, Jeremy called Christophe—better to get to him before Pietro did, if possible. But no one answered. It was the 14th and he was no doubt out in the middle of the festivities. Christophe always loved a

218

party.

In fact the whole Bicentennial day seemed to be morphing from one type of party to another. On the Champs-Elysées they would have barely cleaned up after this morning's parade when the evening's events would start up. Even Jeremy's metro ride home had been a party, with a banjo player strumming Dixieland music and several French youths attempting to sing "Sweet Georgia Brown," while sharing swigs from a bottle of champagne. Before Jeremy had got off the train, the banjo player passed through the crowd collecting coins in a straw hat, and another group of merrymakers struck up an umpteenth version of the Marseillaise.

If Christophe were celebrating somewhere, Jeremy wondered how far Stefania strayed from his thoughts. And then there was the absence of Mirko. What would it have cost Pietro to tell Jeremy where his companion had gone? Suddenly, he had a feeling it wouldn't be Christophe that Pietro would contact right away, but Mirko. Mirko and Stefania—both curiously lost to the picture at the moment...

A presentiment gripped Jeremy in the chest—vague, not yet fully formed, yet sharp as heartburn. In a burst of energy he slammed the windows shut and grabbed his keys. *Gruber*—or whatever that *putain de Grand Blond* was called—might he be involved with both of them?

Chapter 20

On the way out, Jeremy called Haley in order to cancel his rendezvous with her and the girls at eight o'clock. But she didn't answer. What did he expect, with two visitors to guide about town on the day of the biggest celebration in French history?

He took the metro at the Temple station, just a few paces down from his building—destination 112 rue Didot, the address of Horst Gruber. He had to cross a good part of the city but managed to find a route that required only one line change. Even so it took him almost an hour to get to the Porte de Vanves station in the Fourteenth. Along the way, so many people insisted on muscling aboard the cars at each stop that the drawn-out warning horn became deafening. Carriage seats were never empty; no sooner did one person make the slightest move to vacate than another lunged to snap up his place. Jeremy remained fastened to a pole by the doors. Whenever the train stopped (twenty stations all together) he leaned out to breathe a change of air, be it merely the smell of metal and industrial grease native to the metro system. Still, every so often a draft of air would rush through the platform area from parts unknown, fluttering hair and skirts in a cool, delightful surprise.

At Porte de Vanves he began his trek down boulevard Brune, fifteen minutes later turning the corner into rue Didot. This time he didn't bother pressing the buzzer next to Gruber's name. He waited until a woman exited, then slipped into the foyer and checked the mailboxes. Gruber was listed on the third floor. Jeremy climbed to the landing, and choosing between two different doors, picked the one that looked slightly rundown. He thought: If this residence is the *Grand Blond's*, will he answer? And if so, will he try to slam the door in my face when he recognizes me?

In that case Jeremy would have to push back—insist on getting an answer about Stefania. And if his opponent turned aggressive he would be obliged to resort to his fists. It would be the only way to match him, particularly given the bastard's penchant for low blows. Jeremy flexed his left knee. It was finally feeling normal—he'd been suckered once and he wouldn't let it happen again. Whatever the result, he would get some good licks in.

He inhaled deeply, feeling his lungs expand to their limit, rang the doorbell, and waited. Seconds that seemed minutes went by, Jeremy eyed the second door, then thought he heard a noise behind the one he faced. He put his ear to it, made out the metallic sound of a radio voice. Then, as he prepared to deliver a series of hard knocks, he heard footsteps treading on a creaky wooden floor. A pause, followed by the extinguishing of the radio voice. Then more footsteps and another spell of silence. Jeremy clenched his fists as the door finally inched open.

He took a step backwards, utterly astonished, blinking rapidly at a veritable apparition: Stefania, holding the door open a mere crack, but doing so with no apparent fear. She leaned against the doorframe, wearing a pair of faded jeans and the yellow T-shirt with the forlorn pink flower he'd seen before—her eyes betraying barely a trace of the initial surprise she must have registered upon sighting him through the peephole.

"So you've found me," she said quietly.

Jeremy shook his bewildered head. "How did you

get here?"

"It's complicated..."

"Might as well invite him in and tell him." The *Grand Blond* had suddenly materialized behind her to fill the top of the doorway. He pulled the door open and Stefania obligingly stepped aside, sweeping a strand of limp hair from her makeup-less face.

Jeremy advanced haltingly, all the more befuddled by Gruber's invitation and Stefania's not acting like a captive. On the contrary, they both seemed relaxed and *at home*. Gruber, in his tracksuit and stocking feet, his gait loose and nonchalant, displayed nothing of the menace Stefania had once feared and Jeremy had not only anticipated but had already experienced. With a dispassionate shrug, he indicated an armchair to Jeremy, Stefania softly closed the door, and they all sat down, Gruber and Stefania at opposite ends of the sofa. Other than the nondescript sofa and chair, Jeremy observed no other furniture in the sitting room besides an end table on which stood a transistor radio in a dog-eared leather case. *Improvised living?* And though his thoughts still hovered in a semi state of shock, he estimated there to be only one bedroom in the flat. *A bad break-up?* Louise Cholot's conjecture echoed stingingly in his mind.

Stefania avoided Jeremy's regard, her gaze wandering off toward the window, while Gruber's pale eyes scanned him with aloof interest. "*You* tell him," he said to Stefania, without looking at her.

She took her time, her attention gradually returning to Jeremy. With a nod at the *Grand Blond*, she began, "You obviously know this is Horst Gruber. He's Italian, from the South Tyrol..."

"*Alto Adige*," Jeremy finished with a flinty stare, having recalled the name of the autonomous region in Italian. "Where they speak German as well as Italian."

She returned a small nod. With three different ethnicities represented in the room (four, considering Jeremy's dual American and Belgian parentage), all of the participants spoke French: Gruber with his thick German accent, Stefania's Italian accent much milder, and Jeremy with that odd instance of American flavor to his speech, though Stefania had never seemed to notice it. Jeremy pictured Gruber and Stefania speaking Italian when they were alone.

Stefania shifted her weight and crossed her legs, both stiff gestures, while Gruber on his side of the sofa gazed ahead past Jeremy, almost bored. When Stefania went on, her tone was weary. "Gruber works for the Italian security services." She shook her head as if disgusted with herself. "We Compagni tend to live in perpetual paranoia, but this time mine wasn't extensive enough." She responded to Jeremy's widening eyes with a helpless shrug. "Seems they want certain Compagni back in Italy at all costs. You could call it kidnapping, though Gruber here hasn't manhandled me, apart from forcing me into a car and bringing me here. That *did* scare the shit out of me."

Jeremy remained speechless, glaring at Gruber, who matter-of-factly explained, "We've apprehended her for crimes committed in Italy. It's a *police procedure*, Monsieur Winters."

In his tracksuit and stocking feet Gruber didn't look like police or anyone else from the authorities. "But you've detained Stefania in a country where you're *not* the police," Jeremy said, crossing his arms tensely and leaning forward. "To me, that still amounts to kidnapping."

Gruber tilted his head at an inquisitive angle. "Maybe so. But then it's a kidnapping sanctioned by the French authorities."

Imperceptibly Jeremy's knotted arms loosened, and

with a look both shrewd and uneasy he sat slowly back against his chair. Rébert's name resounded in his mind like a fire alarm. Though the Renseignements Généraux were technically an intelligence service, they had dealings with security forces working independently. "So you were right," he said to Stefania with a woeful shake of his head. "About the French being involved."

"That's my hope." She suddenly sounded urgent, sitting up straight and leaning toward Jeremy. When Gruber shifted down the sofa next to her, projecting his bulk so she could move no further, Jeremy's stomach muscles contracted.

"You'd really prefer going to prison *here*?" Gruber demanded, sarcastic as he faced her.

Stefania sat back and waved him away like an annoyed aristocrat. She turned her attention back to the open window, where music drifted in from the boulevard below, perhaps a marching band in the distance.

Icily Jeremy eyed Gruber until he finally edged back from Stefania. In disbelief Jeremy said to him, "So the French gave you *permission* to capture Stefania?" The thought of Rébert's conceivable involvement still astounded him.

It was Stefania who answered. "It seems the Italians and French have made a deal concerning Mirko and me."

Mirko...yes...

"Supposedly, Italy wants *him* more than they want me. I'm supposed to stay here with Gruber and cooperate in helping to capture him. Gruber here"—she gave him a sour smile—"tells me that once he and his men apprehend Mirko I'll be set free to remain here."

Stefania didn't look or sound convinced of the arrangement. Still, Jeremy asked, "So what are you doing to help?"

"She knows of possible hideouts," Gruber answered. "People who might be harboring him."

Questions chased each other through Jeremy's mind—*what did Gruber mean about Stefania preferring to go to prison here?*—while Stefania sat in the corner of the sofa chewing her bottom lip, her face turned deliberately away from Gruber. For a flash of an instant, Jeremy wanted to sweep her up and whisk her out of there. But now Mirko was foremost in his mind, an apparently bigger prize for the Italians—a kidnapper himself during the revolutionary seventies.

"You want Mirko Mazzini," Jeremy directed at Gruber. "And he's on the run. But not just from you..."

Gruber glanced at Stefania who refused him the return courtesy. The sound from the band on the boulevard ballooned closer. Jeremy wished he could shut the window, though neither Stefania nor Gruber seemed bothered by the distraction.

"The explosions," he continued when Gruber gave him a blank look, "at the Louvre and the Bastille...Mirko's work, right?"

Stefania whipped back to him. "Yes, he bombed those buildings—out of protest, and so that maybe the French would find him before Gruber does. I'm not the only one who would prefer being behind bars *here*."

Gruber threw her a smirk. "But it wouldn't be for life, would it—and then what?"

Jeremy ignored the sniping, aiming his question at both of them. "So Mirko planned and carried out the bombings?"

"That seems to be the case," Gruber answered.

Jeremy looked at Stefania, who nodded her agreement. He held her gaze with probing eyes—*we both know that's not the whole story*—until she turned away again.

"Do the French know Mirko's behind the explosions?" Jeremy asked Gruber.

"I'm sure they do; my superiors are the ones in contact with them."

"So if the French catch him first?"

Gruber shrugged. "They don't have Stefania, here, helping them."

Stefania simply shook her head at the open window.

"Which French security service is involved?" Jeremy pressed.

"That's confidential." Gruber squared his massive shoulders and folded his arms against his chest.

Jeremy was still amazed. "So they've agreed to give up Mirko but let Stefania remain in France..."

A brisk nod from Gruber, followed by a crooked smile from Stefania. "As long as *he* keeps his side of the bargain," she said with a distasteful look at Gruber.

The arrangement was peculiar to say the least. And yet, Jeremy observed, Stefania seemed to accept it; there was no sign of her longing to escape. He shot a glance at her. "Any idea as to where Mirko could be? *And*," he added, "whether he's through planting explosives?"

Stefania blinked a couple of times, glanced at Gruber, then said, "We've got hunches about his whereabouts, but I think he's made his point with the explosions."

"He could have stopped after the Louvre pyramid..." Jeremy pointed out.

Stefania didn't respond, and for a time they all went silent. *The Louvre pyramids and the Opéra Bastille*, Jeremy repeated to himself, the eyesores he and Stefania had condemned just a month ago. Had Stefania suggested these targets to Mirko? And what, if anything, did Gruber know of the two Compagni's likely collaboration. Gruber was right, however: though Mirko and, by extension, Stefania might consider justice and imprisonment more bearable in France than in Italy, what would happen upon their release? Extradition to their homeland, most likely, with Mitterrand washing his hands of them. The two Compagni would have put a slight dent in the Bicentennial, but Monsieur le Président would have the last say.

And what of Pietro in all this? it suddenly occurred to Jeremy. No word of him from either Gruber or Stefania. Jeremy was debating whether to mention him when Gruber resumed the conversation. "I thought one bombing would be enough too," he said in a quizzical voice. "Then there was the next, making two, which reminds me that some people are obsessive about the number *three*." He looked over at Stefania who continued to ignore him.

Each absorbed in his own thoughts, none of the three offered anything more. Except Gruber, who cleared his throat and hinted to Jeremy that he had exhausted his time there. Almost polite, this Gruber of late, thought Jeremy with an inward sigh of disgust. Unlike their encounter in the Luxembourg Garden. No hinting around that day, just a direct, crippling kick to the knee.

Finding himself once more on the threshold of the flat, Jeremy looked Gruber up and down. Casually, hands in his pockets, he swung his right leg back and forth, flexing his knee. What Gruber deserved was a massive kick in the gut. But at this juncture, what was the point? Gruber appeared to understand, though, and short of apologizing, said, "Watch yourself out there." Then: "And don't worry about Stefania."

Jeremy returned a cynical grunt. He looked at Stefania. He wanted to pull her to him and whisper: *I know what you've been up to, but do the French?* Instead, with Gruber towering next to her, he let the urge go. There was nothing left for him to do here. As much as he despised the situation, Stefania was a voluntary captive.

On the landing, looking back at the closed door, Jeremy couldn't help concluding that Stefania had plotted with Mirko in the bombings. She may have been on the run with her toothbrush well before Gruber got his hands on her. And now, after seeking Jeremy's help and comfort just a month ago, she stood on the other side of the door, entrusting herself to her enemy. On the other hand, what else could she do? Jeremy wondered if Gruber or his French counterparts suspected her at all in the bombings. Perhaps, with her talk of preferring prison in France. At any rate, provided Mirko was caught and the deal with the French went through, things just might work out for her. And yet, thought Jeremy, if he could get his own hands on Mirko he would be tempted to drag him to Rébert and demand that the RG agent declare what he knew about this business.

Chapter 21

Down on the sidewalk, Jeremy knew he had to dismiss thoughts of dragging Mirko to the RG. A confrontation with Rébert could harm Stefania's chances at freedom. As long as she had merely suggested the targets, with Mirko carrying out the rest, well, her desperation could be forgiven, since there had been no serious injuries. For now Jeremy would wait. He knew where Horst Gruber lived; the French were already looking for Mirko, as were Gruber and Stefania, even though the latter two hardly seemed kindred spirits. With all their chafing and sniping, in fact, Jeremy was certain one of them slept on the sofa.

The music infiltrating Gruber's flat had now taken up bodily form in a marching band pounding up boulevard Brune. Traffic had been diverted, and the brass section roared in Jeremy's ears as if rudely announcing that events had overtaken him, reinforcing the jarring sense of anticlimax he now felt; he needed to get away from here, away from Gruber, from Stefania, away from the intrigues of the French security services. Away from his own sense of futility, an empty feeling growing inside him whose weight he could barely tolerate.

Six o'clock: it looked, after all, like he would be able to meet Haley and the girls at eight. In the meantime, why not tell Louise Cholot that he'd discovered Stefania's whereabouts? Eager for company to fill the void inside him, he caught the bus back to her neighborhood, and while it lumbered along the noisy, congested streets, his mind went over the extent of what he would report to her: that he had found Stefania at Gruber's, that Madame had been spot-on in suspecting the *Grand Blond* was Italian, and that Stefania was now working with this Gruber, a member of the Italian security services. He would go on to say that Gruber and the French sought to apprehend another Italian, known to Stefania and wanted for kidnapping, and that, *mistakenly*, Stefania had been the original target of the investigation...then...then...*No, nothing more*—no digging himself into new lies with Madame. She would understand when he told her the Italian agent Gruber refused to reveal anything else. And frankly, considering Stefania's attitude toward Gruber, Jeremy sensed the *Grand Blond was* holding something back.

The bus squealed to a halt on Madame's street, Jeremy squeezing through the clots of passengers to hop off. Then for the three-block walk to the telephone booth to call her—

Never mind: he would head straight to her building, punch in the codes to enter, and ring her bell. After all, he only planned to stay ten minutes or so before making his way up to the Champs-Élysées.

He rang the bell on the fourth floor. Almost at once he heard voices and quick steps approaching the door.

Then, it opened. "Jeremy, *quelle surprise!*"

Madame looked dressed for a party. And, he could hear a male voice talking in the background in staccato spurts, as if into the phone.

"Sorry to drop in unannounced," Jeremy said, mustering a jaunty tone that belied disappointment in not finding her alone. Given Madame had company, he decided to save the meat of Stefania's story for another time. "I was crossing the neighborhood and thought I'd give you a quick 14 July greeting..."

The voice in the background halted, followed by the

sound of a telephone receiver dropping onto its base. A tall slender man appeared behind Madame, and Jeremy immediately recognized him from the photo in Madame's living room.

Warmly, she said, "This is my son Hervé," and stepped aside so the two men could shake hands. "Hervé: my friend, Jeremy Winters. Come in, Jeremy. Hervé was just booking a taxi to take us to a restaurant this evening. And *bien sûr*, you're invited to join us if you're not busy."

Along with the handshake, Jeremy gave Madame's suited son an imperceptible once-over. He was a good half-head taller than Jeremy and his sallow skin and dark receding hair lent him a mature air. Once a smile began to crinkle the corners of his eyes, though, Jeremy recognized Madame and her youthfulness in him.

"Yes," Hervé agreed. "*Do* join us this evening if you're free." His arm swept toward the flat's interior as if to usher Jeremy in.

Gracious, like your mother, Jeremy thought, returning an affable smile. "Thank you, but unfortunately I have plans."

"*Un petit apéritif, peut-être?*" suggested Madame.

Jeremy slipped a glance at Hervé then aimed an obvious look at his watch. "I'd love to if I didn't have to be somewhere. I just wanted to wish Louise *bonne fête*."

"Another time, perhaps," Hervé concluded genially. "I'll leave you to *Maman. Bonne soirée*."

Jeremy waited as Hervé withdrew into the flat, then said quietly to Madame, "I've found Stefania and confronted the *Grand Blond*—Horst Gruber from the South Tyrol, in fact. I just wanted to tell you before I headed home."

"And Stefania's all right...?"

"Yes, but I won't go into it now."

"Well, come back tomorrow if you can," Louise said,

with a mingled look of surprise and delight. "Anytime in the afternoon."

For the second time in an hour, Jeremy was visited by a sensation of hollowness. The lower he glided in the elevator, the deeper the feeling of futility sank in him. *Futilitarian*: he had come across the term in a British magazine and looked it up—"a person who devotes himself to profitless pursuits." That described his role in the Stefania-Gruber affair to a tee.

As the elevator approached the ground floor, he wondered whether he should have accepted Madame's offer of an aperitif, but with her and her son dressed to the nines he felt out of place. Plus, he wondered what the polite and attentive Hervé thought of his possessing the door codes to his mother's building; whether he was now quizzing *Maman* about exactly who this new friend of hers was. Would his tone be reasonable or demanding? Might he bring up Jeremy's defective eye, which he'd had to wipe there on the spot? He wondered how he himself would react if his mother suddenly introduced him to a young male friend. Probably, a tad suspicious. He left the building giving a curious shake of his head.

Shadows were shifting as he set off for the metro, the sun on the decline, though it wouldn't start to get dark until well after nine, which was probably when the evening parade on the Champs-Elysées would begin. Jeremy had a little over an hour before his rendezvous with Haley and her friends and decided to walk up to Place d'Italie to take the metro. From there he would go straight to the Rond-Point des Champs-Élysées, where he and the girls would grab something to eat before the parade commenced.

Walking always helped him clear his head, but now Christophe popped into his thoughts. Despite Jeremy's casual promise to keep his friend informed about Stefania, he had no stomach for explaining Gruber and the explosions. If Stefania loved Christophe, let *her* contact him and explain once she was free. Jeremy was through meddling with the two. On the ride to the Champs-Élysées, however, he couldn't get the hunt for Mirko out of his mind. And when he emerged from the Franklin D. Roosevelt station, he weaved through crowds already amassed on the sweeping sidewalks of the Avenue, found a phone booth, and called Pietro.

"*Âllo?*"

"Pietro, it's Jeremy..."

An exasperated sigh came down the line, and then: "I thought you'd finished interrogating me."

"Ha!" Jeremy chuckled. "Actually, not quite..." Apart from Pietro's sarcastic tone, Jeremy wondered at his use of the term *interrogate*. How much did he know about his companion's predicament and whereabouts? "Listen," he said, "I heard Mirko might be in trouble—"

"*In trouble?* What the hell are you talking about?"

"Well..." Jeremy pressed his lips together. Pietro was still in full-defense mode; better not to force the issue. "Okay," he went on, "you probably know more about him than I do..."

"Naturally." Dead weight, like lead on the line. An implicit refusal to continue the conversation, and not even a hint from Pietro that he was aware of Mirko's debacle. Except that his very terseness and sarcasm led Jeremy to suspect he was.

"All right," Jeremy finally said. "Sorry I bothered you."

"Right," Pietro grumbled, and promptly hung up, which made Jeremy curse. *The hell with all of them.* Gruber probably had someone sitting on their place in case Mirko returned. Why take this mess any further— *quit being a futilitarian, and let it go.*

Jeremy sighed and smoothed his hair. He made sure his shirt was tucked tightly in, and then crossed over to the avenue Matignon. There he drew himself up, donning his most festive Bicentennial mood, and entered the Drugstore Matignon restaurant.

The restaurant was packed and he couldn't locate Haley. Then his eyes caught Bernadette sitting alone at a table. When he reached her she greeted him with a broad smile. "Haley's down on the Champs-Élysées. She spotted one of those moveable metal police barriers and she and Kathleen claimed it, together with a Polish couple. We'll be able to park ourselves there with a front-row view of the parade. We'd planned to eat first, but we can only do it in shifts or we'll lose our place on the Avenue."

"No problem," Jeremy said. "I'm not terribly hungry, but if you'd like to order something..."

"I've already eaten—we can head down there now."

Indeed the metal barrier, with its vertical bars and long cylindrical top, seemed perfect for leaning against or even balancing your seat on. With room for four, Haley, Kathleen, and the Polish couple were doing just that amidst exuberant crowds continuing to burgeon on the generous Champs-Élysées sidewalks. Jeremy and Bernadette took up places near the girls, Jeremy exchanging twin-cheeked kisses with all of them. He gave Haley an additional hug, which she returned, planting an affectionate peck on his neck.

Then she turned officious. "Here, you sit now, Bernadette. Jeremy can take a turn later."

Jeremy lifted his hand in a blocking gesture. "Don't worry about me, I've been sitting most of the afternoon."

"You have more friends!" An exclamation in accented English.

Jeremy turned to the droopy-mustached man leaning against the other end of the barricade.

"This is Lev," said Haley, "and his wife Stella," she added, indicating the woman between the now-seated Bernadette and Lev. "They're from Poland."

When Jeremy smiled at the couple, Lev pranced forward and thrust a bottle at him. "Good Polish vodka," he said with a ruddy grin. "Your girls don't drink, so it's up to us men."

Jeremy glanced at Haley whose eyes rolled innocently upward. Evidently, none of the three girls wished to swap spit with Lev, who either alone or with Stella had already consumed more than half of the clear, swishing spirits. Yet there was Lev, brimming with merriment; so with a good-natured smile Jeremy accepted the bottle and bent his elbow for a sip.

When he returned the bottle he asked, "Is this your first trip to Paris?"

"Yes, Stella and I are much excited." Lev took another stiff swig and handed the bottle to his wife, who gave the cap a secure twist and stowed the bottle in a large canvas bag settled on the ground next to her. At most, the couple might be in their late thirties, their foreign voyage a further possible benefit of Glasnost. *Good for Lev and Stella*, thought Jeremy. Even Stefania would have to recognize that the relaxing of strong-armed Soviet control proved a boost for the morale of the common man and for humanity in general.

Stefania. What were she and Gruber doing right now in his flat?

Lev, who had returned to the barrier, swayed then slipped off. Stella laughed affectionately.

"No good for me up here," he blurted, beaming and pointing to Haley. "*Ladies* must sit."

"I'm fine," Haley assured him with a friendly grin.

Lev tugged the bottle out of his wife's bag and passed it back to Jeremy, who took another light sip while observing the milling crowd. As he gazed up, down, and across the Avenue, he figured there had to be hundreds of thousands of spectators amassed. He had read in *Le Parisien* that a gathering of dignitaries from all over the world would be sitting on bleachers at Place de la Concorde—a prime vantage point from which to view the parade, and where Jessye Norman, the famous American dramatic soprano, would sing the Marseillaise. At their spot at the Rond-Point, Jeremy and his friends weren't too far from Place de la Concorde and he hoped they would be able to hear Jessye Norman. She had soared above all singers, French women included, to be chosen for this extreme honor. Tall, black, and stunning, he remembered her from the newspaper photo and description.

All around Jeremy the din was increasing as the sun sank behind the Arc de Triomphe. Lev tossed his empty vodka bottle on the sandy ground. Haley, Kathleen, and Bernadette chuckled at him. Stella grinned shyly, then scooped the bottle up and stuffed it conscientiously into her big bag.

Stefania and Mirko crept back into Jeremy's thoughts. How many Italian agents could be searching for Mirko in Paris at this moment? And were they at least communicating with the French as they went about their pursuit? Somehow this type of collaboration didn't sound right...

Suddenly a tidal wave of sound mounted through the loudspeakers—drums and brass. The parade had finally begun.

Before long floats made their way through the Arc de Triomphe, advancing down the Champs-Élysées toward them. One was an enormous bamboo drum on wheels, accompanied by scores of youths walking bicycles in front, behind, and on either side of it.

"A Chinese drum," shouted Lev as the float neared. "And Chinese young people. Remember Tiananmen

Square?" he added in a solemn voice.

Jeremy nodded.

Lev turned to his wife. "Stella, the other bottle! We must drink to the Chinese who stood against repression and paid for it with their lives."

"And to Lech Walesa and Solidarity," Stella added with a firm nod. "Or we wouldn't be here tonight." She produced the second bottle of spirits from her bag and handed it to Lev, who twisted off the cap and offered the first drink to Jeremy. Jeremy gave a gracious smile and took a pull, though his thoughts kept darting to the communist Compagni.

More drums on the Champs-Élysées. This time marching drummers in tartan kilts; hundreds of them, their barrage ever-amplifying, reverberating and deafening in concert with the boisterous, shrieking crowd. In Jeremy's head the tumult was topped by dizzying thoughts of Mirko on the run through the side streets of Paris's dodgy quarters. Of the French sitting on their hands, letting the Italians tromp all over their territory. Of Stefania and Gruber, their foreheads pressed together as they tried to discern Mirko's movements. Of Pietro, who might truly know what they were. The three Compagni, now forced into division. *Three*...Gruber's comment about people obsessed with the number three: the Louvre pyramid, the Opéra Bastille, and...

Jeremy's gaze swept the Avenue, anxiety raking him with its claws. In the midst of this clamor, a minor explosion could easily go unheard. He looked at Haley and the Irish girls who had to shout to communicate, yet appeared cheerfully and utterly absorbed in the commotion. He had to take his leave. If he failed to follow up on the hunch he had now, he might never forgive himself.

Chapter 22

To Haley and the girls, Jeremy yelled the excuse that he wasn't feeling well. Haley acquiesced with a curious nod and a slight frown of disappointment, after which he said goodbye and set off to find a way to cross the Champs-Elysées. He had to get to the Seine, but the parade made it impossible to traverse the Avenue. So he turned and pushed through the wall of spectators behind him, making his way back along the strip of sidewalk and woods that led to the Concorde. As he kicked through ankle-deep rubbish, a firecracker went off not three meters from him; about halfway to the Concorde another exploded, its acrid smoke invading his nostrils. Firecracker blasts were common on Bastille Day and normally he would have shrugged them off. Tonight, each one made him jump in prescient fear of what might be happening at his destination—the Orsay museum, the last of Mitterrand's Great Works that Jeremy and Haley had deemed a feasible bombing target.

When Jeremy reached Place de la Concorde he encountered a strong police presence guarding the high barricades enclosing the VIP bleachers. He was forced to skirt the Place, up and around to rue de Rivoli, which channeled him farther yet from the river he needed to cross. Finally he reached the Tuileries, traversed the gardens, then attempted to cross at the Passerelle Solférino but found the bridge closed. He continued along the quai des Tuileries and at last was able to cross the Pont Royal bridge to the left bank of the Seine. There he landed at the quai Anatole France, only meters from the museum. He felt he had been hiking all night long.

Jeremy approached the left corner of the Orsay's long façade. A pedestrian here, another there, making their way back to the bridge, probably heading to the Champs to join its multitude of revelers. Where he now stood he could still hear the roar across the river.

He continued along the sidewalk in front of the long museum facing the Seine. Black bars soldered into grills barricaded the various entrances. Through their small squares, all was dark. He made his way around to the side of the museum, past the animal sculptures to the dark patio corner: everything was quiet under the glass and metal awning. He stopped to breathe in the calm—so far so good; maybe he could go back to the party, tell Haley he felt better. Before that, however, he needed to check out the back of the building. Walking on the raised sidewalk, he observed sporadic traffic below on ribbon-narrow rue de Lille; a merry blare of a horn, a celebratory yell and wave from a car window.

Satisfied with the atmosphere, he returned to the museum's side patio and cast a final glance down the set of concrete steps that accessed rue de Lille. Its cross street to the right was rue de Bellechasse, across which sat the Palais de la Légion d'Honneur. For an instant Jeremy asked himself if that august building, seat of the nation's highest military and civil merits, could conceivably be a Compagni target. But quiet reigned there too and he decided to move on.

Until his relief was interrupted by loud whispering. He stayed put, listening to it drift to the patio corner from the dark entrance, where he had first arrived and now planned to exit. As the sound came nearer it swelled to arguing, and by the time Jeremy perceived two silhouetted figures he had identified both the language and its speakers. The two stopped and faced him.

"Hello, Jeremy," said Stefania, switching from Italian to French. Her greeting was cautious, her voice seeming to sag with weariness. Mirko stood next to her, only a couple of inches taller, though stocky and muscularly built. He remained silent, but as Jeremy proceeded toward them he said, "Don't come any closer."

Jeremy would have ignored the warning if a revolver hadn't emerged from the Italian's pocket. Jeremy stood shocked at the gun pointed at him. It was as though Mirko didn't recognize him, or maybe he just couldn't afford letting the least guard down in his reduced condition of *animal traqué*. He was shorn of hair, which reminded Jeremy of the Monk Jean-Marc on the run. Jean-Marc and Renaud, *innocent*—at least concerning the bombings.

"So you figured it out," said Stefania, a hand indicating the Orsay.

Jeremy didn't reply; at this point, discovering Stefania and Mirko here together seemed practically natural. Except for the gun, which he continued to eye warily, his pulse ticking up. Mirko was already wanted in Italy for kidnapping, and Jeremy hoped not to learn of any further violent proclivities on the Italian's part.

"Why is Jeremy here?" he demanded of Stefania. Without taking his eyes off Jeremy, Mirko slung a backpack off his shoulder and dropped it next to the museum's set of glass doors. Before Jeremy could take step closer he shook the revolver at him, which he now gripped with both hands.

"Because he's clever," replied Stefania.

"*No*," Mirko countered. "You told him everything while you were cheating on Christophe with him!"

In the shadows it was difficult to tell, but Jeremy sensed Mirko tighten his grip on the pistol. He had stepped away from Stefania and the gun now swayed back and forth from her to Jeremy.

"She didn't tell me anything of the sort," Jeremy protested, flexing his fists in nervous spasms. "That was over a month ago, so please put the gun away, Mirko."

"*Sì—metti giù l'arma!*"

Jeremy jerked toward the direction of the new voice—*Italian*, and it was followed by a flashlight beam bobbing to the top of the concrete stairs from rue de Lille. The figure behind it had reached the museum patio, with two other forms appearing alongside it. Jeremy made out weapons, the man behind the flashlight holding a semiautomatic handgun and the two next to him armed with assault rifles with silencers—in their balaclavas and dark clothing the two looked like ninjas.

"What's going on?" Jeremy said in French.

"*What's going on?*" Mirko hurled back at him. "You called the cops, that's what's happening!"

"We're here to pick you up, Mirko," said the man behind the flashlight, this time in German-accented French. "Now drop the pistol."

"Gruber!" said Jeremy.

No one responded to him, but at least they were speaking French again.

Stefania yelled, "Mirko's backpack is next to the window."

Then more Italian, this time between Gruber and his ninja-like agents, followed by a shout from Mirko: "*State fermi o le sparo!*"

Jeremy ran frantic fingers through his hair. Thanks to his Italian studies both at school and through reading newspapers, he understood Mirko's cry—*Stay put*. And with Mirko's pistol now pointing at Stefania, it wasn't hard to conclude the second part of his warning—*Or I'll shoot her*.

Gruber, you fool, why did you let her come here? An icy thought occurred to Jeremy: *because you're double crossing her; you want to spirit her away to Italy along with Mirko.*

Stefania had to know this...she had doubted Gruber back at the flat.

In the distance the thunderous clangor from the Champs-Elysées vied fleetingly for Jeremy's attention. Then Stefania made a lunge toward the glass door of the Orsay—*the backpack*, thought Jeremy. Mirko pivoted toward her, and in the same moment Jeremy heard the *plunk* of a professionally silenced shot, and then a strangled cry as Mirko clutched his shoulder and dropped to his knees. The ninjas charged, but Jeremy was closer and rushed to Stefania's side, kicking the pistol away from Mirko while Stefania snatched up the backpack.

"*Ci sono delle molotov qua dentro,*" she said, pressing the backpack to her chest. "*Non sparate più!*"

Molotov cocktails inside in the backpack, Jeremy understood. *She's warning Gruber and the ninjas to halt their fire.*

Jeremy's breath froze in his chest as Gruber and his team stood with their weapons trained on the two Compagni, along with himself now.

Then out came a lighter. Stefania had plucked it from her pocket as quick as a viper and its flame now flickered in the dark. As he grasped its horrifying significance, the hair rose on Jeremy's neck. If Stefania were hit by a bullet, she would go up like a Roman candle.

More rapid exchanges in Italian. Mirko collapsed on the concrete, groaning and grasping his shoulder. Gruber addressed Jeremy in French: "Get out of here, Winters!"

"What about Stefania?" Jeremy demanded.

"She and I have a deal—you know that."

Jeremy glanced at Stefania, who hugged the backpack more tightly against her. "I'd like to believe that," she said, "seeing you had me come here..." Her tone was cynical.

"Nothing's changed," Gruber insisted. "So put down the backpack."

"You've got Mirko, so let her go," Jeremy said, Mirko now panting next to them.

"*Winters*," repeated Gruber, more menacingly this time. "Step away from Stefania and leave."

Despite his gooseflesh, Jeremy refused to move. "If you abduct her again I'll inform the French authorities...seems you have a deal with them too." Sweat poured down his temples, down his chest, down the crease in his back. His right eye was streaming. He wondered how the men in balaclavas could breathe.

"Go!" Stefania suddenly said to him. "Find a phone and call the police."

She was desperate, Jeremy thought, and he now questioned whether the French authorities actually knew what was going on; whether Gruber had lied about their cooperation merely to manipulate Stefania, then take her along with Mirko once he was caught.

He wiped his eye with the back of his hand, squinting against the sting of sweat and tears. For all practical purposes, he could only see out of his left eye. "I'm not leaving until Stefania does, and if you take her or harm her I'll go to the press as well."

The ninjas remained frozen and inscrutable. Gruber, behind his flashlight, was a Teutonic monolith who could wipe Jeremy from the equation with one muffled shot. Jeremy could smell the gasoline in Stefania's backpack.

As if tuned into his thoughts, she stepped a good distance away from him. "You'd better go, Jeremy.

Whatever happens to me is ultimately my fault, my mistakes, not your responsibility." Her tone was calm. The flame from her lighter seemed to flag in response, but she flicked it back to life without missing a beat. Frantically Jeremy wiped at his eye with his sleeve.

"Gruber," Stefania shouted in staccato, loudly enough for the entire neighborhood to hear. "If you shoot me I'll be a torch that'll rival the fireworks on the Champs-Élysées. So take Mirko and get him help."

Gruber didn't answer. Below the patio on rue de Lille, a couple of cars honked their horns, twice each, as though in festive greeting. The longer Gruber and his ninjas hung around, the more they risked being discovered. After a couple of deliberative seconds, he flashed his beam at Mirko, still prone and muttering with difficulty. He shifted his light to Jeremy then back to Stefania, and finally spoke. "Place the backpack on the ground, Stefania, then you and Winters can leave together."

Jeremy wanted to follow Gruber's advice, to take Stefania by the shoulders and march her away, leaving the backpack on the ground and himself in Gruber's range of fire. Gruber wouldn't kill him—it would complicate things too much for the Italian agent. But when he started to speak to Stefania she shook her head, her fingers palpating the backpack, her desperate bit of insurance, her unthinkable protection. "No, I don't think so," she said to Gruber, holding the lighter steady while slipping an arm through one of the straps of the backpack.

Gruber gave an impatient sigh. "You won't get shot in the back. That would not be in our interest."

Our interest—no mention of the French. *No deal with them*, Jeremy concluded. He extended a hand toward Stefania. "Come on, let's do what he says and get out of here."

She shook her head firmly and gave the backpack's strap on her shoulder a light pat. "I'm leaving with this," she said in Gruber's direction. "I'll dispose of it before the night's over." And at that she hoisted her charge onto her back and moved toward the stairs.

Jeremy stepped between her and Gruber, and a long sigh issued from the *Grand Blond*. "All right then: go," he said, waving them off as he and his men moved swiftly toward Mirko.

Stefania skipped down the stairs and dashed across the dark street, heading away from the river. Jeremy ripped his shirttail out of his trousers, wiping his eye as he hurried down the stairs after her. *Merde—she still had things to answer for!*

Chapter 23

For a couple of blocks down rue de Bellechasse, Jeremy followed Stefania, expecting her to eventually turn back to the noise of his clacking heels. But her pace accelerated, so he swallowed the distance with long strides, catching up and grasping her arm before she could descend into the Solférino metro station.

"Where are you going with that backpack?" he demanded.

Under the dim metro streetlamp, Stefania shook her arm loose and faced him with a determined gaze. "I said I'd dispose of it, and I will."

"Maybe I should help you..."

"Are you used to dealing with gasoline bombs, Jeremy?" Stefania sounded clinically serious, and when he didn't answer she said, "Don't worry, I'm going to get rid of it in a safe area."

"Where would that be, tonight of all nights?"

"Down in the Thirteenth." When Jeremy's stare became more penetrating, she added, "At the worksite for President Mitterrand's new library."

Jeremy grimaced in surprise and Stefania cracked a grin. "Just joking; probably not an appropriate subject, but at this point I really feel the need to shed some stress. Actually, I plan to cross the site and throw this thing in the Seine where no one'll be around. Then I'm finally going home to my flat."

Home to her flat—as if an escapade like this was an every-day event. More of her way of shedding stress,

Jeremy figured. Relieved she had no other dodgy plans, he pressed her for clarification and confirmation of his own conclusions. "So it seems the French never had designs on you. And as far as a deal with the Italians..."

Stefania met his wry tone with a disgusted shake of her head. "I'm sure those bastard Italian spies muscled in here illegally."

Jeremy nodded to himself. "But did you and Mirko really attack the Louvre pyramid and the Opéra Bastille thinking the French would pick you up before Gruber did?"

Stefania granted him a weak smile and a shrug of admission. "It was partly an act of protest. Then, with your information that the Viking was a German speaker, we gradually put two and two together and figured it would be better to go to jail in France than in Italy. I never trusted Gruber and now I'm pretty certain the French know nothing about him and his goons. I'm sure that's why Gruber backed off when you threatened to notify the authorities and the press. Thanks for that," she added, giving his arm a firm squeeze. She fell silent for a moment, looking down at her shoes; then she cleared her throat and resumed: "You know, I truly wasn't involved in planting the explosives."

"But in selecting the targets," said Jeremy with a little snort and a grin. "I figured that."

"*Not* the Orsay, though," she emphasized. "Adding a third mark was Mirko's idea. I told him I was against it. I hated that people got nicked with glass at the Louvre—we were pushing our luck with the Bastille."

"Well, I never heard you criticize the Orsay," said Jeremy

"So how did you know?"

"It was the only one of Mitterrand's Great Works left that presented a natural target— prestigious and located kitty-corner across the Seine from the Louvre."

"*Bravo,*" stated Stefania with admiring eyes.

"By the way," said Jeremy, "I talked to Pietro, and he denied knowing anything about Mirko running off."

"Well, he *would* keep his mouth shut, wouldn't he?"

Jeremy reckoned so. "You know," he said, casting Stefania a dubious smile, "you could have warned me before disappearing..." He almost admitted how worried he had been, but at this point what was the purpose?

Stefania's eyes turned sober. "I'm sorry about that."

In the misty spray of streetlight Jeremy thought he could also detect a reddening of her cheeks. What was certain was her fingering the straps of her backpack, adjusting them for comfort or simply out of anxiousness to get rid of the load. Yes, it was time she did just that.

"Sure you don't need help with your charge?" he asked, inclining his head toward the backpack, knowing full well his question to be rhetorical.

She shook her head, sending him an amiable smile. "Thanks, but you've helped me more than you can know. I won't forget it."

Right—including with Christophe. Jeremy was tempted to ask about that: whether she would be contacting Christophe, *whether they would*...but no, not even that mattered now.

"I hope to see you around, Jeremy." Her tone seemed earnest as she shifted the weight of the backpack.

Jeremy stepped forward, took her shoulders, bent and kissed her solidly on each cheek. "An *au revoir* for now," he said, stepping back promptly.

"*Au revoir,*" she repeated, her voice solemn. "That's how life should be—never *adieu.*" She shot him a last, quick smile, then turned and briskly slipped down the metro stairs.

He watched her descend until her dark silhouette disappeared. *Poof*—she was gone again. Her exit recalled the enigmatic journey they had shared all along.

Rather than trail Stefania down the stairs to catch his own metro train, Jeremy decided to tuck in his shirt and head back toward the river, where he would go home via the Assemblée Nationale station. As he strolled amidst the clangor still coming from the Champs-Élysées, he imagined how Stefania would go about her self-appointed task of disposing of the gasoline bomb. Come to think of it, there was a metro station right next to the river, not far from the Mitterrand library site. No need to traverse all the construction mess. He shrugged: maybe she preferred the shadowy, isolated cover of the gullies and giant dirt mounds, which slumbered far from any Bicentennial revelry that could occur at a metro stop. Or maybe she didn't plan to go all the way to the river after all—just light the Molotov and fling it at an idle tractor or backhoe. He shook his head, unable to suppress a twitch of a smile. No, he thought, Stefania now knew the Mitterrand government had never planned her deportation, so there was nothing left to protest.

In any case, the disposal of the backpack did not require his help, and Jeremy could only reckon that Stefania had chosen once and for all to continue along her path without him. Which was for the best. Once the backpack was eliminated Stefania could then cross the Thirteenth back to her flat, and hopefully her concierge wouldn't berate her for disappearing for a while. She could always give the woman a quizzical frown, saying she'd merely been out of town for a few days. And who could blame her at this time of year? Mirko, on the other hand, would be on his way toward transport to Italy, with, Jeremy hoped, his wound somehow taken care of. And that would be all.

No, it wouldn't. Jeremy took a drop seat in the metro carriage, oblivious to the festive energy continuously erupting around him. What of the jailed Monks? How long would it take the police to dismiss them as suspects in the explosions for lack of evidence? They could still be held for defacement of public monuments, but even if they confessed they'd probably receive only a light punishment (depending on their history with the law). So the two would be free soon enough, and Jeremy hoped they didn't harbor serious suspicions about him.

He returned to thinking about the plot on the part of the Italians to infiltrate France and kidnap both Mirko and Stefania. Gruber had made a deal with Stefania, and it seemed he'd almost reneged on his promise to let her go in return for her help catching Mirko. Jeremy felt relieved at having at least been instrumental in foiling that.

He shook his head: if only Rébert and the RG had known! They'd be furious as baited bears. Soon they would have to look beyond the Monks for the authors of the Louvre pyramid and Opéra Bastille explosions. And considering the complexity of his involvement in the Compagni imbroglio, Jeremy would be keeping a low profile for a while—no phone calls to Rébert for now.

Rather, the next morning Jeremy called Haley with apologies for leaving the parade prematurely. Bernadette and Kathleen were departing for Ireland this afternoon, with Haley driving them to the airport. Would he like to accompany them? she asked.

Indeed he would.

"Too bad you missed the best part of the parade," Haley said, and went on to describe the magnificent fireworks, stupendous floats, and, believe it or not, a steam engine chugging down the Champs-Élysées. "And the Marseillaise. 'Course we couldn't see Jessye Norman singing it, but we could hear it, and it was fantastic!"

Jeremy listened as Haley went on to quote an

estimated attendance of 800,000 people at the parade. Getting home had been a long slog with all the metro stations along the Champs-Élysées shut down. She, Kathleen, and Bernadette had ended up walking all the way to the Madeleine—only to let train after train go by until they finally forced themselves into one. "But it was worth it," she concluded with a contented sigh.

True, the evening had paid off, Jeremy agreed inwardly—for him as well. Someday he might even tell Haley about his parallel adventure across the river. But not now: he lacked the energy and ambition to embark on such an extraordinary narration from scratch; and, of course, there would have to be key edits.

Yes, 14 July 1989 had been the celebration of a lifetime, rendered all the more unique since no one would live to see a *Tercentennial* of the French Revolution.

Haley suggested they leave early for the Orly airport so they could take the time to show Bernadette and Kathleen the palace of Fontainebleau.

They made the rounds of the palace exterior and lake. At one point Jeremy embraced Haley and waltzed her over the cobbles next to the splendid Renaissance structure, to the accompaniment of giggles from Bernadette and Kathleen. The outing was a light-hearted affair he truly appreciated and needed. Time constraints kept them from visiting the palace interior, and they instead had lunch in a *crêperie* where Jeremy insisted on treating. He ordered hard cider to go along with their *galettes*. "We have to see Bernadette and Kathleen off in style."

The Irish sisters safely in the air, Jeremy and Haley headed back to Paris with Jeremy slouching in the passenger seat. At lunch he had ordered a second bottle of cider and drunk most of it himself, after which he asked for a Calvados to put the final punctuation on the Norman-Breton meal.

Now he was brooding again...

"You've celebrated more today than you did last night," Haley commented from behind the wheel of her second-hand Peugeot. "Making up for your stomach cramps?"

"Mm," Jeremy murmured, his gaze glued to the Route Nationale ahead.

"Sure that's all it is?"

He exhaled heavily. "Just thinking about the arrest of the Monks..."

"Seems to have worked," Haley observed. "No more explosions."

"Right..."

"You've got reservations..."

Might as well get what little he could off his chest. "I still don't think they did it."

"Well, they've done other crap, and the police will release them if they don't have evidence on them for the explosions. Right?"

"Mm-hm," Jeremy said. Hearing Haley repeat his own conclusions made him feel tempted to open up about the true plot, limiting what he said about Stefania to his role with the RG. Yet he was just sober enough to know he was tipsy, and decided better of it.

"Anyway," Haley resumed, "the Bicentennial is over, it was successful, and we can all go back to our normal routines, boring as they may be."

Jeremy nodded and closed his eyes. Haley liked to drive fast and he was beginning to feel carsick. What a shame it would be to lose the satisfying lunch he'd just enjoyed.

He slept the rest of the afternoon and woke sober enough for work. With the club closed for the *Grande*

Fête yesterday, tonight they were reopening with an African-American jazz guitarist. Jeremy had heard Jack May before in another Paris jazz club, and admired his talent in taming the electric guitar into a subtle but passionate stalking panther. His style reminded Jeremy of the legendary Wes Montgomery, and for Jeremy, Montgomery evoked memories of Margie. When he was thirteen—and Margie twenty-five, and his father's girlfriend—she had lent him her album, *A Day in the Life*. Montgomery's music shimmered like Margie's river of red hair, and this style of jazz remained evocative to Jeremy, particularly after his lightning affair with Margie nine years later.

Now, as he stood against the club's wall downstairs, listening to May's rendition of "Angel," Stefania revisited his thoughts. Her resemblance to Margie seemed more vague at this point, after all that had transpired. And yet it suddenly occurred to him whether her concierge had mentioned the police visit instigated by him and Louise Cholot. Whether, surprised, she might call him. Though they had parted amicably, he didn't know whether he would like to hear from her again or not.

Then there was Louise. Jeremy reckoned he should pay his friend and co-investigator the visit he'd promised after barging in on her and her son yesterday. She knew he had found Stefania at Gruber's and he would now have to figure out the extent of what to tell her.

In the meantime, after work, he went out for a drink with his friend Didier. Outside of work at the club, he hadn't spent time with him since the whole Bicentennial business had started.

In the ambience-dark Pub Saint-Germain, sitting in a moleskin booth, the two friends clicked glasses then settled in to small talk. Jeremy had to search his mind to contribute, as not much could qualify as "small" in his life these days. Though he had known Didier two years, he'd ruled out narrating his recent adventure with all its ambiguity and names that needed protecting—Didier knew nothing of his work for the RG.

Even so, the Bicentennial couldn't help infiltrating their chat—the parades, the parties, the expense and hassle of it all. "The bizarre explosions," as Didier had already put it a couple of days ago at the club. Both then and now Jeremy just shook his head in feigned wonder.

Then Didier asked, "Might Haley be coming to the club again soon?"

Over his Affligem, Jeremy's amused gaze met his friend's knowing smile. "I wouldn't be surprised, as much as she loves jazz."

"And *you*, maybe." Didier shot Jeremy a wink as he took a sip of his port.

"Haley's all right," Jeremy responded, hedging, as usual, when it came to talk of female companionship.

"All right? She's pretty and she loves jazz." Firmly, Didier set his glass down. "And any girl who shares a passion like that with you should be sharing your flat as well. Wish I could applaud my wife's taste in music."

Didier was four years older than Jeremy and had been married ten years. His wife Marine, whom Jeremy encountered whenever he was invited to the couple's home for dinner, had been to Woodstock in 1969. She enjoyed recounting the wild experience, and the fluid, carefree way in which she talked and moved reminded Jeremy of a hippy attached to the old ways. Except perhaps in her dress, which evolved according to style—a French trait that was probably anchored in her DNA.

"Marine's a beauty who should be the poster-woman for classic rock 'n' roll," Jeremy insisted. "Plus she's a hell of a cook."

"Okay—Marine may rock, but Haley *jives*, or at least

I imagine her doing that."

Jeremy's smile broadened.

"She isn't squeamish about your eye, is she?" asked Didier, with a mingled look of doubt and sympathy.

Jeremy gave his cheek an automatic swipe for stray tears. "Not that I know of."

"And she's not afraid of *these*—" Didier punched the air with playful fists.

"Course not," Jeremy scoffed. "I'd never hit a woman."

Didier gave Jeremy's shoulder a friendly slap. "Just joking, *mon vieux*."

He knew that Jeremy boxed, had tried out the punching bag in the bedroom; but Didier had no idea that Haley had never set foot in the flat. Plus, Jeremy mused, he'd never told Didier about being locked up in Virginia five years ago, even though he'd known Didier much longer than he had Haley, or Stefania, for that matter. The thought made him marvel at the strange workings of his psyche.

"Okay, *merde*," said Didier, making a show of folding his arms. "Are you in love with her?"

The question elicited a variety of French *euh's* and puffs of breath from Jeremy. Then he threw his hands open: "I think I might be..."

"Then don't be such a wimp—ask her to move in!"

Things weren't that simple and Jeremy chose not to explain *why* to Didier. Still, after his friend drove him home and he was climbing his stairs with a couple of drinks in him, he felt closer than ever to inviting Haley to spend the night. Funny how he could face down Gruber, Mirko with his pistol, hardballs bounding up at his face from home plate and runners barreling toward him, cleats up, from third base, not to mention various toughs in his work for the RG—and still fear that first sketchy step toward commitment. Or, for that matter, breathing into the mouthpiece of Walt Winters' saxophone and producing one measly note. He shook his head and resolved somehow to remedy things.

Chapter 24

A couple of weeks passed with Jeremy still avoiding the subject of inviting Haley to his place. First, he would need to take down the punching bag—make love not war, should be a bedroom's message—and move it. But to where?

In compensation he invited Haley to accompany him to Belgium during the August vacation period. Le Prince Blue Note would be closed for two weeks and Jeremy's conscience sent him the gentle but firm reminder that he should visit his mother. With Haley he could enjoy the thrill of being tour guide by day and lover by night as they explored Flanders. Then they would make a quick two or three-day visit to Namur, where he would introduce Haley to his mother. Béatrice always worried about her son's solitude, and Jeremy figured this way he could kill two birds with one stone.

He would also call Rébert before they left, he decided, as he climbed the lighted stairs to his flat after work, whistling "Old Devil Moon," the last song of the evening at the club. By now things would have settled down, he could inquire about the Monks, and test the terrain for the right moment to ask about that upgrade in his work status.

Almost to his floor he began the song again, attempting to hit that pesky high note—"it's that *old* devil moon in your eyes..."

He reached his landing.

And found the door to his flat ajar.

For an instant he stared dumbly at the crack of

257

darkness leading into the apartment. Mechanically he wiped his eye, then advanced slowly, fists tensed. As he stepped over the threshold he let his left hand unball to flick on the entrance light. Cautiously he stepped into the illuminated entryway—only to find his telephone yanked out of the wall by its cord and sprawling demolished on the floor in front of him. Shock made him blink rapidly, before he took a deep, stabilizing breath and trod softly on into the living area. Between the light reflected from the entryway and the dull glow of the streetlamps through the window, he could see no one. Braced for an intruder's lunge from the shadows he turned on the lamp next to the sofa.

And witnessed a second wave of destruction.

Jeremy wrenched his eyes from the chaos on the floor to sweep the room and the doorways with a vigilant gaze. Still, no one made an appearance. Perfect silence reigned next to the disaster site of which he now took tremulous inventory.

His television lay on its side on the floor, its screen kicked in. Next to its shards he found his boom box, cracked and crushed like his telephone. Books from shelves lay in a heap on the floor, some splayed open, others in willy-nilly piles. A framed photo of his mother and father on their honeymoon in Nice had landed near the books, its glass apparently shattered by the hefty heel of a shoe. His framed Gauguin print of the Breton countryside had suffered the same fate. Fury shook his limbs, and it took slow seconds for it to recede enough for him to judge the scene rationally: the glass could be replaced, the photo and print reframed and restored pristinely to their respective places on the bookshelf and wall. The shattered television screen didn't matter, as the TV didn't work anyway. The boom box and the phone would have to be replaced. At least the cassette tapes that had been hurled to the floor, along with the books, looked undamaged. The vandals had probably feared taking the time to crush each one underfoot.

But what else? He stepped over the mess on the floor to get to the kitchen and give a quick look inside—nothing seemed out of place and still no sight of an intruder. He crossed to the hall and checked the bathroom, yanking the shower curtain aside but finding no one hiding within. He almost wanted to find someone so he could drag him out, hurl him into the wreckage in the living room, and force an explanation from him. With leaden steps he continued on to the bedroom—something told him there was worse to come. And when he pushed open the door and turned on the light he was met by two sights that made him tremble anew. His first glance caught his punching bag. Riddled with slash marks up one side and down the other, it looked like a gyros butchered by a maniac.

When his eyes shifted to the floor, however, he fell to his knees. There lay his father's tenor saxophone, snatched from its case and mauled by a hammer that was left next to it—the hammer Jeremy kept in his toolbox in the kitchen closet.

His shaking hands hovered over the instrument. Its bell had been collapsed by multiple poundings, the mouthpiece and ligature crushed with probably two vigorous blows. The mother-of-pearl keys had been similarly smashed and the whole of the instrument's brass body pocked with vicious dents. And as if the demise of Walt Winter's saxophone hadn't been completely achieved, Jeremy found its case caved in. As if to deny the deceased instrument a decent resting place.

Unaware of tears welling in both eyes, he suddenly burst into sobs, rocking back and forth on his knees. When he had wept himself dry and utterly spent, he stumbled to his feet and staggered back into the living room where he dropped onto the sofa and covered his eyes. *He would murder them—he would bash their fucking skulls in, the way they'd bludgeoned to death his most precious possession!*

If Jeremy needed confirmation of the authors of this crime, it was sitting on the coffee table in front of him. A note in scrawled, distorted handwriting with the simple message: *traître chiant!*

He dropped it on the floor and fell back against the sofa. So the Monks considered him a "fucking traitor." *Fine, then—we'll see about that!*

At length, racked, he got up and went to the bathroom to wipe his eyes and blow his nose. Both eyes shone red now. Two bright embers—ominous looking. To pull himself together he splashed water on his face, then left to survey the place more closely. He found the front door unforced; the lock must have been picked. In the kitchen he saw nothing amiss other than his toolbox, open but otherwise undisturbed in the closet. He checked all the drawers and cabinets in the flat but nothing appeared to be missing.

Revenge: that's what the Monks had sought.

Which led him back to the bedroom and the mutilated corpse on the floor—Jean-Marc and Renaud could never guess how successful they'd been. Once more Jeremy knelt, and with dry sobs lifted the mangled brass body and placed it in its crushed coffin. Then, too exhausted to think or do anything else, he collapsed onto the bed.

The next morning his eyes opened to slits, and in that fluid, filmy landscape between sleep and wakefulness a vague hope filtered through him...that the previous night had been a nightmare. Then he slowly rolled onto his back, and his first glimpse was of the slashed-up punching bag. Weak with the nausea of reality, he rose and stepped gingerly over the demolished saxophone, whose sight drove reality's stake deeper into his sunken heart.

Jeremy had no appetite though he downed a cup of coffee to take the edge off his headache. Then he dressed and went down to see his building's concierge. Shocked, Monsieur Barnier assured him that he would send for a locksmith to reinforce the door with a more secure lock, though in all his years as concierge, he could not remember the building ever suffering an intrusion of this type. Had Monsieur Winters called the police? No, Jeremy replied. He had come home late after work, and since nothing was missing from the flat he had gone to bed exhausted.

"All the same, I'll need to go up and take a look, then file a police report on behalf of the building."

"*Merci,*" Jeremy offered politely, more in concession than in gratitude. "I'll be out, but do go up at your convenience."

He wished Monsieur Barnier a good day and returned to his flat to dispose of the Monks' incriminating note. Then he left the building for La Gitane, where he paid to make a couple of calls: one to have a new telephone hooked up and another asking Didier to help him haul away the shattered television and the sliced-up punching bag, which now truly did look like a slaughtered animal.

By the time he returned home to clean up the mess, his rage had subsided to a grim simmer, a seething undercurrent preserved specially for the Monks. He gathered up the shards of beautiful mother-of-pearl keys and laid them to rest with the remains of the broken saxophone. The bashed-in case would serve as a drawer in the morgue under the bed. Coolly, now, he could see the Monks' actions as tit-for-tat destruction, directed at the place where they were supposed to be granted refuge. And if they had only left the saxophone alone he could possibly call things even. Instead they had descended into barbarity, annihilating what could never be replaced. A beautiful, vibrant instrument, a *being* that had come to life under his father's fantastical fingers, an entity that had held both intimate history and future potential—and *that* he could not abide.

He would deal with this crime in his own way.

The police did stop by while he was out and left the concierge a copy of the vandalism report for him to sign, which he absently did. Then, once the locksmith had come and gone, Jeremy left again, this time for a telephone booth in which to have a private conversation with Rébert.

"Finally got the city back on the rails?" he asked the RG agent, consciously keeping his voice level.

Rébert responded with a brusque laugh. "Who says this city is ever on the rails? But at least we're back to monitoring the usual crap."

"And might that include the antics of Jean-Marc Robinet and Renaud Lenoir?"

"Oh," said Rébert, a hint of fluster in his voice. "I forgot to call you; they confessed to defacement of public property though not to the explosions. We had no evidence on them of the latter, so we charged them with the former and released them. They haven't bothered you, have they?"

Jeremy let this sink in and swiftly weighed what he had already considered this morning. He would not report the conscienceless Monks to Rébert. To the RG, the two would deny the break-in and vandalism as easily as they would to the police; no doubt they'd worn gloves, which would leave their note—*traître chiant*—the only clue to suggest their miserable guilt; a note in distorted handwriting they would deny having written as well. Granted, Rébert might see to it that the two were run through the justice system again. But that would bring no gratification to Jeremy. The pieces of shit didn't deserve another interrogation, they deserved...

His reply to Rébert was reserved. "No, I haven't heard from them. Any other ideas about the bombings?" he added innocently.

"We're working on it," Rébert said, a defensive edge to his voice.

"And the upgrade to my work status?"

"Working on that too; takes time."

"I see. Well, I'll be in Belgium for ten days starting next week. Maybe when I get back...?"

"I might have more work for you myself then...with a raise," Rébert added, an upswing to his tone. "At any rate we'll talk when you return."

Jeremy hung up with a sigh. *Okay: you take time to sort out my situation and I'll do the same with the Monks.* Rébert had mentioned neither Stefania nor her two Compagni Mirko and Pietro, and that was fine too.

Next, he figured he should call Haley, but he shrank at the idea of recounting the malicious destruction the Monks had wrought in his home—he couldn't talk about it right now, especially to someone who would feel sorry for him. He didn't need the kind of sympathy that could provoke his emotions. He needed to make the bastard Monks pay. A centrifuge in his mind began to spin out thoughts of where to get them alone and what to do to them. Such as, perhaps, visiting each in his respective abode and using his hammer to pulverize their fingertips, one by one, the way they'd done the sax's mother-of-pearl keys. Viscerally, the idea pleased him. Rationally, he acknowledged that they probably wouldn't open the door to him. In that case, he could follow them home separately from the Hairy Monk, and, in the shadows of one of the backstreets near the church Saint-Étienne-du-Mont, whale into them so that they would have to crawl home.

If they didn't take the metro, that is. Jean-Marc, no doubt, often walked home since he lived in the *quartier* Mouffetard; and Jeremy could plot out, street by street, the Monk's probable route: from rue de la Harpe up to rue des Écoles, and over to rue Descartes. From there, Jeremy would drag the fucker into short, narrow, rundown rue St.-Étienne-du-Mont and give him the thrashing he deserved. Renaud, on the other hand, would probably take the bus or metro to Gobelins in the Thirteenth. However, if Jeremy could follow him, then slip into his building behind him, maybe something could be accomplished.

He shook himself with curiosity: his thinking seemed to be progressing toward the analytical, away from the kind of spontaneous passionate rage that had come and gone when he fought his cousin Walter. He rolled his tense shoulders, frowning to himself with unease.

During the remainder of the week, before he and Haley left for Belgium, Jeremy's hostility knotted into a tangle of anxiety and moroseness. He made daily visits to rue de la Harpe. Not to confront the Monks—that would have to be done privately—but to get a glimpse of Jean-Marc and Renaud through the windows of The Hairy Monk. He'd gone beyond assigning random, wild maniacal expressions to the two as he pictured and re-pictured them mutilating his father's saxophone. He needed to look at their faces, see how they acted *now*; whether they dared still sport those prancing-dick grins of theirs, especially that clown Renaud.

Each day as he strode past the windows and looked through the door, he spotted Al, though not the Monks. Jeremy tried arriving at different times, even planting himself on the terrace of the café across the street where he could see the two coming. But they didn't appear. Perhaps he would have to follow them from their buildings.

Al never noticed Jeremy when he poked his head through the Hairy Monk's doorway. The Monks' spindly friend went about his business behind the bar as if nothing had happened. Not that Jeremy suspected his involvement in the break-in; Al could even be in the dark about his friends' perverted act of revenge. But Jeremy doubted it.

And yet, when he recalled that last conversation with Al, during the chaotic night of the Monks' arrest, when Al had called, desperate to see if Jean-Marc and Renaud had made it safely to Jeremy's place...when Jeremy recalled his frantic voice...well, the hot steam of his anger underwent a slight change of pressure—the return of a sense of guilt. Something, that when he went home, left him sitting on his bed in semi-paralysis, staring at the floor in a trance of indecision as he imagined the martyred corpse under the bed. Afternoons of funereal vigil, in which he was loath to look at the victim in the battered coffin.

Then, one noontime as he stalked past The Hairy Monk, Jeremy started at the sight of the perpetrators themselves. He passed the window then pivoted to retrace his steps, feeling an unexpected numbness come over him. The Monks were poring over their newspapers, occasionally reaching blindly for their cups or cigarettes. They sat slouched at a table right across the glass from him, and Jeremy stood rooted in silent fascination.

Did he want them to glance up so he could peer murderously into their alarmed eyes? Did he wish to simply startle them, or go further and mouth a silent but clear threat through the glass—*I'll fucking kill you.* He didn't know which direction his drive for revenge was now taking. He could only feel that curious numbness holding his rage in check, keeping him from banging his fist on the window to jolt the Monks into quaking attention. He waited a few long seconds more, gripped by the mystery of how he would react if the Monks raised their eyes. But they continued their placid reading, and Jeremy at last walked on. He didn't know what he wanted to do, and that troubled him in a different way.

Jeremy didn't leave for Belgium without calling on Louise Cholot, who received him for their habitual tea. She looked fit, with a glow that led Jeremy to surmise she was spending more time outdoors since the weather had cooled a bit. She listened eagerly to a tweaked version of Stefania's association with Gruber. "So it *was* a settling of accounts going back to Italy," she pronounced in a semi-satisfied tone. "But you say this Italian investigator Gruber didn't want *her*..."

"No," he affirmed, "Gruber was investigating her acquaintance, a rather sketchy individual named Mario." At this point, Jeremy had no choice but to give Mirko a pseudonym and refer to him as *sketchy*, what with the stakes involving the French vis-à-vis the Italian security services. He couldn't risk the former getting the slightest whiff of the latter and Stefania's role in the embroilment. "Stefania was safe and well when I found her at Gruber's," he told Madame. "He only needed her help in locating Mario. He wouldn't say what he wanted with him."

Louise cocked her head wryly. "Seems Stefania has strange acquaintances."

"Yes," Jeremy said, his eyes and voice even. "As a result, I've put the whole lot of them behind me."

To his slight discomfort, Louise continued to study him, a shade of a smile in her intelligent eyes. No doubt she suspected more than he had revealed, though her impeccable manners kept her curiosity at bay.

"Yet you still have an air of malaise about you," she said with feeling. "I noticed it when you walked through the door. Almost as though you've suffered a loss."

His eyes shifted away but she pressed on: "Might Stefania still have a claim on your feelings...?"

Jeremy met her eyes with an uncertain frown. Time to end the mystique of Stefania, his involvement with her having been quixotic at best. Louise was on to something, however. He *had* suffered a loss, and suddenly he felt like speaking about it—with someone who didn't know all of his baggage, someone who knew him but would maintain a respectful distance.

"Not Stefania," he said. "But you do seem to have guessed something. You're aware I work at Le Prince Blue Note..."

"*Bien sûr*. Creative cocktail master and jazz aficionado!" Her enthusiasm was sincere. "I really must go back there sometime."

"My father's picture is on the wall in the bar," Jeremy continued. "They respect him there, from when he played at Le Tabou and other jazz clubs in the fifties and early sixties."

Louise bent forward in interest, her legs gracefully crossed. And so he told the story of the blacklistings, his father unable to keep solid work in America, Walt's sympathy for
communism stemming from the fascist slaughter he had witnessed firsthand during the war in Europe, the partisans and resistance fighters he had met and befriended, the renewal of several of those friendships upon returning to France.

Alas, making a living and supporting a family was not easy, he went on to explain. As Louise knew well, France, like the rest of Europe, was still in economic tatters for many long years after the war. So they returned to America, where communist-bashing had not ended, nor had the financial situation much improved for the Winters family.

Skipping over Walt's infidelities and his own youthful difficulties, Jeremy got straight to the heart of the matter: Walt Winters' leap to suicide, which had stunned both family and friends. Who could understand it? Certainly not Jeremy.

"I guess you had to be in his shoes," he uttered to Madame, also omitting that he had been the one to discover his father in that chilling state of finality.

Louise had listened gravely. Her sage comment: "Suicide defies human reason, my friend, and loved ones in their grief and incomprehension are tempted to feel guilty over it. Which, as tempting as it can be, is also irrational and very destructive. Remain on guard against it, Jeremy, even though twenty years have passed."

She gets it, Jeremy thought, as if he had indeed related all of the family's turmoils. He went on to tell of the break-in at his flat and the destruction of Walt's tenor saxophone.

"It was the most important thing I had left of his," he concluded with stoic effort.

"And I imagine it was like losing your father all over again," Madame said quietly.

He looked up from studying his hands and nodded.

"And you probably feel that you never really knew your father..."

Right again.

"Well, that's another thing you mustn't feel guilty about. You were only fourteen and none of us can know our parents until we've completely grown up—and that can take several lifetimes," Louise added with a sympathetic twinkle in her eye. Jeremy returned a grateful smile.

At the door, as he took his leave, and after he and Louise had exchanged kisses on the cheeks, he suddenly hugged her. Warm and tanned and firm with wisdom, she felt to him, and he appreciated his beating heart against hers. When he released her, she didn't seem in the least surprised at his gesture. She pressed her hand to his cheek. "You'll get through this," she said, in a tone rich with solidarity and encouragement.

Chapter 25

The martyred saxophone continued to lie under the bed in eternal sleep, while Jeremy, day by day, managed to attain snatches of peace of mind. Didier had helped him haul away the shattered television and shredded punching bag. Though the police report had been taken care of, an officer later contacted Jeremy with follow-up questions. When asked about possible motives for the vandalism to his domicile, Jeremy continued to feign ignorance.

On the eve of his and Haley's departure for Belgium he still felt that his silence about the crime made sense. Although he had ceased conjuring up images of intricate revenge against the Monks, he would never go through normal channels and report their break-in; that would only fling open the gates to an uncomfortable investigation of his RG activities. And the various French security and intelligence services enjoyed their respective independence and privacy.

As he packed his suitcase, his gaze flickered occasionally to the dark gap between his bedspread and the floor, the ghostlike sax pushed far under the bed— *out of sight, and, perhaps, out of mind for a couple of weeks?*

When he finished packing he sat down with a cup of tea and scanned the *Le Parisien*. Over two weeks and still no mention of an explosion at the Mitterrand library worksite, or anywhere else for that matter. It seemed he had reasoned correctly about Stefania calling things quits. At least he could leave on vacation with a clear mind as far as that was concerned.

Jeremy and Haley retreated to Belgium by train just as another heat wave was expected to roll into Paris. They settled into their hotel room in Brussels and the next day took the day train to Bruges. Sitting at an outdoor café in the vast Market Square, surrounded by gothic and gabled Flemish architecture, fondled by cool breezes fluttering down from the North Sea, Haley and Jeremy sipped the beers Jeremy enthusiastically selected for them. But while Haley relished the view, a pesky thought buzzed back into Jeremy's mind, one he had batted away before leaving Paris. *Might the Monks come back for a second round of mayhem while he was gone?* Highly unlikely, he reconfirmed to himself, as little was left to demolish. *Unless they wanted to go full out and torch the place.* He shooed the ridiculous fly away; a fire would endanger the entire building, everyone in it, and the Monks had never expressed attitudes anywhere near that diabolical, or ambitious, for that matter. They were nothing but pathetic delinquents.

For the most part Jeremy was able to let himself go in Belgium: lose himself in the pleasure of showing Haley the sights, in dining on mussels and fries washed down with strong Belgian ale, in making carefree love in a foreign hotel. Still, at unpredictable times, that lone fly would return to pester him. Such as the afternoon he and Haley were motoring tranquilly through Bruges's canals on their boat tour. The wind turned chill, and as he sat gazing at the ancient, vine-covered stone bridge ahead of them, he was suddenly reminded of the numbness and paralysis he fell prey to while glaring at the Monks through their café window. *What must he ultimately do about the two? He had to take some action.* The harrying reminder left his face frozen in semi-rictus, and Haley looked at him with a slight frown.

"Is something wrong?"

Jeremy turned to her, his face slowly relaxing. Would he ever feel up to telling her about the Monks' savage coup?

"No, nothing," he said, injecting deliberate cheer into his voice. "I'm just amazed at the design of that pinkish brick building we just passed. The way you could dock your boat next to it and enter right through the red door."

Yes, things were idyllic here, as they motored gently through narrow waters depicted in oil paintings hundreds of years ago. Houses with their roofs grazed by the leaves of arching tree boughs, their bases lapped by lulling little waves. He tried to impose this tranquility on the blaze for retribution flaring once more inside him. *Keep the fire banked*, he ordered himself. *Deal with it later.*

The little sightseeing boat chugged on, with Jeremy and Haley sending each other respectful smiles colored with faint curiosity, before returning their gazes to their enchanting surroundings.

They both loved exploratory walks and the next day they scoured the city of Brussels. With a guidebook he'd bought, Jeremy led them to alcoves of significant culture he hadn't known existed. He and Haley agreed to split the hotel bill, though Jeremy insisted on paying for dinners and the Belgian beers he took pride in proposing, while she paid for lunches. When she questioned the financial fairness of the deal he responded, "In the evening I should pay, like in Paris; it may seem old-fashioned but it makes me feel more comfortable." Haley returned a fond smile and they made a further step toward working out the mechanics of their relationship.

Then, one afternoon, when they were sitting on the terrace of a café at Brussels' Mont des Arts, Haley asked for the latest about the Monks.

"Released from jail," Jeremy stated in a level voice, adding a shrug of one shoulder. "No evidence on them, it turns out."

He was gazing at the city's giant outdoor clock whose base arched over a street accessing the Mount and its several museums. The clock's elaborate stone façade included figurine soldiers that spun out from gilded niches at the striking of the hour. The spectacle had delighted Jeremy from boyhood and for now his eyes remained purposefully fixed on the clock.

Haley was watching him. "Then you must feel better now that they're free."

"Mm." Jeremy gave his neutral murmur without shifting his gaze. He wished it were twenty minutes later so the clock's show would begin.

"So the hunt for the bombers must still be on ..." said Haley.

Jeremy returned a placid expression. "I'm sure it is," he answered in all sincerity. As Haley indulged in further speculation about who the true culprits might be, he stayed mostly quiet, offering his take on the logic of her suggestions but proposing none of his own. Finally he diverted the discussion to where they would dine this evening. "A Flemish restaurant I hope you'll like," he said. "We'll eat late, then take a nighttime stroll through the Grand-Place. Oh, and before we go back to the hotel we'll pick up our train tickets for Antwerp and Louvain. And while we're at it, the tickets to Namur. Which reminds me, I'd better call my mother. She'll be put out if she doesn't know the exact hour we get in."

Haley listened, her head ever so slightly atilt; an inquisitive glint remained in her eye that Jeremy felt had nothing to do with their travel plans.

He chose to ignore it. "And don't mention the Monks to her," he ordered gently.

"I wouldn't think of it." For an instant Haley's lips remained parted and through them Jeremy heard a subtle intake of breath. He expected more questions...instead her chin dipped and she communicated a knowing smile. "I *do* understand, Jeremy. For the longest time I kept my grandmother in the dark about my involvement with the CIA." She paused, a delicate hesitation in which her eyes narrowed to a slight frown. "How much does your mother know about your other...um...troubles...?

Jeremy's brows rose in question.

"The history with your cousin, I mean..." Haley's cheeks colored, her smile was awkward.

"She knows it all," Jeremy said. "And I have to say she supported me once she got over the initial shock of the situation."

The shock had been profound, with Béatrice shedding desperate tears over the telephone when she learned her son was in jail; that he had sent his cousin Walter to the hospital in critical condition. It had been the hardest conversation of Jeremy's life, revealing that crime of passion to his mother—his terrifying loss of control. He feared she would have a nervous breakdown. Instead she had offered to book a flight to Virginia to occupy his corner in court. But he couldn't bear facing her, the grief he'd caused her, his shame. He declined, assuring her of his lawyer's good judgment that, given the fight had been mutually instigated, Jeremy would be charged with a misdemeanor and serve minimal incarceration time. So, in the end, she had offered to console his fractured spirit, and perhaps her own, somehow: by helping to bring the saxophone back to him.

The latter was what Jeremy confided to Haley. "She intervened with Walter's family. And without that..." Jeremy halted. He had almost said: *without that, the saxophone wouldn't be sitting safely in my flat as we speak...*

"Without that," he resumed softly, "I wouldn't have got it back."

Haley smiled warmly. "At least now it has a good home."

Jeremy gave a mechanical nod, his face a mask whose gaze returned to the scenery.

"It's been months since I've seen him and I've no idea what he's been getting up to," Béatrice Winters informed Haley about her son.

Maman's style of banter, reflected Jeremy, one that preserved a haughty distance since she avoided both his and Haley's eyes.

Haley expressed a polite little laugh and sipped her coffee, as she and Jeremy sat at the table of Béatrice's gleaming tiled kitchen.

"*Work*—that's what I've been up to, *Maman.*" He couldn't help responding to the bait, turning a thin yet indulgent smile on his mother.

Once more avoiding eye contact, Béatrice gave a long-suffering nod. Her dark eyelashes fluttered playfully against her pale complexion, however, and the image complemented the cheery, flower-patterned dress she wore. Her hair had aged naturally grey though she kept it full and teased. "Jeremy still doesn't understand a parent's constant worry," she tittered, still addressing Haley.

Jeremy shook his head inwardly and reserved comment. Haley looked awkward at being subjected to this female-commiseration game and he didn't want to cause her additional embarrassment. Plus, he doubted she perceived the serious *lack of humor* floating barely below the surface of Béatrice's banter; that she lived with recurring anxiety that her son might once more do something drastic enough to land him in jail. Needless to say he wouldn't be informing *Maman* about the break-in and the destruction of the saxophone. She might fear him capable of...

He shook himself and returned his gaze to the two women. He looked forward to getting them all out of the house.

And so went the three-and-a half-day visit, replete with daily outings to the Walloon countryside, Jeremy driving his mother's Renault. "Belgium actually has more Dutch than French speakers," he informed Haley.

"But we got along fine speaking French in Brussels," she said. "That's all I heard. And it's neat how they say *septante* for the number seventy, instead of *soixante-dix* like in France."

"And *nonante* as well," Béatrice added, regarding the number ninety. "Much more sensible, although we do say *quatre-vingts* for eighty, instead of *huitante*. I confess I don't know why."

Exposed to both usages all his life, Jeremy offered no opinion on numbers in French versus Belgian-French, and instead resumed the original discussion. "Brussels is actually in Flanders, though it's true that it now has more French than Dutch speakers. Partly due to immigration, partly because the European Community is headquartered in Brussels, and French, along with
English, is an official language of the institutions." He really did enjoy his role as tour guide, smiling off and on as he drove through the hilly green land, dotted with crops and cows and small towns with steepled churches.

From the backseat Haley asked, "In addition to French and English, do you speak Dutch, Madame Winters?"

"No, dear. Dutch wasn't studied here in Wallonia when I was a girl," said Béatrice. She might have intended to sound matter-of-fact, but her tone hinted a defensive prejudice before she changed the subject. "By the way, did Jeremy point out the Walloon parliament building when he showed you Namur's historical center?"

"He did, but my favorite sight was the citadel overlooking the river."

"The Flemish and Walloon cultures don't tend to mix much," Jeremy felt obliged to explain. "Once you count the German-speaking minority, Belgium's got five different levels of government. Each group tends to be concerned with its own."

"Yes, ours is actually an artificial state." Béatrice turned to the backseat. "It's a younger nation than the United States, Haley."

"Mm," Haley mused, nodding her head. After a moment she asked, "Do you miss things about America, Madame Winters?"

Innocent and inquiring as Haley's question was, Jeremy cleared his throat and hooked her gaze in the rearview mirror. His slight frown caused her to return a contritely crinkled brow. She knew Béatrice's experience in America had not always been wonderful, especially as the wife of a Communist sympathizer, not to mention as a widow who'd lost her husband to suicide.

Yet Béatrice appeared unfazed. "Of course, dear. But once a foreigner, always a foreigner. Naturally I feel more at home here." Then she promptly tapped Jeremy's arm. "When we get to Liège we'll stop immediately for a refreshment in a café."

But Béatrice didn't always handle things blithely. The second evening of their visit, after his mother had gone to bed, Jeremy confided as much to Haley as they sat in the living room speaking in low voices.

"She may *seem* offhanded, but she's a closet worrier.

You might hear her complain about the roof before we leave. Nothing's wrong with it, I've been up there twice to check and she got a professional to do the same."

"She's a woman on her own," Haley said. "Give her a break. *We* live in apartments and only have to ring the concierge if something goes wrong."

"True," Jeremy granted. "Sorry she's so puritanical, though, putting us in separate bedrooms." To be precise, Haley had got the spare bedroom and Jeremy was relegated to the sofa in Béatrice's tiny sewing room.

"My grandmother would have done the same," Haley said. "Anyway, I wouldn't feel comfortable sleeping in the same bed with you after just meeting your mother."

"Agreed." Briefly pinching her chin with his thumb and forefinger, Jeremy grinned at Haley and joked, "Be on your toes, though, about swearing or obscenities. She can't tolerate any of it."

Haley pulled a face, as if to say *Do you really think I'd let fly a raft of "putains" and "merdes" in front of your mother?*

He got the message and chuckled. "So far is there *anything* you don't like about Béatrice?"

Refusing to be drawn in, Haley cast him an ironic smile. "Your mother's very hospitable, and that's what counts with me."

"True," he said with a little sigh. "She's even given up daily Mass while we're here."

"Well, if she wants to go on Sunday I think we should accompany her."

"We're leaving Sunday."

"Not till the afternoon."

Jeremy knew Haley had been raised Catholic like himself, but in Paris she'd never mentioned attending Mass. More of Haley's good manners concerning Béatrice and her hospitality, he thought; and reciprocity. He couldn't fault that. Rather, he was beginning to feel a tad immature with his complaints about his mother. Béatrice was kind to Haley and he greatly appreciated that. All the same, he wanted to distinguish himself from his mother and her irritating ways, particularly now, with mother and son on display side by side for Haley's review. And he felt slightly vindicated in this when during dinner, on the eve of their departure, Béatrice made a derisory comment about Flemish cooking.

"Beer stew—how quaint," was her response to Jeremy's praise of the excellent lunch he and Haley had consumed in the Flemish city of Bruges.

Jeremy countered her calmly. "I know you don't like beer, *Maman*, but they used a delicious dark ale to steep the beef and vegetables in." He then reminded her of a similar stew made in Wallonia.

"Unfortunately even we're not immune to imitating," was Béatrice's final word.

And, the final word for everyone. Haley hadn't offered a comment and Jeremy considered it wise to fall silent as well.

On the subject of Sunday Mass, Béatrice was adamant that Haley and Jeremy sleep in. "I'll go to church early and be home before you two are even up. Your train's not until four so I'll have time to treat you to a nice lunch. I'd like Haley to try La Bouche Allègre." She turned a gracious smile on her. "It's a restaurant in Namur's historic center with photos of Paris' ornamental balconies. I thought you might find it interesting considering the book you're translating."

Haley assured her she would, and Jeremy, perhaps for the first time during their visit, nodded his unreserved approval of Béatrice.

On the train home Haley summed up the delights of their ten-day journey: the exploration of a country brand new to her, its serendipitous sights, and last but not least, the overall satisfying visit to Béatrice Winters in Namur. "She really does have your happiness at heart, Jeremy."

Jeremy squeezed her hand, enjoying their bit of privacy as they sat side by side in the train's two-seat configuration, with non-paralleled seats across the corridor. Haley sat next to the window, and as on the Paris-to-Brussels leg of their journey he enjoyed watching her soak up the scenery, this time that of the return route. He felt more content than he'd expected with their sojourn at Béatrice's. Haley and his mother had gotten on pretty well. He had carried off his dual goal of traveling with Haley and looking in on Béatrice. Now, if only she wouldn't proceed to nag him about his relationship with Haley.

As the train continued its gentle rock and rattle on its rails, and the green of the countryside marched inexorably in reverse, Jeremy finally sank in his seat and rested his head back. He and Haley would be in Paris by seven p.m. Then they would go their separate ways home. He opened his eyes, the thought filling him with that particular form of emptiness that could turn oppressive. Haley would resume her translating job with Madame Kérouac, and he...

He...Angst gripped him as once more the faces of the Monks muscled into his thoughts. There they dangled, like a couple of grubby coats waiting for him on the brass hooks in his entryway—reminding him to *do something*.

His dour stare was drilling the seatback in front of him when Haley's voice jerked him to attention.

"You've gone pensive again," she said with an irritated frown. "Now what's bothering you?"

He looked at her for an instant, shook his head, and flung out his palms. After dropping his hands in his lap and releasing a helpless sigh, he told her. He spared no details in describing the Monks' spree of violence, only avoiding reference to the banked fire for retribution within him. It helped that she sat next to him, that he could direct his eyes and purposely-monotone voice at the seat before him, and that his tone blended with the overall droning of the train.

When he finished his account he closed his eyes and accepted Haley's all-encompassing hug, her assurance of moral support. For the time being, he felt neither the welling of tears nor a flare-up of his desire for revenge. Just a welcome moment of serenity. He lifted his eyes to the window and gazed out at the green countryside, a sprig of hope in his heart. Yes, perhaps he could just let it all go...

Then, as his eyes returned to the seat in front of him, he felt a slight twitch of mood. Shifting his weight, he added to himself: *as long as I never catch sight of those bastards Jean-Marc and Renaud again.*

Chapter 26

The next day, back in Paris, Jeremy called Rébert. Time for the RG agent to make good on his promise in the matter of the work permit.

"Have a nice time in Belgium?" asked Rébert pleasantly.

"Always do." Jeremy's voice was low, his jaw working. *Time to get to the point.*

"Well, you might like this news: I've obtained permission to restore your fulltime work status..."

Jeremy breathed out and blinked hard; he sensed there was more.

"...The thing is, the deal's still contingent on your keeping your hand in with us."

Jeremy lifted the phone's base from the entryway table. "I see..." he said, placing a foot on the table's chair and resting the phone on his thigh.

"You'll be getting a raise, though."

"Yes, you've already mentioned that," Jeremy responded evenly. "How much?"

"You'll make enough to pay half your rent each month, or more, if the jobs keep coming."

"And they always seem to," said Jeremy with a wry smile. Not that he was disappointed. The situation might actually prove advantageous, since he foresaw no fulltime job prospects at the moment.

"So are we in agreement?" said Rébert.

"How can I say no?"

Rébert gave a brusque chuckle. "So let's get down to business, then. The new job is something you'll already find quite familiar. Remember our friends the Compagni?"

Jeremy set the phone back on the table and slowly sat down.

"Now," Rébert specified, "we'd like you to question Pietro Grimaldi."

After Jeremy hung up he sat in silence at the entryway table, his mind reeling with this new assignment. *Oh, he had experience*—Rébert was right about that. For once more the RG agent was instructing him to cozy up to someone in order to extract information. This time the target was Pietro, however, and it had taken all of half a second for the various snags involved to jump out at Jeremy. For one, Pietro had turned stubbornly uncommunicative of late, verging on antisocial during Jeremy's visit to him, as well as later on the phone. Then there was the second catch, which made the first one arguably a moot point; for the RG wanted to know one thing, and one thing only—where had Mirko Mazzini gone? And who was better placed than Pietro to provide the answer? That Jeremy knew that answer, knew it intimately, would make this new job a sticky challenge to say the least. What in hell could he report to Rébert?

It seemed Mirko was no longer living with Pietro, Rébert had duly informed Jeremy. And the RG must always keep on top of the various Compagni's whereabouts in France. Rébert himself had had no luck in questioning Pietro, who insisted Mirko had simply moved out without leaving a forwarding address. "Pretty strange, eh?" Rébert had said to Jeremy. "As close as those two are?" Jeremy could picture Rébert's virtual wink. "Anyway, now it's your turn to try to figure it out."

Pretty strange indeed. Mirko moving on without a forwarding address: why did Pietro say that to Rébert?

With deliberation Jeremy stood up and returned to the living room. He executed a few circular paces, his narrowed eyes tracing the scratches on the floor, then went to the open window and leaned onto its black railing. It was the 16th of August and the sun's position in
its seasonal cycle was clearly on the wane. Summer's brash and domineering light was easing up, the heat spells dwindling. Twilight approached earlier each day, gifting softer, cooler nights. Yes, the shifting season merited a bit of lazy meditation, and in letting his thoughts wander as he breathed in August's drier air, Jeremy came to a realization that brought a subtle smile to his lips. "Operation Pietro" might be easier than he'd thought, if he played it right.

He spent the day tidying up and ironing. Before his departure for Belgium he had gotten his framed photos and Gauguin print restored behind glass and back on the wall and bookshelf. He hadn't replaced the boom box yet, but, in compensation, the living room looked more spacious without it and the TV. Regarding television, for now he could go on muddling through without it. But music—well, he absolutely had to have it. His soul craved it—demanded it. As soon as Rébert handed over that promised fatter pay, he would go over to BHV and check out their selection of music devices. And speaking of music, when the moment proved favorable he would ask Pierre, manager of Le Prince Blue Note, about increasing his hours. He didn't want to abandon the jazz scene, and still harbored hopes of eventually netting a position booking gigs. As things stood, perhaps Pierre would let him come in to tend bar at six p.m. versus eight. The doors to the club opened at that hour, and even though the performance didn't start until nine, locals dropped in for aperitifs, lounging at the little round wooden tables next to the floor-to-ceiling windows that gave onto the boulevard Saint-Michel. As autumn approached and the club's habitués straggled back from vacation or retired from long days spent outdoors, demand might tick up, be it for an aperitif or a cocktail, or even a restorative cup of hot tea in the warm, intimate, wood-paneled bar. Jeremy would like to be the one to unlock the doors and welcome them in.

As he left the window to dress for work, his eyes performed another cursory inspection of his living room. Today, he had even vacuumed the furniture. As soon as he bought a new boom box he would invite Haley over. As much as his, her soul nourished itself on music, and he wanted the atmosphere in the flat to be as inviting as possible.

Now that vacation had ended, Haley would be busy at Madame Kérouac's the entire week. And Jeremy would have to plan how to start his assignment. Rébert had mentioned no time constraints regarding the job. He was a professional who understood the ticklish dance, the drawn-out maneuvering required in obtaining sensitive information. And this understanding would play to Jeremy's advantage.

His first move was to call Georges Sauvebelle, an acquaintance of both his and Christophe's. As much as Christophe, Georges would know what kind of wind might be blowing through the communist community of Paris: whether a rally was in the making or a festival, or even a house party. Flipping to Georges's number in his address book, Jeremy felt his stomach sink as he passed over Christophe's name. It would be a long while, if ever, before he might again feel comfortable in asking a favor of his oldest friend in Paris. If friends they still remained. Judging from their last phone conversation and Christophe's sincere, almost humble plea for information about Stefania, an ember of hope still burned.

Jeremy rang Georges, indulged in preliminary pleasantries, then moved on to the subject at hand.

"Hmm," Georges drew out, in his ever-reflective way. "Don't know of any rallies coming up, but there's a get-together next Saturday night at the Club Écarlate. Some of us sons of the resistance fighters decided it's time for an impromptu little reunion. You're welcome to join us; you know the *Club Écarlate*—rue Linné, near the Jardin des Plantes?

Jeremy did.

"We haven't seen you around in a while," Georges commented.

"Yes, it'll be nice to catch up." And Jeremy meant it. The various sons and daughters of those with a leftist bent, who had fought the Nazis, remained bonded by both camaraderie and nostalgia for their fathers' war. "What time will you get started on Saturday?"

"Around ten."

"So you'll still be there when I get off work about eleven-thirty..."

"Without a doubt, *mon vieux*. Drop by when you're done."

"I'm looking forward to seeing you, Georges, it's been a long time."

Jeremy had always liked the gangling, good-natured Georges Sauvebelle. Bespectacled, often rumpled-looking, he was an ardent student of communist and socialist history, his father having fought the Fascists like Christophe's, Stefania's, and Mirko's fathers.

Like Pietro's too. Before ending the call Jeremy asked, "Do you think Pietro Grimaldi might join us?"

"Pietro? Very likely, especially now that he's living alone. You know, Mirko's gone..."

Jeremy shifted the phone to his other ear, intoning a veiled "I heard..."

"Pietro thinks he's been kidnapped by Italian spies, but who knows?" Georges added with a bemused chuckle.

"It *would* be remarkable..." Jeremy agreed.

After he hung up he went to the kitchen and made himself a strong cup of coffee. He took it to the living room and sat on the sofa from which he was vaguely content to see no dust rise after his thorough vacuuming.

So Pietro had an idea about the Italian conspiracy and was spreading the word. Who knew how many of his fellow Communists believed him? And did he suspect Stefania's involvement in the kidnapping of Mirko? Jeremy took a sip of coffee and tried to cobble together his last two conversations with Pietro—the one in the Compagni's flat and the phone call he made to Pietro the day after, on the Bicentennial. Pietro surely knew Mirko was on the run when he and Jeremy had talked, but had he by then figured out that Mirko was fleeing *Italians* and not some French security service, which had been Stefania's previous fear?

The rest of the week passed in a stream of grey clouds and whipping winds that ushered in a series of aggressive rainstorms. One night, on his way to the metro station from work, rain-ridden gales lashed every which way, turning Jeremy's short, compact umbrella inside out, into the shape of a distorted trumpet, its ribbing bent and utterly useless. When his metro train pulled in at Place de la République, he stuffed the broken umbrella in the trash. But instead of exiting the station, which would require another five-minute, drenching walk to his building, he decided to make another change and wait five more minutes for the Line Three train. It would take him only one stop further but save him four minutes of deluge. He accomplished this last leg with his sodden head down, eyes alert for murky puddles, while a couple of late-night pedestrians trotted past, jostling him as they squinted in the dark. All in all, it took him over half an hour to get home and dry off.

And his mood didn't improve the next day, his day off, when Haley declined his offer to go to dinner. *Too much to do*—she would be staying on this evening at Madame Kérouac's. At this point he looked forward to Saturday and his night out at the Club Écarlate—the "Scarlet" Club, with its promise of both socializing and the kind of quirky work he was becoming accustomed to. For he was determined to discover what Pietro knew about the kidnapping, and if the Italian showed up, Jeremy would consider phase one of his plan commenced.

Like Le Prince, L'Écarlate was a cellar club, only its specialty was old-style *musette,* a music that blossomed from an accordion player sitting on a wooden chair in the corner of the basement room. As he fingered his notes the seventyish man smiled euphorically, stretching wide the bellows of his instrument; and in the smoky, yellowish-lit space Jeremy found it hard to distinguish whether the old musician was a permanent feature of the club or had merely dropped in to offer his endearing tunes while humbly collecting coins in a hat. But Jeremy could see neither a hat nor the glint of coins in the accordion case—if so, he would have walked over and contributed a couple of francs.

Instead he moved on to where he did catch sight of three wooden tables pushed together in a line. Georges Sauvebelle and another Communist son of a *Maquis* fighter sat on one side. Across from them Jeremy identified two others he was acquainted with, and next to them at the end, and to Jeremy's satisfaction, sat Pietro. No appearance of Christophe or Stefania, and that was a relief, for he had worried how the two would affect the group's dynamics in terms of both himself and Pietro.

As Georges called him over and indicated the empty seat he had saved next to him, Jeremy briefly locked eyes with Pietro. He still wore the guarded expression Jeremy had last seen on his face. Now that he had nothing more to hide regarding Mirko, he might have shed his snit, thought Jeremy. Or maybe it was his way of grieving the loss of his companion. That thought made Jeremy assume a sympathetic smile as he shook hands with him and the other sons of the resistance before sitting down.

Having spoiled himself for ten days straight with rich Belgian ale on his trip, he ordered a Kronenbourg and entered into the camaraderie and chatter of youngish men who revered heroic fathers, some of those living, others buried on the field. And one father persecuted to death by fascist foes on another continent. That was the unvarying refrain of the young Communists' tribute to Jeremy's father, and as his thoughts flashed on the martyred saxophone still lying under his bed, he accepted the salute with renewed appreciation.

Across the room, "Sous le ciel de Paris" ("Under Paris Skies"), "La vie en rose," old standard after old standard rose from the big red accordion, which held its own against shrill female voices and competing male voices in the smoke-thickened room. A few older couples, skilled in javas and two-steps, danced to the spirited rhythms. The club encapsulated wartime and post-war nostalgia for many and sundry a patron, especially now that the war had been over for almost forty-five years.

While indulging in his share of jawing, Jeremy kept one eye on Pietro. The Italian was engrossed in a conversation about volatile Eastern Europe. He brushed his black wavy hair off his tightly corrugated brow, adding more drama to the intenseness of his dark eyes. "You all know I'm no Stalinist," he stressed, "but those idealistic Poles and Hungarians better be careful what they wish for." His companions frowned and nodded, some thoughtfully, others adamantly. Pietro hadn't mentioned Mirko or the Italian spies, Jeremy noted; most likely those at the table already knew his astounding claim, or they had talked about it before Jeremy arrived. Tomorrow he would report this evening's encounter to Rébert—his first official contact with the target. He would initiate a few others to make things look as if he were truly inquiring after Mirko's whereabouts. And, more urgently, throughout this patient process, he would glean what Pietro knew about Stefania and Mirko's Bicentennial escapade.

As the party broke up towards two a.m. Jeremy rose and shook a stone-faced Pietro's stiff hand. "Good to see you—we should get together more often." Step one completed.

Chapter 27

Ideally Jeremy would have waited a little longer to report to Rébert, to simulate the extensive process of real investigative work. But with the news of Mirko's kidnapping already in circulation, he knew he needed to act before Rébert found out through another source. He would have to tread cautiously, both in his approach to Rébert and with Pietro.

Rébert scoffed at the news which Jeremy reported over the phone. "You're joking—I'm supposed to believe that some Italian spies swooped in here and snatched up Mirko?"

Carefully, Jeremy countered this. "Not necessarily...but that's what Georges Sauvebelle heard. I'm skeptical myself, as is Georges."

"*Sauvebelle...*" repeated Rébert, and Jeremy could picture the RG agent scratching his chin. "From what I know he's a serious type. Still, it sounds like an urban myth."

"I agree, though I haven't talked to Pietro Grimaldi about it yet."

"He should be the first you make contact with."

"I have—I just need to question him alone."

"You do that; and continue to ask around. Christophe Branger—he's close to Mirko...Stefania Perin too. They might know something."

"Right," Jeremy obliged mechanically.

"This kidnapping story might be a cover for something else, so keep sniffing around."

Jeremy agreed to do so.

After hanging up he sat brooding for a while. At least in alerting Rébert about the "alleged" kidnapping, he had stolen a march on the rumor-mill, and it suited him that Rébert considered the claim preposterous. Jeremy would let things play out accordingly, cull what he could from Pietro: most importantly, what exactly Pietro knew about the Italian agents and Stefania. From there, if absolutely needed, he would extend some kind of censored version to Rébert. The whole process was beginning to make Jeremy uneasy. Even more so, the thought that Rébert might pull Pietro in for official interrogation, with the threat of deportation.

He needed to get to Pietro as quickly as possible.

He called him. But instead of Pietro's live voice, Jeremy was greeted with a tinny recording. He couldn't distinguish if it was Pietro's or Mirko's voice, but one of them had obviously purchased a modern answering machine—a *répondeur*. The announcement was formal, assuring the caller he had indeed reached the Compagni's number, and suggesting the caller leave a message.

Jeremy hung up. These machines were mainly used in professional offices, Pietro and Mirko being the only people he knew who owned one. Yet who was it that had recently told Jeremy he himself should get a *répondeur*? *Al*, from the Hairy Monk, Jeremy grimly confirmed to himself—two nights before the Bicentennial, when the barman had called to appeal for help for the Monks. Jeremy felt an unpleasant lurch in his stomach, before deciding to ring Pietro again and leave a message.

He mulled over just what to recite to the machine and decided on a neutral, gadget-appropriate greeting, followed by, "There's something important you should know."

After leaving the message he hung up with an annoyed sigh. Now it was Pietro's turn to make a move.

Three days later, Jeremy was still waiting for the Italian to return his call. In his message he had even specified Pietro call back in the morning, when Jeremy was sure to be home. After the fourth day Jeremy called again, only to have to deal with the irritating *répondeur* once more. He repeated his message, this time substituting "urgent" for "important."

Three more days passed with no results. It was already the beginning of September, and when Jeremy got together with Haley for dinner he vented his frustration.

"You know," she replied, as they were sitting at the counter of the Drugstore Matignon restaurant, "I've heard of people using answering machines to screen their calls." She took a bite of bread, her inquisitive eyes on Jeremy. "Maybe this Pietro doesn't *want* to talk to you."

By now, given his revelations regarding the Monks, Haley knew he worked part time for a French intelligence service; still, he could not (per Rébert), nor did he desire, to reveal details about the Pietro job, only that he was tasked with helping to locate an Italian political refugee from the 1970s who had now gone missing. A fellow he knew from communist circles that dated back to his father's time in Paris.

"Yes," he agreed, "he's probably *screening* his calls."

"Have any idea why he doesn't want to talk to you?" Haley asked.

He did: lingering guardedness concerning Mirko, continued despisal of Jeremy over his betrayal of Christophe with Stefania. Perhaps Pietro felt embarrassed about lying to Jeremy the day before the Bicentennial, when he'd insisted Mirko had left town to get away from the festivities. *Or*...might Pietro be the one who was now "out of town?"

As Jeremy distractedly mopped up sauce from his

piperade omelet with a piece of bread, he heard Haley ask again why Pietro might be avoiding him.

"Who knows?" he said, evading her eyes and popping the chunk of bread into his mouth. It had been over a week since he had seen Pietro at the Club Écarlate. And if he had run off for some reason? Jeremy felt his pulse tick up a notch. "I think I'll go straight to his flat early tomorrow morning," he said, more to himself than to Haley.

"Hopefully he'll answer his buzzer," said Haley, "since he won't answer his phone." Nonchalantly she added, "What time were you thinking of going over there?"

Jeremy didn't answer right away. He hadn't yet said anything, but he'd planned to invite Haley to his place tonight, had even done a spot of last-minute cleaning. Now he felt a surpassing urgency to meet Pietro face-to-face—Jeremy's standing with the RG depended upon it, not to mention the risk he was running at being exposed in the kidnapping affair. He had to find out what Pietro knew.

"I'd like to get to his place by seven," he said, "before he has a chance to go out."

"So you'll have to get up around..."

"Six."

"Then it might not be convenient for us to have a late night..."

With a sigh of regret Jeremy nodded. Inviting Haley to his place would have to wait. Along with their first night of intimacy since Brussels.

They agreed to make it an early evening. Jeremy searched Haley's gaze for signs of disappointment. He thought he caught one in the brief lowering of her eyes, though her tone when she spoke remained entirely understanding.

"How well do you know this Pietro guy?" she asked

with genuine interest.

"Not too well, he's a friend of a friend. But since I'm also acquainted with the man who lived with him, the one who's now gone missing, it helps—I can sympathize."

"Sympathize?" Haley wondered.

The waiter behind the counter arrived to clear away their plates and ask if they'd like dessert.

"Go on," Jeremy urged Haley. "Order the Charlotte aux poires, I know you love it."

She gave a little grin, and he told the waiter to bring two Charlottes.

"What do you mean by *sympathize*?" she asked again.

Jeremy considered the question and carefully weighed his response. He decided it couldn't hurt to mention the two Compagni's relationship, and said, "The two Italians are together—a couple."

"A gay couple," Haley construed matter-of-factly. "And both communist refugees?"

"Right."

"That could certainly be tough for them," she said, nodding thoughtfully.

"They've been together for about fifteen years."

"So they must really depend on each other...love each other as much as a regular couple."

"I imagine," Jeremy agreed. Maybe, in his grief, Pietro couldn't bring himself to talk about Mirko other than in righteous anger, a hardness and distance afforded by announcing he'd been kidnapped.

"What did these two do in Italy to have to flee to France?"

At this point Jeremy knew he had spoken enough about the case. Rébert would probably disapprove of his revealing the little he had. And, naturally, even with Haley he had to steer well away from the truth of the story.

He offered an apologetic frown. "I really can't go into that. It's confidential."

"Oh," said Haley, her voice on the downswing. He could now both hear and see disappointment in her. More, it seemed, than when he'd had to cancel the rest of the night with her.

"Sorry," he said, his frown deepening.

But her voice was already tilting up. "Well, I guess I *am* a little used to your secrets, your telling me things in your own time...*You know,*" she said, when Jeremy canted his head: "your past, your secret job, the Monks. And maybe there's more, but I won't insist."

He was finding it hard to read her, to distinguish what the lilt in her voice actually meant. "Haley," he said in frustration, "I really *can't* disclose certain things about my assignments, especially this one."

She gave a soft little laugh. "Then I'll just have to believe it's only your job that you're secretive about."

When he reached for her hand, he did so with a weak smile. Exactly *how* content she was with their relationship, he truly didn't know.

The next morning Jeremy rose before six and was down in the Temple metro station by six-twenty. On Line Three he traveled directly to Père Lachaise Cemetery, then walked a block further into the Twentieth Arrondissement to Pietro's building. It wasn't yet seven o'clock and he hesitated before ringing. Idly he gazed up at the modest façade of the building: the window railings and shutters needed varnishing, and some of the stucco was peeling. Still he judged the general area a decent place to live, with the renowned Père Lachaise Cemetery only two blocks away. Last spring he and Haley had made an outing to the woodsy, village-size cemetery, crisscrossed with cobbled paths flanked by chipped and tilting headstones as well as sculpted and statued tombs. The trees had been budding, so had their relationship.

As he stood waiting he again thought of last evening's conversation with Haley. When had she started to sense he was hiding things from her? Maybe after his abrupt departure the evening of the Bicentennial parade, or it could have easily started when he abandoned her in the taxi the night of the Opéra Bastille explosion. Concerning the latter he had come clean about his dealings with the Monks, whereas the excuse of a stomach problem the night of the Bicentennial...well, even he could recognize the feebleness of it in hindsight. Ideally it would be nice to have a relationship that wasn't pitted with secrets, like so many holes distancing people from each other. And yet certain of his RG jobs required just that. Perhaps his own personality did as well. After all, who in this world lives without secrets? As for giving Haley an edited version of the Bicentennial episode, he would rather not, for it would require lies. Lies and dancing around Stefania's role. He didn't regret his affair with her; it had served a purpose for each of them, they had enjoyed it, then had mutually agreed to put it behind them. He valued that kind of freedom and privacy. Certain things warranted keeping in separate compartments, in different worlds, whether they were work-related or otherwise. That was how he felt, and, perhaps, it explained why he didn't mind continuing to carry out Rébert's little jobs.

At last, when the minute hand on his watch reached seven, Jeremy pressed Pietro's buzzer. When no answer came he tried twice more. Nervously he waited, until finally he heard the click of the interphone, and a croaky "*Oui*?"

"Pietro, it's Jeremy."

"Christ, you've yanked me out of bed. What are you

doing here at this hour?"

Jeremy rolled his shoulders uneasily, feeling a flush of embarrassment at having woken Pietro. But at least he now knew the Italian had not taken flight. You never knew these days...

"I left a couple of messages for you," he said tentatively, "but I haven't heard back..."

"Oh..." came another croak.

"You *did* get them? I never know with these new machines..."

"Yeah, I would've called you back...but what's so important that you're on my doorstep at seven a.m.?"

Right, Jeremy said to himself, feeling slightly on the back foot. He could picture Pietro, jolted and disoriented by the persistent buzzer; scratching himself, rubbing his eyes, half-consciously untangling himself from the sheets to get to the interphone.

"I just need to talk to you," Jeremy said, his tone apologetic.

"About what? I'm not up for company this early."

"How about later on—it won't take long."

A crackly, grumpy sigh followed. "I'm busy all this week..."

Doing what? Jeremy wondered irritably. *You don't even work.* "Can't we just meet for a quick coffee? Really, there's something I'd like to talk to you about."

A pause ensued: either Pietro was thinking through his schedule or pondering how to continue stalling.

"What about this Saturday, around two?" When Jeremy didn't answer right away, Pietro added a grudging "If it works for you..."

It would have to, Jeremy complained to himself, though he agreed to meet Pietro at the Café Saint-Maur, roughly half way between both of their neighborhoods.

When Pietro hung up, Jeremy stood there for a moment, staring absently at the mute, paint-chipped interphone speaker. *Five more days*: by that time it would be the beginning of September—a new month, and, Jeremy hoped, one that would bring finality to this uniquely awkward RG assignment. Rébert would consider realistic the two weeks Jeremy had devoted to it, Jeremy would maintain that Mirko's kidnapping was a rumor, and Rébert could decide once and for all whether he believed it. If he didn't, Jeremy decided while heading back to the Père Lachaise metro station, just as well. Rébert could go on searching for Mirko on his own. Jeremy would have done his best.

He sighed and corrected himself: *No*, Rébert would probably think otherwise.

Chapter 28

With the arrival of September, Jeremy found a moment favorable for having a word with Pierre at Le Prince Blue Note. The club's manager seemed pleased to hear of Jeremy's attainment of fulltime work status, though he cautioned, "Let's see how the month goes; if we have a boost in customers, you'll be the first we give extra hours to."

Encouraged by the prospect Jeremy passed the news on to Haley, who congratulated him. "So you would almost be fulltime at the club," she said.

They were sitting on the sofa in his flat. They had dined on *choucroute royale* at Chez Jenny at Place de la République and were now sipping *génépi, a* digestive Jeremy kept on hand in his liquor collection. From his new boom box (purchased with Rébert's payment for the Monks job), placed on the table formerly occupied by the television, came the syncopated piano music of Duke Ellington.

"Or," Haley continued, "you could look for a fulltime day job."

"True..." Jeremy said after a slight hesitation, his voice distant in a speculative way. He felt good about Haley's first visit to his place. She had admired his Gauguin print, commented on the attractive post-war photo of his parents on the bookshelf, even remarked approvingly on a couple of the novels behind the photo— Camus's *L'Étranger* and Le Carré's *The Spy Who Came in from the Cold*. In short, she seemed to feel comfortable in his home and he didn't want to contradict her right out. So he finished his liqueur and casually added, "My current schedule's not bad—night work at the club, days free to pursue other things. Plus, I'm hoping to someday get a chance to book gigs for the club."

"That sounds super," Haley replied, setting her glass next to his on the table and snuggling against his shoulder. "Do you know how long it would take to get a position like that?"

"No..." he confessed, a quizzical lilt to his voice.

"But you like your days free..."

"I do," he said, glancing at her from the corner of his eye.

"So you can remain on call for the intelligence services..."

"It's been an okay job."

"Except for the Monks' arrest..."

The embers of resentment flared. Jeremy could feel their heat and shifted a fraction away from Haley so he could meet her square in the eyes. "That was no one's fault but their own. *They* made themselves a target with their persistent graffiti."

"Of course," she quickly agreed. Her gaze moved discreetly to the wall and Gauguin's green and burnt-orange Breton countryside. Then it returned to him. "I just wonder whether you might be setting yourself up for more of, well...the Monks' style of retaliation."

He observed her calmly now, then rose to fetch the bottle of *génépi*. "I wouldn't worry about that—I've already lost the only possession of real value to me." He sat down and offered the bottle to Haley. She declined, and he refilled his own liqueur glass. She had spared correcting him on the "loss" of the sax; after all, the broken, battered body still lay under his bed.

"What I meant," she said, "in terms of 'retaliation,' was harm to yourself, considering the element you

301

sometimes have to work with...I don't know about the case you're on now..."

"Don't worry yourself," he said with a dismissive little laugh. "I'm a boxer, remember? And now that the weather's cooler I'll probably get back to the gym."

"Right." Her smile was aloof, and he wondered whether deep down she disapproved of his boxing. And whether there might be more to her comment on his working for the intelligence services. She didn't even know which service employed him, and he hoped she wouldn't ask, for he was obliged to keep that confidential. Another secret...

Then again, he recalled her excitement in helping him identify the Bicentennial bombing targets. She enjoyed being involved in a mystery, no doubt about it; ten years ago she had been unofficially engaged by a spy service herself, though it had ended in the tragic death of her friend. Maybe she feared something similar in his future, or perhaps she just resented being excluded from his new assignment...as she had voiced at the counter of the Drugstore Matignon the last time they'd met: *having to get used to you hiding things from me.*

He could always ask her to clarify things, but he didn't want to risk an argument. He preferred the status quo for now: his apartment's soft lighting, the slow, pulsating jazz, the warm, loosening liqueur...the further intimacy he was counting on...

He slipped his arm around her and pulled her closer to him. "I love this song," he murmured of Ellington's "Long Time Blues."

"Mm, it *is* beautiful." Haley paused for a heartbeat. "But I'm mostly glad I'm listening to it with you. That you've finally let me into this part of your life." She indicated Jeremy's flat with a wave of her arm. "Listening to it by myself tonight would remind me of the loneliness of life." Jeremy looked deep into her eyes as she continued: "the solitude we all have to face, and that never goes away no matter what." Jeremy nodded, ever so knowingly. "Listen to the arrangement," Haley said. "It's haunting—bittersweet. Do you feel it, Jeremy?" Then she kissed him.

"*Bittersweet*," Jeremy echoed softly, taken by her plaintive tenderness. And indeed he did understand the music's mood, recalling something elegiac he had himself once perceived in it: a chorus of trumpets, a low growl heralding the arrival of early nightfall in winter; then the high voice of a clarinet. Although it relieved the trumpets, its notes were a lone, piercing plea in the darkness, a darkness that had already fallen outside Jeremy's apartment window. He closed his eyes and let the sweet melancholy soak into his marrow. Then he took Haley in a *frisson*-filled embrace.

The following Saturday, at one forty-five in the afternoon, Jeremy left the house for his two-o'clock rendezvous with Pietro at the Café Saint-Maur. After a ten-minute metro ride he was sitting in the café at the crossroads of avenue de la République and rue Saint-Maur, waiting. Pietro arrived twenty minutes later, greeted Jeremy with a cheery "*salut*," then, without excusing himself for being late, sat down and ordered a glass of hard Norman cider. Having already finished an espresso Jeremy joined him in a cider as well.

"It's autumn," Pietro declared with a wide smile: "apple time."

Jeremy granted a polite nod. Naturally, he had noticed it was autumn, and had spent a good part of his twenty-minute wait for Pietro in gazing out the window at the gleam of half-green, half-golden leaves of trees on the rue Saint-Maur. That is, when he wasn't worrying Pietro would stand him up.

"So what's up?" asked Pietro, taking a pack of

cigarettes from his pocket before slinging his jacket over the back of his chair. He extended the pack across the table. *Royale menthol*, the same cigarettes Jeremy used to smoke. He declined with a dutiful "*merci*." Resisting a smoke seemed to be getting easier as the months wore on.

The waiter arrived with the two glasses of cider, giving Jeremy a bit more time to gauge his approach to Pietro. He waited for the man to leave, then said, "We haven't had a chance to chat for some time...since I called you on Bastille Day..."

Pietro passed a hand through his hair, smoothing his black waves before lowering his hand to rub his chin; there was a recent-red nick there, as though he'd performed a hasty shave before clipping out the door. "Is that what's so important," he asked, checking his finger for traces of blood, "Bastille Day?" He flashed another smile, this time with wide, wondering eyes.

Jeremy went on, "That phone call I made to you on the fourteenth, do you remember? I said Mirko could be in trouble..."

Pietro's dark eyes flickered for an instant before settling with dispassion back on Jeremy.

"So now I've heard the rumor that Mirko's been kidnapped by Italians," Jeremy continued evenly. "And Georges Sauvebelle said it came from you..."

Pietro sat back and took a sip of his cider. "Mirko *was* kidnapped." He set the glass down with a clunk. "*Now*, are you telling me it could have been avoided if I'd listened to you? Are you here to say 'I told you so'?"

His voice had pitched higher, the defensive, irritable posture was back (or had never really left), and Jeremy needed to offset it. He took a strong gulp of his own cider. His nerves were *à fleur de peau*—at his skin's surface; he wanted to confront Pietro directly about his knowledge of the kidnapping plot but felt the Italian might retrench, shut down completely. He had to prompt him subtly. So he said in his most earnest voice, his gaze sympathetic, he hoped: "I only came here to find out the truth about the kidnapping. Not everyone believes it, but I don't think you'd make up something like that."

Pietro took a hard pull off his cigarette. As he released a long stream of smoke, he gave the cigarette a couple of taps against the rim of the plastic ashtray on the table. "And that's what's so urgent to you?" he asked, now focused on shaving the remaining ashes and rounding the tip of his cigarette.

Jeremy had to justify his concern. "You know," he began in a tentative voice, "I was worried that something sinister might happen to Stefania. Remember, in your flat, I mentioned that even Christophe was worried. I'm now thinking that the guy who was following her was Italian as well." Jeremy inhaled a silent breath then asked, "So, what all do you know?"

Casually, Pietro returned his gaze to Jeremy, looking him up and down with raised eyebrows as if Jeremy were a lab specimen he was about to dissect. At length he said," I know everything."

Like that insect, Jeremy began to squirm inside, waiting under Pietro's clinical regard. But Pietro offered nothing more, and so Jeremy broke the silence. "So is it true?" he asked. "There was an Italian plot to kidnap both Mirko and Stefania?"

"Humph," uttered Pietro with an arid laugh. "Still *sooo* obsessed with Stefania."

"It's been ages since I've seen her," Jeremy emphasized. "But it would be nice to know whether she's out of danger..."

"So you know nothing of her these days...you're not in touch with anyone any longer...not even Christophe?"

Pietro's tone was mocking and Jeremy decided not to be baited into defending himself. His affair with Stefania was history—why did Pietro care anymore? He ignored the question and said, "So how do you know for a fact Mirko was kidnapped?"

Slowly Pietro stubbed out his cigarette, pressing and twisting it repeatedly against the green ashtray, systematically extinguishing any remnant of smoke and ember. Until finally he pronounced, "I heard it directly from the source."

Jeremy shifted his weight, leaned slightly forward though not so much as to appear overly thirsty for the scoop. "And who would that be?" he asked warily.

Pietro's wide, innocent grin returned. "Well, Stefania of course."

Jeremy blinked twice then slowly sat back in his chair. He tried not to show either shock or confusion, both of which he now felt galloping through him.

"Didn't she tell you?" Pietro asked, shaking his head in semi-amusement.

Jeremy aimed his gaze at the bustling bar past Pietro's shoulder. "Why should she, we haven't talked in over a month."

"Well then I guess it's up to me."

With that, Pietro proceeded to recount, almost blow by blow, the events of the night of 14 July: how Mirko was shot and hauled off by the Italian security services, how Stefania was spared, having made a deal. In short, most everything, minus Jeremy's part in the play, for which he felt heartily, though somewhat guiltily, grateful.

"You see," said Pietro at the end of his narrative, "I *made* her tell me. I knew she and Mirko had been followed last July, that they went off together to plot some kind of revenge against the French; so why, then, should only one of them disappear?"

Jeremy's tone and frown were accusing. "You *forced* her to talk to you?" he said, fearing just how Pietro might have accomplished this.

"So to speak. I threatened that if she didn't tell me the truth, I would denounce her as a traitor to all the Compagni and French comrades in Paris, in France, and through the grapevine to everyone in Italy. That she'd given Mirko's whereabouts to the French to save herself, and then got him arrested. On the other hand, I promised that if she came clean I would leave her alone and the subject would be dropped. But what did I discover? That she truly *was* a traitor, that she'd sold Mirko out after all, only instead of to the French, to the rotten Italian fascist regime. At first I wanted to throttle her. But I'd made a promise, and I came to realize that she was only saving herself from maybe a worse fate in Italy than Mirko's. She's wanted for accessory to murder, you know."

Jeremy nodded somberly: and you for robbery and Mirko for kidnapping—*kidnapping, how ironic!*

"Anyway," concluded Pietro, in a philosophical tone that seemed painfully forced, "instead of capturing two Compagni, the Fascists were only able to get their putrid paws on one."

During the account, Pietro had kept his eyes trained mostly on the ashtray, grinding his spent and crooked cigarette down to the nub of filter, leaving a small pile of paper and ash and un-smoked tobacco. He didn't want to look at Jeremy, something Jeremy found pathetically reminiscent of himself, when he had focused on the train seat in front of him while confessing the Monks' revenge to Haley. Yes, Pietro had suffered a great loss as well, plus he still must be in a state of worry over Mirko's injury. Jeremy wanted to assure him that the Italians would have taken Mirko straight away for medical help, but obviously he couldn't offer that. Instead, after displaying amazement at the account, he sought a bit of reassurance for himself. "So you've been telling people Mirko was kidnapped by Italian agents, and nothing more?"

Pietro nodded glumly. "He deserves some kind of justice."

"And what if the French get wind and start making their own inquiries?"

"Don't worry, I'll keep Stefania out of it." This time Pietro pronounced her name without sarcasm. "I may have been a thief at one time, but that doesn't mean I break my word. Plus I'm in no mood to rock the boat and risk any of us Compagni getting deported, including myself."

Pietro was looking Jeremy in the eye now. It was a strange gaze, thought Jeremy, mixed with pain and something else. Something ruminative, or wry: as if Jeremy might not understand the sum of things as they stood. But Jeremy did understand and nodded back with both appreciation of Pietro's grief and thanks for his protection of Stefania. He only hoped Pietro would continue to honor the latter. *And*, that he would not somehow discover that he, Jeremy, had played a part in the intrigue himself.

Chapter 29

Instead of taking the metro, Jeremy chose to walk
home from the Café Saint-Maur, along the wide
avenue de la République. He needed to ponder
things in the open, let his whirling thoughts air in the
company of racing automobile traffic and the purposeful
strides of his fellow pedestrians. His first urge was to
contact Stefania, verify she was all right and had truly
received no rough treatment from Pietro. Then, thank
her for leaving him out of her account. A simple, friendly
phone call would do the job, they could wish each other
well once more, hang up, and continue along their
individual paths like before. But Stefania didn't have a
telephone, and Jeremy did not wish to go out of his way
to seek her out; his pride rebelled against the idea, even
though a small seed of desire still lingered under his skin
and would have no doubt been watered by seeing her in
person. That was the problem: Stefania knew his desire
all too well, could sense it, he was sure, and this made
him put the kibosh on the idea of seeing her. And yet he
wondered if she knew Pietro was circulating the
kidnapping story...which made his thoughts swivel to
the RG. It was time to call Rébert with news about
Mirko's disappearance.

The remainder of the afternoon, Jeremy considered
how he would present things to Rébert, finally deciding
to go with what Pietro had suggested if he himself were
to be brought in for questioning. Jeremy would report
that Pietro had only *heard* of Italian spies looking to
pluck political refugees from France in defiance of

President Mitterrand's doctrine of asylum. That the Compagni lived in fear and insecurity of either being deported by the French for some infraction or snatched up by Italians; that unless the French happened to have arrested Mirko for some reason, the word was out that he might have fallen prey to an Italian conspiracy. No proof, of course—as long as Pietro continued to hide what he knew of the kidnapping. Still, Jeremy worried that if pressured by the authorities Pietro could crack and spill the entire story, a revelation that could lead to Stefania's involvement, and down the line perhaps to his own.

Those thoughts continued to harry him when he finally met Rébert for a tête-à-tête in a café at the Place du Châtelet.

"Sounds like paranoia," was Rébert's take on the story. "The Compagni have a right to stay here; those French on the political right may not like it, but that's the way it is."

Jeremy's gaze was glued to his soggy, dripping teabag as he carefully transferred it from his cup to his saucer. "Well," he said, dabbing his fingers on his napkin, "that's just it, you see. The Compagni know they're not exactly loved by all the French; they live here at the pleasure or, some would even say, the displeasure of the French government. They know they could be deported at the drop of a hat—so they're edgy, skittish, always suspicious."

"Nothing we can do about that. They got themselves into their messes on their own; they should at least be grateful they're here. Which reminds me, whatever happened with Stefania and the *mec* who was following her?"

Jeremy shot Rébert a deliberate frown of confusion.

"The big blond *stalker*, remember?" said Rébert with an impatient sigh.

310

"Right," Jeremy mumbled. "He must have given up the game; Stefania hasn't mentioned him in ages. You were probably right about his pestering her for fun."

"Mm," Rébert grunted. "Stefania's not paranoid about rogue Italian spies—is she?"

"No." *No longer*, that is. For an instant Jeremy gazed out the window at the yellowing leaves that thicketed the Place. When he looked back at Rébert, he said, "I'm the one who over-reacted." Then, to further nudge Rébert off the subject, he added, "I guess I got a little too protective with that job."

Jeremy winked and Rébert returned a dry chuckle. He didn't comment, and Jeremy asked himself what else could be percolating in the RG agent's mind. He had given Rébert that snapshot of the big blond Gruber and wondered if it was still floating around the RG offices.

Thankfully, Rébert returned to the issue at hand: "So Pietro has nothing more to offer about Mirko's disappearance than a conspiracy theory?"

Jeremy shook his head, affecting disappointment with an added shrug of his shoulders. Then he made a suggestion, a tack he'd come up with before meeting Rébert. He leaned in, forearms on the table. "On the other hand, I've been mulling it over, Pietro's surly attitude every time I mention the subject...could be that they've split up—if you get my gist. He could be smarting from it, embarrassed, so he's given over, at least in public, to hypothesizing this bizarre kidnapping."

Rébert's eyes narrowed in interest. "Do you know if Mirko's stuff is still in the flat?"

Jeremy claimed to have no idea.

"Well, I'd like to find out. If the two had a 'lovers' quarrel' and Mirko moved out, I still need to get a location on him." He drained the rest of his Kanterbräu lager, then asked, "Have you gauged anything suspicious as far as Pietro goes, anything he could be hiding that the two might be up to?"

"No. *Although*," Jeremy added shrewdly, "when he lets his guard down he seems to lapse into a kind of depression, as if Mirko's died or something, which could be consistent with whatever kind of loss he feels."

Rébert threw him an amused grin. "You should be a shrink, Jeremy." Then his ruminative frown returned. "On the other hand, if Mirko abandoned Pietro of his own accord..."

"*Exactly*," Jeremy agreed. "He would want to avoid losing face."

Rébert sat back with a sour expression, sighing and massaging his temples. He appeared to have had his *sacré* fill of the Compagni drama, which allowed Jeremy to feel a bit of cautious relief...

Until Rébert cleared his throat and straightened in his chair. "See if you can find out whether they *have* had that lovers' spat and if Mirko flew the nest completely. If that's the case, Pietro might not, in fact, know where he's gone. And that still puts the ball back in our court. In the meantime I'll pass the word around the Service that the Compagni fear Italian spies are after them." He emitted a cynical little laugh and checked his watch. "I've got to get going."

Rébert rose, buttoned his jacket, and reminded Jeremy that he would expect an update. Then he headed for the door, leaving Jeremy behind in dismay. *Would this business never end?*

A *messy* break-up: that's what he could confirm to Rébert about Mirko's disappearance. Mirko had taken a good part of his belongings from the flat and left without a word. And Jeremy would add that it took an agonizing amount of time to worm this much out of the humiliated and depressed Pietro.

But of course that wouldn't be enough. Jeremy

would then be tasked to track down Mirko's new address, plus Rébert might still pull Pietro in for an interrogation which could reveal too much. As he sat on a dark-green bench in his little neighborhood park, Square du Temple, he gazed about him as if hoping to telepathically receive an inspiring idea—from a child doing somersaults on the grass, from the chrysanthemums still hanging on as autumn advanced with plunging temperatures, maybe from the changing leaves whose growing goldenness spelled the death of summer.

Death. What if the RG could be manipulated into thinking Mirko had died...might that put an end to things? Jeremy sat back and crossed his arms in disgust. The notion was utterly absurd and merely reflected his desperation to be done with an impossible assignment—one he had once foolishly thought might be easy. Nevertheless, Pietro did seem to suffer, as if he were grieving for the death of Mirko. Jeremy had expressed as much to Rébert and, unlike other things he'd fudged with the RG agent, he hadn't made this up.

Another week went by, with the end of September approaching and Jeremy continuing to put off a call to Rébert. He still hadn't obtained extra work hours at Le Prince, although one day Pierre asked him to come in early to cover for a colleague. Immediately Jeremy noted a change of atmosphere in starting work at six p.m. The relaxed tempo, versus the scurry and rush he felt when people poured in for a performance. The lazy chatter he could exchange with patrons who enjoyed the mood and ambience of the club even without the live jazz. And he had the freedom to set the background music, choosing from bar's collection of dozens of jazz cassettes.

He had put Artie Shaw and his big band on the sound system when a customer arrived whom he'd never seen later in the evening; a woman who looked at

313

least sixty, judging from her mildly sagging skin. She had short, thick grey hair and wore large rectangular spectacles that lent her hooded eyes an owlish air. When he brought her glass of Dubonnet she said, "If I'd known big band was played here I would have come in more often." Smoke rose vine-like from the long cigarette in her ashtray, and through it she cast Jeremy a nostalgic smile.

"Well, that's just *my* choice—the Artie Shaw," he said, smiling back and transferring his tray to his right hand.

"And a better one than some of the modern jazz I've heard. Why don't you set that down for a moment," she politely suggested, indicating the tray. "You don't seem to be in a rush."

"No," he agreed, resting the tray on her little round table. "We've barely just opened."

"And luckily I happened in while you were playing 'Out of Nowhere.' She gave a sigh that was as nostalgic as her smile. "It was just short of this same time of year, in 1944. I heard the song for the first time and it still takes me back to the Liberation. An American band playing down at Place Saint-Germain-des-Prés—such a lovely saxophone solo."

Jeremy's ears pricked up, his eyes brightening.

"And the wonderful black woman singer—no black person dared sing in public under the Nazis. I was twenty years old and I'd never witnessed such a bold, romantic piece of music in my life."

Jeremy thought hard; he couldn't recall his father talking about playing outdoors during Liberation. But it was possible...

"Do you remember what the saxophone player looked like, or his name?" he ventured.

"I wish I could, but after forty-plus years I'm afraid not. I hadn't heard many big band tunes before," the woman went on, dividing her wistful smile between Jeremy and the bar from where "Out of Nowhere" emanated. "Anything jazz-like, including big band, was banned under the Occupation. We listened to our radio in secret, caught the BBC when we felt it was safe. That's how I heard snippets of big band."

"And de Gaulle's speeches," Jeremy offered, warmed by the woman's personal account, and still imagining that it could have been Walt Winters entertaining the euphoric crowd at Place Saint-Germain-des-Prés.

"Of course. But I was young and preferred the music, so you can imagine what a treat it was to hear it live on the streets of Paris after all those dark, oppressive years." She paused to take a delicate drag from her cigarette, then said, "Why did you ask if I remembered the saxophone player?"

Jeremy smiled modestly. "My father played the sax here during Liberation."

"How lovely—an American, by chance?"

"Yes."

"Well, tell him I'll never forget the incredible joy he and others brought us during that time; such a treat, on top of what the American soldiers did for us. I know it's not always fashionable to praise Americans these days, but I can guarantee that the people of my generation will always honor the sacrifice men like your father made for our freedom." Her eyes sparkled when she asked, "Does your father still play?"

Jeremy's response was almost apologetic. "No, he died some years back."

She turned a sad smile on him. "I'm so sorry. Such a loss in more than one way."

Jeremy gave a respectful nod. *Liberation*: after France, Walt played in Belgium, where he and Béatrice fell in love. It was that same heady atmosphere, according to Béatrice—the intoxication of newfound freedom coupled with exotic big band rhythms—that had attracted her to Walt Winters. In the days before Walt got involved with the communist party and his liberal lifestyle began to complicate things for the devoutly Catholic Béatrice. Jeremy wished he could have known his parents in those halcyon days of innocence, before everything fell apart and the worst came to pass.

The door to the club opened and in filed two more customers. With a tinge of reluctance he picked up his tray and politely took his leave. Not, however, without feeling the burn of a lump in his throat.

Grief. For a short interlude, while listening to the woman in the club, the unpredictable emotion had returned to him. He continued to imagine that forty-four years ago, in Place Saint-Germain-des-Prés, Walt Winters had serenaded the woman who was then a fluttering twenty-year-old girl. All because he had played Artie Shaw's "Out of Nowhere" in the bar. The song had set off an emotional chain reaction, gripping the woman and transporting her back in time. Jeremy knew the feeling well, knew what music was capable of. How a song could seed an emotion in you, stoke it, indeed become master of it; so that, *voilà*, years later, the song could summon that feeling, and every detail of time and place associated with it, back to life like a hypnotist with his powers of suggestion. *Right out of Nowhere.*

And the chain reaction continued when Jeremy went home to bed, his thoughts now gyrating in the dark like a child's mobile above a crib. The genuine sorrow the woman had seemed to feel upon hearing of Walt Winters' death. The Monks and the grief he still felt over their despicable deed...the brutalized saxophone, helpless and unavenged under his bed; lying there the way some Americans kept the ashes of a loved one in an urn at home. Only Jeremy had benefited from no funeral, no "closure" as the Americans liked to put it. He wondered if it was the same for Pietro and his grief...

Jeremy turned onto his side, uttering an accusing sigh at the tedious darkness that stubbornly refused him sleep. *Grief*: perhaps another visit to see how Pietro was getting along, considering Mirko was now most likely in an Italian jail awaiting trial...*yes*, and Jeremy could also express an additional concern: his wish for them to be on the same page in case of an eventual interrogation of Pietro regarding the kidnapping story...*right*: in fact he would tell Pietro that he himself had been approached by a security agent who had asked what he knew about Mirko's whereabouts. "They might be asking everyone acquainted with Mirko," Jeremy would claim, knowing full well Pietro would find the notion reasonable, since he himself had been questioned about Mirko's whereabouts by Rébert a couple of weeks after the abduction.

Sympathy, solidarity, and unity in the face of a possible inquiry: that would be the tone Jeremy would bring to his next meeting with Pietro. In the meantime the idea of *closure* stole back into his mind. He tried to banish it, for when it came to a resolution of his own grief, all he could see floating across the screen of his closed eyelids were the bloodied faces of Jean-Marc and Renaud.

Chapter 30

Jeremy was relieved to hear the live voice of Pietro on the phone, felt even surprised, for he had dreaded another round of evasiveness on Pietro's part via his damned answering machine. Jeremy asked if they could meet again, stressing his concern over "a new issue" that had cropped up. "I could come to your house..." he suggested.

Silence down the phone line, then a sigh. "Can't you tell me what's going on right now?"

"I'd rather not talk about it over the phone..." Jeremy hoped his tone conveyed a certain suspense. He wanted to engage Pietro in the intimate surroundings of his home—see how he was getting along, ask if he needed a hand in dealing with Mirko's stuff. And, of course, report the all-important *news* of the police "questioning him out of the blue;" how he and Pietro must now align their stories carefully. "I really don't mind stopping by your place..." he insisted.

More silence. Then, "...All right. Friday afternoon at two, *if that's not too late in the day for you.*"

Of course it wasn't, and when Jeremy hung up he shook his head at Pietro's ongoing edginess. Everything seemed an inconvenience to the man. He hadn't always been like this; he was reserved, to be sure, but always kind. If only he would soon find a satisfactory way to fill the hole represented by Mirko's absence.

Another five days Jeremy would have to wait—so much for his ability to arouse suspense in Pietro. He wondered what was keeping him so bloody busy. He

318

considered phoning Georges Sauvebelle again, just in case their mutual communist friend had heard something interesting about Pietro since their night out at the Club Écarlate. But he didn't want to push his luck: two phone calls concerning Pietro within a month, after at least a year's silence, might make Georges wonder what was going on.

Then Jeremy came up with the idea of tailing Pietro—just for a couple of days, in order to satisfy his curiosity about the Italian's comings and goings.

He knew Pietro was a late-riser, and so the next morning he arrived in his street at eleven a.m. *Le Monde* in hand, he ducked into a café across the way, ordered a café au lait,
paid for it immediately per his habit when tailing people for the RG, and drank it at a table next to the window.

At one-fourteen Pietro finally exited the premises, heading toward Père Lachaise Cemetery. Maybe to the metro stop, thought Jeremy, slipping out of the café and falling in behind him, leaving a couple of fellow pedestrians to fill the gap between them. The sun shone off and on through clouds nudged along by a chilly wind, and Jeremy wore the bomber jacket he had bought the previous autumn. He was sure Pietro had never seen the jacket whose collar he pulled up stiff against his chin, a black stocking cap covering his hair and ears—a pair of sunglasses disguising his defective eye.

Jeremy was right about the metro, Pietro reaching the Père Lachaise station and trotting down the stairs with Jeremy discreetly at his heels. Throughout the tunnels, commuters hastened along like ants with a purpose, all but Pietro who advanced at a leisurely pace. Jeremy jockeyed accordingly, hanging back as sober-faced commuters consistently marched past them both.

At the platform Jeremy stood in the shadow of an archway leading to connecting tunnels, eyes on Pietro.

When the train arrived Pietro stepped into the nearest carriage, Jeremy entering the one next to it and stationing himself at the door where the two cars connected. Through the grimy half-window he peered about for Pietro in the adjoining car, but a thicket of travelers obscured his view. So he moved back to the main doors, where he stood, hand gripping the pole, and where at each stop he cautiously leaned out so as to spot Pietro as he exited. At length the Italian got off, only to change lines, which necessitated a repeat of the same subterranean game.

Finally he debarked definitively, surfacing on the Left Bank at Odéon, where Jeremy followed him to a café on the street that led to the Odéon Theater. Jeremy waited on the sidewalk until he felt Pietro had time to get settled inside. Then he carefully slipped in the door, scanning the crowded space from the short entranceway hall. When he couldn't spy Pietro he crossed the café to where he found the entrance to yet a second room. A stolen glimpse inside revealed Pietro on the far side, seated at a table facing another man. Jeremy pulled back; Pietro's companion looked vaguely familiar, an older man, though he could only see him and Pietro in profile. Slowly he peered back around.

Now he recognized the guy: a Frenchman who used to show up at rallies and demonstrations with the rest of the communist community. Jeremy withdrew behind the wall again. *Richard* was the guy's name, though he now looked old enough to be the grandfather of Richard. Jeremy gazed back: poor *mec*, he had fallen into shocking decline since Jeremy had last seen him some years ago. He couldn't be older than forty, but seemed sixty or more. His hair, dull and stringy, was losing significant ground to both advancing greyness and baldness. White stubble frosted his gaunt cheeks, and his emaciated shoulders, hunched over the table, reminded Jeremy of a couple of bent and brittle weeds, especially next to Pietro who was both taller than Jeremy and more robustly built. Most telling of all was the network of angry little veins on his cheekbones and the bulbous red nose that looked like raw meat. Instinctively Jeremy surmised the reason for Richard's transformation, and as a waitress passed him, heading into the room, his suspicion gained justification. On her tray sat a large carafe of red wine and two glasses which she set on the table between the two men. Jeremy waited for her to return before glancing into the room again, where Richard was pouring wine into the two glasses with a shaky hand. Under normal circumstances the sharing of a carafe of wine in the afternoon wouldn't have raised one single hair of an eyebrow. But Richard's reputation as an inveterate alcoholic went way back, explaining why the likes of Christophe and Georges Sauvebelle agreed long ago that he had ceased being of help to the cause. Little by little Richard had melted away from the communist scene.

Yet here he sat knocking back a carafe of red with Pietro, whose face also had a grubby aspect. He too had neglected to shave today and his hair hung lank and matted. He was letting himself go, thought Jeremy, and he had Richard to keep him company. Jeremy retreated once more and leaned against the wall, sighing inwardly. He eyed his watch. Now that he was here he might as well order something and wait to see where Pietro might go next. He nabbed a free table in the corner of the crowded first room where Pietro wouldn't notice him when he left. There, he took off his hat and sunglasses and ordered a cup of tea, something he could draw out for close to an hour, since the little metal pot contained extra water.

Less than forty-five minutes later, his eye caught the same waitress heading to the backroom with a fresh, brimming carafe of red. When she returned with an empty carafe on her tray, the corner of Jeremy's mouth drooped cynically. The pathetic duo had ordered another round. Jeremy slipped away from his table to check, peering round the corner just in time to see Pietro and Richard clink full glasses a second time. He ducked back, shaking his head. So this was what kept Pietro "so busy"—*getting sodden drunk in the afternoon*. Jeremy checked his watch again. It was a little past three-thirty, and who could guarantee the drinking bout would end after this round? He grimaced at the idea of finding out; it was demoralizing at best. At worst Jeremy cursed himself for wasting time playing spy. He returned to his table and gathered his stuff. No more following Pietro today, or any other day, *bon sang*.

The rest of the week passed, with Jeremy wondering whether Pietro might be turning into a lush; or maybe he was drowning his sorrow over Mirko.

The latter thought hovered in his mind when Friday finally arrived and he stood in front of Pietro's building, waiting to press the buzzer. He frowned in anticipation. He felt genuinely concerned about how Pietro was getting along and planned to open the conversation by expressing just that. Then he would move on to the issue of the kidnapping and how to limit potential damage that could arise from Pietro's heralding the news.

It took less than five seconds for Pietro to pick up the interphone and buzz Jeremy in, a mild surprise considering he half expected Pietro to try to postpone the visit with one excuse or another. And when the door to the flat opened, Jeremy felt relief to see Pietro clean-shaven, well-groomed, in a pair of corduroys and a pullover sweater, and seemingly sober. "You don't have to dash out soon, do you?" he asked doubtfully.

"I've got a little time." Pietro waved Jeremy in,

accepting his tweed jacket, which Jeremy had immediately shed as a hint he wasn't to be rushed through the visit. "So what's so urgent *now*...?"

Pietro's hands were hooked on his hips, again the irritated posture. Jeremy waited to be invited to take a seat. Pietro indicated the sofa, Jeremy sat, then thought he might be offered a refreshment. Finally he asked. "Do you have anything to drink?"

"Right," Pietro grunted and headed toward the kitchen. "Is lager okay?" he voiced across the room, more a statement than a question.

Jeremy's *sure* was also a formality; he didn't really care what he drank as long as he could get Pietro talking. Pietro handed him a bottle of beer then sat in a chair across from him. He took an immediate swig from his own bottle; not even a polite little *cheers* beforehand, Jeremy observed, recalling Pietro's clinking of glasses with the poor, booze-diminished Richard.

Which brought Jeremy to his first point: "How've you been doing lately?"

"Me?"

"Yeah. I've been a little concerned since...you know, Mirko..."

"Mm," Pietro replied, then gave a placid smile. A smile that looked detached...*manufactured.* "I've been fine—couldn't be better."

False cheer in his voice as well, Jeremy detected. He returned a civil nod.

"So what's the *main* concern that's brought you here?" Pietro insisted.

Jeremy shrugged and took a sip of his lager. "Just a small matter of security I think you should be aware of."

Pietro angled his head, and for the first time his eyes betrayed a touch of uncertainty.

Pleased, Jeremy went on: "Last week, while I was at work, I received a visit from some *mec* from the security services—asked if I had any knowledge of the where-abouts of Mirko Mazzini."

Pietro took his time responding. Perplexed, he frowned, his mouth tightening into an annoyed line, before he countered, "Why would he ask *you*?"

Jeremy took another pull of his beer, let his reply sound matter-of-fact. "They must be questioning various people who know Mirko. Stefania once told me that you Compagni are supposed to check in regularly with them..."

"She's right. Naturally Mirko hasn't checked in for a while. As a matter of fact the bastards came knocking on my door. I told them he'd left and I didn't know where he was."

"Then they didn't mention any kidnapping..."

"No, it was last month when they came. Did they bring it up with you?"

Jeremy decided to lend a dose of irritation to his voice. "Yes, thanks to your spreading the news. The guy said they'd heard a rumor Mirko might've been abducted—didn't say by who—but I told him it was only a *vague* rumor; the thing is, now I'm even more concerned they might pull you in for questioning..."

"Or pull Stefania in..." Pietro eyed Jeremy wryly. "You're still worried about her..."

"I trust you'll maintain your word about keeping her out of it," Jeremy reminded Pietro. "Anyway, you should seriously think about preparing a statement, just in case—"

Pietro set his bottle on the coffee table with a clang; he leaned toward Jeremy. "Maybe you *don't* trust my word." His dark eyes flickered defiantly. "It's a funny thing, *trust*, and *loyalty*. You never know who might double-cross you..."

Though Pietro sounded speculative in a clinical way, his eyes had turned scornful, and Jeremy felt renewed angst, not only for Stefania but abruptly, and inexplicably, for himself. Did Pietro wish to somehow punish *him* for Stefania's betrayal of Mirko? He flashed back on Pietro's stubborn avoidance of him. His enduring defensiveness whenever they spoke. The despisal in Pietro's voice whenever Jeremy mentioned Stefania...

Passive-aggressive, wasn't that how psychologists described this kind of behavior?

Pietro continued to sit forward, observing Jeremy with a cold and critical eye.

Blackmail, or extortion? Jeremy asked himself nervously. In some way he wants to damage me, make me pay...

Then it struck him, like a blow out of the blue to the solar plexus. *He already has...*

Slowly Jeremy set his bottle down and got to his feet, stepping away from the coffee table. Pietro matched the gesture and they now stood facing each other, Jeremy's flashing eyes lifted a fraction to meet the taller Pietro's. "How did you get into my flat last July," he demanded. His hands had gone icy as the revelation careered through him, but now that they were balled into tight fists, hot blood began to course back through them.

"Funny thing to ask a former thief," Pietro said with a sneer. He drew himself up and squared his bulky shoulders before adding, *Traître sciant!*"

Pounding blood reached Jeremy's temples. In front of his eyes danced the crooked letters scrawled on the white scrap of paper he'd found on his coffee table after the break-in. They gyrated mockingly—*fucking traitor*—and his fists, almost of their own accord, sprang forward to strike Pietro in the stomach—*one, two, three.*

Pietro grunted and expelled a stream of air, wheezing and buckling like a slashed tire, remaining bent and deflated for a second or two, then straightening and throwing a punch to Jeremy's face. Jeremy blocked it with his left arm and delivered another blow to Pietro's midsection. The Italian staggered then lurched forward, aiming once more for Jeremy's face, his knuckles instead striking Jeremy in the chest. Jeremy winced, fell back a step; Pietro, powerfully built, was capable of doing him serious damage...

Again Pietro charged, shoving Jeremy onto the arm of the sofa where they grappled, Pietro still trying to strike Jeremy's face, Jeremy seeking to paralyze Pietro with a solid punch to the diaphragm. They only succeeded in short jabs, and the two managed to stagger back to their feet. Jeremy eyed Pietro's nose, which along with the eyes and groin were the most vulnerable parts of the body. As if guessing those thoughts Pietro let fly a kick to Jeremy's crotch, which Jeremy barely blocked, taking the kick to his knee—this time, to his right one. Once more he winced and stepped back, thankful *this* kick was not expert. He set his sights on Pietro's aquiline nose. One blow there would end this scuffle, avenge the slain saxophone, and leave Pietro to mop up the blood from his crushed nasal cartilage...

But Jeremy balked—so far he hadn't touched Pietro's face. He retreated another step, shaking himself: *no, he would not strike Pietro in the face or head, would not risk putting him in the hospital*, even if the Italian, who measured half a head taller, continued to attack him.

Again Pietro seemed to sense Jeremy's thoughts. "What's the matter," he taunted, "afraid to hit me like a boxer?" They were both breathing raggedly. "I'm expecting one of your *hooks* to the jaw. Waiting to see how low you'll stoop for a saxophone when I've lost my best friend."

The pause in the fisticuffs allowed Jeremy to catch

326

his breath, for the pulsing pressure in his temples to slacken. *Indeed, how far would he go?* Lips still parted, head atilt, he considered Pietro with a fresh eye. "You destroyed the saxophone to get back at Stefania?" he wondered aloud.

Pietro wiped a film of sweat from his brow, his chest still heaving. His voice was hoarse. "In a way...what does *she* own of any value? Plus I promised not to pursue things with her, and someone had to pay..."

Jeremy shook his head, astonished. "So you came after my father's instrument?"

Pietro looked surprised. "It was your father's?"

Furious and exasperated, Jeremy delivered a powerful punch to Pietro's torso, striking between the ribs to the diaphragm. He glared at Pietro, who was doubled up and gasping for breath. *Finally*, he said to himself as Pietro sank back onto the arm of his easy chair, no doubt feeling he would never be able to breathe again.

But in a few seconds, of course, he did, and wheezed, "I didn't know..." His distressed gaze was aimed at the floor, his brow heavy and furrowed.

Was that *remorse* Jeremy heard in his voice? He continued to glare at Pietro.

"Are you claiming no fault of your own?" Pietro suddenly demanded, sitting up straight on the armrest.

Jeremy's eyes narrowed in uncertainty.

"No fault *in the least*?" Pietro persisted. When Jeremy didn't answer, he barked a sarcastic laugh and stood up. "Remember, I told you I know *everything* about Mirko's kidnapping."

Jeremy stared hard, worry beginning to gnaw at him.

"*That's right,*" Pietro said, nodding askance, his eyes and lips forming a painful expression.

"I wasn't quite ready for this moment the last time we

met, so I lied to you. In truth, Stefania told me you were there when those bastards shot Mirko. And you obviously did nothing to help him, but did everything to free the person who set him up. So you see, now she's betrayed you as well."

As the shock set in, Jeremy wheeled back and dropped onto the arm of the sofa. He felt exhausted, but Pietro was wrong about his feeling betrayed. After all, why *should* Stefania have hidden his part in the 14 July debacle? If he had ever considered her an altruist, he would have been deceiving himself.

Inwardly he sighed and looked out the window. For the first time he noticed that rain was spraying the panes in little bursts. As it fell on the roof of Pietro's top-floor flat, its ponging sounded like tiny rubber balls. The room had suddenly darkened.

With a wary look Pietro slid down into his armchair.

"Why did you hide what you did for so long?" Jeremy asked, shaking his head.

"I might never have told you," Pietro answered in a quiet voice. "It's not something I'm proud of, if you want to know the truth. But you wouldn't leave me alone, calling constantly, wanting to meet...Georges Sauvebelle told me you'd asked if I'd be at the Club Écarlate—you'd think you suspected me, or at least had a guilty conscience..."

No, Jeremy countered numbly to himself: in pursuing you I had a job to do, *and the party I suspected of wrecking my place seemed eminently logical*. But he should have looked beyond the Monks, rather than keep them fixated in his head. Jean-Marc and Renaud couldn't have had a clue how dear the saxophone was to him. Although Pietro claimed not to know the sax belonged to Jeremy's father, he still knew of Jeremy's love of jazz, and therefore how valuable the instrument would be to him. Pietro had alluded to Jeremy having a *guilty conscience.* And he had, in a sense, but toward the Monks. The feeling had been fleeting, though he now realized it had probably reinforced his suspicion of them. "I should have known..." he told himself in a half whisper.

The rain was now drumming against the windowpanes in staccato bursts, and as the room slipped into penumbra, Pietro silently observed Jeremy from his armchair.

Jeremy slid down onto the sofa. *God, he felt tired.* Not in terms of his muscles or his stamina—just tired inside his head, inside his heart. And when he was tired his eye watered all the more. He wiped away another wandering tear.

Pietro might have taken it for a tear of grief. He didn't apologize, per se, about the saxophone, but he did reiterate something expressed more than once by various Compagni: "We all know your father was a good man, Jeremy."

Jeremy nodded dumbly, staring at his hands: his fists were now laced together in repose between his knees, his forearms resting on his thighs. He was starting to feel calmer, subdued by the shadowy room and the rhythmic pattering of the rain.

Then Pietro said something that made him arch to attention. "In reality things could be worse. Mirko could be rotting in jail as we speak, but instead he's escaped."

Chapter 31

What?" Jeremy uttered in disbelief. Mirko had *escaped*!?

Shadows obscured Pietro's face while the rain continued to batter the windows with its rubbery beat. He turned on a lamp next to his chair. "That's right," he said, "I only just found out. Evidently those fascist fuckers never got him to Italy. He evaded them when they stopped over for medical assistance in Vichy—*Vichy*, how's that for irony. From there he made his way to Marseille, with the help of comrades. They set him up with a fake passport and credit card, then he got on a flight to Cuba. He's been safely tucked away in Havana for two months."

Pietro took a large swallow of beer and set the empty bottle down with a satisfied sigh. "So if the security services come knocking at my door again, I'll tell them I was wrong about the kidnapping and heard that Mirko took off for Cuba. Anyway, who wouldn't prefer living in a country where you're welcome?"

A fake passport—Pietro would never realize the *irony* in that for Jeremy! He shook his head in marvel. Mirko might even have possessed one in Paris (finding out would have been the next step in Jeremy's job concerning Stefania); he could have had it with him on the run, though Gruber would have surely confiscated it when he apprehended him.

"And you waited until *now* to tell me?" Jeremy said.

"It took a while for the news to get through the grapevine, then I got a letter from Mirko, using a

330

pseudonym."

Jeremy regarded him gravely. "I understand—still, you could have told me when I first got here, we might have avoided..." He stopped, noting Pietro's scowl. "Never mind," he said. In his gut Jeremy knew the confrontation between Pietro and him had needed to play out the way it did—for both their sakes. Jeremy had ultimately prevailed in the fistfight, but that didn't ease his ache regarding the saxophone.

And, of course, Pietro must still be aching inside as well. "Do you know if Mirko got patched up all right?" Jeremy asked. He would have liked to express his worry over Mirko getting shot, how he wished the Italians had let both Stefania and him go, but instinct told him to keep his mouth shut on that score. Pietro might not believe him and could once more be roused to aggression. Plus, Jeremy admitted to himself, he couldn't remember exactly what he'd felt on the night of 14 July, in that hurricane of confusion and desperation. Everything had happened at whirlwind speed, now that he was revisiting it in his mind. The only feeling he could be certain of was his fear for Stefania's fate, something, he suspected, Pietro would find difficult to entertain.

"Mirko got his wound treated in Marseille, where we have friends," Pietro confirmed. "Then the doctors took over in Havana. You know, they have excellent health care there."

Jeremy nodded. "I imagine he's a celebrated refugee in Cuba. Smoking Montecristos and drinking daiquiris under the palm trees—good for him!"

"Mm," agreed Pietro, a touch sullenly. Jeremy understood his mood though he didn't hazard to offer sympathy for Pietro's newfound solitude. Instead, Pietro went on to give his own take on the matter. "I might just join him there...I'll have to see."

Jeremy nodded again, wondering whether Pietro

had a fake passport. *Dieu merci* Rébert had taken him off that job.

And as far as Rébert was concerned, Jeremy would have to once more beat the rumor mill and relay Pietro's news. It would be his final report on the subject: that Mirko had left France for Cuba. And if Rébert didn't find this truth plausible he could investigate all he wanted—all the way to Havana, if he felt like it. In one way or another, Jeremy's account would be confirmed and nothing would matter any longer. The Cubans would refuse to give Mirko up, given it was highly doubtful the French even wanted him back. It would then fall to the Italians, if they dared make things public, to complain and demand and threaten Fidel, and good luck with that!

Jeremy wished he could share this last bit with Pietro but judged it better to go on keeping silent. He looked out the window at the rain-blurred day. Within a couple of weeks it would be fully dark by seven p.m. Already he felt a degree of relief with the dispersal of tourist congestion and the retreat of the heat. Shrinking days, with night pulling up its anonymous hood to shadow private thoughts, shortcomings, sketchy accomplishments.

His gaze drifted back to Pietro, who had also sunk into silence and was staring at the coffee table with a certain bleakness in his eyes. It was probably time for Jeremy to leave. As he uncrossed his legs and sat forward, Pietro said, "Would you like another beer?"

Jeremy regarded him with surprise. "Sure...it'll give the rain more time to calm down..."

Pietro nodded and stood up. For an instant, without moving, he watched Jeremy. So Jeremy rose as well. "Are we all right?" Pietro asked him, a tinge of red in his coloring.

"We're all right," Jeremy answered soberly. The

coffee table stood between them, precluding a facile handshake, if either of them truly felt the need for one. Jeremy, still uneasy, followed Pietro into the kitchen so that he wouldn't have to be served.

This time Pietro poured out two lager glasses. Jeremy accepted his and, inclining his head, clicked it against Pietro's glass. "To Mirko and his new life." He paused, then added, "And to both of yours if you decide to join him."

Pietro raised his glass in acknowledgment.

By the time Jeremy took his leave, he and Pietro did shake hands at the door. Outside, he zipped up his jacket and lowered his head against the rain that had calmed to a dark drizzle.

The next day Jeremy called Rébert and gave him his news.

"*Nom de Dieu*, so he got his hands on a passport..."

In the silence that followed, Jeremy pictured myriad more curse words shooting through Rébert's mind. "Do you know the alias he used?" Rébert finally asked in a flat voice which sounded forced.

"Pietro didn't say."

"Well, what else did you hear?" The flat tone was giving way to frustration.

"He traveled to Marseille, got someone to set him up with the passport, and from there took a direct flight to Havana."

"...So he got the passport there..." A slight softening of tone: *at least he didn't get hold of one in Paris.*

"That's what Pietro said."

"Anything else?"

"No, that's it," said Jeremy.

"Well, I'll pass the news up the chain and see if they want to do anything with it. They might want to get the name of that alias."

"On the other hand," Jeremy offered, "one fewer Compagni to deal with..."

"*Ouais*, drawled Rébert, "that's how they might see it. But the Italians will be furious as hell when they find out—and I'm sure they will."

"Right," Jeremy agreed, then added to himself: but they won't be telling *you people* the true story.

"Did Pietro say *why* Mirko left?" asked Rébert in an afterthought.

Jeremy hesitated, then decided to repeat Pietro's own words. "He wanted to live in a country where he was truly welcome."

"Ha! Well I hope he likes it there because he'll never be able to return to Europe a free man."

Jeremy didn't comment, and Rébert ended up thanking him and arranging for a wrap-up meeting in a week's time, during which he would present Jeremy with another assignment.

Wrap-ups, Jeremy repeated to himself when he got off the phone. He thought of Stefania. During his go-around with Pietro at the Italian's place, Jeremy had worried once again about her, stressing that Pietro keep his word and not bother her. Heated confrontation had followed, then the brief brawl, after which Jeremy's thoughts had shifted elsewhere. Later, once he and Pietro had calmed down and were indulging in their second beer, Pietro mentioned her. "Incidentally, you might want to know that Stefania's moved in with Christophe."

Just like that, Jeremy had heard it from Pietro. Not from Stefania, not from Christophe. He wondered if the two, now officially a domestic couple, would ever think to call him sometime, would still consider him a friend. Naturally, Jeremy knew that any such decision would have to reside with Christophe. Whatever the case, at least Jeremy could finally consider Stefania safe—that she had gotten what she desired.

A week later Jeremy received what he had expected as well. A big bonus from Rébert and an official sign off of his work on the Compagni job. "We've put out feelers in Cuba," he told Jeremy. "Seems you could be right about Mirko living in Havana. We also have him on film in the Marseille Marignane departure terminal—his arm in a sling with a jacket thrown over it."

Jeremy acknowledged the news with a nod of faint curiosity. *Perhaps he'd broken his arm?* Rébert's shrug was eloquent: *wouldn't we like to know.*

Ten days later found Jeremy behind the bar of Le Prince, chatting with Haley who was enjoying her first evening of jazz at the club since July. Like the last time, she and Jeremy planned to spend the rest of the night together. Unlike the last time with the firebombing of the Opéra Bastille, he would not abandon her in a taxi.

Haley had just headed downstairs when someone else familiar appeared at the entrance. With a bright smile and an elegant stride, Louise Cholot approached the bar and exchanged cheerful greetings with Jeremy. It was a cold mid-October night and she wore a long, tan camelhair coat with a matching cloche set at a jaunty angle. She entered alone, which made her image all the more striking and attractive, thought Jeremy.

He shook her hand vigorously. "So you've finally decided to visit the best place for jazz in the city!"

"I've conceded to the expert," replied Madame, indicating Jeremy with a flip of her hand. "Plus I love a muted trumpet." This addition, referring to the evening's performer.

Jeremy considered her warmly, though not without a small thought to how she and Haley had almost stood side by side at the bar, and still might meet in the foyer at the end of the performance. Not that any real conflict existed between the two women; he would simply prefer to avoid explaining his friendship with Louise and the entailing link to Stefania.

"I'm glad to see you, Louise," he said. "I've been on vacation and meant to get in touch when I got back..."

"Oh," she scoffed good naturedly, "you don't have to tell *me* how time flies. I've been away myself, but I'm glad to get settled back in for the autumn and winter. Which reminds me, have things settled down for you?" Her gaze revealed a fleck of concern, but mainly a knowing look that Jeremy found not only appropriate but something he appreciated. "Everything's fine, back to normal. All's turned out well, thanks to your help."

"Good," she said. "If you ever need a sounding board again you know where to find me."

"You'll be the first to be consulted." He felt a nip of guilt saying that, as if contacting Louise in the future would depend on the need of a favor. He wished to add how he valued her friendship in general, but the noisy, crowded bar wasn't quite the right setting for it.

His expression, part frown, part smile, must have said as much, for Louise cast him the slightest though warmest of winks, then asked, "Are drinks served downstairs?"

"They are." At that moment Didier pulled up at the bar with his tray. "And my friend here will take your order when you get to your table. He introduced Madame to Didier, who smiled brightly at them both before offering to escort Madame to the jazz cellar.

The evening moved along at its usual brisk tempo, with Jeremy taking a break to catch a song downstairs. This time he leaned against the back wall with an ulterior motive. And with satisfaction he noted Haley sitting at the back of the room while Didier had settled Madame near the performers.

At the close of the evening Madame rose from the cellar before Haley, stopped briefly at the bar to say goodbye and tell Jeremy how she had enjoyed the music, then left to catch the taxi she'd arranged.

Jeremy stood reflecting for a moment, rubbing his hands absently with his bar towel well after they were dry. Haley was still downstairs, probably chatting with someone from the club; she knew Jeremy couldn't leave immediately after the performance. Eventually she would come up and take a seat at a table in the bar until he finished tidying up and they could leave together. He had dodged a sketchy situation and was relieved not to have to prepare a story for Haley. Better they remain separate, Louise and Haley.

He looked over and saw her mounting the stairs, safely in her metaphorical compartment with Louise taxiing away in her own. She beamed at him and he shifted his weight uncomfortably. Tonight he would have to tell her about his upcoming absence out of town—the new RG assignment—and he had little stomach left for obfuscation. He had arranged for a leave of absence from work to pursue the job, with vacation time still owed him from the summer. Pierre had frowned and scratched the back of his neck but offered no objection; he still hadn't granted Jeremy more hours and Jeremy felt no obligation to forego Rébert's lucrative offer.

He wished things to go smoothly with Haley tonight. Her smile was so welcoming, the night was cold and he desired her warmth and company. He would tell her enough about his assignment to allow them some mutual speculation, to put their heads together in that same spirited way they had when discussing Mitterrand's Great Works. He wanted to keep her on his side in all ways.

Chapter 32

Two mornings later, Jeremy sat across from Rébert in the Café des Sphinx in Place du Châtelet. He handed Jeremy an envelope filled with cash for his next assignment, including reimbursement for the train ticket Jeremy had bought for Amsterdam, where his next job would play out. In three days he was to travel to the city of canals and diamonds and Rembrandt, to escort the daughter of an assistant at the Élysée Palace back to Paris. The eighteen-year-old had run off the rails and headed for the Netherlands, slumming it in Amsterdam for the last two months, supposedly up to her eyeballs in cannabis and other forbidden delights for which the capital was also famous. Word had it, however, that perhaps the girl was ready to come home. *Perhaps,* being the operative word. She had a Dutch boyfriend, according to sources, and since dissipation enjoyed company, he might not want her to leave. Maybe Jeremy, in his low-profile status, could convince her to cut ties with the Amsterdam drug scene and return to Paris unhindered by the boyfriend. Jeremy was willing to give it a shot, particularly since the job included an all-expenses paid sojourn out of the country. He had only visited Amsterdam once in his life—mainly the city's museums and famous homes with his mother when he was a teenager—and looked forward to seeing more.

Which reminded him, he needed to renew his passport at the beginning of the New Year. The process had proven easy the last time, a simple jaunt to the

American embassy in the avenue Gabriel, bringing his old passport and two new pictures snapped in a self-service *photomaton* booth at the train station.

Conversationally, Jeremy mentioned the passport business to Rébert. "Hopefully there aren't any new requirements...it'd be convenient to have a French passport as well...dual citizenship, you know."

It wasn't the first time Jeremy had hinted as much to Rébert, who responded with a sympathetic half-smile. "Ah, that again. In time, *mon vieux*. Everything in its time."

Which Jeremy took to imply the indefinite: *maybe in ten years or so.*

"Anyway," continued Rébert, "I'm sure the American embassy will tell you if they require anything new. The important thing is that your present passport's good."

Jeremy assured him it was.

"By the way," said Rébert, "I heard there was an earthquake in San Francisco yesterday."

At ten in the morning Jeremy had yet to read that day's newspaper. "Downtown, or just somewhere in the Bay Area?" he asked.

"Don't know, but they say it was a big one—six-point-something. Have you still got family there?"

Jeremy didn't, and since the two men had nothing left to cover they parted ways, freeing Jeremy to head straight for a news kiosk. He bought a copy of the American-published *International Herald Tribune* and scanned it while standing on the sidewalk. His eyes widened with every line he read, culminating with a paragraph on the buckling of the Bay Bridge wrought by the earthquake. His thoughts streaked toward his drummer friend Monty and his family, other neighbors back in North Beach, plus one or two kids he had gone to school with.

He turned a couple of pages and read feverishly on:

WORLD SERIES INTERUPTED BY 6.9 JOLT:
Pieces of concrete fall from top of Candlestick Park.

Jeremy blinked repeatedly in dismay. In the *Herald Tribune* he had been following the San Francisco Giants' progress against the Oakland A's. The Giants had finally made it to the World Series (conveniently dubbed the Bay Bridge Series, though now that moniker seemed macabre) and Jeremy nursed a keen delight in it. Though so far his team had lost the first two games he had been counting on their producing a win in the third, then charging on to take the Series.

Now he read that yesterday, right at the beginning of that third game, Candlestick Park had had to be evacuated, luckily with no injuries. The same could not be said for the victims on the Bay Bridge. Numbly Jeremy folded the paper and continued on to the metro station.

Late that night after work, when the time difference was more suitable, he called Monty's old number in North Beach. A stranger answered: "Never heard of the MacLean family; I've had this number for ten years." Jeremy apologized for the mistake and rang off. Who knew where Monty and his parents and sister might now be living? He considered calling directory assistance but it was one o'clock and he was tired. He would try tomorrow morning.

When the morning came, however, the urgency had strangely subsided, and the prospect of hearing more bad news made him shy away. The last time he had seen Monty, almost twenty years ago, their friendship was already on the wane, with Jeremy having left their combo and his mother Béatrice suspecting an affair between her husband and Monty's mother. The two boys hadn't communicated since Jeremy and his mother's return to France. Still, it was an uncomfortable feeling, the awareness that his drive, or will, or whatever it was, to discover Monty's current status had disappeared overnight. For a few more seconds he stared at the phone. It was eight a.m. in Paris, making it eleven p.m. the night before in San Francisco—too late to call. As daylight beckoned through the window, he headed to the kitchen for breakfast, then back to his bedroom to pack for Amsterdam.

He kept his light travel bag under the bed, and as he squatted to reach for it his fingers grazed the saxophone case. He withdrew his hand and stood up, staring uneasily at the dark strip between the floor and the bedspread, imagining the still blackness under the bed that shrouded the body of the battered and dismembered saxophone. *Body, corpse*: terms his mind had latched onto since the destruction of the precious instrument. Louise Cholot was right: initially he'd felt his father had died all over again.

Only the saxophone was *not* a human being, something Pietro had not-so-subtly pointed out. Those who perished in the San Francisco earthquake and the hundreds, if not thousands, of injured, *were* human beings...

Jeremy squatted back down, pulled out the crushed case, and lifted its wobbly lid. The instrument appeared no different from the last time he'd had the guts to look at it, some two months ago. Same cracked mother-of-pearl keys, shards of which lay littering the felt-lined bottom of the case. Same fractured mouthpiece and caved-in bell. A thoroughly demolished instrument which could never be played again but that had belonged to his father, and therefore would stay put until...until...

He didn't know. He picked up one of the mother-of-pearl shards, felt its shiny smoothness as he rotated it between his fingers. Stiffened as he registered a sharp prick. He examined his middle finger where a drop of blood slowly spouted, no bigger than from a paper cut, a shaving nick, the thorn of a rose.

He dropped the shard back into the case, smearing the trickle of blood between his middle finger and thumb. For a moment, almost philosophically, he stood watching as another drop stubbornly took its place. He rubbed that one away in turn. *There would never be another fight over this instrument.* He shut the case, pushed it back under the bed, and went into the bathroom to rinse his hand. He dried the cut and placed a plaster on it to avoid getting stray blood on his clothes, then left the bathroom to pack. His train was scheduled to leave at nine the next morning and he still had errands to run.

He needed to pick up a couple of sweaters from the cleaners, so before closing his bag he struck out through the Passage Saint-Élisabeth over to rue du Temple. The street hosted a variety of useful stores, including a Monoprix which he ducked into to buy toothpaste and disposable razors. Then he resumed his way down the street to the cleaners, at the corner of rue du Temple and rue de Perrée.

The owner, the Moroccan-born Monsieur Saïd, greeted Jeremy with a droopy-mustached smile. After exchanging a pleasantry or two, he collected the sweaters—a forest-green pullover and a grey turtleneck—and wrapped them in a paper package, taped then tied with string, the better to carry on foot. "Not a moment too soon," he stressed, extending the package to Jeremy and nodding at the low clouds out the window. "Tomorrow it's supposed to be colder."

Jeremy agreed. *Probably even chillier in Amsterdam.*

He left the shop with his two packages but stopped

before turning right to make his way back up rue du Temple. The plaster on his middle finger tip was flapping open. He pulled it off, wadded it up, and almost stuffed it in his pocket to dispose of at home, until he spotted a trash receptacle a block down the street on the left. He headed that way. After flicking the balled plaster in the metal-barred trash bin, he stopped again. A few paces beyond stood a music store with instruments on display in the window, an establishment he had passed many times on his way toward the center of Paris. He'd never entered it, though he absently kept track of what sat enthroned in the window at any given time, of late an accordion, a clarinet, and a violin. He consulted his watch, decided he had time to check the window again, and clipped down the sidewalk.

As he stood verifying the existence of the same three instruments in the window, he wondered what else the store might boast of. *Just a quick peek inside, then.*

The small space was crammed full of goods, though he instantly spotted a row of saxophones mounted on one of the walls. He approached, examining the attributes of both the alto and tenor versions. Perhaps the store had a "bari" or even a bass saxophone for sale as well, crowded into some backroom ample enough to accommodate them. As it was, no clerk appeared to ask, and he leaned in to scrutinize the prices, a wide range of them he discovered. One instrument, an alto, sported mother-of-pearl keys...

"The prices are different because some instruments are new and others are used."

Jeremy swiveled to meet the gaze of a young girl he judged to be no more than twenty years old, and who appeared to have materialized from nowhere.

"*Excusez-moi, bonjour,*" she quickly added, apologizing for her initial abruptness. "It's just that you seemed to be checking the prices. We also rent

343

instruments, I mean if you're interested in the saxophone." Her small hand swept toward the instruments on the wall, her fresh face gleaming proudly. "They're all top quality."

"I'm sure they are," Jeremy said graciously, before turning back to the wall and pointing to the alto sax with the mother-of-pearl keys. "Is this one for rent?"

"As a matter of fact, it is."

He nodded thoughtfully.

"My name's Odile," said the girl. Her stature was petite but her voice mature and confident. "I can help you with any of your music needs."

Jeremy smiled and adjusted his packages. "Well," he said offhandedly, "I'd probably need to start lessons if I did anything. I've played the sax but it's been eons."

"That can be taken care of too," Odile said cheerily, and flung one loose end of her wool scarf over her shoulder. It was chilly in the shop, though the dusty premises still smelt of warm, aged wood. "We, in the store, can recommend a very good saxophone teacher. He lives in the neighborhood and gives lessons from his home."

"Sounds like you have the answer to everything here," Jeremy replied, feeling a fondness for the girl. "Do *you* play an instrument?"

The girl took a step backward and placed her hands on her hips, as if to allow herself added space and poise to present her answer. "The viola. I'm studying at the conservatory, but I can tell you pretty much anything about all the instruments in the shop." Ever the sunny countenance.

"I like jazz..." Jeremy said.

"*Bien sûr*," Odile affirmed in the manner of an expert. "You've got to like jazz if you're interested in the sax. The teacher I mentioned, Brian Jordan, is an excellent jazz saxophonist. He's American but he speaks very good French." She paused, though not long enough for Jeremy to comment. "The alto sax that you like," she went on, indicating the specimen on the wall, "is a used instrument as well as a potential rental, so it's convenient price-wise. Some people even *prefer* the sound of a used versus a new saxophone. Anyway, Monsieur Jordan also teaches his students music theory." She gave a modest little shrug. "I'm not very good at math so music theory was hard for me, but Brian helped me—he's very kind and patient...we've got his card if you're interested..."

The academic rigor of music theory notwith-standing, there was no way Jeremy could refuse this bright, knowledgeable and delightfully enthusiastic young woman. "Thanks," he said, "I'll take the card." He glanced at his watch. "And now I've got to go."

He exchanged *au revoirs* with Odile and exited the store, striding briskly back up the street, where at the corner of rue du Temple and rue Perrée he halted at the red light. Balancing both bags in his left hand and arm, he plucked the business card from his jacket pocket:

Brian Francis Jordan
Clarinet – Saxophone – Flute
Performance and Instruction

At this stage, Jeremy mused, *"Instruction" would be all I could handle.* The light turned green and he pocketed the card. This fellow expat Jordan could be an interesting *mec.* Maybe he'd give him a ring when he returned from Amsterdam. As he crossed the street the melody to "Satin Doll" flitted into his head and he whistled a few bars. It was one of Haley's favorite standards. She'd expressed good-natured envy when learning he was headed for Amsterdam, or at least it had seemed good-natured; the way she'd smiled with her mouth but less with her eyes made him unsure. Once he gave her a vague outline of his assignment, though, she'd muttered that maybe she wasn't *that* envious of his getaway, and wished him good luck. *Oui*, he would probably need it. Who knew what kind of fuss the presidential advisor's daughter might kick up when he confronted her to return home. He pictured Odile, the girl in the music shop; if only a young girl like her awaited him in Amsterdam—pretty, cheery, yet with a good head on her shoulders. *Dream on*, he told himself in English, and went back to whistling "Satin Doll."

Acknowledgements

Many thanks to the city of Paris for hosting such a marvelous bicentennial jubilee. In terms of festivities, everything described in this novel is accurate. It was a celebration to remember across the years, especially since I won't be alive to partake in another!

Many thanks to my critique partners, with special thanks to author and friend Paula Riley. Much appreciation to beta-readers Angela Sell, Cora Robey, Barbara Stephano, Livia d'Andrea, and Arlette Lessig. Once more, your sharp eyes have proved invaluable! Much gratitude, as well, to my friends in France and Belgium, Hervey L'Hostis and Steven Tijdgat, respectively—such marvelous sources of cultural nuggets you are!

Excerpt from *Paris in Black*, sequel to *1989*

Chapter 1

Jeremy Winters swore he would never again accept an assignment involving a teenage girl. Give him blackmailers, counterfeiters, even would-be terrorists, and they could not come close to the deceptive charm and dumbfounding pluck of eighteen-year-old Solange Gautier. At first he had thought the Renseignements Généraux insane to assign him the job. The RG handled French police intelligence, not kids who turned eighteen while on summer vacation, then refused go back to school in September. Only the *kid* in question just happened to be the daughter of an assistant to President Mitterrand of France, and Jeremy Winters just happened to work for the RG in an unofficial capacity—a part-time "little-jobs" man—which, he eventually conceded, had proved a convenient match-up to the delicacy of the operation.

That was back in October of 1989. Now it was four months later—February, the start of a new year—and as he listened to a message from the same Solange on his answering machine, he marveled once more at his efforts to wrangle the wayward teen back to France from a commune in Amsterdam. "You remember me?" came the perky voice. "From Amsterdam and Brussels, last October?"

Remember? How in hell could he forget? *Solange*, who had hopped off the train in Brussels on their way back to Paris, leading him on a not-so-merry chase. Overall he would remember the job as a fiasco, if not for one penetrating ray of sunshine. He had met *Ghensie*. The thought of the Albanian beauty still brought on a sensual sigh.

But *Solange*—what could she possibly need from him? The question sent his thoughts spinning back to that October morning in 1989.

It was the 12th, Columbus Day in America, Jeremy always remembered from his boyhood in the U.S. He had rolled into Amsterdam on the train on a quiet autumn morning. The sky shone a marbled blue and white, the leaves on the trees a shuddering gold in the cool breeze. As he walked to his hotel alongside the rippling waters of a canal he couldn't help seeing it all as a good omen. Didn't his RG boss, Benoît Rébert, assure him that Solange was already tilting toward returning to her parents and school? That the gentle pressure of a fingertip would turn the teen in the right direction? It might, Jeremy thought, be like gliding an iron over a wrinkle in one of his shirts, applying just enough pressure for the right number of seconds to smooth the crease without burning the garment. As a thirty-five-year-old lifelong bachelor, Jeremy had done plenty of ironing and the image made him crack a small smile.

When he managed to meet Solange in an Amsterdam café, his gentle but steadfast iron seemed to be doing the job. She'd talked to her parents beforehand and seemed receptive to Jeremy's benevolent presence.

"Yes, I'll be coming home," she affirmed to him.
"Good. I'll buy the train tickets."
"I just have to take care of one little issue."
And there his iron hit the first crease.

"I need to say a proper goodbye to Henk."

"*Henk...*" Jeremy echoed uneasily.

"The guy I've been living with." A matter-of-fact statement from a girl who reminded Jeremy of a 1970s hippie—long lank hair, grubby-looking jeans, fingernails needing a good cleaning and filing. Still, she didn't look completely worse for wear from her communal living. Her blue eyes were clear and lucid, her face full with youthful freshness. Her parents shouldn't be too shocked when they saw her, and Jeremy was determined they would see her soon.

She assured him she would come back to Paris after tying up a few loose ends. "You don't need to wait for me."

If Jeremy's iron suddenly lost steam he tried not to show it. He cast Solange a wary smile. *Oh, he would wait all right*.

She might have read his mind. "Don't worry, Henk's okay with me going home."

Of that assertion Jeremy could hardly be certain, so he waited the three days it took Solange to finish her business and finally get to the train station. Thank goodness she looked clean and groomed, though he couldn't say the same about the young man who'd accompanied her, his blond hair long and stringy, his jeans frayed and mopping the platform.

She gave Jeremy an absent glance, then looked back at her companion. "Henk," she indicated to Jeremy, "came to see me off."

"Needed to see who she's leaving with," the young man said, drawing himself up. He spoke good English, like all the Dutch, and probably spoke it with Solange. In fact he looked like a West Coast beach boy, which inspired Jeremy to slip into another persona, one he'd abandoned almost twenty years ago—the youthful Californian.

"I'm from San Francisco, a friend of the family," he said. "Just volunteering to check on Solange."

"And to take her back to Paris..." The tall, lean Henk ran a hand through his hair, catching and working at a knot as he seemed to mull over Jeremy's words.

"If she wants," Jeremy said casually. "Her choice, since she's eighteen. But really, I was dying to get away from Paris. I miss California, but Amsterdam's a cool place too. I'd really dig staying on if I didn't have to get back to my bartending job in the Latin Quarter."

Henk stared. Solange looked astonished in turn. She knew Jeremy wasn't a family friend, knew he had been sent in some kind of vague official capacity, though she clearly hadn't let on about it to Henk. Alone with her, Jeremy had spoken in perfect French but was now conversing in the most colloquial American English.

"You're from *California*?" Solange said.

Jeremy nodded. "It's the coolest state in the U.S. I really miss surfing in Santa Cruz." Though he had never surfed in his life, he let out a nostalgic sigh, then shrugged and nodded toward the train parked next to the platform. "Anyway, I'm going to board now. I've got the tickets, Solange. I could load your duffel while you chat a little longer." He glanced at his watch. "Got about another three minutes before departure."

After a long couple of seconds Solange and Henk finally tore their gazes from Jeremy, shifting uneasily from one foot to the other as they looked at each other. Solange handed her duffel to Jeremy. "I'll be up in a minute."

Jeremy climbed aboard, the duffel in one hand and his own valise in the other. From the doorway he smiled at Henk. "You should check out California sometime." Then he headed into the corridor and found an empty compartment, where he swung the bags onto the luggage rack, then went to the window to peer out.

Solange and Henk were locked in a hug, after which they disentangled themselves and held hands. At last their fingers unlaced and they moved a touch further apart. Jeremy checked his watch again, raising a knuckle to his teeth as the conductor blew his whistle. *Her bag's onboard; she won't leave it behind*, Jeremy assured himself. And in fact Solange hopped onto the train just in front of the conductor, who slammed the door behind her. The train lurched forwards, Jeremy met Solange in the corridor, and as the train picked up speed he could almost exhale a sigh of relief. *Almost*.